BECOMING WILDE

HK JACOBS

D1410491

BECOMING WILDE

Copyright © 2021 HK Jacobs

All rights reserved.

ISBN: 978-1-7358156-4-0

DEDICATION

To my patients and their families, who have taught me that life is
infinitely precious, and hope abounds when one least expects it

HK JACOBS

CONTENTS

ACKNOWLEDGMENTS

Thank you to the following beautiful people, without whom, this
book would not be possible:
Erin for your friendship and unwavering support
Amy Partain for your fabulous editing
Angela Wingard for your keen eye and the cover art
Tammy and Emily for being willing to slog through my rough draft
Katie Hagaman for bringing Alex and Ian to life on Audible,
and my team at the children's hospital for encouragement beyond
reason.

BECOMING WILDE

ONE

Everything felt swollen—her eyelids, her cheeks, her lips. Especially her lips that had been kissed furiously and desperately the night before. A reminder of her transgressions in the form of a single copper strand of hair rested lightly but resolutely on her sleeve. Alex picked it off and flicked it to the floor.

Despite the warm shame from the memory of the previous night, her skin prickled with an interminable cold. Frost had spread across the airplane window, reaching inside with its icy fingers and permeating her skin. Alex huddled deeper into the leather-backed seat and scrutinized the details in the snow-covered landscape that had become more visible over the last hour. They would be landing shortly.

She stared down at her nails, short and bitten almost to the quick over the last few months and hid them inside the sleeves of her aubergine wool coat. As a physician, long nails had never suited her. She had to position her hands on tiny bodies and place catheters into blood vessels no bigger than a stick of spaghetti. Her hands were constantly dry from the onslaught of disinfecting foam and her fingers frigid as if she had just pulled them from a deep freeze. In her haste to leave, she hoped she had remembered to pack gloves.

The plane dropped another hundred feet of altitude, revealing a distinct patch of grass pushing its way through the frost and a herd of sheep trotting merrily toward a cluster of felt-lined dwellings. A lazy river wound its way through a vast meadow until the terrain abruptly morphed into a mountain range with peaks still dusted with snow. The climate was unbearably cold in the mountains where the altitude rose and the air thinned. Alex shivered, grateful that they would be spending most of their time in the city.

After living in Botswana most of last year, she had been spoiled by the semi-arid climate and the spectacular sun that baked the land and her skin during the day. Even the hospital where she worked had open-air corridors and a central courtyard so that transitioning between wards allowed a moment of fresh air. Alex briefly wondered how the pediatric ward was faring without her. If she hadn't promised Ian that she would do this, she would be in Gaborone right now, probably up to her elbows in the onset of fall weather and the childhood respiratory infections that usually came with it.

Alex glanced around the plane at the rows of empty seats, pausing on the few occupants. Lydia, her red hair wound tightly in a bun, was the Scottish powerhouse behind the inner workings of the Devall Foundation. She clicked away on her laptop, oblivious to her surroundings. Rachel and Rahul, work colleagues who had evolved into a couple, were huddled tightly together, her head lolled over on his shoulder. He leaned over and kissed her hair gently. Ian's father, George Devall, swiveled in his rear-facing seat and stretched his giraffe-like legs into the aisle. The bulk of the Devall Foundation— the most philanthropic entity on the planet. People who cared about changing lives and making a difference. They had certainly changed hers.

When Alex had met Ian Devall on the outdoor patio of Ex-Pats almost two years ago, he had charmed her and repelled her at the same time. In his black leather jacket, black jeans, and aviator sunglasses, he was the epitome of sex appeal and charm...and he knew it better than anyone else. She expected to be attracted to him. What she didn't expect was to fall madly in love with him. He had slowly but effectively deconstructed her barriers until she had had no choice but to leap into the flames of a consuming, life-altering love affair.

A tall, fine-boned flight attendant with tightly coiffed ebony hair strode through the cabin with a red-lipped smile, revealing a set of perfectly polished teeth.

"May I offer you a beverage before we land, Dr. Wilde?"

Although tempting, her stomach lining had been excoriated by champagne the night before, and it had not yet regenerated.

"No, thank you," she answered.

The woman eyed her critically and handed her a bottle of water anyway.

After taking a quick sip, she placed the water in the cupholder of her highly accessorized plane seat. Alex had only been on a private plane once before. Ian had scooped her out of Haiti after an unfortunate incident involving an aftershock and a collapsing school. A school that she happened to be inside. Alex had flown to Port au Prince on a rescue mission to provide medical care for kids after a devastating earthquake. Instead, she had become the one needing emergency medical treatment. Fortunately, the only reminder of the accident was a single jagged scar on her scalp, usually covered by waves of chocolate brown hair.

Unlike Alex's small-town upbringing, Ian had grown up in the privileged universe reserved for heirs to billion-dollar mining fortunes. A few years ago, he had been named chairman of the Devall Foundation, which allowed him to spend his days flitting across the globe working to build partnerships with animal preserves, educational organizations, and hospitals, including the hospital where she worked in Gaborone. She had always marveled at the freedom Ian possessed being able to command sky travel according to his will.

When Alex had arrived in London yesterday, she had been ushered through Heathrow airport and driven in a black sedan to a private hanger. Gentlemen in white coats had stowed her luggage into the deep underbelly of the Learjet. They directed her up a set of rollaway stairs where individual alcoves with white leather armchairs awaited each passenger. The service provided by the stylish flight attendants had been impeccable, complete with a wide array of beverage options and light meals offered every few hours. Alex had pretended to sleep through most of the concierge service, preferring dreamless solitude to mindless snacking.

Now, out of the corner of one eye, she saw a pair of gray trousers striding down the aisle, and, shortly, George Devall settled into the chair opposite her. His face appeared thinner than the last time she had seen him but had maintained its distinction. His snow-white hair was perfectly combed and thick despite his age. His chocolate brown eyes, set deep into his face, were always a combination of kindness and perception.

Ian had inherited none of his characteristics from his father apart from his height. From the few pictures Alex had seen of Ian as a child, he resembled his mother. He had her jet-black hair and eyes the color of an ocean's sky.

"How was the flight, Alexandra?" George said in a soft voice that always seemed to surprise her given his gargantuan stature.

She straightened in her seat and tucked a loose strand of hair behind her ear. "It was fine, thank you." Her voice sounded thick and strained like she had swallowed the gravel coating her mom's driveway.

He nodded, accepting her answer into the depths of his eyes but not believing it. Clearing his throat, he reached into his jacket pocket and removed a small leather portfolio, splaying it open in front of her.

"This is our schedule for the next few days. I trust that Lydia sent you a copy?"

Alex nodded. "She did."

"Excellent." He pointed to a highlighted event on his printed itinerary. "I was hoping that you might be able to say a few words at the dedication tomorrow."

Alex felt her throat constrict as the words fought to scrabble past her vocal cords and leave her swollen lips. "Of course."

She expected the tears to come then, unbidden and shameless. They didn't.

"Wonderful. Did you have a nice time at the charity event?" He offered her a weak but gracious smile.

Alex swallowed past her sandpaper throat, clutching the water bottle in her hand.

"I...it was lovely."

Ian's signature phrase popped into her head—*I drink, I dance, I donate.* She had outdone herself with the first one last night. The fresh memory of hands gripping her hair erupted into her pounding head. She had been swallowed into a moment, the first moment in forever that had not been excruciatingly painful and indulged in a slice of physical pleasure for the purpose of analgesia. But instead of making her forget, it had made her remember.

George kept his eyes trained on her face, seeming to wait for words that she didn't plan to say.

When Alex had met Ian, he had been exiting hedonistic highway after a decade of indulgence in order to dull the pain of losing his younger brother and then being abandoned by his mom. After living life from one social event and exotic international location to the next, he had come to rest on the precipice of change, as was Alex herself.

Right before meeting Alex, Ian had been named chairman of the

Before Alex could respond, the SUV picked up speed.

"Don't do anything I wouldn't do," called Rox as she and Nic disappeared around the corner.

Giddy with the intoxication of what the future held, Alex tossed her head, letting the night sky swallow up her laughter. Ian tucked her into his side so that his leather jacket became a cocoon for her face. She could feel his heart pounding beneath his ribcage against her cheekbone, an erratic rhythm of hope and desire that made him intensely real. Ian raised his other arm to signal a cab driver, and Alex disentangled herself to pull it out of the air.

"We don't need one. I have a car." She reached into her purse and then dangled her keys in front of his face. "Come on."

"When did you get a car?" he asked as they traipsed through the dusty parking lot to the even dustier black Land Rover.

As Alex shoved the key into the keyhole, Ian stood behind her, close enough that his heat warmed her through the air. She twisted until the silver knob popped satisfactorily out of its hole, reminding her of the whack-a-mole game she used to play when she was a kid.

"I'm renting a house from a South African couple, and they left their truck for me to use."

She tugged the handle, struggling as the door creaked open. Before she could fling it wider, Ian pressed the entire length of his body into hers, the latch clicking back into place with their combined weight. Devoid of a streetlamp, the parking lot was nearly pitch black, the only ambient light a constellation or two hovering above them. Shocked into temporary paralysis, Alex was sandwiched between the immovable truck door and Ian's formidable midsection.

He leaned down until his lips brushed her ear and whispered, "You have an important choice to make, Alexandra."

She couldn't see his face, only feel his slow smile, his breath caressing her exposed neck as a pulsating need grew between them.

"What choice is that?" she asked warily.

If sexual tension had a visible aura, it would have settled over them like a cloak right then.

"Here in the parking lot, here in your car, or..." He encircled her waist with his arms and bent his head to the tender spot above her clavicle. "In your bed?"

Her entire being resonated with a dizzying rhythm. For a moment, she was tempted to start unzipping, unbuttoning, and discarding anything within her reach. She shook her head to clear it.

A few nagging thoughts clamored for attention in her brain. Ian had always been a master of distraction, but she didn't want to be distracted tonight. She wanted this moment to be solid so that when she remembered it months and years later, she could hold onto its perfection—not as a dream but as her new reality.

"Jump in," Alex whispered hoarsely. "I'll take you to my house."

Without hiding any of his disappointment, Ian relaxed his hold and shuffled around to the passenger door. Once the dashboard dials bathed his features in a luminous glow, she appreciated the very large pout displayed across his beautiful face.

Alex twisted the key in the ignition and threw the truck into gear.

"Mongolia didn't grow your patience," she teased.

"I can be patient...when I have to be," he retorted, eyeing her sideways. "I have demonstrated a saint-like degree of patience given the circumstances."

Alex tilted her head, weighing his response, and wondered how he had coped with the last six months. She had hurt him deeply. Although it wasn't fair of her to judge, she wondered if he had taken his pain and evolved...or devolved into his previous behaviors, seeking a salve for his wounds with pleasure. And by pleasure, she knew that included women.

Even though she didn't want to know the answer, she had to ask. Alex glanced over at Ian's form, reclined casually in the leather seat, ever the sex magnet with his dark tousled hair and lean, muscled body that was even evident through his layers of black jacket, black t-shirt, and black jeans.

From their very first encounter, his sarcasm and wit had magnetized her. Once Ian flipped on his charm, he was impossible to resist. She remembered Celeste at Rox's wedding, shamelessly flirting and undressing him with her eyes. Alex wondered how many more Celeste's had happened since that traumatic day on the bridge when she had told him to let her go.

"This is it," she announced softly, as the truck rolled to a stop and she cut the engine. The ensuing silence created a void for all her runaway thoughts.

By the time Alex unclicked her safety belt, Ian was already striding around the truck and wrenching open the door. He reached in with long arms, scooping her up like a child, and carried her to the door.

"I'm not five," she laughed.

"Sometimes you act like it," he teased. "Give me your keys."

With one free hand, he twisted the key in the lock and shoved open the door.

"Oh no! I forgot to warn you about McCartney," Alex yelped as their entrance was met with frantic whining and barking.

On getting a whiff of Ian, McCartney paused and then, hackles raised, let out a low menacing growl.

"It's okay, boy. I'm okay," she soothed and slid out of Ian's arms.

Ian bent to one knee, proffering a tentative hand toward McCartney's nose. He took a gentle sniff and then another before wrapping a long pink tongue around the extended fingers, a shiver starting in his muzzle and extending through the end of his tail. He pushed his nose into Ian's chest, siphoning up whatever delicious scents lingered there.

"So much for my watchdog and protector," Alex muttered.

Ian grinned and pulled the giant head into his hands for a solid ear scratch. "Animals love me, and I love them. Are you a good boy? Yes, you are."

Alex rolled her eyes and smiled as McCartney tried to shove his head inside the small space between Ian's armpit and his unzipped jacket.

"I met Clementine," Alex said as she hung up her jacket and kicked off her shoes. Clementine was Ian's Jack Russell Terrier who lived a posh life at his dad's house outside London.

Ian rose to his feet, much to McCartney's disappointment.

"I know. My dad told me."

"What else did he tell you?"

Amidst their conversation, Alex could hear the *thwack* of McCartney's tail on Ian's legs.

"That you talked, and he gave you my letter."

The letter Ian had never sent. The words that solidified Ian's intent to let Alex go like she wanted. Only that wasn't what she had wanted at all.

"I sat in your car and read it." Alex's eyes focused on the top of McCartney's head.

"You really are an emotional masochist. I wondered who had cried in my front seat and completely ruined my leather upholstery."

His mouth twitched with humor, and Alex gently punched him in the bicep.

"I didn't ruin anything."

Ian chuckled as he led her over to the couch where he sprawled out, sandwiched between McCartney on one side and Alex on the other.

"Why didn't you say anything at Rox and Nic's wedding about going to my house?"

His questioning eyes implored hers. So many questions hung in the air between them. So many answers as well—answers that stubbornly refused to wait until morning.

"I had bigger fish to fry," Alex replied evenly, and Ian's face lit up in amusement.

"So wicked tuna, now that you've got me here, what are you going to do with me?"

He ran the tips of his fingers across her inner wrist, and she tried to suppress a shiver that started in her lower back and spread up her spine. *Everything I've been dreaming of doing for the past six months.* She groaned audibly.

"I need a drink...and then I have questions," she said, leaping off the couch and bustling into her kitchen.

"Always questions. Are you sure you want to take right now to be Nancy Drew?"

She didn't want to, but she didn't have a choice.

"I'll have one too," Ian called from the living room.

Alex opened a bottle of wine that had been lounging in her fridge for a few weeks and splashed it into two glasses. She chewed her bottom lip, suddenly overcome with shyness. The possibility of her dreams coming true was a heavy weight to bear.

As the ball of nerves in her stomach unraveled, a nervous tingle rose to the surface and settled between the layers of her skin. Taking a deep breath, she slowly made her way from the kitchen to the couch, balancing the wine glasses between her clammy palms. Ian was cuddled up next to McCartney, who whined appreciatively as his ears were scratched.

"Here you go," Alex said, again settling into the spot on Ian's other side, purposefully keeping a section of cushion between them.

He took the wine and lifted it to his lips. Lovely shapely lips molded around the glass like they had molded around various parts of her body. The tingle in her spine extended to her face, and she hastily gulped her own wine. He reached out the hand that had been waggling McCartney's ears and placed it on her knee. For once, he was wordless, outwardly calm and still, but she could see a flicker of anticipation in his irises. As her courage mounted, he continued watching and waiting in silence, poised for whatever might come out of Alex's mouth.

"Why did you come back, Ian?"

"Short version—I came to terms with who I am. A truly selfish man who cannot live without you."

He narrowed his eyes at her, a smile flitting across his features before a look of consternation overtook it. She peered into her wine and indulged a moment of elation before her next inquisition.

"And the long version?"

He nodded, turning the question over in his mind for a moment before responding. "How much do you want to hear?"

"Everything," she whispered, willing herself into a state of resolve.

Ian removed his hand from her knee, and she frowned at the immediate disconnect she suddenly felt. His warm palm had been a constant reminder of how real this moment was. Leaning his head back into the couch cushions, he closed his eyes, and she waited for his lips to move and bring to life the story that was unwinding in his head.

"You hurt me, Alex. I left you in Texas with the intention of never seeing you again."

She shuddered at the memory and the tumultuous aftermath of that day.

"I needed space...a lot of space. There is no greater space than the land of the eternal blue sky, so I asked my dad if I could oversee our new mining cooperative in Mongolia, and I left."

"You never sent the letter you wrote. Your dad found it in your car."

He sighed through his nose. "I know. I meant to, but I didn't want the situation to be real ...and mailing the letter would have made it real. I wasn't ready yet."

"What did you do in Mongolia?"

"I worked—boring stuff like meetings. But then I traveled and saw the country. I even stayed in a ger for a while in the mountains. I did everything I could to get you out of my head."

"Everything?"

Alex's insides were clenched so tight that they felt deprived of blood flow. Ian had always used women as his analgesia—his distraction. When his mom had abandoned him at age fifteen, he had spent more than a decade roving those lips over an endless stream of beautiful women. Alex emotionally prepared for what might exit his lips next.

His eyes popped open, their sky-blue hue divulging a sense of wariness. "Are you asking how many women I used to dull the pain?"

Alex closed her eyes, letting the brick-like tension root her to the couch. His answer wouldn't change how she felt, but she had to know. She opened her eyes and locked them with his.

"Yes."

His hand vacated its spot on her knee to push up the sleeve of his black long-sleeved t-shirt, revealing a neat script-like tattoo in a language that Alex very much recognized.

"That's traditional Mongolian script," she breathed.

When Russia had occupied Mongolia, they had demanded a transition to the Cyrillic alphabet. There wasn't much evidence of traditional writing left in Mongolia apart from old books and wall art, but Alex had seen it once or twice during her brief time there.

"It's your name," Ian said, tracing the black writing that starkly contrasted with his alabaster inner forearm. Alex inhaled sharply, her nose burning with emotion as the bricks, one by one, crumbled to the ground.

"Even though I thought I'd never see you again, I promised myself that I would never forget you...that I would never forget the man I was with you."

Alex bit her lip to staunch the tidal wave of regret, relief, and revelation threatening to flood her with emotion and the tears that came with it. She had no words—only a fierce connection to this other human that had evaded her for a lifetime.

Reaching out a tentative finger, she traced the black writing, permanent ink dwelling right beneath Ian's first layer of skin. Exactly where he resided in her. He shifted and reached his other hand to tip up her chin. When his eyes met hers, they were alight with a familiar blue flame.

"The answer to your question is not a single one."

Her eyes widened in surprise, and her fingers inadvertently tightened over his forearm.

"Not one?" Alex asked, regaining her voice.

"Not one," he replied firmly, searching her face for absolution.

When she said nothing, he continued. "Come on, Alex. Tell me what's going on up here." He tapped her gently on the forehead.

"It's just hard to believe...knowing your past." She gulped her wine for courage. "And knowing how much I hurt you."

He flitted his gaze to his own glass and shrugged.

"Well, I'm not going to say it was easy—living like a celibate monk. There were plenty of opportunities."

He cast her a devilish half-smile and she rolled her eyes dramatically despite the tension. "It just didn't have the appeal that it once did."

Alex inwardly rejoiced while she steadied her face and tried to chase away the smile threatening to erupt like a homing beacon.

"What about you?" Ian asked.

"What about me what?"

"Did you find something that provided more distraction than running or working yourself to death?"

"No. Of course not," Alex stammered as a quick vision of Tim on the steps of the Philadelphia Art museum flashed into her consciousness. Ian eyed her speculatively and swished his wine around his mouth like mouthwash. He swallowed with an audible gulp, his thyroid cartilage bobbing up and down like a fishing accessory. She scrunched up her face and averted her gaze into her wineglass.

"I kissed Tim," Alex murmured.

"What was that?"

He put a hand behind his ear and craned his head toward her. She stared hard into her wine, wishing she could jump in and drown herself in its golden depths.

"I kissed Tim," she repeated and allowed one eye to drift upward to his face.

Surprisingly, Ian bore an expression of extreme amusement at her discomfort. He took his time before answering, studying her features before he narrowed his eyes and simply said, "And?"

"And I basically told him that he would never be enough." Alex felt the epitome of sheepish, imagining her face appearing in a wooly hooded cape complete with a ribboned bell.

"Ouch," remarked Ian, taking another enjoyable sip of wine.

"I know," Alex groaned. "I'm a terrible person."

He weighed her comment, shifting his head from side to side before answering. "But you're my terrible person."

A smile flickered across her features, the first one since the interminable couch conversation had started.

"Yours?" she breathed, feeling the rest of her tension take flight.

He stood abruptly and held out a beckoning hand.

"Yes. Now take me to bed or lose me forever."

THREE

Alex's insides somersaulted with anticipation. Ian's reference to their time in Paris flooded her with a torrent of desire that would not be contained any longer. On her way home from Botswana last year, she had met Ian in Paris. At the time they barely knew one another, their attraction raw but deep, even then. The weekend had culminated in sensual dream sex amidst the provocative melody of the *Top Gun* soundtrack, their intertwined silhouettes framed by a backdrop of the Eiffel Tower. It had been her first time with a man. And not just any man—the man she was hopelessly in love with.

Plunking her half-empty wine glass on the side table, she grabbed Ian by the hand and whispered, "with pleasure."

He was as docile as a Sunday pony when she led him by the hand up the short flight of wooden stairs to her rented bedroom. With the creak of each step, Alex's confidence rose. One more step. Then another. Into the life she had chosen. Yearned for. Fought for. She would make it a life of dreams.

Lost in her imagined fairytale, Alex startled when they arrived on the threshold of her room, and Ian's lips tickled the tender spot below her ear. He ran his nose up the back of her head, inhaling the scent of her hair before letting go of her hand and entering the room.

Alex lived in what she referred to as "controlled chaos." Books littered the surface of her bed, and a pile of folded laundry decorated one corner. Her desk exploded with stacks of medical journals on which sat framed photos separated by various artifacts—a blown glass penguin from Cape Town and a painted wooden bowl from Guatemala.

Surveying the chaos through narrowed lids, Ian sauntered over to the bed where he carefully cleared off the books, stacking them against the wall. Spying the lion pendant, he cast Alex a carnal look and walked over to pluck it from its spot draped over the picture of her and Ian from New Year's Eve last year. Alex joined him in the middle of the room and eyed him quizzically before he spun her around.

"What are you—?"

"Shh," he whispered. Alex felt the weight of the lion on her sternum as Ian deftly attached the clasp. "I am going to strip you naked of every single thing you have on—except for this." He adjusted the rose gold lion so that it hung delicately from the end of its chain.

Letting out a slow even breath, she waited while he curled his warm fingers under the hem of her sweater, biting her lip while a current of desire electrified even the tips of her toes. Her black cashmere top sailed through the air like a crow and landed neatly in the doorway.

Expert hands unfastened the top button of her jeans, and she heard the distinct buzz of unzippering right before a sharp tug sent her pants into a puddle around her ankles. She daintily stepped out of them, a surge of feminine power—instead of what a year ago would have been timidity—overtaking her. She heard Ian's quick intake of breath at the sight of her posterior and smiled to herself as she took out her hairband to send her long dark chocolate waves rippling down her back.

Turning around, she encountered him in a statuesque stance, so still that his chest was barely moving when he breathed. Her undergarments were simple but as black as night and contrasted with her porcelain skin. She felt anything but made of porcelain. His eyes hungrily roved her form as she watched the blaze in their depths escalate to an inferno.

"I don't know about you," she said, "but I've had enough slow burn for one night."

His eyelids fluttered in surprise at her boldness, but then his features quickly transformed into a salacious smile. That was the last thing Alex saw before they collided with each other.

The next several minutes were dominated by sensation after exquisite sensation. He crushed his lips into hers, and she immediately opened her mouth to let lips and tongues wind together in silent, erotic conversation. She slid her hands under Ian's black t-shirt and flung it over his head in one smooth motion, then started on the waistband of his jeans.

Experienced fingers hastily unclasped her bra then slid between her hips and the lace of her panties. Alex paused in her tenacious homage to Ian's lower lip when the sound of ripping met her ears and her bare bottom met with the cold draft leaching through her window.

"Did you just—" she asked, seeking an audience with Ian's face.

"I absolutely did," he answered wickedly.

"If you keep ripping my underwear, I'm going to run out," she replied, mockingly stern.

"That's the point," he groaned into her ear, and she erupted into a fit of giggles—the laughter of a woman in love with her man and the world at her feet.

Strong forearms hoisted her into the air. Her laughter faded as she wound her legs around Ian's waist, and he walked them both over to her bed. She siphoned up his smell—freshly washed skin, the hint of wine on his breath, and the distinct pheromone musk of a man who wanted what he wanted. *Her.*

What ensued next was a several-hour marathon of an explosion of carnal need followed by passionate interlude and concluded by lingering lovemaking. The sear of Ian's lips had traversed every inch of her body—twice—and she had gladly returned the favor. Their synergistic desire for one another would not be satiated until each bundle of nerve endings had fired in recognition. In reacquaintance. In resolution.

Side by side, they huddled under Alex's floral comforter, an icy draft cooling the flush from their most recent escapade. This most recent romp had left tendrils of hair stuck to Alex's cheek, and Ian gently stroked them free with his thumb.

"I love you," Alex whispered as she imagined actual sparks leaping from Ian's eyes and sizzling as they landed on her bare skin.

"I know you do," he replied, grinning happily.

"You're supposed to say it back," she said with narrowed eyes, and he responded by dragging his thumb across her bottom lip then taking it between his teeth.

"How about I show you?" he murmured, his other hand already finding the bloom of desire happening between Alex's legs.

She arched her back and closed her eyes and came very close to purring as pleasurable tingling heightened into sensory overload. Ian covered her mouth with his own as he settled himself over her bare form. Lips to lips. Skin to skin. One soul to another.

A painful yet gratifying feeling swept over her as he entered her again, her inner thighs shaking with anticipation. He moved achingly slow, never pausing as his hips connected with hers and released, little by little pushing her closer to a blissful precipice that she was more than happy to fall over.

"I love you, Alex," he said, and, in that instant, her life resembled nothing less than perfection.

For once, Alex slept through the predawn rooster's obnoxious crowing and only awoke when incessant scratching threatened to splinter her bedroom door. Ian's limbs wound around her, his natural heat warming every single part of her body except for her nose, which remained exposed to the morning chill.

"McCartney, I'm coming, boy," she called and groaned when her bare feet struck the floorboards. Quickly pulling on a cozy pair of sweats, she leaned over to deliver a swift kiss to a barely stirring Ian. "I'll just be a minute."

Outside, the sun was barely peeking her golden halo over the horizon, nicely silhouetting the lanky puppy utilizing the sparse brown grass for his morning routine. The events of last night settled into Alex like bits of treasure. She had to keep reminding herself that it hadn't been a dream. She inhaled sharply, and the cold bite of winter permeated her lungs, where the engulfing blaze of being in love quickly melted it into nonexistence.

McCartney shot between her legs, scrambling to get inside the house once he detected a whiff of Ian. He whined dramatically until a certain hand had placed itself between his ears. Alex ambled over to Ian and managed to wrap her arms around him despite a thrashing russet-colored tail.

"Can I make you some breakfast?" she asked, leaning her head into his muscled chest, and inhaling the traces of cologne and desire lingering on last night's t-shirt. Underneath a rumpled mass of hair that was black as night, his face broadened in a bright smile.

"Sure. What do you have?"

Alex wrinkled her nose and tried to conjure a vision of the interior of her fridge. "Not much."

"I'll eat anything at this point. I burned a lot of calories last night. You have a surprising degree of stamina."

Alex flushed a bright shade of hibiscus pink and hustled into the kitchen. "I *am* a distance runner," she called, hastily pulling various porcelain bowls from under the island. "How about pancakes?"

"Only if you have chocolate chips."

He smiled boyishly, and Alex's insides melted as if they were a mound of milk chocolate turning to ooey-gooey liquid in a hot pan. How could one human make her feel so many life-altering emotions all at once?

Ian pulled out a barstool and parked his statuesque frame on the seat, his elbows casually resting on the island. McCartney circled once, sniffing, then settled onto the linoleum, his body wrapped around Ian's chair.

"Lucky for you, I recently became addicted to baking. So, yes, I have chocolate chips."

Alex paused, reflecting on her first several weeks in Botswana. Freshly wounded from Ian's rejection at Rox's wedding, she had discovered therapy in the form of a perfectly dense chocolate cake. While she whisked pancake batter, her mind mulled over the events of the last few weeks, pausing to skirt around the manholes that belied logic and reason. In a starlit courtyard with wedding festivities as her background, she had emptied her heart at Ian's feet, but he had retreated into indecision and let insecurity fester. What had changed his mind and propelled him to come find her?

The question tugged at the corners of her consciousness while she poured lumpy batter into a sizzling pan and watched the air bubbles pop on the surface. Taking a cue from the pancake batter, she decided to let her own thoughts escape into the atmosphere. Tossing in a handful of chocolate chips, she turned to face Ian, who was busy scrutinizing his phone screen.

Alex leaned over the soapstone island and studied Ian's features—the tufts of dark hair artfully decorating his forehead, the way his lids narrowed as he scrolled through his messages, the carved jawline with its narrow trail of stubble that she had run her tongue over multiple times last night.

"Alex?" She apparated out of her salacious daydream at the sound of her name.

"Uh-huh," she called, turning to flip the pancakes as an intangible timer sounded in her brain.

Ian had put his phone face down and was massaging his left palm with his thumb. The same palm where she had once removed a very large acacia thorn that had attacked him in the Kalahari. Alex placed a topsy turvy tower of pancakes in front of Ian, complete with a melting square of butter and a ring of amber syrup that Rox had gifted her from Canada.

Alex let him gobble up the pancakes in silence for a while, watching him stuff tender forkfuls past his lips.

"These...are...amazing," he said between bites, closing his eyes in gastronomic bliss. When his fork paused, Alex leaned over to wipe a smear of melted chocolate from the corner of his mouth.

"Tell me something," she started tenderly.

"After those pancakes, I'll tell you anything," he replied, putting a hand on his abdominals that remained flat as a washboard despite the massive carbohydrate load he had just inhaled.

"You went to Mongolia, lived in a ger, avoided the opposite sex." She reached over and traced the black script on his forearm, furrowing her brows in concentration. "Tattooed my name on your arm and then came to Rox's wedding."

Alex could sense him watching her face, and she seized the moment to lock her eyes with his and steady her breathing. They were so blue—like an ocean's sky. They made her flit into the air and grounded her at the same time if that was even possible.

"I told you I was in love with you, and you weren't ready to accept it. What changed?"

Alex let the question dangle in the air like the flicking end of a fly fisherman's rod, hoping he would bite. He stared into the pile of sticky crumbs coating his plate as if he could divine his thoughts from the image they created. Knowing Ian, he was probably visualizing a bottle of bourbon...or a naked French lady.

"I decided to trust you," he said simply, using his fork to draw tiny lines into the remaining puddles of syrup. Alex remained quiet, her insides squeezing with a yet unnamed emotion. "I went back to London after the wedding, and everything felt wrong. A life without you felt...wrong."

The emotion in his voice caused McCartney to pick up his head and emit a throaty whine.

"What happened then?"

"I went to see my dad to talk to him about the Mongolia project, and he suggested we go for a drive. That's when he told me you had come all the way to his house to find me, and I asked him a...question."

Ian focused harder into the remnants of his breakfast.

"What question was that?"

"What was it like to love someone so much and not be loved like that in return?"

Alex blinked as the words settled into her skin. Ian was referring to his parents—how his dad had let his mom pursue her dreams at the expense of his happiness and how she had slipped away from him after Ryan's death, ultimately abandoning Ian. Alex tried to contain the singular tear spilling over the outer corner of her eye—a tear concentrated with empathic grief.

"What did he say?"

Ian pushed his plate to the side and turned to face her, his long legs barely able to fit in the narrow space between the barstools. "He said that it was terrible...and wonderful." Ian reached down to wind his fingers through Alex's. "He said he had no regrets." Ian closed his eyes, plucking the conversation out of his memory. "Because epic love is rare and requires a man to let go of his fear. But once he does, he is free to love recklessly."

His lids parted to reveal a depth in his irises that Alex had only seen once before, and their flames scorched her very soul.

"I am terrified of losing you again, but I am more terrified of a life without you."

His lips were moving again, but the words were scattered by Alex's quick exhale right before she pressed her mouth to his. In her kiss, she infused all the warm, tender sweetness that bloomed in her heart. Their meeting of lips was a sacred vow made amidst the leftover scent of maple syrup and the gentle whine of a concerned canine. Alex pulled away, opening the drawbridge to a fortress filled with emotion that rushed to the surface, leaving a warmth to her skin and a brightness in her eyes.

She placed her palms on either side of Ian's face. "You will never have to imagine a life without me."

Although he remained speechless, his expression, one of adoration and spectacular love, provided Alex the answer to her heart's final question—an answer written in the glowing embers of his flame blue eyes.

FOUR

"We're almost there," shouted Ian from the front seat of the open-air jeep that bounced erratically along the narrow strip of dust masquerading as a road.

Alex gave him a quick thumbs up and stuffed her Phillies baseball cap farther down on her head, tucking in a few strands of wayward hair that had been caught in the tornado-force wind. She was stuffed into a tiny square on the rear bench, sandwiched between duffel bags of supplies and Ian's leather luggage.

In a baseball hat of his own and fitted black sweater, Ian was seated casually in the front passenger seat, braced by his foot on the dashboard and his hand gripping the jeep's olive-green metal frame. The driver, an older gentleman with patches of white at his hairline and ebony skin that stretched tightly across an angular bone structure, seemed completely unmoved by the rocking vehicle. He remained still as a statue as he navigated them through bumps and ruts in a range of heights and depths.

One tire-sized divot sent Alex airborne, and she briefly imagined the luggage exploding and burying her under a pile of Ian's black t-shirts. Buried under a pile of anything related to Ian was highly desirable. Just two days ago, after making him pancakes and finishing a rather weighty conversation, she had ended up naked on her kitchen island. It had taken a deliberate scrubbing in the shower to remove the syrup from her backside.

"Allow me," Ian had offered, and she let him use his hands to remove the stubborn stickiness.

They had made love again in the shower, the scalding hot rivulets of water no match for the heat generated by the friction of their skin. Later, sprawled out on her comforter with only a blanket and Ian's nearness for warmth, Alex had laid her head, damp locks and all, in his lap and dozed while he scrolled through his messages.

"Anything interesting to report?" she asked sleepily, drinking in the smell of his freshly washed skin.

"What are your plans for the next few weeks?"

Alex sat up abruptly, her hair cascading over one shoulder. "I don't start work until the end of August, so none right now." She hesitated then added, "But I was hoping to spend time with you."

She glanced at her bare knees and chewed on her bottom lip, wondering when asking for what she wanted would become less awkward.

"My thoughts exactly," Ian said. Alex smiled without meeting his eyes. "How would you like to come with me to Tanzania?"

So here she was, not even forty-eight hours later, holding on for dear life in the back of an old military jeep, careening toward her next adventure. They had taken a twin-engine Cessna from Gaborone to Arusha and from there hopped into their current mode of transport to their intended destination, an exclusive elephant reserve supported and maintained by the Devall Foundation.

Despite being in the heart of the dry season, the tender hand of spring had sprinkled the landscape with a few lush mounds of greenery separated by baobab trees. Even through the curtain of dust cloaking her visual field, Alex could appreciate the silhouetted forms of zebra, wildebeest, and a few giraffes on the horizon. Shielding her eyes from the sun's glare and the wind's incessant pummeling of her corneas, she squinted to see a baby giraffe trotting unconcernedly behind its mother.

The jeep took a sharp turn that sent Alex grappling for a hold on the front seat, but instead, she collided with Ian's bicep. He reached over to grasp her hand with fingers warmed from sun exposure. He didn't look over, but she could see the tiny lines at the corners of his eyes crinkling as his lips grew in a smile. The rugged look suited him. And every single image of him suited her insatiable libido.

Finally, after what seemed like more than a mere two hours, the tossing abruptly abated as the jeep crunched to a halt in the middle of a tree-lined clearing where a two-story structure towered over the landscape. For all intents and purposes, it was a tent—a tent on steroids—and a far cry from the yellow pop-up where she and her mom had pretended to camp in their backyard. A skeleton of hewn logs covered by thick khaki canvas created a building that allowed the breeze in while keeping the rest of the elements out. Clusters of men in khaki uniforms elbowed one another and joked in Swahili as they carried bales of hay to a nearby flatbed truck. Their voices resonated with fresh air and sunshine. Even though she had never been to Tanzania, it already felt like a friend.

Ian hopped out of the passenger side to greet a smiling gentleman who strode toward him with outstretched arms. He had prominent cheekbones and skin the color of seal's fur. There were grace and purpose to his lean frame and strength that belied his height, which was not much taller than Alex herself.

"Welcome, friend," he shouted and caught Ian's palm mid-air, his other hand grasping him firmly by the shoulder. "It has been too long."

"Good to see you, Josef."

Ian pulled the gentleman in for a quick hug. Josef's lips parted in a pearlescent smile, and he separated from Ian to run a quick hand over his bald head. Alex loitered a few feet behind Ian, carefully observing their casual friendship and the monogrammed badge on the man's canvas pocket that read "Manager."

"This is my girlfriend, Alexandra Wilde."

Ian opened his stance and gestured to where Alex stood. Josef eyed her curiously for a moment, as one would an interesting animal at the zoo, and then, regaining his composure, extended his hand toward Alex.

"Very lovely to meet you, my dear." He grasped her hand gently but firmly, a distinct amusement growing in his walnut-colored eyes. "Welcome to Uhuru Elephant Preserve."

"I'm thrilled to be here," she replied, finally finding her voice.

"We'll talk later, Josef," Ian called as he took Alex by the elbow and steered her toward the gaping entrance to the building.

Josef nodded curtly and then purposefully strode toward a group of jeeps gathering in the pebbled drive. Ian slung his arm around Alex's shoulders, slowing his stride so they could walk as a unit.

"What was that all about?" she asked teasingly.

"What was what?"

"He looked at me like I was an exotic animal on display."

Ian squinted up to where the sun was peaking in the sky. "He's never seen me bring a girl here before."

Alex's insides melted in delicious satisfaction. Her mouth twitched into the inkling of a smile.

"Oh." She cast her eyes upward at his beautiful face. He was smiling as well. "And why did you introduce me as Alexandra?"

"Alex is your 'save the universe' doctor name, whereas Alexandra—" He narrowed his eyes and bent his head so that the exhaled breath from his parted lips tickled the tiny hairs of her ear. "Is a name reserved for my exceptionally beautiful, adventurous, off-duty girlfriend who can't get enough sex."

The fuchsia roses in vases marking the entrance were incomparable to the spreading flush across Alex's cheeks.

Their pace slowed as they stepped onto a stark white stone walkway, and Ian had to duck his head as they entered a grand anteroom. A peaked ceiling with exposed wooden beams towered above them, and the ground transitioned into plank wood flooring that bore the scuffs of many pairs of boots underneath its polish. They skirted around an unoccupied desk filled with notes scribbled into a spiral notebook and an olive-green rotary telephone to exit onto an outdoor patio.

Alex walked into a bright shaft of sunlight and her own personal version of heaven. The patio was filled with comfortable leather furniture boasting cream-colored pillows, side tables stacked with books, and a bar running the entire length of one side. But the true miracle of the moment was the small herd of elephants casually grazing mere feet from the edge of the patio. Her eyes riveted to one mother-baby pair, their trunks intertwined in a loving embrace. Placing fingers to her lips, she breathed an unexpected "oh."

"Aren't they spectacular?" Ian asked, extending his arm toward the herd, the pride in his voice unmistakable.

"I've never been this close to an elephant before." Alex took another tentative step forward as Ian eyed her with amusement.

"Watch this."

He strode gracefully over to the edge of the grass, cautiously stepping out into the sunlight as if he couldn't bear to disturb even one blade of grass. Standing there underneath the cloudless sky in front of a herd of elephants seemed like the most natural thing in the world for him. Pieces of his hair ruffled in the light breeze that wafted through the airy space.

Alex was struck by his ease in the presence of animals, especially how they seemed to understand one other. Maybe that was why she responded to him; by breeding, she was basically a rescue dog.

As she watched incredulously, one of the larger females lumbered over to where Ian stood, blocking out the sunlight with her gargantuan form and extending her trunk to rest on his shoulder. His hand immediately caressed the side of the writhing gray tube, which caused her ears to flap ecstatically. It seemed that even females of the *Loxodonta* species could not resist Ian's charm. Alex was not surprised, but she was impressed. She inched over to stand directly behind Ian as he and the *she*-pachyderm became reacquainted.

"It looks like I may have some competition after all," Alex teased.

Ian glanced over his shoulder as the elephant used the sensitive end of her trunk to rove over his cheek. He emitted a carefree laugh. "Possibly. Princess Diana has a jealous streak."

Alex grinned and gingerly stretched her hand toward the creased gray skin. "Could I—?"

She let the question hang in the air as she inched ever closer until she could feel warm, exhaled breath on the tips of her fingers. The matriarch's skin was warm from the sun, rough but supple at the same time. Alex traced the geometric crevices along her trunk, her arms taut with the thrill of such an intimate moment with a creature thirty times her size.

Emboldened, she stepped closer until nothing stood between her and an enormous head containing the largest, most curious brown eye Alex had ever seen. They stared at one another for a moment— not as elephant and human but as two females who were empowered by strength, wild at heart, and free to choose their own destiny. And apparently in love with the same man.

In the next moment, Alex felt the high-velocity spray of an elephant snort coating her face in a fine mist of snot mixed with gritty particulate matter. As she heard Ian chuckling behind her, she felt certain it had been deliberate.

A short while later, Alex stood with Ian at the entrance to their accommodations for the next few days, and they were nothing short of magazine-worthy "glamping." The stand-alone tent was located a short walk from the main structure and designed similarly with thick olive canvas stretched across pale wooden scaffolding.

The furnishings were simple and thematically appropriate. A large four-poster bed with crisp white sheets and leather pillows filled most of the space surrounded by a few immaculately placed items like a leather trunk and a cushioned occasional chair with an ottoman. The bed faced a curtained wall that Ian pulled back to reveal a small sitting area and nothing but meadow for the eye to see. The landscape before her was a lush green carpet dotted with trees that worshipped a cloudless blue sky. It was heaven on earth.

"Can you see any animals from here?" she asked excitedly, squinting into the distance.

She felt Ian press his body into her posterior and place his chin on top of her head.

"If you sit here quietly, the animals will usually come to you."

"Oh, I hope they do," Alex said wistfully.

"Alex, you don't seem to have a problem attracting wild animals."

Alex felt what had become a very familiar surge of heated desire spread through her middle and then glanced down at the splattered elephant secretions decorating the front of her t-shirt. She groaned inwardly.

"Please tell me that this luxury tent thing has a shower."

Ian laughed into her hair. "Princess Diana really doesn't like you," he said, then pointed to a scraggly bush as tall as a person hiding the doorway to an enclosed structure. "It's right through there."

Even in her careful observation of the patio, Alex had completely missed it.

"Outside?" She half-turned into Ian and raised one eyebrow.

Feeling like a lioness on the prowl, she secretly hoped he could detect the hidden agenda in her voice. Turning around to meet his eyes, their familiar flames scorching her lashes, she desired nothing less at that moment but to explode with every carnal instinct she had.

His phone buzzed in his pocket against her thigh, and she saw the hesitation in his expression. She bit her lip, intending to stoke the flames in his irises, and surged with satisfaction when he took her bottom lip between his teeth. Repetitive buzzing like a pesky insect emanated from Ian's pocket, and he dropped his head in resignation.

"Give me one minute," he sighed. Extracting his phone, he slid his thumb across the bottom and put it to his ear.

"Only one," Alex mouthed, holding up her index finger and sidling toward the mysterious door encased in shrubbery.

Once inside the hidden shower, she marveled at the neatly lain teak flooring and the rough-hewn tree limbs acting as the perimeter. In the corner, the wall changed from wood to coarsely stacked limestone with two twin shower heads jutting from their crevices.

Alex removed her mud-caked shoes and dingy clothing, carefully piling them on a convenient bench that stretched along the sidewall.

Fully disrobed with the warm sunshine playing on her backside and the breeze beckoning her lady parts, she felt genuinely wild. The water was just warm enough to cast off the chill in the air, and she tipped up her head to let it caress her face and stream through her hair.

Since her sweet reunion with Ian, the last few days had flown by so quickly she had scarcely had a chance to grasp their strings before they floated away like balloons in the summer breeze. As much as she could manage it, she had willed her brain into focusing on the present. The wonderful now. The exquisite moment.

Occasionally, however, the trepidation of the future took hold, and she wondered what would become of them. Her job was in Botswana now, and she had no idea where the Devall Foundation would be sending him next. Geography and her professional life still loomed as potentially insurmountable obstacles. Not to mention that there was still much to learn about one another.

Alex still had not told him about her childhood. About JR. Closing her eyes, she ran her hands through her hair, sending a cascade of water droplets—and errant thoughts—toward the drain.

Warm hands closed over her breasts pulling her into the solid form waiting behind her. She gasped then settled into the familiar midsection. A few solid silent seconds ticked by, which was enough time for her to release the minimal hold she had on her inner lioness. Without a trace of timidity, she turned and lifted her hands to the back of Ian's head, pulling him down to her hungry mouth. He met her lips in mid-air.

Strong hands lifted her off the stone floor, and she wrapped her legs around Ian's middle as he positioned them against the shower wall. Alex dove into his mouth, experiencing the sensations of rushing water, lips on fire, the earth at her back, and the wind cloaking them—all of the elements aligned in approval of their union. She would never get enough of this man.

As they rocketed toward ecstasy together, Alex heard the din of voices behind her, and she froze as her thighs shook around Ian.

"Who is that?" she whispered and strained to detect the traces of a conversation in English in a notable American accent.

She couldn't make out the words but heard the tittering laughter of a woman mixed with low-pitched commentary. Her face, already pleasurably flushed, deepened to crimson, and she attempted to dismount from Ian's waist. He said nothing but shook his head "no" and tightened his grip on her bottom. Alex's eyes widened as he slid into her just a fraction deeper.

Tightening her hold on his shoulders, she tilted her head toward the crescendo of voices. He shrugged nonchalantly, his eyes betraying his mischief as he balanced her on one arm and placed his other hand over her mouth. He ground his hips into her, slowly and deliberately, seeking and finding the epicenter of pleasure just inside her pelvis.

A tingle grew along her hairline as she heard the distinct phrase, "I'll meet y'all at the bar," booming from a male voice immediately on the other side of the shower wall. Wicked laughter grew across Ian's face as he increased his cadence with no intention of pausing.

"Let go," he whispered, and she did.

Without her voice as a release, all the luxurious erotic bliss erupted up her back and down to the tips of her toes and into the depths of her irises where she was sure the flames would threaten to compete with even Ian's.

FIVE

Freshly showered and still pink from embarrassment, Alex reclined back into the leather pillows of the cozy sofa where she and Ian watched the last rays of sun coat the horizon. She watched the light play off his cheekbones as he swirled a glass of bourbon, noticing that a fine row of stubble had popped up on his jawline in the last few hours. She took a sip of her potent elixir—a fizzy champagne cocktail that matched her mood. How could she not be legitimately effervescent after their *sexcapades* of late?

A solitary elephant, a young male with an exploratory trunk, stood silhouetted against the sagging orange ball in the sky. Alex swallowed, letting the pink liquid bubble merrily down her throat, and found Ian's hand. He brought it to his lips and savored one of her knuckles for a moment before resting their intertwined fingers on his knee. He inclined his head toward hers.

"Happy?"

"Ridiculously happy," she sighed, watching Ian's smile stretch across his features and spill into his eyes.

"I can't believe the Devall Foundation built this place," she mused. "It's phenomenal."

"Luckily, my dad had the foresight to purchase the land decades ago, even though he had no idea what it would become."

Alex had browsed the brochure on the bumpy ride from Arusha and learned the history of her current location. The Devall Foundation had created the Uhuru Elephant Preserve as a sanctuary and breeding ground for the rapidly declining population of African elephants in Tanzania. Ian's dad, being the magnanimous philanthropist he was, had gifted the twenty thousand acres back to the Tanzanian government but continued to support the preserve with grants from his successful non-profit organization.

Due to the convenient paucity of local predators, it was the single largest concentration of elephants in the entire sub-Saharan region. The only predator that remained were people—illegal hunters on gaming trips or criminals that would capture the babies to sell to foreign zoos.

"Have you spent much time here?" Alex asked, her eyes flitting to the nearby chairs that were filling up with patrons, ready for a drink after a dust-filled day on the savanna.

"Off and on over the last few years," Ian replied with a shrug.

Alex saw the tiniest flicker of recognition spark in his eyes as a woman edged around the guests to make a purposeful beeline toward Ian. She was tall—taller than Ian—and statuesque with skin the color of ebony wood and a pair of eyes black as night that sparkled with their own stars. Ian stood and accepted her casual embrace, allowing her to peck him deftly on each cheek.

"*Karibu nyumbani*, Ian my dear. It has been a long time."

"Good to see you, Imani."

Alex watched, mesmerized by the woman's graceful movements as she adjusted the turquoise beads around her neck.

"You must be Alexandra," she said smoothly, peering around Ian to where Alex was observing the scene playing out in front of her.

"Just Alex is fine," Alex blurted and stood up so quickly that a few drops of champagne cocktail splashed onto her jeans.

Imani placed her hands on Alex's shoulders and kissed both of her cheeks in quick succession. "Very nice to meet you. Take care of Ian," she said, casting a backward glance as she floated toward the bar.

"Didn't you brag to me earlier about your lack of female companionship here?" Alex asked through mildly clenched teeth.

Ian clinked the ice in his empty bourbon glass. "Technically, I've never actually brought a girl here." Alex glared at him through slit-like lids, and he shrugged. "What? Imani works here—she manages the reception desk."

Alex groaned and plopped back down into the welcoming sofa cushions indented with her backside. "What am I going to do with you?" she huffed in mock-disgust.

His expression wavered for a second then erupted into his characteristic salacious half-smile. He sat down smoothly and molded his body to hers. "I can give you an entire list of things I'd like you to do with me."

Alex felt the burning rush of being in love and simultaneously in lust. She tilted her head so that her lips brushed his earlobe.

"Like?"

"Well, let's see. We can check off the front seat of a car, hotel balcony, and kitchen island. Next would be a rooftop at sunset, and since I know you are a morning person, the beach at sunrise..."

"I didn't realize you were such an avid outdoorsman," Alex commented with a smirk.

"You have no idea what you have been missing."

He leaned over and placed a succulent kiss right underneath her jawline, his tongue still cool from laving over the ice in his drink. A shiver started at her hairline that accelerated down to her lower back. She was invisible from the outside buzz of the bar scene—cloaked in a cloud of desire and exhaled bourbon.

"Maybe you should show me," Alex replied brazenly, reveling in the wit of their banter.

He slid his hand to the top of her leg, precariously close to where the apex of her thighs betrayed her composure with its insistent throbbing.

"I plan on having a lifetime of showing you."

Wait? What? Alex reeled for just a second before she lost herself in a set of warm beckoning lips. Her runaway thoughts could be shelved for the moment.

An insistent throat-clearing halted their shameless public display. Beyond Ian's shoulder stood Josef, hands clasped in front of him and completely expressionless. He rubbed a hand over the back of his neck. "May I have a word, Ian?"

Ian straightened, and, leaving a lingering kiss on the sensitive corner of Alex's mouth, stood to face the silent overseer of the reserve.

"Absolutely." He turned to Alex, his expression lighthearted enough that it concealed a subtle flare of concern in his eyes. "I'll only be a minute."

Alex blew him a kiss carrying all the aching tenderness in her heart and settled into her thoughts and the rest of her champagne. She let her eyes drift to the verdant sheets of grass tucked into a gorgeous pink ombre horizon and the massive lumbering inhabitants of this little participle of heaven on earth.

The male elephant from earlier had been joined by a young female who grazed a casual distance from his swinging trunk. She plucked a bundle of grasses from a nearby patch and placed it delicately in her mouth while the male, who was a good bit larger than her, circled her with rhythmic flapping ears. Her tail swung back and forth, like the pendulum of a clock. Tick tock. A gesture to give him hope that it was only a matter of time before his pursuit became fruitful. Alex flushed pink at their obvious intimacy and her front-row seat to pachyderm foreplay at its finest.

Alex crossed her legs to stifle the incessant throbbing between her thighs. Ian's minute was stretching into many, allowing her thoughts to unravel like thread on a spool, collecting in a snarled pile on the floor of her consciousness. *Lifetime.* The word expanded in her brain until it became nothing less than a space-occupying lesion. She had barely processed that she and Ian were together—much less what waited for them on the other side of tomorrow.

As a couple, she and Ian fit together like lock and key, but melding together two very different lives seemed overwhelming right now. Where would they start? What would have to change? She frowned into her empty champagne glass. She wasn't ready for anything else to change. They had a delicate bubble of happiness right now, and she wanted nothing more than to exist within its whimsical walls, floating above the necessary reality awaiting them below.

A high-pitched trumpeting sound erupted from the male as he pursued his pachyderm princess trotting into the sunset. Alex glanced up in time to catch him fondling his prospective mate with the tip of his trunk. Elephants did not mate for life, nor were they completely monogamous, but the bonds of friendship, especially among the females, lasted for a lifetime. She wondered what a lifetime with Ian truly entailed.

She heaved a sigh and flipped the trunk lid closed on the future. Sliding her empty glass across the woodgrain bar, she surveyed the neat display of spirits on the shelves towering above her, noticing several varieties of uncoincidental bourbon.

"What will it be, love?" asked a smooth velvety voice coming from a set of full red lips. Imani was tending the bar, her long torso towering above Alex and the scent of warm vanilla emanating from her flawless skin.

Alex knew Ian's past was complicated, but she had come to terms with the fact that she loved who she loved. She had chosen him, and he had chosen her—even when she had sent him into a spiral of hurt. However, it would be a tremendous help if the universe could stop maneuvering Ian's exes into her path. She plastered her face with the brightest smile she could. *Damn.* She should have worn Rox's shiny pink lip gloss.

"I'll have a shot of tequila."

"Make that two."

A solid shape wearing a cornflower blue shirt with the sleeves rolled up to his elbows landed in the empty space next to her at the bar. Through her side-eye, Alex observed his clean-cut chestnut hair styled to perfection and an oval-shaped face with the hint of a strong jawline. He sported a light growth of facial hair that surrounded a mouth set in a cocky grin. He stared at her comically, amusement growing in the hazel eyes flecked with gold set under full brows. "That's a strong drink for a lady of your—" He looked her up and down, pausing periodically to blatantly assess her physical features. "Stature."

Alex recoiled from both embarrassment and recognition. She would know an accent from her home state anywhere. He was the man whose voice she had heard while in the outdoor shower with Ian as she silently lived out her sexual fantasies. A rush of heat crept up the back of her neck, and she plucked her brimming shot glass from the tray Imani had slid in front of them. Narrowing her eyes, she daggered a look in his direction and put the fiery liquid to her lips, swallowing it in one gulp.

"I have a lot of fortitude."

He wrinkled his nose at her and smirked. "I bet."

The man tipped his head back and released a dramatic sigh when the glass was empty. He picked up a tiny white cocktail napkin and dabbed it on his lips, and she noticed the large ring he sported on the fourth finger of his right hand—an overly ostentatious college ring from Texas University. Alex scoffed internally. She had spent a decade steering clear of men like this and felt newly awash with gratitude that she no longer needed to cast her line into a sea brimming with male specimens who thought every woman wanted to be rescued and wooed and then patronized.

Somehow, Ian was different. He had always been different. Although detest spread across her stomach lining for this genteel Texas boy in a plaid button-down and overly shiny boots, her outward countenance and good manners refused to betray her.

"Where are you from?" she asked casually, although she felt

confident she already knew.

"Texas," he said, a complete smile stretching across his features. "Dallas actually." He motioned a hand to the solemn bartender who had replaced Imani. "You?"

He cut his eyes down at Alex briefly.

"Texas," she replied with an almost apologetic shrug.

"Really?" his eyes bore into hers with renewed interest. "You don't look like you're from Texas." He averted his gaze to the stately bartender who had appeared in front of him.

What's a Texas girl supposed to look like, Alex mused. Visions of fluffy-haired, tiara-toting, ex-sorority pageant queens carrying monogrammed makeup bags floated through her head. Despite her growing annoyance, she plastered a smile on her face.

"I'll take a beer—Shiner," the man said.

"We are literally thousands of miles from anywhere that carries Shiner beer," Alex scoffed.

Shiner was made in Texas in the same town that bore its name. With limited exportation, she hadn't even been able to find it in Philadelphia apart from Baby Blue's. Yet seconds later, a satisfied grin parted the man's sparse facial hair when a cold sweating bottle of Shiner was slid across the wood toward his waiting palm. He put the bottle to his lips and gulped, emitting a content, embellished sign when he was done.

"For you, miss?" inquired the bartender gesturing toward the empty space in front of her.

"I'll take the same," she muttered but couldn't help feeling giddy with nostalgia as the cap to her favorite beer flew off and landed neatly in front of her. Her face must have given her away as she took a sip of home because her preppy bar companion offered the answer to her unspoken question.

"I'm here quite a few times a year, so they keep some around for me."

He took his next generous gulp, expectation evident in his side-eye gaze. She refused to be impressed, letting all emotion drain from her face, and focused on her beer as the invisible wall that had served her so well in life rose into position.

"I'm Logan."

He failed to proffer a hand, instead throwing his statement out like a baseball expecting someone to catch it and lob it back. Alex could play along for now. She had been pretty good at baseball once upon a time.

"Alex Wilde," she said simply, taking a long drag of the ice-cold beverage between her palms.

Where was Ian? Her cordiality had an expiration date.

His face crinkled in admonishment. "What do you do, Alex?"

"I work at a children's hospital."

"No kidding! My sister is a pediatric nurse too."

Alex rolled her eyes and failed to see the point of correcting him. Not that she minded. Some of the smartest, most competent women she knew were nurses. But it was excruciatingly common for any woman in her field to be underestimated, and she felt a surge of disgust that took considerable effort to stifle.

"That's great," she replied in a flat tone and mentally willed Ian to show his beautiful face. "So, are you here on vacation?" she asked, trying to change the subject.

"Vacation? Nah. Business, actually. I pretty much keep this place afloat."

Alex let out light but audible snort and physically bit her tongue. Miraculously, before she could reply, a solid arm belonging to the person who did maintain the reserve slid around her waist. She melted into it like it was a lifeline to freedom. Fervent lips brushed her cheek.

"Can we take a walk?"

"Of course," Alex breathed.

Logan's brow raise was subtle but perceptible as he observed Ian's proximity to Alex. Recovering quickly, he thrust out his gold ringed hand to Ian.

"How you been, Ian?"

"I've been amazingly well."

Ian met him halfway and grasped his outstretched hand for a moment before dropping it and shoving his own in his pocket.

"I can see that." Logan's eyes flicked to Alex and lingered there.

"I'll see you around, Logan."

Without any further wastage of oxygen molecules, Ian intertwined his fingers with Alex's and tugged her behind him into the night.

"Nice to meet you, Miss Wilde," he called into the rapidly expanding space between the bar and her retreating form.

She shouldn't...but she couldn't resist.

"Dr. Wilde, actually."

When they had exited the bright space of the patio bar, Alex inhaled the cool purity of the night air and shed her negative vibes into a puddle at the base of her quickly moving feet. Blades of grass swished past the hem of her jeans with a rhythmic melody as she kept pace with Ian, who strode purposefully toward a glowing spot in the distance. As they drew closer, Alex could make out the weathered boards of a barn door.

"Where are we headed?" Her breath came easily, albeit quickly.

"Storage building of sorts," he replied enigmatically. "How were you and Logan getting along?"

Even in the starlight, she could detect the hint of a smirk tainting the corner of his mouth.

"He is—" Alex tossed a few choice adjectives around in her mind before she answered. "Insufferable."

Ian erupted in a quick staccato laugh. "Excellent word choice," he said, casting an approving look back at Alex.

Letting her annoyance from earlier resurface, she continued ranting.

"He is a preppy, spoiled, patronizing—" She let the words hang in the air while she searched for a proper non-four-letter word to describe him.

"Wanker?" Ian finished.

"Yes!" Alex raised her hand that wasn't bound tightly to Ian's to the night sky in a salute. "He even claimed to be the one keeping the elephant reserve—what did he say—afloat."

Ian shook his head. "Ridiculous," he muttered.

"Who is he anyway?" Alex asked.

"He is from old money. His grandfather is some rich Dallas oil tycoon. They own this exotic travel company, and he just made Logan the CEO. Our elephant preserve is one of the stops on their seven days in Tanzania tour."

Ian halted for a moment and dropped Alex's hand so that he could wrench open the side door to a wood-planked structure that resembled the barns dotting the landscape in her part of Texas.

"Apparently, he has made this place his stomping ground. Quite a hit with the ladies I hear. A real country song love 'em and leave 'em."

Alex didn't even try to contain the laughter that bubbled out of her throat. Tears rained across her vision as the laughter forced her to bend in half like a pretzel.

"So, basically, he is a Texas version of you?"

Ian whipped around, a disgusted yet adorable tint to his features. "Hardly."

The door popped open with a creak, bathing them in a golden glow.

"I'm richer, meaner, and much better looking."

Alex shrugged and followed him inside. She couldn't argue with two of those things.

Once inside, she was enveloped in a warm sweet, musty scent as she eyed the stack of hay bales that reached the top of the ceiling like a rustic Egyptian pyramid. The concrete floor was mostly swept clean except for a few wisps of hay that had found their way to the ground and an occasional scuff from the sole of a rubber boot.

Brightly colored pails and rope were hung neatly along one wall interspersed with giant coils of green water hoses that resembled dormant pythons. A military-grade all-terrain vehicle with deeply treaded tires, its doors splayed open, was parked in the building's central corridor. Josef's head appeared above one of the dented passenger doors.

"The truck is almost ready, Ian." Alex watched him hoist a zippered canvas duffel into the backseat.

"Where are we going?" she asked excitedly.

"You aren't going anywhere."

Alex involuntarily recoiled. Ian didn't look at her. He was busy surveying the contents of the barn as if trying to remember something.

"What's going on, Ian?" Alex asked.

He rubbed his chin thoughtfully.

"There's been some...trouble...at the perimeter of the park. Someone has been trying to get inside the fence to get to the elephants."

"Like poachers?"

Josef cleared his throat. "We think they may want to steal a few of the younger elephants for illegal sale to zoos. It has been happening at a few other parks nearby."

Alex's mouth was set in a grim line and her fists clenched at her sides. Maybe it was because of her traumatic childhood and the abuse she had experienced at the hands of a tormentor. Whatever the reason, a cold rage rushed through her veins.

"I'm going with you," she said firmly, cutting a glance at Ian that encouraged him not to argue with her. His eyes continued to scan the supply wall.

"No. No, you are not," he responded with equal firmness.

Alex decided to try a different tactic.

"I'll wait in the truck the entire time. And it never hurts to have a doctor along. Just in case."

Ian wrinkled his forehead in thought.

"I'll do everything you ask me to do. No arguments. Ian...please."

He exchanged a look with Josef that Alex could not decipher and then jerked his head toward the truck.

"Get in, Wonder Woman."

Meanwhile, Ian had found what he was searching for on the wall and stepped over to grab it. As Alex piled in the backseat, she watched him through the window taking a thick barreled high-power rifle from where it hung on the wall.

SIX

The trio was swallowed into the black night as the glow of the glamorous campsite faded behind them. Alex squinted upward through the crack in her window into the star-studded sky and marveled at the skill Josef demonstrated as he navigated them through the twisting terrain. If the protruding boulders weren't threatening to upend their vehicle, the skeletal underbrush was.

Ian appeared thoughtfully tense in the front seat, most likely in consternation over his choice to allow Alex to accompany the mission. Staying behind had not been an option for her. A force beyond her control compelled her to protect these elephants. Even though it sounded delusional, Alex thought her presence kept Ian safer too. From what, she didnt know.

The engine's gears made a guttural noise as they downshifted and swerved to avoid a solitary zebra that had gotten separated from her herd. The mare kicked up her heels in disgust and disappeared into the brush. Josef brought the jeep entirely to a halt, and an eerie silence descended over them like a veil.

"We are near the north perimeter. I can turn on the floodlights so we can see if there is damage to the fence line," Josef said.

Ian nodded, and in the next second, a bright beacon of light from the top of their vehicle created a runway of photons the length of a football field. Beyond the glowing eyes that scattered into the night to escape the beam's glare, Alex could make out a high-profile security fence that resembled nothing less than a structure from Jurassic Park. With its steel-reinforced cables strung between thick wooden poles, the fence looked like it would deter even the most determined animal...or human.

Josef delicately pressed the accelerator, and they began to creep toward the formidable border. Tailpipe exhaust tickled the back of

Alex's nasal passages as she extended her head through the half-open window to peer into the horizontal plane where light met darkness. Even with heightened senses, she didn't notice it immediately—the mound of flesh inside the fence line and just out of the light's reach. Josef maneuvered the jeep into a sharp ninety-degree turn to bring the dome-like mass into view.

As they drew nearer, the shape grew in breadth, and Alex was able to discern distinct features. She sucked in a breath of night air tinged with exhaust just as Ian cursed under his breath. It was an elephant—a young one—probably not quite a year. Josef threw the jeep in park and killed the engine, leaving the animal bathed in light and noiselessness.

"Stay in the truck," Ian commanded as he pushed open the passenger door with a wailing creak.

Alex barely heard him. She was already ankle-deep in savanna grass and striding purposefully toward the calf. Ian beat her there and immediately crouched down in the dirt, placing a hand on the animal's oversized cranium.

"Is she...?" Alex whispered into the night, kneeling in the dirt beside Ian.

He hung his head until his sculpted chin almost touched his chest. "I have no idea, but probably." He opened his lids to slits to glare in her direction. "I thought you were going to stay in the truck."

Alex shrugged and placed a hand on his shoulder to push herself into a standing position. Brushing off the knees of her worn jeans, she casually asked, "Did I ever tell you that I'm terrible at following orders?"

Despite his stern expression, a grin peeked through. "No, but you keep making it abundantly clear that you do whatever you want."

Alex's lips stretched into a smile, but inside, her heart wrenched. Her adamant passion to care for sick kids all over the globe had consequences, and, unfortunately, Ian had borne some of those. And now he had chosen to continue to bear the consequences of her decisions, including the reckless ones. Would she continue to make those decisions knowing how it could hurt him?

She thought of Haiti and lying in a medical tent after sustaining severe injuries in an earthquake aftershock. Ian had come to rescue her, and she knew he would do it again. She just hoped he never had to. It had been hell for both of them and led to the downfall of their relationship.

Josef had crept up behind them so quietly that Alex started when she noticed the brilliant white of his sclera examining the hindquarters of the elephant.

"It's a female. Probably not quite a year." He ran his hand carefully along her back, trying to evoke signs of life in the form of a shiver or a tail swish or a heaving side that indicated a quick intake of breath.

"Where is the rest of the herd?" Ian asked, his tone dripping with concern.

"No idea. She is too young to be on her own."

Ian nodded in grave understanding, and Alex flicked her gaze from one man to the other, trying to decipher their unspoken meaning.

"Cows never leave their calves unless—" Josef explained gently, gesturing a hand into the stillness that surrounded them like an impervious bubble.

"They're killed," Alex finished.

"That's how these despicable people operate. They kill the mother so they can steal the baby," Ian added, rising to his feet, his hand still perched protectively on the young female's forehead. "Except, in this case, it looks like something happened to the baby as well."

He put his arm over Alex's shoulders, and she felt every bit of Ian's emotions in the weight of his bicep.

"Come on. We better get back. Josef can come out with a team in the morning and take care of her."

Alex stared down at the beautiful mammal, who probably days before had been happily romping among her herd and nuzzling with her mother. She was filled with an empty vacuum of grief that threatened to suck everything tangible into its vortex, unable to tear her eyes away from the still form.

At first, Alex thought her emotional spiral was causing her to hallucinate, but then she saw it again—a patch of grass bending to and fro in the windless night. A patch of grass located right next to the tip of the elephant's splayed-out trunk.

Wordlessly, she fell to her knees, her fingertips finding the floppy end of a trunk and lifting it to her cheek. The end was dry instead of moist, giving Alex a clue to the elephant's degree of dehydration. She stilled her own breath for a moment...then two...then three until she felt a light but definitive *whoosh* of air tickle the tiny hairs on her face.

"Alex, what are you—" Ian started, but Alex cut him off.

"She's alive."

"What? How can you tell?" He joined her in the dirt.

"I can feel her breathing. It's shallow, but I can feel it."

Alex took his hand, positioning it in front of the delicate twin abysses of her nostrils. She watched his face transition from incredulity to fascination as he too felt the warm condensate of breath on his outstretched palm.

"Josef," she called to the stately gamekeeper who was keeping watch over their little epicenter. "Can I borrow a flashlight?"

Seconds later, a thick black cylinder was thrust into Alex's hands. She pressed the button with a click and, using the tips of her fingers, lifted the excoriated skin of one eyelid. When she swung the light, an amber iris with the tiniest speck of a pupil was visible. In response to the light, it slowly constricted. Any reactivity meant she was still in there.

"Hold this, Ian," she commanded, passing him the flashlight and transitioning into critical care mode. Alex worked her upper half between the elephant's front legs to reach the horizontal struts of her ribcage and the coveted sounds of a heartbeat.

"Did I ever tell you how sexy you are when you're bossy?"

"Shhh," Alex chastised as she listened attentively but couldn't help but smile at the shred of hope in his voice.

She pressed her ear into the formidable gray chest wall until she felt a resounding thump. She counted one one thousand, two one thousand, holding her breath until right before three one thousand when she detected another soft *whump*. Untangling herself from elephant appendages, Alex sought and found Ian's expectant face.

"Her heart's still beating, but it's slow. Probably twenty times a minute."

Ian's brows furrowed as question after question popped into his head and escaped his beautiful lips. "What do you think happened to her? Can you fix it? Will she wake up?"

Alex had a sudden flashback to just about every single day of her medical career. Having just completed pediatric critical care training, she was an expert at sick children and their worried parents. She took one of Ian's hands in her own, infusing calm with her eyes, and said, "I will do everything possible to make your baby better."

At first, Ian acknowledged what she said by squeezing her hand, his face awash with tenderness, then, noticing the seizure-like twitch at the corner of Alex's mouth, dropped her hand in mock horror.

"You *are* a terrible person."

"But I'm your terrible person," she crooned and leaned over to connect her lips to his. They felt deliciously warm in the cool night air. "Seriously, though, I take care of baby humans not baby pachyderms. I have no idea what I'm doing. Isn't there a vet close by?"

Josef had entered their intimate elephant-human semi-circle. "He stops by once in a while but is on holiday at the moment." His hand, so dark that it blended in with the velvety night, rubbed the elephant's head vigorously but received not so much as an eye flutter in response. "An elephant's heart rate is slow. Much slower than ours. I think, in time, she will be all right."

Ian blinked a few times as if a thought was shaping itself into an actionable plan. "We have a flatbed truck with sides. Do you think we could get her onto it and take her back to the main house?"

Josef nodded agreeably. "Yes. We have used it before for some of the babies who needed medical attention."

Ian swiveled his head over to Alex. "Head back to the house with Josef. Once he brings the flatbed, he and I can get her loaded and bring her back. Then you can Florence Nightingale all night if you want."

Alex folded her arms across her chest in absolute defiance. "I'm not leaving you out here all alone, and I'm definitely not leaving a sick baby."

Ian tilted his head back to the endless sky, seeming to glean guidance from the heavens. "I thought you were a baby human doctor...not an elephant one."

"I am but...a baby is a baby. This just happens to be the biggest one I've ever taken care of." Alex smiled sweetly, and he dropped his shoulders in resignation.

"You will be fine," Josef reassured him. "Our park has not had predators in a decade."

Half an hour later, Alex sat huddled into Ian's armpit for warmth, using their elephant's broad backside as back support. Encircled in the gaslight glow of lanterns set equal distances apart, she hummed with excitement, her sense of adventure flaring like the flames dancing in the glass lantern closest to her feet.

Despite her chilled exterior, her inner thoughts raced on a track of firing neurons fueled by adrenaline. Like any ardent medical professional who lived to make the correct diagnosis, Alex ticked off the possibilities in her head.

The young female didn't seem to be injured on the outside, so it had to be something sinister happening in her bloodstream—dehydration, hypoglycemia, sheer exhaustion, or a toxin. Alex bolted to her feet, causing Ian, who had been nodding off, to startle and reach out for her hand. Always the protector.

"Are you okay?" he whispered, and she saw the lines of his jaw grow tense.

"I'm fine, but I had an idea about what's causing the elephant's encephalopathy."

He brought her hand to his warm lips. "I have no idea what you said, but it definitively sounds sexy."

A small smile formed on her face amid the furrowed concentration as she separated from Ian and began walking a perimeter around the elephant. "There are only a few possibilities for her condition. She's breathing, but she won't wake up. Her pupils are small and reactive, but she doesn't respond to painful stimulation."

"Your brain really works overtime," Ian remarked admirably.

"A blessing and a curse," Alex muttered as she crouched to the ground at the fringe of the lantern-lit circle and began sweeping her palm over the dirt.

Her hand brushed over the stubbly ends of dried grass, and the grit of the soil began to collect under her nails. She duck-walked back and forth, and even though she knew exactly what she might find, she still shuddered in shock when her hand closed over the cold metal cylinder half-buried in the dirt. She offered it up to the lantern's glow, allowing Ian to observe the syringe encased in metal, a hypodermic needle extending from one end with the other end decorated in a plume of faux red feathers. Exotic and deadly.

"That's a—"

"I know," Alex said solemnly as she turned the tranquilizer dart over in her hand to see the imprint on the side. *Wildnil.* She wasn't incredibly familiar with the cocktail, but she knew it contained a massive dose of a high-potency synthetic narcotic called Carfentanil.

As if Ian had picked up on her thoughts, he blurted out a

question. "What did they use?"

"Carfentanil. It's a narcotic about ten thousand times more potent than morphine."

"Enough to take down an elephant?"

"Yes," she replied. "Enough to sedate but not necessarily kill a baby elephant."

Several startling emotions lit their fuses and skittered into existence at once. The little elephant was going to be okay once the sedation wore off. Elation erupted but was quickly drowned out by a nagging dread. Whoever did this would be coming to collect their prize.

As if her worst fears were materializing, a truck engine roared in the distance. Her gaze flicked to Ian's, whose expression appeared grim in the dim flickering of the lantern light. He strode over to Alex and grabbed her by the arm, positioning himself between the truck noise and his two precious wards, the baby elephant and his woman.

Alex felt oddly calm as the truck ground to a halt about fifty yards in front of them. Her career had trained her to oppose the anxiety of oncoming disaster, like when she was in charge of a sick child whose heart or lungs had stopped working. Her own heart rate obediently slowed, and her mind absorbed every single detail around her so that every response was planned...calculated...perfect.

Alex peered around Ian's lean shape. Two men approached, lumbering along through the grass and slowing to a snail's pace once they caught sight of the humans standing guard over their bounty. One of them called out into the silent night, his foreign words failing to register in Alex's vocabulary. She mentally flipped through the myriad of foreign languages that she had a handle on, and this was not one of them.

Ian, however, lofted a return response into the night, and the men gestured in understanding. Something clicked into place in her brain like a pin in a hole—Portuguese. Despite her gnawing fear, she couldn't help but be impressed at Ian's fluency. She supposed it was Nic's doing.

As the men edged closer, their dark shapes evolved into detailed caricatures. While one was slim and the other hefty, both of their faces bore features that were edgy and harsh. Ian remained still, his feet dug into the dirt, his lips the only part of his body in motion. Verbal warfare in Portuguese occurred over the lantern's incandescence.

The more dominant of the two men motioned to Ian, and he stepped over to the border of their circle where light met dark. Ian continued to communicate via gestures and words that she couldn't decipher, but she had the sense that he was not backing down.

Alex shifted her weight uncomfortably. Conflict was not in her nature, probably because of her traumatic childhood. In fact, she avoided it like the plague. Not surprisingly, Ian seemed much more adept at "negotiating." After a thorough berating by Ian, the slimmer man nodded his head and shrugged in resignation. Alex stood rooted to her spot between the elephant and Ian and allowed a flicker of internal rejoicing.

The back of her neck suddenly prickled, and she flicked her gaze over her shoulder. The more solid of the two men had edged his way around the circle until he was directly behind them. The night's shadows swayed in a grotesque dance across his face—a face that bore a murderous glare, directed primarily at her and the precious baby she was protecting. His pupils, black as death, seemed to suck her soul into their void as he crept closer.

Her insides crumpled inward as his predatory stare reminded her of another man, and her feet erupted in a cold sweat. Her heart thumped a soundtrack of inevitable tragedy. She knew there was nowhere to run. An evil plot played over his features as he edged closer. Somewhere in her brain, she thought she should scream, but it died in her throat like in a nightmare where every sound comes out as a hoarse whisper.

"Ian."

Her voice was low and scratchy and not at all heard above the raised voices. Slowly, the man adjusted his course, and she could see what he intended seconds before it happened. He reached around behind Ian and slung his swarthy arms around his neck.

The rage she had felt earlier whipped through her like a tornado, spurring her into action—the only action that would make a difference at this moment. Her hand tightened around the metal jacketed dart in her hand, and she drove it decisively into the man's thigh.

SEVEN

Hatred spread over the man's face like a wildfire racing through the dry brush, and he pushed Alex forcefully, right in the middle of her chest. She landed on her hind end in the dirt and accepted a ringside seat to the onset of ataxia and stupor right before the hefty man collapsed in a heap at her feet.

Utterly shocked, Ian's eyes flared with admiration as his gaze darted from the crumpled-up human to Alex. Alex stared at the prostrate form of the man who moments ago had been her absolute nemesis—a predator and a criminal. Yet with one swift motion of her wrist, he had become nothing more than a fragile human with enough narcotics coursing through his system to tranquilize an elephant, literally. In a flash, she had transitioned from victim to defender to doctor. And now he had become her patient.

Scrambling over a rock-studded patch of dirt, Alex, still shaking from adrenaline, willed her disobedient limbs into action and heaved her body weight into one of the man's shoulder until he flopped over onto his back.

"Alex," Ian said evenly, positioning himself between her and the slim man who stood wide-legged with his mouth agape.

"I have to open his airway," she grunted, placing one hand under his meaty chin and the other on his sweat-slicked forehead.

Please be breathing, she prayed silently. She bent her ear to his mouth and slipped her fingers down to his carotid, where a slow but steady pulse thrummed. She thought she saw the faintest of chest excursion, but before she could be certain, several things happened at once.

The world suddenly became illuminated like some alien ship was descending on them, and the roar of engines filled the night like a warrior's battle cry. The slim man was so astonished that he glanced from Ian to the onslaught of vehicles and then into the direction he had come. An army of four-wheeled vehicles encircled them like a civil war cavalry, and uniformed men, their rifles trained on the slim man, barked orders in Swahili as they exited like a stream of ants on a mission.

Forceful arms hooked themselves under Alex's armpits and thrust her into a vertical position.

"Time for us to go," Ian commanded.

Alex felt like time was happening both quickly and at a snail's pace at the same time. She stiffly allowed Ian to lead her away from the supine man, briefly unsure of what action to choose next.

"Wait," Alex yelped, but Ian either didn't hear her or chose to ignore her. Wait," she repeated more forcefully.

Ian sped up his pace, his momentum propelling them through the dust cloud of authoritative voices and brandished weapons to the safe haven of the open truck door beckoning them in the distance. She could practically smell his fear and determination. Digging her heels into the soft dirt, she used the anchor of her sneakers to retract her hand from Ian's. He immediately whirled on her.

"Get in the truck, Alex."

"I just injected that man with enough narcotics to sedate a large animal. I need to make sure he is breathing." She clenched her fists into her thighs.

"No, you don't," he replied coldly. "The police will take it from here."

"I did this, Ian, and last time I checked, I was the only doctor within a hundred miles of here."

His posture relaxed, and she unclenched her fists, confident that he would understand her need—her duty—to rectify the situation. He took a step toward her, close enough so that she could feel the electrified stress crackling in the air between them.

"You," he murmured, rubbing her bottom lip with a cold thumb, a look of utter adoration painted all over his face, "are done making decisions tonight."

And with that, he picked her up like a rag doll and tossed her into the truck, closing the door behind her with a definitive click.

After a solid hour of high-pitched requests, shameless pleading, and logic-driven arguments, Alex found herself back at the main house, pacing a figure eight into the floorboards of their room. Ian had poured himself a glass of bourbon so full that the waves amber liquid undulated millimeters from the top of his glass. Tiny droplets cascaded over the side onto the floor as he elevated the rim to his lips. Muttering to herself, Alex tried to focus on the swirling grains of wood under her feet.

"What did you say?" asked Ian, not turning around as he leaned into the open frame of the patio, letting the bourbon and the night air soothe his distress.

"*Primum non nocere.*" Alex enunciated each word, allowing them to rebound off the walls of the room and fill it up with the depth of their meaning. "First—"

"Do no harm," Ian interrupted.

She had forgotten Ian's fancy education required two years of Latin.

"It's the oath that we all take in medical school and I just broke it."

"Don't be so dramatic, Alex."

Ian leaned on the sturdy log framing the opening to the outdoor patio, staring out into the black void of night, its silhouetted shapes more sinister now under cover of darkness, or maybe it was the aftermath of the ordeal they had just undergone.

"I don't think situations of self-defense apply."

"No," she replied evenly, "but I am required to attend to the injured." She took a deep, steadying breath. "Even if I did the injuring."

Ian took another long swig of bourbon. For once, his preferred elixir was failing to release the tension in his posture. "I should never have let you come."

"You can't protect me from everything all the time. I chose to go. I chose to stay with you. I chose to shove a dart in that horrible man's leg." Her voice had risen at least two octaves. "You need to learn to support my choices and understand that you are not responsible for the consequences."

He visibly winced. The conversation sounded too familiar, too much like the one after the accident in Haiti. It had been the catalyst for Alex's decision to let Ian go, convinced that choosing him would create strife and unhappiness for them both.

Ian downed the remainder of his bourbon, twisting the glass in his hand as he often did when he was tense. His brief tide of anger had subsided and left a somber thoughtfulness that she detected in the sag of his shoulders. His gaze appeared vacant as he watched the lamplight dance off the crystal in his palm.

"When has supporting your choices ever made either of us happy?"

His voice was quiet with a razor-sharp edge that could have sliced into a tire. Without any further words or glances in her direction, he shrugged on his jacket and strode into the night.

After he left, Alex stood fingering the edge of his glass. She put it up to her nose and inhaled deeply. The leftover molecules of spiced bourbon and distress filled her nostrils. She and Ian had come full circle—back to the very issue that had driven them apart in the first place. She wanted the freedom to choose her path, but by also choosing Ian, she was asking him to deal with the fallout of her choices. What was different this time?

Alex knew exactly what was different, but Ian didn't and it was past time that he did. She had never spoken about her childhood to anyone, not even her closest friends. Not even Rox. Her heart rate kicked up its pace as she let the words she would say to Ian settle in her brain. But somehow, instead of wanting to stuff them back into an old dusty trunk, committing them to lock and key, she found herself willing to coexist with her past. She would let it refine her instead of define her.

Alex was done running from something. In fact, she had been running toward something for some time now. That something, or rather someone, was worth the sacrifice of her vulnerability. *Could Ian exist in the epicenter of her pain and not be burned by it?* She set down the glass and set off into the night with a singular purpose—to take down a wall and build a bridge with the pieces.

Alex entered the curtained patio bar, finding it completely empty except for one solitary patron. He slumped in a structured chair, its trappings made of stretched animal hide, his feet propped up on a leather ottoman. She had indeed found someone but not her someone.

A brown leather jacket lay casually tossed on the chair next to him, and his plaid shirt, still rolled up to the elbow, revealed a surprisingly ropey forearm. He nursed a beer in his hand, and his heavy lids remained in place even as Alex edged closer. Despite his grating personality, he actually bore a sweet expression, like he was having a pleasant dream. His hair had remained perfectly coiffed throughout the evening, one chestnut shock flopping over his forehead, reminding her of a horse she had once ridden in her youth. A horse who was beautiful on the outside, a real prima donna, and nearly impossible to train.

In her concentration to avoid the random glassware littering the floor, her thigh brushed against a side table, sending a not quite empty bottle of wine crashing to the floor. Topaz eyes popped open in time to observe her clumsy half-hearted effort to curtail disaster. She had managed to slow the bottle's momentum as it glanced off her outstretched palm, leaving a splatter of blood-red droplets on her palm and, as she found when she licked her lips, apparently her face.

"Looks like I've caught you red-handed," Logan remarked, a smirk spreading across his face. "Here."

He stood quickly, graceful despite the amount of alcohol he must have consumed over the last several hours and reached in his pocket to procure a folded blue handkerchief bearing the initials *LP*.

Alex was too shaken to respond at first. The unexpected noise had burned up the last of her adrenaline. The argument with Ian and the fact that she might have actual blood on her hands was too much to bear. As Logan reached over to wipe the wine droplets from her face himself, a switch flipped on in her brain, and she snatched the monogrammed cloth from the air.

"Thanks," she murmured, running the soft fabric over her face and then her hands until she revealed the stark white of her palms again.

Logan had disappeared behind the bar and began rattling through the contents on the lower shelves, emerging seconds later with two glasses and a handful of oranges. Still unsettled by the night's events, Alex tottered over to the bar where an orangish-red concoction awaited her in an overly tall glass. Wearily, she slid into a barstool.

"Have you seen Ian?"

"Tall, sarcastic dude who thinks he's God's gift to women and doesn't know how to dress?"

Alex attempted a glare, but even such a small gesture required too much emotional energy.

"Funny, that's exactly what he said about you."

Logan quirked a smile and became absorbed in his task of peeling an orange. "Haven't seen him—other than earlier—when he came to stake his claim."

I don't have time for this. Alex inwardly groaned. The male imperative to challenge each another for the coveted position of alpha had never impressed her.

"Ian doesn't need to stake anything. I'm taken."

"From what I hear, Ian isn't the one who's been staking people."

Alex's head jerked up. "What did you say?"

"Folks are actually comparing you to Black Widow—a regular femme fatale. Of course, I said you seemed more like a Jean Grey to me."

Whatever color was left in Alex's face drained back into her central vasculature, leaving her skin feeling clammy. She tried to stabilize the shaking in her voice.

"Where did you hear any of this?"

"Josef stopped by when he got back from your little late-night adventures, and I treated him to a well-deserved stiff drink."

Alex glanced down at her hands, made pristine again by her aggressive wiping. Her hands were small with petite fingers. They were the hands she had placed on numerous tiny abdomens and shoved in tons of sterile gloves for procedures. Not the hands of someone who would hurt someone else, even if they deserved it.

Red and orange layers sloshed about as a glass was shoved toward her.

"He's going to be fine by the way." Logan casually dropped an orange slice into her drink.

"You don't know that," Alex responded quietly.

"I do," he replied, taking a swig of his own drink and plunking it down on the counter in front of him.

"How?"

The dominant part of Alex's brain did not want to believe that this could be made right, not until she was forced to suffer and self-flagellate a bit more.

Logan looked positively giddy at the revelation he was about to make. This tiny gift of absolution that Alex so desired.

"The Tanzanian police had been after those guys for an entire year for elephant theft. They hog-tied them and tossed them in the back of their truck...but not before Josef saw your friend wake up and wonder what the hell had happened."

"Really?" Alex asked incredulously, allowing her burden to lighten the tiniest amount like the release of a single balloon.

"Yes ma'am." His Texas accent accentuated the phrase, and they shared a brief but meaningful smile.

"Wow. Thanks for letting me know."

Relief flooded through her, and she tipped the tall glass rim to her lips in a semi-celebratory gesture. Syrupy sweetness met her tongue, and she swallowed quickly before she could process the aftertaste.

"This is terrible," she choked, wiping her sleeve across her lips. "What's in here?"

"Tequila sunrise," Logan replied, draining his own glass in one fell swoop. "I guess I mistook you for someone who preferred something sweet."

"It's never my first choice." Alex tried to hide her disgust behind a wry smile.

"Noted. It seems like you do prefer...complexity."

His expression had changed, golden irises drinking her in by the eyeful. Despite their mineral color, they were soft, like a ray of sunshine on bronzed skin. Eyes that had only known pleasure and comfort. The playful lock of chestnut hair on his forehead glinted in the dying embers of firelight in the corner.

"Can I interest you in something else?"

Was he talking about drinks or himself? *Not in a million years.* Alex broke the tension with a forced laugh.

"I only need one thing tonight."

She hopped off the barstool, leaving his handkerchief crumpled in a tight ball next to her unfinished drink.

After circling the main building twice and checking their room once more, Alex determined that there was only one more place that Ian could be emoting. She pushed open the heavy side door to the barn-shaped building she had visited only hours earlier. It seemed like a lifetime ago. With a definitive shove, she was bathed in amber light from a solitary hurricane lamp that hung from the rafters.

With one terrible problem behind her, she set out to face her second, much more delicate one. One quick glance around the central area of the oversized shed failed to reveal the object of her affection, so she ventured down a dim-lit side corridor with a row of sliding doors constructed of steel bars. Only one was occupied.

Ian sat on a squatty stool made from a tree trunk in what appeared to be a gigantic horse stall, only intended for a much bigger mammal. The baby female elephant rested on her side, nestled into a pile of straw that surrounded her like a pillow. Her side rose and fell with regularity and much-improved depth, which meant that she was hopefully nearing wakefulness. Ian's head reclined back resting on the wood paneling behind him, a light snore emanating from his flaring nostrils, a half-empty bottle of bourbon at his feet.

Alex smiled and wrapped her hands around the cold steel. He really did keep a bourbon stash readily available all over the world. She tugged forcefully at the bars. They remained in place, impervious to her efforts until finally, she heard a faint click and was able to wedge herself through the narrow gap.

Ian had one eye open. One beautifully hued eye that reminded her of an ocean's sky. Limitless and depthless. Eyes that she had willingly been consumed by. He rubbed one hand over a face etched with exhaustion.

"She hasn't woken up yet."

Alex cautiously picked her way over to the elephant and kneeled in the straw, placing one hand gingerly on her leathery forehead. She used two fingers to gently pry open her eyelid and illuminate the pupil inside. It was quite a bit bigger than the last time she had checked and responded briskly to the light exposure.

"She will. It's just a matter of time now," Alex said confidently, brushing her hands over her jean-clad thighs.

"Good. That's good." Ian reached down for the bourbon bottle, pulling out the stopper with a notable pop, releasing the vapors inside. He took a sip and set it back down in its previous position in the dirt. "The guy's going to be okay by the way."

"I know," Alex said quickly, eager to navigate the conversation to the imaginary elephant in the room rather than the actual one. "Apparently, I am being compared to a certain Avenger."

Ian arched one brow quizzically before his features settled back into melancholy.

"I saw Logan in the bar earlier. Word travels fast, I guess." She screwed up her face, intense relief washing over her once again, grateful this had become a satirical comedy instead of a tragedy.

"You tried the bar, first?"

"Of course," she replied, her eyes drifting to the bourbon bottle on the ground, firmly nestled into a mound of dirt.

He curled his lip and nodded like he couldn't dispute her decision and then flattened out his palms on his thighs to steady himself. She heard a deep indrawing of breath and braced herself. For what exactly, she didn't know.

"I'm not sorry," he said quietly, his voice calm but hard like a river stone.

She could imagine his emotions swirling around it like rapids, bubbling around its solidarity. Before she could respond, he continued.

"I'm not sorry for dragging you out of there and I would do it all over again. I will never support choices that put you in danger or hurt you or threaten you, so if that's your expectation, I'll never live up to it, and you should do us both a favor and walk away right now."

At a different time in her life, Alex would have obeyed. The fear of rejection...the feeling of being unworthy of such love would have carried her out of the barn, slamming shut a physical and emotional door that she would have kept closed for an eternity. But she wasn't the girl she once was. She was choosing to live a life that rose above her most basic fears.

Put on your phoenix wings, whispered her subconscious. She stood but didn't make a move toward Ian, not even a gesture. Instead, she stayed perfectly still, breathing in the sweet smell of hay and elephant musk.

"I don't always make the best...decisions. And I don't expect you to like all of them, but there is one that I will *never* give up."

"And what's that?"

She sensed him steel himself for her answer.

"You."

The steel began to bend as his expression transitioned from apprehension to astonishment. A spark of hope ignited in his eyes, and his lips parted in involuntary surprise. Alex wanted to go to him then, to bury herself in his scent and meld herself to his skin as sinewy arms wrapped around her middle. She wanted nothing more than to lose herself in the intoxicating feeling of sensation apart from logic, but he wasn't reaching out either physically or emotionally, and she faltered.

Ian closed his eyes briefly and tipped his chin upward.

"I'm not...right for you, Alex. Nothing has changed. I haven't changed. I still don't even know why you changed your mind about us."

The moment had come. The door had opened. All she had to do was walk through it. She mentally scurried to the other side before she could change her mind.

"It was never about me wanting to live a life of freedom and self-sacrifice," Alex said. "I thought that if I couldn't make you perfectly happy that I didn't deserve you...that I couldn't possibly have you and the life I wanted...that my love would never be enough, and eventually, you would leave me."

"Why in the world would you ever think that?"

"Because I had a terrible childhood."

"How terrible?" he probed.

Alex was saved from elaborating further by the thunderous heave of a giant head and plate-sized feet striking the ground.

EIGHT

Alex was thrust backward when the giant baby reared her head and swung it to and fro as she emerged from her sedated state. Her body stiffened as she plummeted through space, preparing for the inevitable connection with the dirt floor. But instead, she connected with a solid mid-section and a strong pair of hands that caught her in mid-flight.

"Thanks," she murmured.

"Any time."

Ian's face was motionless except for a slight brief upward movement of his lips, but his eyes burned into hers with cautious hope. Any time. She knew in the depths of her soul that he meant those words. In times of good and bad. During sacrifice and bliss. He would love her through it all.

A wayward trunk struck him in the arm, coaxing them both into action. They each took a side of their precious baby as she staggered back and forth, using their own body weight to stabilize her trajectory.

Alex had a flashback of herself as a gangly teenager in another barn in the humidity of summer with an equally gangly chestnut horse who didn't quite know what to do with his size. Her left foot still ached sometimes where he had crushed it the summer before her senior year. She glanced down to ensure that her boots stayed out of the path of an even larger set of feet.

"How are you doing over there?" Ian grunted.

Alex couldn't see anything but the top of Ian's head, but she could hear him breathing heavily on the opposite side of the elephant.

"Better than you," she replied, and he snorted in response.

The elephant had finally stabilized on her shaky legs and

extended her trunk to explore the straw-covered floor.

"Do you think she's hungry?" Ian asked and bent down to gather a handful of hay, which he extended toward her eager trunk.

"Maybe we should start with fresh water." Alex chewed her lip, extrapolating her pediatrician training to her pachyderm problem.

"I'll get some," Ian replied, moments later returning with a red plastic bucket.

A puddle of water sloshed onto the sandy floor when he settled it into one corner. The elephant skated the tip of her trunk across the surface but didn't drink. She dipped her head back and forth several times making weak trumpeting noises of distress. Ian ran his hands through his hair.

"What's wrong with her?"

"I'm not sure, but she's dehydrated, so we need to get her to drink somehow." Alex bent down and swirled the tips of her fingers through the bucket. "Sometimes when kids are stressed, they won't eat or drink, even if they need to."

She held her hand up to the elephant's flaccid trunk and rubbed some of the cool liquid on its tip. The elephant brought the trunk to her mouth, and Alex's excitement built as she shoved it forcefully into the bucket.

Right as she exchanged a broad smile with Ian, the elephant whipped her trunk out of the water, sending the bucket flying and soaking the front of Alex's white t-shirt. She swore under her breath while squeezing the excess water from her hair, rivulets dripping down her cleavage.

"What do we do now?"

She glanced up and caught the sight of Ian's face awash in lust.

"Wet t-shirt contest?"

"What do I get if I win?" Alex asked playfully.

"Me. As your personal tour guide to ecstasy."

He smirked, and Alex blushed crimson as her face, as well as the rest of her, pulsed with desire. When she stood, a giant ear smacked her in the face, followed shortly by nothing less than an idea of pure brilliance.

"Ian, does the vet keep any supplies here?"

"Yes," he said slowly. "In a closet at the end of the hallway."

"Be right back."

Alex pressed a quick kiss to his cheek and trilled with excitement as she strode down the concrete passageway and flung open the door to a storage closet. When her pupils adjusted to the dim interior, Alex began examining the contents of the haphazard stacks of cardboard boxes. She pulled out vitamin supplements, antibiotics, and deworming supplies, none of which she needed. After shoving almost every box to the back wall, she spied an orange plastic toolbox and flipped open the hinges to view what was inside.

"Jackpot."

"Elephants have really large veins in their ears," Alex explained to Ian as she pushed another syringe of isotonic saline through the IV catheter dangling from the floppy gray skin.

Within the orange box, she had found an elephant emergency kit, including large-bore IV catheters and a few bags of fluid. Ian had stabilized a large territory of leathery ear, and she had poked the biggest vein she could find. He watched from a stool in the corner, intrigued by her efforts to push syringes full of life-giving fluid into a flapping appendage.

"You made that look so easy."

He looked at her appraisingly, and she snorted.

"Well, usually I'm putting catheters into vessels the size of a strand of thread, so this was a piece of cake. I just hope it works."

What was the proper dose of resuscitation fluid for a baby elephant? Alex had no idea, but she could wing it. She continued pushing fluid until the pink mucosa at the end of the elephant's trunk felt moist, and her amber eyes seemed a touch brighter. After three entire bags had been infused, the baby elephant dropped to her knees and tucked her head, her side heaving with deep, regular respiratory cycles.

"Is she okay?" Ian asked, his forearms resting on his thighs, hands clasping and unclasping with nervousness.

"Yeah. I think she's going to be fine."

Alex felt a surge of contentment and protectiveness that could only be explained by the most primitive source of emotion there was—maternal instinct. Her hand trailed over the enormous cranium, the skin under her fingertips sweetly warm.

"What now?" Alex asked.

Ian placed his hand next to Alex's, and they stroked the giant head in unison like a pair of proud but exhausted parents. Eventually, Ian found her grimy hand, clumps of dirt under her nails, and clasped it in his own.

"Come on. I know where they keep the fresh hay. She might be hungry when she wakes up."

Ian led her to the opposite end of the barn, where they climbed a ladder to the second floor of the structure. He flipped a switch, and an entire floor was illuminated by an overhead chandelier hanging from a peaked roof. Barrels of grain lined one wall, but most of the space was filled with a towering pyramid of sweet-smelling alfalfa that was still green from being freshly cut and tied into square bales.

The smell alone propelled Alex back over a decade to her summer job as a stable girl for an English barn near her hometown. Moonlight streamed through the only window and, with it, the exact quietude of night that Alex needed to tell her story.

"I'll be right back," she said, leaving Ian with a quizzical look as he began to separate some hay for the baby.

When she returned, he was seated on one of the bales closest to the window, his face bathed in starlight, his lips full and parted as he inhaled the night air. She flipped the light off, plunging them both into darkness except for the moon's glow.

"You once told me," she said, edging toward him over the piles of hay, "that story time deserved proper refreshment."

A wry grin crossed her face as she proffered the retrieved bottle of bourbon, taking a quick swig before relinquishing it to Ian. Sensing the tension of the moment, he said nothing but took the bottle and put it to his lips while she settled into her thoughts.

"Once upon a time, there was a girl who lived in a house on a river..."

Alex tried to leave nothing out, fishing memories from a dark pool whose surface had rarely been broken. She told him of her childhood home and the horrors it witnessed until it was washed away by a merciful storm one fateful night while her father took last call at the local bar. She and her mother had escaped drowning only by wading through miles of water to reach help.

"My father was a terrorist. He was selfish and cruel, and the more cruel he became, the more impermeable I became."

Ian had not moved a muscle, his eyes trained on her face. She couldn't read his expression and couldn't rid herself of a fleeting fear that being this vulnerable might have been the wrong decision.

"Do you have scars?" he asked, his voice soft but raw.

"Only on the inside."

Alex focused her gaze on the moon, comforted by its impartiality. "My mother called me last spring to tell me that he died of liver cancer, and I went back home for the funeral. We buried him in the cemetery behind the church that I took you to...and when I walked across that bridge...something changed."

Alex closed her eyes to sink further into the sensory memories of that day—the spring breeze carrying scents of bluebonnets and the sun kissing her face as she tipped it upward.

"I realized that my entire life—the good and the bad—had happened under his influence and that I could choose to live differently...to believe that I was worth loving...to accept more love than I thought I deserved and return it."

She stole a glance in Ian's direction, encouraged by the brightness of his eyes and the tenderness in his face. "This was the freedom I had always searched for. So, with this gift and a twelve-hundred-dollar inheritance, I bought the last seat on a flight to London."

Ian shook his head as if trying to shake all the pieces of a puzzle into place when they wouldn't quite cooperate. "I can't believe you endured all of that and didn't end up..."

His eyes narrowed as he struggled to find the word he sought.

"Broken?" Alex finished.

"Yes."

"I'm completely broken," Alex confirmed. "But I'm really good at hiding it."

She smiled, but it failed to reach her eyes. A sadness had seeped into them and, along with it, a heap of doubt. Maybe it would have been better to keep this part of herself confined to memories. Another person knowing her past elevated it from a forgotten nightmare to something much more real.

"You're not broken. You are the most...formidable person I have ever known."

"Here's to fortitude," she said, reaching for the bourbon bottle and the precious burn that would quench her other senses for a moment.

"You are not who I thought you were," Ian mused.

The words themselves stung, and Alex momentarily felt her insides crumble. This reaction was her worst fears realized. Who wanted to buy a broken toy? Who would voluntarily take on the burden of someone else's pain?

She made herself look him in the eye to accept the inevitable blow of rejection from the man she loved. She stared critically and found something she did not expect. Acceptance rather than judgment. Adoration rather than pity. He took the bottle back from her and drained the last remnants of amber liquid.

"When I met you, I was intrigued and maybe even a little intimidated." He held his thumb and index finger about a millimeter apart, and Alex rolled her eyes. "I was drawn to your wit, your passion, your...many other assets." He grinned wickedly and squeezed Alex's knee. "You were composed and beautiful but a complete mess at the same time. I thought you needed someone to sort you out. To protect you from yourself."

Alex shrugged. Some of that was probably true.

"But I didn't realize that you had been protecting yourself for a long while before I came along," he whispered, dragging his thumb across her cheek. "And that what you needed was something else entirely." His voice was thick with emotion. "I love you, Alex. I love every good and terrible part of you, and I will love you every single day of your life. Every second I am on this earth come hell or high water."

Alex's heart swelled as it thundered inside her chest and she let out a shaky laugh.

"Did you just say high water?"

His face fell as he searched hers with concerned eyes. All the emotion welling up inside her needed an outlet, and she burst out laughing at his unintended wit. He smiled and shook his head as she laughed and then cried, because one heightened emotion begot another. A pair of warms palms gripped her cheeks, and gentle thumbs began to wipe the tears collecting at the rims of her eyes.

"I love you," she whispered hoarsely.

"I love you," he repeated firmly, reverently, as he raked his eyes over her face. "Now kiss me."

Their lips met in midair, the tears and grime staining Alex's face all but forgotten. Her mouth became the conduit to her soul. What started as a gentle meeting of lips quickly evolved into a desperate attempt to lave the raw edges of vulnerability.

Alex opened her lips wider, desperate to feel his wanton tongue against her own and to taste his promises and offer hers in return. Ian's lips moved at a frenzy-like pace as he pulled her into a standing position and reached his hands underneath her damp t-shirt. He barely broke his connection with her mouth to tug the shirt over her head and then again to rid himself of his own.

Her entire body caught fire when the bare patches of their skin touched. She could feel her nipples hardening underneath her bra, and suddenly even a thin strip of cotton was too much separation from Ian's heaving chest. She shrugged it off, letting it drift delicately to her feet. Nothing in the universe existed except for two bodies clamoring to be made whole.

His eyes surveyed the space, frantically searching for anything suitable to use as a barrier between a pair of lovers and the rough straw. Impatience surged as Alex pulled his head down to her mouth, and he groaned as her teeth caught his bottom lip.

"This is perfect," she whispered. "Just this."

She broke apart from him reluctantly to separate a bale of hay and spread it in a thick pile on the flooring, and then added another layer in the center as he watched curiously.

"You act like you've done this before," he said in amusement, but she caught the ravenous look building in his features.

Alex shrugged guiltily. Ian was her one and only, but she hadn't been opposed to physical interaction her entire life.

"Alexandra Wilde," he teased in mock horror.

She blushed and continued fluffing a pile of hay. "I worked at a barn in high school, and—"

"Say no more," he said flatly.

"Stop," she chided, tossing a handful of straw in his direction. "It was my first kiss and completely innocent."

Ian began moving toward her with the grace of a predator, his lithe body floating through the wedge of moonlight on the floor. When he reached her side, he pulled her to a stand and tipped her head back, letting her hair cascade over her naked back. He exhaled over her lips without kissing her, the scent of bourbon lingering as he moved to bury his face in the exposed skin of her neck.

The heat of his mouth in the space right above her collarbone sent a delicate shiver down her spine, and she moaned. He worked his way up to her ear, his teeth grazing the tender spot beneath her earlobe.

"You aren't innocent anymore, Alexandra, and we are about to do much more than kiss."

Alex squeezed her eyes closed, unwilling to exit the blissful afterglow. She could feel Ian beside her emanating the heat of spent desire as she flipped through the reel of their tryst.

A hand unbuttoning her jeans and slipping past the waist. Her fingers digging into the muscles of Ian's upper back. Searing lips on her face then her neck then a wayward tongue on her nipple. The incredible, beautiful ache being massaged into ecstasy. The feel of Ian's skin under her teeth as she released. All of the mental imagery—every tactile sensation, every breathless moment—she gathered up and imprinted them in her memory in a fireproof, waterproof box.

"I think we'll name her Ujasiri. Siri for short," Ian murmured into her hair.

Alex was propelled from reliving her sexual fantasy-turned-reality.

"What? Who?" She flipped onto her side to gauge Ian's expression.

"Our baby."

Her stomach flipped before she realized he was talking about the elephant.

"What does that mean?" she asked, drinking in the sheer beauty of his eyes alight with promise and purpose. He winked at her and grinned.

"Fortitude."

NINE

Alex peered closely at the plastic-wrapped box that was the size of a nice weekender roller bag. Her fingers tingled with anticipation as they stripped the wrapping to reveal a pixeled screen surrounded by uniformly shaped knobs and square buttons. It might as well be Christmas in September. She was giddy with excitement as she ripped the last of the plastic off the smooth white surface of the machine's base. She could hear the throaty exclamations behind her coming from the cluster of new interns as they beheld the pediatric ward's first mechanical ventilator.

As promised, the pediatric department now had a fattened budget thanks to the Devall Foundation's generosity. Alex had met with Dr. K every day during her first week back at work to stratify the requests and order the necessary supplies. Alex and Lesedi, the ward's nurse manager, had set aside a small square of geography in the corner to serve as the "ICU bed" for the one child who was sicker than all the rest. Luckily, during the hospital's construction, the engineers had possessed enough foresight to provide the basic structural components for wall oxygen. Without it, running a ventilator was near impossible.

"Let's try it out, Dr. Alex," exclaimed Lucia, an intern who had appeared from the back of the group and had started fiddling with some of the knobs.

"We will. I just need to figure out where everything connects," responded Alex.

Electrical equipment had never been her forte, but with an instruction manual, how hard could it be? Two hours later and several forays into Google translate for the instruction manual written in German, Alex had still not achieved her goal. The air and oxygen hoses had been attached successfully, and the screen depicted a ridiculous infographic of a stick person hooked up to a ventilator, but she had not gotten the machine to push any air through the accordion-style tubing.

One of the interns had jogged down the street to a multi-purpose store to pick up a balloon and a set of rubber bands that could serve as their surrogate "patient lungs." The red balloon sat in a deflated heap as Alex's lips were tempted to spew a few choice curse words at the screen. As much time as she had spent twiddling the various knobs and pressing the buttons of this machine, she had thought that dealing with the actual mechanics would be easier.

Of course, in fellowship, she had been spoiled by the diligent expertise of the respiratory therapists, the true unsung heroes of the medical world. A group of specialists that not only commanded authority over all types of respiratory machinery but also provided life-saving lung clearance therapies that awarded them immense gratitude in the form of expectorated secretions of various shades of green. A groan of desperation started in her chest and exited her lips.

"I'll be back in a minute," she said, thrusting the dog-eared instruction manual to the nearest white coat in her peripheral vision.

Warm air enveloped her as she loped across the courtyard to the administrative offices, not pausing until she was outside the wood paneling bearing the inscribed label, Dr. Kefentse. She could hear voices rising and falling from the inside. She knocked anyway. The voices stilled and were replaced by the scraping noise of chairs being pushed back and footsteps inching toward the floor near the door.

When the door swung inward, Alex was met with two pairs of inquisitive eyes—one belonging to Dr. K, her boss, mentor, and longtime friend, and the other belonging to a female face that she failed to recognize.

"Dr. Alex," boomed the familiar baritone of Dr. K. "I was just mentioning you to our newest staff member."

Alex averted her gaze from the kind, smooth lines of Dr. K's forehead to the flat, expressionless face under a crown of a spiky red pixie cut that peered over his shoulder.

"This is Dr. Samantha Drake. She will be taking over for Roxanne until we can hire a local head of obstetrics."

"Hi. It's really nice to meet you," Alex offered.

She held out her hand and was met with a reluctant grasp and a forced smile. Dr. Drake's hand was uncomfortably warm and her grip just a little too intense for the circumstances.

"I go by Sam," she said in an East coast accent, dropping Alex's hand and shoving her own into the pocket of her white coat.

She was tall, almost as tall as Dr. K, and solidly built, like a female version of Gaston from Beauty and the Beast. A vision of her seated at breakfast with a plate of six hard-boiled eggs in front of her covered in hot sauce flashed through Alex's mind, and she had to stifle a smile.

"I go by Alex," Alex replied, searching the girl's face for even the hint of a smile.

Without Rox here at PM, Alex's life had felt incomplete. Sam was no Rox, but maybe they could strike up a congenial friendship.

"That's what I hear," Sam replied, not bothering to hide the disdain dripping from her words like grease from the fat cakes in the PM cafeteria.

Her eyes, the color of malachite and just as rock hard, revealed nothing. There was no depth to them, like every word and emotion around her deflected right off. Alex had seen more displays of emotion in the geckos at the Houston Zoo.

Without waiting for Alex to step aside, Sam exited the cramped office and marched out of the glass doors into the courtyard like she had just been called into surgery, even though no semblance of an emergency was waiting for her on the other side of the doorway. Alex blew out a breath.

As a socially-challenged introvert herself, she could choose to disregard this entire interaction. After all, where would anyone be without the benefit of second chances?

Dr. K cleared his throat, his typical polite sign for "I have something to attend to, so get on with it." Alex tried and failed to fill up the doorway with her frame.

"I need something," she started. "Or rather someone."

"Mmm. I guessed as much."

She had his attention, albeit briefly, and she forged ahead.

"The new ventilator for the pediatric ward," Alex started, then paused to chew on her bottom lip. "I'm going to need some help calibrating it and maintaining it, not to mention teaching the staff how to use it."

"Mmm," he repeated and picked up his spectacles from behind the desk, running the lenses over his crisp button-down before placing them on the bridge of his nose. "As a physician, I want to say yes. Whatever we need for the kids. But as an administrator, I need to think broader. We need to be wise about the grant money, Alex. The hospital has many needs."

"Of course," she stammered.

Asking for what she wanted had always made her uncomfortable, and a familiar clamminess spread to the insoles of her feet. This was different, though. Children's lives were at stake—children who would otherwise perish at the hands of pneumonia or sepsis, or drowning.

"Please try to be creative and, for now, use the resources you have to achieve your goals."

As he settled into his worn leather desk chair and picked up the rotary phone, Alex took that as her sign to leave. As she rounded the first brick pillar of the standalone office building, an unexpected shape with crossed arms and the aggressive stance of a hyena guarding a kill was waiting for her. Alex's white trainers made a squeaking noise as she skidded to an abrupt halt, almost falling off the curb in the process.

"Hello again, Sam." Alex sighed internally, swallowing her disappointment while she trying to ascertain what this anti-Rox-like female might want.

"I bet you're used to getting everything you ask for."

"I don't have any idea what you're talking about," Alex replied.

She had no clue where this conversation was headed and mentally began building a demilitarized zone between her and the red-headed hyena.

Sam snorted derisively. "I seriously doubt that. You're pretty smart from what I hear. And pretty convincing."

"Pardon me?"

"Screwing the head of the Devall Foundation is a sure-fire way to get exactly what you want...in more ways than one."

Where the hell was this coming from?

"I suggest," Alex said coldly, her voice resembling the sound of ice skates skirting across a frozen pond, "that you stop talking."

"I mean...whatever...I hear he's hot as hell and just as good in bed."

Sam narrowed her gaze and uncrossed her arms to shove them down into the abyss of her mammoth white coat.

"But when your extracurricular activities interfere with the success of my department, the situation becomes inappropriate and unprofessional. Trust me, you don't want me as an enemy."

Her red hair blazed a trail of fire behind her as she turned on her heel and stalked in the opposite direction.

The cool air that blew through the courtyard contrasted with the warm pink flush crawling up Alex's neck. Despite a brisk walk around the square and a trip into the cafe to get paper cup of warm tea, her discomfort only worsened. She inhaled the vapors from the thick lava-colored concoction of red bush tea and then let the bitterness coat her tongue much like the previous conversation had. Sitting down on the bench where she and Rox used to share sandwiches and bits of gossip, she replayed the conversations from this morning in her head.

In a way, she was accustomed to getting the things she asked for, where medicine was concerned, at least. One of the things she loved about the pediatric ICU was the lack of boundaries...the limitlessness.

In Philadelphia, at one of the best children's hospitals in the entire world, she could summon a massive outpouring of resources, at any time of the day, any day of the year. She had once even put a pregnant teenager with severe pneumonia on ECMO on Christmas morning. While the rest of the world was unwrapping gifts in the pajamas, her team had been saving a life. Two, actually. She loved that about her profession.

In Botswana, where the resources were scarcer, but the dedication to the children no less, she had committed to build a program that addressed pediatric survival. A program that focused not only on the children surviving but thriving and returning to an enhanced quality of life after their serious illness. They would not be able to save every kid, but she had to start somewhere. She had to start with one.

Ian had encouraged the foundation to donate the money to PM, and Dr. K had promised her that most of it would be used for the pediatrics department. Her relationship with Ian had absolutely zero influence on how the money was distributed, or did it? As she peered into the abyss of her tea, she realized she had no idea how the foundation's internal structure worked.

From Sam's vehemence, she surmised that the obstetrics division was somehow being slighted and Alex was the natural blame target. Dr. K., in his wisdom and diplomacy, had asked her to be creative, which was probably a plea to stretch the grant money as far as possible. Her tea had become lukewarm as her hands had siphoned up its heat, and she dumped it into a nearby patch of dried grass. *Be creative.* That's precisely what she would do.

With a renewed sense of purposeful calm, she strode into the pediatric ward where the interns in their white coats resembled a flock of sheep as they huddled around Alex's mechanical nemesis of the day.

"Any luck?" she asked, raising up on tiptoes to peer over their hunched shoulders.

They remained silent, emitting a grunt or two as Lucia flipped the pages of the instruction manual. The red balloon remained a deflated, poorly compliant blob. She stared it and then at the blank screen of the ventilator, stubbornly unwilling to give her the blue pixeled peaks and valleys that rose and fell, indicating that air was actually moving through the plastic tubing. Somewhere behind her, a door burst open and struck the drywall so violently that a particulate cloud of dust puffed into the open doorway.

Lesedi and one of the other young nurses who was fresh out of school were pushing a stretcher toward her, the gyrating wheels careening over the cracks in the linoleum floor. The stretcher contained a girl of around three with braided hair clutching a stuffed toy that was so worn Alex only realized it was an elephant by its yarn-like tail.

The girl lay reclined on two pillows, her chest heaving with each breath that was only interrupted by rasping bursts of coughing that sounded like machine gunfire. The noise spurred the entire room into a flurry of activity as the stretcher wheeled into the bed space containing the ventilator like a formula one car making a pitstop.

"I need oxygen on her," Alex called into the frenetic din and noticed that Lesedi's junior nurse had already placed a mask on her face and was dialing up the flow on the bulky green tank at the foot of the bed.

Grabbing her stethoscope from around her neck, Alex shoved it under the girl's shirt, which was damp with sweat from the exertion of breathing. She heard rhonchi everywhere inside her chest, like the sound bubble tea makes when a person blows into it with a straw. With every breath, precious air molecules were straining to diffuse through the copious lakes of mucus filling up this girl's lungs.

One of the interns, a quiet, studious young man with heavy, black-rimmed glasses, clipped a portable pulse oximeter machine to her finger. Alex studied his face as he waited for the digits to light up and then saw his look of consternation right before he flipped the screen to show her the result. Seventy-nine percent and falling. Alex cut her eyes over to the blue screen of the ventilator and the dormant red balloons.

"I guess it's sink or swim time, guys," she said wryly.

They divided up into two teams: Alex took one of the interns, planning to stabilize the child and place a breathing tube, while the other team was assigned to troubleshoot the ventilator. She needed a respiratory therapist. Quickly punching in the digits she knew by heart into her phone, she waited for the ring while mentally praising Ian for encouraging her to upgrade to a global plan on her cell phone.

"Pediatric ICU, how can I help you?"

"Audrey, can you put me through to one of the RT's?" It was still night shift in Philadelphia.

"Anything for you Dr. Wilde," she cackled, and Alex could imagine her long manicured nails punching in the numbers on the keypad.

"Hello, it's Ritu with respiratory."

"Ritu, it's Alex. I need your help."

Alex glanced up once while managing the child's airway, long enough to see the interns excitedly programming buttons as Ritu instructed them via speakerphone. The young girl, whose name she had learned was Keeya, had been ill for two days with high fevers and progressive respiratory distress, most likely some type of pneumonia. When pneumonia was this severe and progressive, it didn't matter what type. Her lungs begged for relief. When Alex placed the breathing tube through her vocal cords, a torrent of yellow mucus surged up the tube and out the end.

"Take the bag and squeeze it just like this," she instructed the junior nurse, Botshelo, who had placed a trembling hand on the end of the inflated green rubber bag. "Just make sure the chest is rising, and the bag is emptying." Alex smiled at her in encouragement.

Botshelo turned her attention to the sedated young girl, now dependent on them for every single breath, as Alex maneuvered herself over to the mechanical ventilator. A miraculous sight met her eyes. She watched the red balloon inflate and deflate in consecutive turns as the screen captured the various pressure and flow waveforms in beautiful symmetry. She sent a silent prayer of thanks to Ritu and all respiratory therapists who were saving lives all over the planet with their expertise at this hour.

Less than an hour had passed since little Keeya had rolled into their ICU. As Alex connected the ventilator tubing to her breathing tube, the gravity of the moment tumbled over her like a tidal wave. A year ago, this beautiful young lady would not have survived the night. Now she had a chance—Alex would make sure of that. Her survival not only meant an incredible miracle for her family, it also meant that Dr. K would see what a difference they were making with the grant money.

"Congratulations everyone. We did it. I'll see you all in the morning."

The interns finished their day under a beautiful sunset seen through the picturesque window along the west-facing wall. Alex watched them as they walked away. Some were engrossed in their phones while others talked animatedly about the events of the day. She smiled as she pressed her back against the wall, sinking into a sitting position right next to the beeping ventilator.

As the sun was enveloped by the night sky, swallowed up into the mouth of its blackness, Alex watched the steady rise and fall of the girl's chest and listened to the mechanical chirping of the machine that kept her alive. Every so often, an alarm would sound, rousing her out of a semi-sleep, and she would leap to her feet to silence it and then troubleshoot the problem.

There were so many variables to adjust and maintain—the airflow, the oxygen concentration, the respiratory rate. When the ventilator alarmed "high pressure," she had to pass a suction catheter into the breathing tube to clear it of secretions. Without performing this seemingly easy task, the ventilator would just stop delivering the desired quantity of air into Keeya's struggling lungs.

The moon rose and cast its silvery light onto the stained yellow floor. It brought the rest of the ward into quietude. Except for a nurse's occasional murmuring to a fussy baby or the shuffling of papers on the desk, Alex could detect no other sounds apart from the noises in her corner. Having just adjusted the pressure knob and raised the oxygen level, she was granted a reprieve from the incessant dinging, and her brain drifted into a state of brief tranquility.

Thoughts of Ian unfurled like a clean cotton sheet in the gentlest of breezes. After their adventure in Tanzania, they had parted ways.

She had returned to Gaborone to start work and Ian went back to London to fulfill the multitude of tasks Lydia had compiled in his absence. Before, Alex had existed on the high of their romantic interludes for weeks while easily slipping back into her work and her life, but this time was different, and she knew why.

Work had always been a surrogate for who or what she was missing in life. It was thrilling and fulfilling and required her utmost attention, both physically and emotionally. Previously, it had been easy to swap her profession out for Ian and vice versa. She only had so much emotional bandwidth, didn't she?

After her revelation about her past, Ian had gripped her entire body with strong arms and even stronger unspoken emotions that settled into her very bones. In her mind, she pictured a Venn diagram. They still existed as two whole individual circles but now with intersecting arcs that created a shared elliptical sliver. For the first time in her entire life, her constructs of home—of security, of life, of her past, present, and future—were intertwined with someone else.

TEN

Alex reclined on a slatted bench. Its once brilliant green paint was peeling in several places and had faded to the color of Oscar the Grouch's fur. She squinted into the sun's glare, partially blocked by a rickety playground set. From her perch, she could hear the bustling noise in the pediatric ward through a window cast open to welcome a springtime breeze. The playground was rarely used. Most of the kids were too ill to consider tromping up the slide, and those that were well enough could be sent home with their parents. Apart from an older woman in a canary yellow skirt flipping through a leatherbound Bible, Alex was the only patron here today.

After two days and two nights camped out by little Keeya's stretcher, the tiny hair cells of her ears vibrated from the high-pitched alarm symphony. Even the sound of muffled children's voices and a short, sweet tune from a bird on a nearby branch seemed too much for her overworked eardrums to process. Tonight, she was definitely making it home to sleep in her own bed. Maybe.

Luckily, Alex's baking adventures had paid off and solidified an acquaintance, if not a friendship, with her neighbor down the street, a retired social worker from Kentucky who lived in Botswana half the year and had a predilection for anything chocolate. Mary Lou seemed to prefer canines to humans and was happy to watch McCartney while Alex's shift at the hospital stretched into the following day or days. She glanced at her watch. Ian would be at the office buried under Lydia's demands, but another Londoner she desperately missed might be free.

When the ring was picked up, an explosion of commotion involving scraping metal and animated voices filled her ear.

"You're on speakerphone with Dr. Clarke," said a monotone

75

voice.

Alex stalled for a second. "It's just me, Rox. I can call you back."

"No need." She heard the voices fade as she was taken off speakerphone. "Just cleaning up after a C-section. Mum and babies are doing fine."

Rox breathed heavily into the phone, and then Alex heard the squeak of vinyl as she settled herself into a chair.

"Babies?" Alex asked.

"Twins—one boy and one girl."

"A perfect set. What an overachiever," Alex joked.

"I don't know...two of each might be nice," Rox mused, and Alex could picture her examining a set of neatly manicured pink nails as she talked.

"You want four kids?" Alex exclaimed.

"Maybe," she admitted. "How many do you want?"

"I have kids," Alex said wryly. She made a mental loop around the pediatric ward, performing a summation of the kids that were currently admitted. "Thirteen at this moment."

"You'll see. Once you and Ian get married, the baby bug will strike."

Alex let out a laugh that bordered on a guffaw. "Ian and I have literally been back together for—" She glanced at her phone. "Forty-three days. Getting married isn't even on our minds right now."

Rox said nothing more, and they settled into a pause that was pregnant with some secretive knowledge that Alex didn't necessarily want to know. Before the discomfort completely filled the pit of Alex's stomach, Rox changed the subject.

"How are things at PM?"

"Good, I guess."

"You're a terrible liar. Spill it."

As Alex launched into a monologue of the ventilator saga, her uncomfortable meeting with Dr. K, and the public display of disdain from the new obstetrics director, she realized how long it had been since her snarled-up emotions had worked themselves free.

"And she thinks that my relationship with Ian is affecting the distribution of the grant money...which it's not." Alex huffed out a breath, enough to send a buzzing gnat whizzing in the opposite direction.

"Well, it is, and it isn't," Rox remarked.

"What does that mean?"

"I don't think Ian has direct input, but Dr. K knows you are together, and I'm sure he has entertained the idea that keeping you happy keeps Ian happy, and therefore, the hospital happy."

"But our relationship would never—"

"It already has," Rox added quietly.

"How?" Alex challenged

"Dr. K shut down the surgical skills lab for the obstetrics program."

"Why? You worked so hard on that."

"He said there was a funding issue...but I imagine it had something to do with fattening the budget for the pediatrics program."

No wonder Sam, her red-headed nemesis, had spit fire at her outside of Dr. K's office.

"I can't control every—" Alex started and then halted mid-sentence when a blinding flash of light descended on her retinas. "I have to let you go, Rox. Call you later?"

"Later," she yawned into the receiver right before they disconnected.

While Alex was engrossed in her conversation with Rox, two children in flapping hospital gowns had ventured onto the playground and were taking turns pushing each other on the tottering merry-go-round. Their smiles revealed unadulterated glee as they swung around at top speed, ignoring the bumps and squeaks of the rarely used equipment laden with rust at every joint. Sitting near them on the ground, a pale girl with golden hair thrown up in a bun was capturing every moment with a click of her Nikon.

Staunching a flare of irritation, Alex approached the girl. She was seated cross-legged on the hem of her white coat, one eye pressed into her viewfinder with such intensity that she failed to respond when Alex cleared her throat. Alex sighed and, instead, stepped into her line of sight to create a barrier between the camera and the thankfully oblivious children. The blonde girl dropped her camera into her lap and cocked a well-plucked brow in Alex's direction.

"Excuse me?"

Alex sized her up; she was young with wide eyes, an unblemished face and an American accent wearing a short white coat that read "Katherine Mackenzie" in blue stitching.

"What are you doing?" Alex asked politely but with narrowed eyes.

77

The young woman stood up and, at full height, was several inches shorter than Alex with petite features that resembled a porcelain doll. She brushed her hand over the seat of her slacks and looped the camera around her neck.

"Taking photos of the kids. I have really gotten into photography since I got here. These are going to look fantastic!"

Glancing down at the weighty black box around her neck, she started scrolling through a set of digital images. Alex peeked over her cupped hands at the still images of the kids on the playground, babies in cribs in the ward, laboring mothers clutching their backs as they walked the halls of the obstetrics ward.

"What are you doing here at Princess Marina?" Alex asked, trying to tame some of the bite in her voice.

"I'm a third-year medical student," she boasted proudly in a singsong voice. "I'm here doing a rotation with Dr. Drake."

Fantastic.

"Do you have permission to take these photos?" Alex asked pointedly.

A rosy bloom filled the girl's cheeks. "I..." she stammered and began studying the ground for anything remotely interesting.

Alex folded her arms across her chest but regarded the girl gently. She was young and naive but teachable. Probably not so different from Alex herself at one point.

"Please ask Dr. Drake to teach you about respecting the people whose country and hospital you are visiting. And if she's too busy, you can find me in the pediatric ward. Just ask for Dr. Wilde."

As the girl turned on her heel to leave, her bun glinting in the sunlight, Alex caught the eye of the older woman in the yellow skirt, absently flipping through the tissue paper-thin pages of a worn Bible. The woman motioned to her with a withered hand.

Amid the joyful noises of the two children, who had now moved on to the swings, Alex casually walked over and slid onto the bench next to her. The woman's hair was trimmed short, and the sprigs sprouting over her crown were purest white like fallen snow. The years had etched wisdom and possibly even more beauty into her face and, underneath heavy lids, her mocha-colored eyes sparkled with life. She brought her hands together atop her Bible, long bony fingers coming together in the shape of a church steeple. Her pencil-thin lips coalesced in the beginnings of a smile, and Alex simply waited for the words underneath them.

"Everyone comes to Africa wanting pictures of wild animals and suffering children. We are so much more than that."

Alex let the words sink in. "I know," she replied solemnly.

When she was growing up in her small Texas town, Alex's church asked for volunteers one spring break to ride on a van for thirteen hours to a remote village across the border in Guadalajara. They held a Bible camp for the kids and set up a tent for praise and worship in the evenings. As teenagers, Alex and her best friend Justin had been placed in charge of handing out water bottles and plastic baggies of expired over-the-counter medications and vitamins. During one of the sweltering evenings, while the sun dipped behind the dilapidated buildings and gnarled shrubs that were too complex to be called trees, she sat on a bench sharing a sandwich with Justin.

"Hey, you want the rest? Earth to Alex?" Justin flashed her a smile, the sunlight highlighting the copper streaks in his hair.

"I was just thinking."

"Oh no, here we go." He stuffed the rest of the sandwich in his mouth.

"Do you think what we did this week...did it matter?"

"Of course, it did," he said through a huge bite of turkey on white.

"How do you know?" Alex challenged. "How do we even know what these people need? We barely know their language, much less their culture...their beliefs. Handing out expired aspirin doesn't seem helpful at all, and then we leave tomorrow, and we'll probably never see them again. Something's missing."

"You worry too much, Lex." He extended a sinewy arm and ruffled the top of her head.

Justin was the only person who had ever called her Lex.

During medical school and residency, Alex had used every week of precious vacation time to travel to low-income countries for various excursions—medical missions or surgical trips or short courses that taught pediatric resuscitation. Traveling taught her resilience and resourcefulness and stoked her passion for global health. After repetitive trips to the same locations, she felt like she was at the beginning of something rather than the end. She imagined herself as a partner rather than an outsider.

Her heart swelled as she considered the dignified woman now

seated next to her. Somewhere along her global health journey, Alex had learned to serve for the sake of serving rather than for primary gain. Her involvement was never the answer. She was merely the tool that provided a way to reach a solution. Investment was the key, not only in patient care, but in the culture of a place. Its people. Its language. Its heartbeat.

Alex had to stop her hands from reaching over and grasping the brown ones, wrinkled like a pair of raisins left in the sun to bake.

"You seem like you do know," the woman responded, closing up her leatherbound book and dropping it into the embroidered bag that lay at her feet.

Alex hoped she was right. Otherwise, what was her purpose here?

After a quick trip home to shower and change scrubs, a layer of cleanliness rested atop Alex's weighty fatigue. The savvy group of interns had taken responsibility for the mechanics of the ventilator during the day, assigning one person to remain at the bedside in shifts. Nights were different. Only one intern remained in the hospital overnight to handle every single aspect of patient care—issues on the ward, new admissions from the emergency department, and phone calls from outside hospitals hoping to find a bed for a sick child.

No matter how many nights it took, Alex had agreed to perform sentry duty next to the wily contraption keeping Keeya alive while her body recovered from a nasty Streptococcal pneumonia.

Her sneakers had just struck the grit in the parking lot when her phone rang, and a familiar voice sent her insides into a cascade of butterflies.

"I can tell you're missing me."

"How?" Alex tucked the phone into her ear as she pulled her Mary Poppins-worthy tote out of the truck and kicked the door closed with the sole of her shoe.

"Because, if you miss me half as much as I'm missing you..."

His voice trailed off, and she could hear the clattering of dishes in the background. His words had a vice-like grip on her heart. Her response was there circulating in her chest. *Yes—I do miss you, and it's killing me.* But instead of saying the words, she held them tightly inside.

"What are you doing? Are you cooking?"

"Maybe." His voice was quiet, suggestive.

"What are you making?"

"Curry."

How could a two-syllable word that meant sauce-covered meat and vegetables sound completely erotic when uttered by Ian's lips? He must have heard her suck in a quick breath through her teeth because a muffled laugh resounded through the phone receiver.

"And I'm naked."

That was how.

Long after their phone call, the vision of Ian *sans* clothing crouched over a stove of simmering Indian curry refused to be edged out of Alex's consciousness, even when she stepped onto the pediatric ward wearing a lovesick grin. With the subtle cock of one brow, Lesedi honed in on Alex's face, a smile teasing the corners of her mouth.

Once Alex had run through all the lab values and put a stethoscope to each chest, she flopped down on a makeshift pallet in the corner next to the ventilator. Shivering, she pulled her fleece jacket onto her shoulders. Alex could almost smell the scents of cardamom and turmeric wafting through the air instead of antiseptic and dirty sheets.

As much as she loved her job, she had to admit that spending a night in a warm kitchen eating spicy Indian food while gazing at a naked Ian was highly preferable to another night camped out at her patient's bed space. She rubbed her hands together, eking warmth from the ventilator heater exhaust. A question tugged at the hem of her thoughts, and she pulled out her phone.

Awake?

Yep. Lying here thinking of you.

Can I ask you a question?

Anything

Alex faltered before she started typing and then forged ahead. She would rather know the truth and deal with it than otherwise.

Do you have any input into how the foundation money is distributed at PM?

Her next exhale circulated in her trachea while she watched the words "typing" flash a few times on her screen.

No. Lydia gets a spreadsheet once a month but otherwise I don't know much about it.

The brick in her chest suddenly dissolved, and she felt a few days' worth of tension release in her hunched shoulders.

Everything okay there?

She replied quickly, this time, fingers flying over the keypad.

Yes—nothing for you to worry about. And then added—*Peachy*

Ian responded immediately.

Peachy? Erotic. I like it.

A delicate flush spread across her chest. Only Ian could transition a commonplace phrase into something explicit.

Peaches are not erotic
Well, what is erotic? Do tell.

As she attempted to extract some sexual wit from her brain, a high-pitched whine erupted from the square pulse oximeter attached to her patient's finger. Alex leaped to her feet, her stomach falling into the floor when she processed the digits flashing on the screen. Sixty-nine percent. Keeya's oxygen levels had been in the nineties all day.

Shoving her phone deep into her scrub pocket, she disconnected the breathing tube from the ventilator and attached a green rubber bag that would provide a vital supply of oxygen. She began the rhythmic squeezing that would deliver life-preserving bursts of air into Keeya's lungs.

"I need a hand over here," she shouted into the sleepy calm of the ward, and several child-sized heads popped up from the comfort of their cribs to survey the action in the corner.

The young nurse who Lesedi had been precepting appeared at

her side within moments, eagerness and a touch of fear beneath her long lashes.

"What can I do?" Botshelo asked, a noticeable waver to her voice.

"Take this bag just like we practiced and squeeze it about every three seconds," Alex instructed.

Her mind began whirring with the possibilities for the low oxygen saturations. Ironically, it didn't seem like it had started with a ventilator malfunction. She glanced at the pulse oximeter reading again, and it had fallen farther. *Damn.* Hand ventilating her from the wall oxygen supply was making no difference whatsoever.

Unwinding her stethoscope from her neck like a snake, she put the diaphragm on each side of Keeya's thorax and listened hard. Squeeze bag—*whoosh* in. Release bag—*whoosh* out. She had never realized how sending mechanical breaths into a patient's lungs sounded exactly like Darth Vader. When she moved over to the left side, she lost the sound and the chest movement.

"Keep doing exactly what you are doing, Shelo," she called, using the young nurse's nickname.

Alex used her bare thumb and forefinger to grasp the breathing tube and assess its position. It was appropriately taped at the proper distance to avoid slippage of the end of the tube into the bronchus instead of remaining in the trachea. She listened again on the left and failed to detect any sounds of air movement. This could only mean one thing—pneumothorax.

A pneumothorax was a well-known and often fatal complication of being on the ventilator. Sometimes, as the patient's lungs improved, the pressure provided by the ventilator caused some of the air sacs to pop like little balloons. Instead of filling the air sacs, the gas flow from the ventilator would simply flow into the space between the lung and the chest wall, causing a pressurized air compartment that squashed the lung into nonexistence.

"I need a chest tube," Alex murmured, mostly to herself, as she observed the cyanotic tip of Keeya's nose in the dim overhead bulb above her bed.

After a frantic search of the supply room, Alex returned with a chest tube tray, thankfully left behind by some well-meaning surgical mission trip a few years back. She met Shelo's eyes as she prepped the child's left chest with betadine solution and passed her a confident smile.

"You're doing great," Alex said.

Shelo nodded and continued diligently depressing the oxygen bag as Alex had instructed.

The alarm from the pulse oximeter twanged repeatedly as Alex found the appropriate landmark and inserted a large bore needle through skin and muscle into the space around Keeya's lung. An incredible whoosh of air met her ears, followed by an encouraging high-pitched tone from the pulse oximeter that proclaimed victory. The oxygen saturations were climbing.

Out of her peripheral vision, she detected Shelo's broad burgundy smile.

"Go ahead and hook her back up to the ventilator," Alex instructed. "We're not out of the woods yet."

Alex replaced the needle in Keeya's chest cavity with a tube that would keep the air from reaccumulating around her lung. *Now, what could they use for a collection system to trap the air?* A frantic heat rushed up the back of Alex's neck before she willed herself into calm.

"Shelo, I need three separate containers—glass bottles if we have them—and a few lengths of suction tubing."

"Be back in a moment, Dr. Alex."

Instead of entering the supply closet, Shelo exited the double doors of the ward and returned proudly clutching three glass bottles. Alex examined the familiar script on the side and smiled at her ingenuity.

"Unconventional...but I think these will work."

In fellowship, Dr. Gibson, her mentor, had insisted everyone learn how a chest tube collection system worked. She was never more thankful for the lesson than right at this moment. *If you want creative, Dr. K, this is it.*

Once the three glass Coca-Cola bottles were properly connected via tubing with the third one connected to a portable suction machine, Alex plugged the whole system into the catheter exiting Keeya's chest cavity, noting a satisfactory bubbling of air entering the second bottle. She checked the oxygen saturations once again and heard the beautiful swish of air in and air out when she listened with her stethoscope.

Shelo was quiet, but her posture was electric with adrenaline and her eyes bright with their success. Alex smiled broadly and placed a hand on her shoulder.

"Excellent job."

The older woman from the bench flashed into her thoughts as she scanned over the ventilator graphics and the favorable numbers flashing on her patient's monitor. Investing. Teaching. Empowering. This was what she could offer. This was what made a difference. She pulled out her phone and fired an answer to Ian's question.

Saving lives, baby.

ELEVEN

The sun glinted off the paper streamers and clusters of blue and black balloons weaving and bobbing in the light breeze. A sheen of moisture had begun to collect on Alex's nose as she and Ian navigated the crowd gathering in the public plaza to celebrate Botswana Day.

Every year on September 30, the entire country paused for a twenty-four-hour period to commemorate the day Botswana separated from the government of Great Britain and became an independent nation. Gaborone held a particularly robust celebration in its largest public park, complete with food vendors, games for the kids, and performances from local musicians. Over the din of the local Tswana clamoring for a spot on the grass, the first notes of a dramatic African beat sprang into the air.

Alex squeezed Ian's fingers, which had remained cool despite the rising heat of the day. The celebration happening all around her seemed like a perfect reflection of the joyous state of her being. All the kids in the hospital were improving, especially little Keeya. Her lungs had improved enough that Alex was able to take out her breathing tube several days ago. Just yesterday she was sitting on her bed playing pretend with her stuffed elephant, requiring only a tiny whiff of oxygen flowing into her nose as a remnant of her recent ordeal.

And Ian was here.

Something just fell into place when they were together. Alex's life grew wings. She had taken him to the pediatric ward yesterday. He had trudged behind her with his head down, taking deep breaths through his nose. She knew that being in a hospital rattled him because it stirred up memories of his younger brother. Ryan had died from heart failure when they were kids. It was a wound that

Ian had tried to bandage with a life of indulgence and only recently had managed to start healing. Alex wanted to encourage the process by showing him the fruits of his generosity firsthand.

Ever so carefully, Ian's hand had reached out to little Keeya, his blue eyes full of trepidation as they met her wary brown ones. She had swatted him away, a completely appropriate response for a precocious three-year-old.

"Still think people can't make a difference?" Alex had asked him. "A year ago, she wouldn't have survived."

He eyed Alex speculatively but then relaxed his features into a look of acceptance. "Trust me. You've changed my mind about a lot of things."

Now, as Alex gazed upward at his profile from under the brim of her baseball hat, catching the gleam of Ian's glossy black hair in the sun, she had never felt more at home. A waving hand caught her eye, and she peered around Ian's frame to catch sight of a handsome couple. The woman motioned to her with one hand while the man carried a sleeping toddler sprawled out over his shoulder.

"This way," Alex said and redirected their path toward the young family.

"Dumela, Dr. Alex," murmured the young lady, and Alex dropped Ian's hand to take both of her hands inside her own.

"Dumela, Mercy." And then she let go to wrap her arms around the thin shoulders in a heartfelt embrace.

Mercy had decided to pursue a pediatrics residency but had taken a year off after her daughter was born. Without a program anywhere in Botswana, she had applied in South Africa at the famous Red Cross War Memorial Hospital in Cape Town.

"This is my husband, Kabo." He nodded in Alex's direction, unable to spare an extremity for fear of waking little Naledi.

"Very nice to meet you. This is Ian."

"Oh yes. I remember you," Mercy exclaimed, assessing him critically before offering a genuine smile.

"Nice to see you again." Ian bowed his head dramatically. "Would you like to join us for some lunch?"

"We are headed home." Mercy shifted her gaze over to her husband and daughter and then placed a hand on her swollen belly, taut with the life growing inside her.

"Come see me soon," Alex replied. "I miss you at PM."

"Of course," she said, as she followed her husband, stepping carefully through the picnickers.

Ian was quiet as he waved at their departing backs, and Alex glanced over at him just in time to catch an expression on his face she had never seen before. It was almost...wistful. And then, a second later, it transformed into a *sextastic* half-smile that never failed to make Alex feel like she had just disintegrated into a warm puddle.

"Let's get out of here," he whispered into her ear, and it took all the strength in her quadriceps to keep her knees from buckling.

"By 'let's get out of here,' I thought you meant to my house," she teased as the evergreen mile markers slid by on a smooth gray highway headed east.

"Surprise." He smirked, tightening his hand on her knee that was casually but purposefully rested on the console of the truck.

She loved being within his arm's reach with perfect striking distance to her skin. The ties that bound them had certainly grown shorter over the last few months.

"Are you going to tell me where we're going?"

"Nope." He turned up the radio, and the beats of a familiar French pop song filled the truck with sensuous chords.

"What's this song about?" she asked absentmindedly, staring at the sun as it dipped lazily behind a clump of acacia trees.

"One guess," he replied, raising his brows and giving her a smirk.

"Aah. I'm not surprised you know dirty French."

He shrugged in a "guilty-as-charged" movement of his shoulders.

"By the way, you never told me you speak Portuguese."

"I picked up a few phrases from Nic over the years. We spent most of the late nineties in Portugal."

Alex couldn't be sure, but she thought she detected a quick twitch develop in the muscles around his left eye. Alex quickly strung a sequence of variables together.

"Let me guess—the hatchet lives there?"

Ian had once alluded to his brother's bond with Nic—one that had survived despite a major schism occurring at one point in their relationship. He flicked his eyes to her in astonishment and nodded.

"Yeah. I was...young."

"Nic's sister?"

"Not exactly. His aunt...his married aunt."

Alex grimaced with the emotional gut punch.

"Add that to the list of things I didn't have to know."

She frowned, her forehead furrowing as she switched tracks and changed the direction of their road trip exchange. "Do you speak any other languages?"

"I speak Alex."

Not diverting his eyes from the road, his face settled into a satisfied smile as he shifted in the leather bucket seat. And she knew that he was absolutely right.

When they finally arrived at their destination, the night sky had unfolded in all its celestial glory, the stars serving as ambient lighting as they trudged down a sandy path toward a thatched roof. Benguerra Island. They had driven the better part of a day to arrive at the coastal town of Vilankulo, Mozambique, and then hopped on a skiff that had ferried them over to the exclusive, remote island of Benguerra. Alex yawned as they rounded a bend and, in her fatigue, tripped over an obnoxious tree root that almost sent her face-first into the sand.

Ian grabbed her waist from behind.

"Careful there," he warned her. "Let's make it to the house before your narcolepsy kicks in."

Alex's feet were leaden weights, heavier every time she pulled them out of the ever-deepening piles of sugary sand, and her duffel bag had gained several kilos by the time they exited the boat. She mentally cursed Ian for insisting they could find the beach cottage on their own.

Fifteen total nights she had slept beside the ventilator, waking periodically to its chirping alerts. The long drive to Mozambique had only succeeded in downshifting her adrenaline into a bone-deep tired. Even her hair follicles rejected being vertical.

Commanding one foot in front of the other, she followed Ian onto a porch, then into a doorway where she spied a four-poster bed complete with a realm of sumptuous indigo pillows. Her duffel hit the floor with a thud and her body, entirely of its own volition, curled onto the duvet, which accepted her curves like it had been fashioned just for her.

With one eye open, she caught Ian as he took a seat on a wicker chair, propped his feet on a leather pouf, and pried open the top to a bottle of bourbon. And then sleep came, easily for once, dreamless and motionless, freezing a perfect life moment into her consciousness.

Alex awoke in the exact position she had fallen asleep, legs tucked into her stomach and her arms cradling her head. Ian had removed her shoes and tossed a cozy throw over her torso but otherwise left her thoroughly undisturbed during her period of slumber. The mound of a marshmallow duvet rose and fell beside her with the excursions of his chest wall.

Rising to a sitting position, she wrapped the azure fringed throw around her shoulders and surveyed the details of their bungalow. It was small but cozy with wicker chairs and occasional tables made from gnarled driftwood that were stacked with books. A sheer linen swathe of material fluttered along one wall, and she rose to draw it back.

The first hues of a pink sunrise skipped along a tranquil ocean before tinting the white crystalline sand along the shoreline. She stepped out onto the smooth teakwood deck, still cool from the night's chill, and kept going until her feet plunged into the warm sugar-fine sand.

They were completely isolated on this stretch of beach with only friendly palm trees for neighbors and the sounds of lapping waves for morning conversation. The ocean teased the shoreline and Alex's toes with its warm wetness and its promise of power...sensation...ecstasy. Somewhere along her path, she had discarded the throw, and several footsteps later, she tugged her white t-shirt over her head and let it drift to the ground like a bird's feather. She dug her toes into the wet sand, letting it ooze into the crevices and unbuttoned her jeans.

The water was as smooth as glass except for a few gentle waves that made it to shore and still warm from yesterday's sunlight. Before she could change her mind, she hurried out of her bra and slid her panties down past her hips to her ankles, kicking them behind her in one fluid motion.

The surf swirled around her calves then tickled her thighs as she waded in deeper, thrilled by its natural prowess. When she was waist deep, she halted, creating a toe hold in the sandbar beneath her feet and slid her hand across the rippling currents. Had she ever known such joy, such freedom, such connection with the world around her?

Her decision to undress her emotions—to bare the naked soul underneath—had created the foundation for her life's happiness.

Speaking of life's happiness.

The current parted as someone approached—her someone. His lean arms encircled her middle, pulling her into a desirable hardness that stretched from his bare chest to his lower abdomen and beyond. For one singular moment, neither of them spoke. They stood there, bathed in the sun's glow, with the sea as their mistress. Two souls with a bond forged in the elements.

Ian's lips, wet from the sea spray, found her ear. "I feel like E.T."

Alex stiffened, dumbfounded for a moment, before responding. "The extra-terrestrial?"

"Mm-hmm." He nuzzled her damp hair and palmed her breasts, pulling her deeper into his middle.

"Why?" She dug her incisors into her lip to stifle a giggle.

"Because instead of Reese's Pieces, I woke up this morning and followed a trail of your clothing."

"And what did you find at the end?"

"You tell me."

Rather than waiting for a response, he bent his head around to meet her lips, already eager and blossoming as the blood rushed into their tiny capillaries. In the water, she was weightless, and he deftly pulled her onto his lap. She intertwined her legs with his so that, to any onlooker, they created some erotic art form—a balanced silhouette of man and woman. Masculinity and femininity.

Ian held her there as the sun lifted her crown above the horizon. All she heard was the sound of his ragged breath in her ear. All she could feel was the warmth of his torso that contrasted with the cool ocean. She licked a salty remnant of Ian's kiss from her upper lip.

Despite the chill of the breeze caressing her damp skin, she felt like a rising inferno as his form grew more prominent between the gentle curve of her bottom. Her pelvic muscles tensed, poised for the deliciously satisfying stimulation they so desired. Still, Ian didn't move except to pull her tighter. Sometimes the only thing more erotic than having sex was not having sex.

"I wish," he murmured, "that I could make up for every bad thing that ever happened to you."

"You can't," Alex replied to the swirling turquoise undulating beneath her chin. "But I don't need you to."

She felt his long exhale, and his hold tightened on her as he put his cheek next to hers.

"What do you need, Alex?"

This was the second time he had asked her this question. It

seemed like a lifetime ago—that day on the bridge when under a gorgeous Texas sky, she had answered "freedom" and asked him to let her go. She had not been honest with herself or Ian that day.

Alex knew what he was thinking, as easily as if the words were scrawled out on paper in front of her. Above everything, Ian feared abandonment. After listening to the travails of her past, he now understood how easy it was for her to disconnect in order to pursue some existential greater good or, in the case of her childhood, to survive. She knew exactly what he wanted and needed to hear. This time, it wasn't at all difficult to let the words slip past her tongue.

"I need...you."

How liberating it was to admit it. Liberating yet terrifying. Exposing her vulnerabilities took considerable effort but the result something she never imagined—a tri-level, soul-soldering bond with another human. Mind. Body. Soul.

Her lower back arched as Ian growled into her ear and slipped inside her just enough to make her want more. It seemed to be a common theme lately. Living physically apart in parallel lives always left her wanting more. But what was more? What could be more right now? As sensation after luxurious sensation cascaded through every neuron, she let her thoughts wash up to the shore and focus on more pressing matters—like Ian.

As Alex lay on the decking outside their bungalow, skin damp and hair splayed out around her like a halo, she relished in the bliss of being at the very fringe of sleep, sandwiched between the sun and the hard surface beneath her. Like a lizard on a rock, a little poikilotherm that required a warm surface on both sides to achieve a comfortable body temperature. She felt both grounded and free. Ian sat in the wicker patio chair beside her, his elegant body pressed into a very lucky blue cushion, occasionally brushing his toes over her shoulder to maintain a sense of physical connection.

"What's going on in there?" he asked, reaching down to drum her forehead with his fingertips.

"Absolutely nothing," she sighed, and it was mostly true.

"Liar," he teased. "Your brain is about as dormant as an erupting volcano."

"I was just thinking," she started, "about this perfect moment of bliss. This little sea of tranquility in the storm of my life and how I love the feeling of the sun scorching me and a hard surface underneath me."

Ian snickered. "You sure do."

She could practically feel the smirk leaping off his face. Rolling onto her stomach, she swatted his calf.

"You know what that makes you?"

"Do tell."

"Very very lucky."

He nodded his assent. "I am. I definitely am."

She noticed his broad smile and the light of a screen reflecting off his corneas. He scrolled and tapped like he was creating an art project.

"What are you doing with my phone?" She eyed him suspiciously.

"Making you a running playlist. What did you call it once? A soundtrack to your life that you keep adding to."

She gulped, frozen by pure astonishment for a second. That's exactly what she had said to him almost a year ago sitting in his kitchen in London.

"I can't believe you remembered that."

He didn't reply but instead focused his gaze on the task before him, continuing to drag and drop to his heart's content.

"I'm surprised you aren't working. Has Lydia relaxed her death grip on your schedule?" Alex grinned, thinking of the ginger-haired powerhouse in a petite Scottish package behind the internal workings of the Devall Foundation.

"My phone is on silent. She knows I'm enjoying my last bit of freedom for a while."

"For a while?" Alex frowned.

While she was in Botswana and Ian circulated through sub-Saharan Africa on his many foundation tasks, she had thought they would be spending more time together...definitely not less.

He placed her phone facedown beside her and grabbed his own off the nearby side table.

"My dad has decided to retire next year, which means, I'll be running the company full-time. If I want to. He's left it up to me."

For such a verbal bombshell, he lobbed it out there like it was a tennis ball, not the grenade it actually was. Rather than dive into the swirling whirlpool of questions about their relationship, she skimmed off the top with the first thing that came to mind.

"And your work with the foundation?"

"I love it too much to let it go completely. I would have to figure out some way to do both."

Alex, who had spent a decade immersed in a professional life and humanitarian work, knew it was possible to balance both. But everything had a price, and she couldn't help but feel that their relationship would be paying it.

Ian reached out and grabbed her hand, brushing warm lips across her knuckles.

"We have some things to figure out," he said quietly, "but not today."

Alex desperately needed to calm the tumultuous state of her brain. Her worries were writing themselves onto her skin for the entire universe to see. Always the master of compartmentalization, she forged a mental dam and plastered a smile onto her sunbaked cheeks.

"Okay," she said evenly, trying to hide the churning under the surface.

When she bent down to pick up her phone, she spied her running shoes tossed casually under a chair. "I'll be back in a bit."

She had already pulled on a t-shirt and one shoe and was headed toward the beach by the time Ian called, "Have fun."

The sand pulled at her feet, sucking the soles of her shoes into its wetness, and it wasn't long before her thighs burned with effort. Alex finally gave up and slowed to a brisk walk, shifting toward the firmer sand near the water's edge.

In the first fifteen minutes of her run, she had already sorted through the various paradigms. Every single algorithm to happiness ended with one common thematic element—Ian was hers and she was his. No matter where in the world they were and what they were doing. Like Ian had said, nothing had to be decided today.

Smiling with the decision to give herself an emotional reprieve, Alex opened Ian's running playlist and let the music crowd out any straggling thoughts. She picked up her pace and laughed as the throaty intro to "Bad Romance" by Lady Gaga started up. Ian had an excellent ear.

She clicked through each song in turn—upbeat and sunny notes from "Good Day Sunshine" by the Beatles and "I'm Yours" by Jason Mraz. Alex had just turned around to make her way back to the bungalow when the smooth richness of Bruno Mars resounded in her ears with his newest hit. Her feet struck the sand with the rhythm, and she was blissfully unaware of the words she hummed until one repetitive phrase made her screech to a halt.

Marry You.

TWELVE

"What in the world did you say?" Rox practically shrieked into the phone.

Alex could hear the distinct clanking of pots and pans as her friend searched for the appropriate receptacle for a jar of spaghetti sauce.

"I was too freaked out to say anything. I just acted completely weird for the rest of the trip."

"What did Ian do?"

Alex sighed dramatically and flopped back into her pillows.

"Walked around like a sex god with a constant smile on his face, like he knew exactly why I was acting like an imbecile."

Typical Ian. Despite her discomfort, she couldn't help but smile at the memory of him doing yoga out on the deck without a stitch of clothing.

Curled up on her bed, with McCartney acting as a foot warmer, she unraveled the remainder of her story to a domesticated Rox who was busily preparing spaghetti from a jar.

While she and Ian were in Mozambique, Alex had said nothing, even though a question was burning its way through her like a match to gasoline. On the way home, however, inside the confined space of the truck, the question invaded every single molecule of space. She had decided on the covert approach. Clicking on the playlist, she let the minuscule speaker in her iPhone do the talking and fill the conversation void with music.

When the upbeat rhythm of "Marry You" had started, she had maintained her cool and concentrated on a clump of trees in the distance. Ian seemed distracted at first, and she mentally chided herself for even thinking he had intentions besides adding a popular song to her running mix.

Halfway through the song, she detected the inkling of a side-eye and the twitch of a smile. And then he caught Alex looking at him. No matter how many times and ways she had seen him, he always took her breath away when his eyes met her own. Like she no longer needed to breathe air. Like she could somehow be sustained by the life in his sky-blue eyes. It was now or never. She opened her mouth to speak, but his lips moved faster than a hummingbird's wings in a Texas spring.

"Interesting song choice."

"What?" She startled and the neat stack of planned sentences toppled over inside her head. "I mean...if you're asking, then my answer is a definite yes."

Too shocked to move anything except her extraocular muscles, Alex cut her gaze to the driver's seat to absorb every detail of his face. He obviously enjoyed her discomfort. Her insides were squirming more than the nightcrawlers she used to buy from the bait shop back home. Ian's lips arced upward in a smile, and he reached over to squeeze her knee.

"It's just a song, Alex."

Then he tapped her phone so that it skipped ahead to the next song, but she had seen the look on his face—the same one she had seen in the park. *Wistful.*

Rox had remained quiet until the end of her monologue, and then Alex heard her voice revving up like a staccato motor.

"I just can't believe my best friend is going to be here in London. We'll do date nights and couple's trips, and our kids will grow up together—"

"Wait a minute. Hold on, Rox. Rox!" Alex said a little more forcefully than she intended. "We're not getting married, are we? No, we're not. I'm not ready. I haven't even learned how to be a good girlfriend—still working on sex goddess—and I'm definitely not ready to be someone's wife." Alex's voice had grown shrill as the panic within rose into her throat.

"It's just a matter of time, love."

"I don't want to move to London, Rox. I just got started here in Botswana."

Until now, she hadn't said it aloud. This dreaded reality had weighed her down since Ian set her lips on fire and then caught a plane to Mongolia.

"He wants you here, Alex. I've seen him. He's lonely, and when he takes over for his dad, he'll have to be in London nearly full-time."

"I...I wish...you were here," Alex finished resolutely. "Being alone with my runaway train of a brain is nauseating." She rolled over onto her side, and McCartney responded with a disgruntled whine. "Can you come?"

Alex heard the clatter of a pot lid, and a choice curse word before Rox answered. "Checking my schedule. How about Halloween?"

"It can't get here fast enough." Alex sighed as some of the weight ascended from her shoulders.

Long after they had hung up the phone, Alex realized she hadn't asked how her best friend was doing. It had been a drastic transition from single gal working in obstetrics in Botswana to married to a pro soccer player in a new city with a new job. *Marriage.* She would cross that bridge when there was actually a bridge to cross.

"Yes...just like that," Alex instructed one of the interns.

All five of them were lined up at a table in their meeting room taking turns placing breathing tubes in bodiless heads.

"The most important skill is proper bag-mask ventilation." Alex demonstrated with her hand forming a "C" shape around the mask, creating a perfect seal between patient and plastic. "Squeeze the bag and voilà!"

The green balloons that simulated a pair of lungs inflated obediently, and the young man next to her in the white coat emitted a broad smile. Picking up the smooth silver handle of the laryngoscope with its battery-powered blade shining like a tiny Christmas light, she demonstrated how to visualize the vocal cords by smoothly sweeping the tongue aside and inserting the blade into a convenient pocket made by the tongue base at the back of the throat.

Pediatric airways could be an adventure, and she had definitely had her share. A lot could happen in the thirty seconds it took to visualize the vocal cords and insert a tube of plastic into the trachea so the lungs could receive air.

Unlike the training mannequins who had nice smooth rubber parts and were dry on the inside, actual patients had floppy tongues and loose teeth, malpositioned tracheas, and secretions of every color and consistency. One time, she had managed to get a breathing tube into an airway through a fountain of blue Gatorade.

"I'm ready to be back here," called a steady but quiet voice from the corner.

Alex turned and clasped the outstretched hands of her very pregnant friend. "Mercy! How are you?"

"Tired," she admitted, removing her hands from Alex's grasp, one to stroke her protruding belly and the other to massage her lower back.

"Sit down. You look exhausted...in the most beautiful way possible." Alex hurriedly slid over the only chair in the room.

Mercy lowered herself gracefully onto the seat of the grade school-sized chair, blowing out a sharp exhale when her body contacted the seat.

"Are you okay?" Alex asked gently.

"Just some Braxton Hicks, I think." She smiled, appearing tired but with her characteristic fortitude. "How is Ian?"

Alex's heart felt like a skipping stone that jolted her with emotion each time it hit the water. Which emotion she wasn't certain. She cleared her throat.

"He's good. We're good."

Mercy nodded, seeming to absorb the details Alex purposefully omitted. The memory of Ian's expression as Mercy and her husband walked away arm in arm at the park flashed into her consciousness, and she unsuccessfully tried to shelve it.

"What are you doing here?"

Mercy shifted in her seat, grasping her back as she did so.

"I...had to...come by...for Dr. K to sign something," she replied, her sentence coming a few words at a time.

"Are you sure you're okay?" Alex eyed her critically, a wheel in her brain starting to turn like the gear on a clock.

Before Mercy had a chance to answer, the sagging door to the meeting room burst open, and a cloud of red rage descended. Sam's voice cut through the room like a saber.

"Dr. Wilde."

"Dr. Drake," Alex replied, summoning the full measure of her patience and grace. She positioned herself between Mercy and the granite stare emanating from under Sam's hooded lids. A sigh escaped Alex's lips, and her shoulders slumped. "What do you need, Sam?"

"My med student said you berated her in the middle of the

hospital the other day."

Alex snorted lightly. "Hardly."

She folded her arms across her chest, a modicum of protection against the dragon breathing fire in her direction. "She was snapping pictures of my patients without permission. I would appreciate it if you would teach her the concepts of cultural awareness and common decency."

Sam's nostrils flared, and her voice lowered an octave. "It's hard to teach anything when one department is receiving all the funding."

She glanced over Alex's shoulder at the interns clustered around the makeshift airway station, quietly practicing their new skill set. Alex's heart rate spiked, and tension like a Burmese python wound its scales up the back of her neck and around her forehead.

"Improving childhood survival is important. We are saving lives with the money from the Devall Foundation."

Sam gave a huff that was worthy of a movie starlet. The puff of air reached Alex's face, and she smelled the morning coffee on Sam's breath. Her stony glare drilled into Alex's ocean blue eyes. Alex half expected her pupils to be elliptical.

"You're not going to have anyone to save if I can't help these mothers deliver healthy babies."

Her words, although delivered harshly, were true. Alex opened her mouth to respond, but her quick inhale sent a new odor billowing past her nasal turbinates. An eerily sterile smell, like dilute bleach. Whipping her head around, Alex spied a doubled over Mercy, her face paralyzed in surprise and her mouth in the shape of an "o." *Oh hell.* She and Sam reached Mercy's flanks at the same time and bent down near the puddle of amniotic fluid pooling under her chair.

Alex snapped her head up to the interns. "Guys, go grab a spare stretcher from the ward."

They rushed out as a unit, flurrying like a pack of pigeons, and were back in a flash with a wobbly stretcher with one bad wheel.

"How far apart are the contractions?" Sam asked, transitioning into MD mode and pressing both of her palms to Mercy's rigid abdomen.

"Maybe a minute...or two. I have...to call my husband. I am supposed...to deliver...across town." Mercy's words came two at a time.

"Well, you're not going to make it," said Sam assuredly.

Alex knew she was right and met Mercy's wide eyes with her own. She tried to infuse some calm into her friend.

"Let me help you on the stretcher," she said gently, and Mercy obeyed like a quiet mare, all her energy directed toward the contractions ripping through her middle.

As Sam and Alex pushed Mercy through the courtyard to the labor and delivery wing, Mercy called her husband, and they shared a rapid hushed conversation in Setswana.

"He is on his way, but the traffic...is bad today," Mercy said after she disconnected.

Alex gripped her hand. "It's going to be okay. I'll stay with you."

Sam shot her a look but didn't say anything, her words halted by Alex's steely expression. As they turned the corner, banging through the double doors, Mercy was in full-fledged stage two labor. Alex's phone began buzzing incessantly, and she ignored it. Everything else could wait for a moment.

Meanwhile, she tried to dredge up any knowledge she remembered from her OB rotation in medical school. When was Mercy supposed to push? When was she not supposed to push? Did the baby's mouth get suctioned first or the nose? Alex felt a rising tide of stress but maintained her calm exterior. She would never let Sam see her bent out of shape.

"Help me get her to the end of the bed," Sam barked, and Alex glanced around for someone else before complying. "I need you to hold her legs up."

While Sam busied herself with snapping on a pair of gloves and donning a blue gown, Alex helped disrobe Mercy from the waist down and then wrapped her arms under her knees and pulled them toward her chest. Her ear was filled with Mercy's groans and jumbled speech as the next contraction sent a spasm of pain through her body.

"What was that?" Alex asked gently.

"I want my husband," she cried, large tears starting to pool in her lids and spill over onto her cheeks.

"I know," Alex said, wiping Mercy's face with a hospital sheet. "I'm not going to leave you until he gets here."

"All right," said Sam, rolling a stool up to the end of the stretcher. "Let's see what's going on here."

With a surprisingly gentle hand, she probed underneath the crisp white sheet. "I feel the head, Mama. You're close. Are you ready to push?"

"Nooo," Mercy shrieked to no one in particular.

"You can do this," Alex said, gripping her knees tighter and continuing to ignore the buzzing in her pocket.

"Ready...here it comes. Push!" Sam commanded from the foot of the bed.

Mercy lifted her head in a half-abdominal curl and cried out, spewing warm air into Alex's ear canal. She struggled and heaved while Alex whispered encouragement and wiped off the sweat collecting on the bridge of her nose. Twenty minutes and just as many pushes later, a wriggling blue bundle entered the world for the first time, sliding into Sam's outstretched arms. Mercy's husband burst through the double doors and took Alex's place by the bed, cradling his wife's head in his arms as she cried silently, smiling the entire time.

"Put some gloves on and give me a hand, Wilde."

Alex obeyed and spread out a fresh swaddling blanket, murmuring to the shrieking infant as she carried him over to the warmer. He threw up his hands in protest as she rubbed off the birth remnants, stimulating him from time to time to encourage him to continue to take the breaths that would transition him from fetus to infant.

"It's a boy," she called, peering back at the tender couple, and their tendrils of emotion strummed her heartstrings. She thoughts briefly flashed to Ian. "Hey little guy," she cooed. "Want to meet your mommy and daddy?"

Wrapping him up in a tight bundle, she carried him over to Mercy, placing him on her chest to absorb all the warmth of her love and the comfort from her heartbeat. "I'll give you a moment before I do his full exam," she said. "Congratulations."

Alex stepped out into the waning day, the fresh air brushing her face and drying the tears that had escaped onto her cheek. Rocking on her heels, she reached in her pocket for her phone to discover four messages from Rox.

Booked my flight.
Pencil me in for Halloween.
Will meet you at the Ex-Pats party.
xoxo Rox

Alex heaved a sigh of relief—relief for Mercy's baby and especially for Rox's visit. Rox would know how to fix the obstetrics division plus she would help Alex navigate her relationship with Ian. Everything was going to be okay. As the sun set on PM, she was filled with a joy she couldn't explain. Perhaps the joy of bearing witness to something so miraculous that everything else in the world couldn't compare to that moment in time.

"Get your ass in here, Wilde."

Alex leaped out of her own head and through the door, already scanning the room for the baby and making a list of potential issues that could be happening. Sam had removed the baby from Mercy's arms and unwrapped the swaddle so that he was splayed out on the warmer bed.

"Something's wrong," she muttered. "I just don't know what."

"Give me some room," Alex said sternly, and Sam nodded and faded into the background.

Alex examined the baby critically as she put her stethoscope to his chest. He had a blue undertone to his skin, one that could only be detected in the tips of his nose and the discoloration of his gums when he cried. Air in. Air out. He had clear breath sounds but she heard a rumbling in his chest that emanated from his heart. A few choice curse words entered Alex's mind before she squelched them and pivoted toward Sam.

"Go get me your ultrasound machine."

Within moments, Sam returned lugging the heavy wheeled contraption into the room and handed Alex a freshly wiped down probe. Amid a modest amount of protest from Mercy's second-born, she placed the probe on his heaving chest and watched the grayscale images leap to life in front of her eyes.

His heart was the size of a walnut, contracting with the speed of a hummingbird's wings as she scanned backward and forward. She swept up and down with the probe twice to be sure before she called out to Mercy, her nerves hardening into steel cables.

"Mercy, do you have any family outside of Botswana?"

Through Mercy's fatigue, a spark of fear caught fire, and she struggled against her husband to sit up in bed. "Atlanta. In the US."

A wave of heroism washed over Alex as she frantically fished her phone out of her pocket. She dialed the numbers that had become so familiar to her the last three years of her life.

He picked up on the second ring.

"Hello? Alex?"

"Hi, Tim. I'm going to need a favor. A big one."

THIRTEEN

"It's called transposition of the great arteries," Alex explained.

Mercy and her husband listened attentively as they glanced nervously at little junior sleeping peacefully in his bassinet, utterly unaware that his life depended on the succinct coordination that occurred in the next twenty-four hours. Mercy nodded in understanding, so Alex directed her attention and napkin graphics toward her husband, Kabo.

"The aorta is supposed to come off the left side of the heart and carry the red, oxygen-rich blood. The pulmonary artery is supposed to come off the right side and carry the blue blood to the lungs. In this case," she paused to draw a few choice arrows on the napkin, indicating the blood flow direction, "the two are switched."

"What does that mean?" Mercy's husband had spoken for the first time, his voice a deathly quiet.

Alex opened her mouth to respond, but Mercy beat her to it. "It means his body is receiving blood with a low oxygen content and he needs heart surgery to fix it."

Although her voice was calm, Alex noticed the fear that flooded her eyes when she glanced over at the bassinet. Kabo's knuckles tightened on Mercy's shoulder. "And without heart surgery?"

The question hung in the air for a moment, and Alex detected an almost imperceptible nod from Mercy.

"He'll die," Alex said softly, letting the reality settle over them like an ensuing storm.

Mercy furrowed her brows in concentration, moving down the mental pathway that Alex had just taken, and when she reached the end, a dim hope turned on in her face.

"I have a plan. It's insane...but it could work," Alex said.

Over the next several minutes, they hung on her every word,

clasping each other in a supportive embrace. Alex explained that, although some centers in Africa were offering neonatal surgery, most were not. Luckily, because of the holes in his heart, the blue blood mixed with the red blood and provided him with just enough oxygen to function, for a while.

Ideally, he would need surgery within the next two weeks before he became sicker. He would have to travel on a plane, preferably a nonstop flight to a center that performed an operation called an arterial switch. Since the hospitalization might be prolonged, even up to a month or more, Alex told them it would be beneficial for them to be somewhere they had family and resources—like Atlanta.

"Can we bring him back after the operation?" Kabo asked.

"Absolutely. This operation will fix his heart. He'll probably never need another surgery for the rest of his life."

Mercy's fortitude had expired during the conversation, and she shook her head vehemently as tears began running in rivulets down her cheeks. "We'll never get there. I don't have a visa. I don't know any of the doctors there."

Alex walked over to pick up the stirring infant who had wiggled out of his bundle and thrown a solitary fist in the air. As she picked him up, his tiny fingers curled around her thumb, and his eyelids opened sluggishly to reveal milky gray irises that were bright with life.

"Dr. K may be able to help with the visa issue, and one of my very best friends just happens to be an ICU doctor in Atlanta."

Alex's face stretched into a contained smile as she thought of Tim, her golden-haired, witty comrade, her co-fellow through three years of fellowship at the Children's Hospital of Philadelphia, her rock after she and Ian had broken up, her would-be love interest if she had never met Ian. After fellowship, he had taken a job at the Children's Hospital of Atlanta, and the timing could not have been more perfect.

When she had called him a few moments ago, he had been in the middle of rounds, most likely with a gaggle of nurses drooling over his every word and swooning over his Southern boy charm. He had listened attentively to Alex's plan, inserting a few comments here and there, and finally finished with "whatever you need, Alex."

"Thanks, Tim," she had replied. "I'll call you when we have the flights."

Her heart squeezed when she hung up the phone. She had

secretly worried that after she her rejection that day on the steps of the art museum, their friendship would fizzle. Instead, despite thousands of miles of distance, it seemed like nothing had changed.

Alex handed the infant to Mercy. His little bird mouth was open, searching for a soft place and an easy meal.

"I think he's hungry."

Mercy eyed her nervously. "Is it okay if I...?"

"Of course," Alex replied. "It's actually a good thing that he wants to eat." She checked his oxygen levels one last time. Eighty-five percent. That would be enough. For now.

Sam was milling around outside Mercy's room, hands stuffed in her coat pocket, eyes focused on a delicate vine that hung precipitously from the metal roof of the walkway.

"Thank you," Alex said pointedly. "For helping Mercy."

Sam let the compliment fly right past her without so much as a blink to acknowledge it. "And the baby?"

"The baby has congenital heart disease. He needs surgery."

Sam picked up her head, spiky pieces of her ginger hair sent in various directions as she ran a hand through it. "That sucks."

"Actually, I think we can make it happen...if we can get him to Atlanta in time."

"Are you always so full of hope and rainbows?" Sam retorted.

Alex shrugged. "It's better than being a raging bitch."

She tipped up her chin and leveled her gaze with Sam's, expecting and girding herself for the onslaught of insults likely to come her way. Instead, Sam tilted her head to the side and curled her upper lip into the beginnings of a smile. For once, she kept her barbed words to herself, turned on her heel, and stalked into the descending night.

Twenty-four hours and just as many phone calls later, Alex nestled into her couch cushions, McCartney warming her from the outside and a fervent vintage from Stellenbosch warming her from the inside. She closed her eyes to focus on the thoughts spinning a web in her brain. Every variable had to be accounted for to ensure success. She would settle for nothing less than perfect preparation with every scenario accounted for. This was her gift—anticipating disaster and avoiding it to prevent the failure to rescue moment. Her friend depended on her. A baby's life depended on her.

Tim proved to be a miracle worker. After an emotionally charged conference call between Alex and the chief of cardiothoracic surgery, she had agreed to accept the baby on one condition: they had to make it there in the next seventy-two hours.

Alex had scoured the flight schedules, and there was one direct flight from Gaborone to Atlanta leaving tomorrow night, which would usher Mercy in just under the wire. A transport team from the children's hospital would be at Hartsfield-Jackson Airport to pick them up and take them directly to the cardiac ICU, where the baby could be evaluated for surgery.

Only one snag had emerged thus far. The consulate office had received Mercy and Kabo's applications for a visa this morning, but they refused to promise a quick turnaround. Alex had encouraged Mercy to buy the tickets anyway. Miracles did happen...if the way was properly paved. She had even been lucky enough to witness one or two.

Alex took a sip of her wine and tilted back her head, remembering a sweet eight-year-old who had been riding an ATV with his sister when a falling tree limb struck him in the head. After a solid week delicately managing his intracranial pressure, which necessitated putting him in a medical coma and removing part of his skull, Alex had told his parents he would never resemble the kid he once was. Once he was well enough to wake up, Alex removed his breathing tube. The next day she entered his room, and he looked right at her and waved hello. She had cried that day...and every other time she thought of this family.

A brusque ring from her phone snapped her back to the present, and she took a sip of wine before answering. "Hi. It's Alex."

"Dr. Alex." The baritone richness of Dr. K emanated from the earpiece.

"How are you, Dr. K? Any news?"

"Still working on it. I have applied my influence. I do not think there is anything else I can do."

"Okay. Keep me posted. And thank you, Dr. K."

"Of course." And then, with a simple click, he was gone.

Alex awoke ridiculously early the following day with a moderate headache from the imbalance in her water to wine ratio. After a solid breakfast of Diet Coke, ibuprofen, and a granola bar, she pulled a brush through her thick brown mane and threw on a pair of powdered blue scrubs stamped with "CHOP"—a souvenir from fellowship training. As she was leaving, she spied her lion pendant on her dresser and reached for it. Wearing it made her feel close to Ian, a reminder she desired more and more these days. After only a few weeks apart, she physically ached with longing.

When she arrived at the hospital, Mercy was seated next to her newborn, hands folded in her lap over a colorful dressing gown with half-closed eyelids. They fluttered open when Alex approached. She knelt at the bed space they had given the baby in the pediatric ward. No one had felt comfortable sending him home under the circumstances.

"Any news from the consulate?"

"Not yet," Mercy answered. "But we are hopeful." Her hand drifted toward her baby's crib. A protective hand. A hand that would turn over the world for her son.

"I'll do anything I can to help you," replied Alex, gingerly placing a hand on Mercy's shoulder as she stood.

"I know you will."

Mercy didn't look at her. She kept her eyes riveted on the baby. The baby who now looked blue even to the untrained eye and was breathing just a little harder than yesterday.

Lunchtime came, and, despite no word from the consulate, Mercy had sent her husband home to retrieve their bags. From there, he planned a personal visit to the consulate to determine the likelihood of obtaining their paperwork for travel. Alex paced through the ward, then out to the courtyard, and once around the parking lot trying to come up with a plan B.

No other hospital within less than a day's flying distance had offered to accept them, and they couldn't leave the country without a visa. Even Ian and his endless resources wouldn't be any help. They had to have permission to enter the US. This plan had to work. An entire team of people was ready to take care of them in Atlanta. Alex glanced down at her phone. *Damn.* It was already after four o'clock.

"Mercy," she called, bursting back through the metal doors that clanged shut behind her.

In her absence, Mercy had gathered her few belongings from the hospital and packed them in a shoulder bag. The baby was snuggled into a brightly colored carrier that she wore over her shoulders.

"I'm ready," she said calmly. "Kabo will meet us there with the bags and the papers."

After bustling her to the truck and weaving through the end of workday traffic, Alex felt like a harried mess on the inside. She had put kids on ECMO with less stress. The airport was relatively empty, apart from a few business suits with compact roller bags. Alex put Mercy in line for check-ins and immediately began surveying the airport for her husband. Not until Mercy was next in line did Alex spot him bursting through the sliding doors like an Olympic sprinter, a duffel slung over his arm, waving a flapping stack of official documents.

"I have it." Kabo bent to his knees to catch his breath for a moment before continuing. "But they would only give us one for you."

Eyes wide, Mercy accepted her passport filled with sheaves of paper from her husband.

"Next!"

She stepped up to the counter and pushed her ticket toward the clerk with trembling hands as fat tears rolled down her cheeks.

"Mercy, what's wrong?" Alex hissed as the clickety clacking of a keyboard served as their soundtrack.

"I can't do this alone. I am so tired. I can't even think."

Alex glanced from Mercy's crumpled-up face to her husband, stilled into silence, and then to the baby, sleeping peacefully, conserving his energies for the tremendous experience he was about to endure. Before she even had time to think through her plan to conclusion, she opened her blue leather shoulder bag to extract two things: her credit card and her passport.

The flight to Atlanta was long and was made even longer by a fussy, cyanotic baby that prevented Alex from closing her eyes for more than a nanosecond. Alex had taken the baby from Mercy to give her a much-needed reprieve from mothering, and they had spent a glorious hour staring into each other's eyes before he had realized that Alex had nothing to offer except for entertainment.

By the time they landed, Alex's bloodstream was coursing with the last remnants of adrenaline, and she had the tremulousness of a hangover, without the benefit of the night before alcohol binge. Thankfully, Tim had thought of everything. She and Mercy were ushered off the plane and sent to a private waiting area where an immigration officer was waiting to stamp their passports.

Meanwhile, an ambulance crew was on standby at the exit to transport them to the hospital.

Once they settled in a few bright orange vinyl chairs, Alex's eyelids drifted closed until a raucous ring from the bottom of her bag popped them open. She fished out her phone. A picture of Ian lit up her screen, his devilish smile and flame blue eyes sending a few sparks shooting into her live wire of a heart.

"Hi," she murmured, unable to stifle a yawn.

"What are you doing right now? And by the way, the right answer is I'm naked in my bed waiting for you to come ravage me."

Alex glanced at her surroundings with the familiar bustle of people with Southern accents and the sight of a city rising in the distance. "I..."

"Well, it doesn't matter because I lucked into a free weekend, and I'm about to get on a plane to come and see my girl."

He sounded so boyish and eternally pleased with himself that Alex cringed.

"Ian, I'm not there."

"You have exactly—" His voice muffled as she heard the ruffling of papers. "Twelve hours and fourteen minutes to finish saving lives and let me come and save yours."

Her ability to explain had dissolved into sheer fatigue. "I'm in Atlanta."

She could practically hear the hammer as it struck.

"Georgia?"

"Yes."

And then she rushed, tumbling over her words, to explain about Mercy's baby and the heart condition and the surgery and how Tim had helped her find a surgeon that would accept them.

"When will you be back?"

"Day after tomorrow. I'll spend the night here and then get on the first South African Air flight in the morning."

The phone was completely silent. Alex imagined he was letting go of his expectations and trying to redirect them like a solitary balloon floating up into the stratosphere until it was gone from view.

"I'm really proud of you, Alex, and unfortunately for me, exceptionally turned on right now.

The pallor of her cheeks was replaced by a deep pink.

"I'll be home soon with absolutely no plans if you want to try again."

111

The thought of seeing him, even for forty-eight hours, intoxicated her, and she felt a delightful rush.

He sighed deeply. "I can't, baby. This is my last time off until Christmas."

Gut punch. "Oh."

"Tell me what you're thinking, Alex."

"I'm just wondering how last year's most eligible bachelor turned into a workaholic?" she muttered.

"I'm dating Wonder Woman. I had to up my game."

The ride to the hospital in the bright yellow and green Children's Hospital of Atlanta ambulance lulled Alex into a semi-trance as they sped down the silver ribbon highway into the small metropolis of Atlanta. Once they arrived at the hospital, Mercy rode the stretcher with her son wrapped tightly to her chest, and Alex trudged alongside with the luggage through the labyrinthine hallways and up an oversized elevator.

As they entered a mechanical set of double doors, Alex's eyes took in the carnival orange and yellow motif of an open concept ICU with cribs lined up as far as she could see. Nurses in brightly colored scrubs scurried about their tasks—silencing monitors, adjusting drip rates, and calming babies who had become irritated by all the commotion.

As they skidded up to the appropriate room, a flurry of activity descended upon them and every type of noninvasive monitoring device was applied to the baby's skin. A perky blonde took Mercy into a corner where she began firing questions and typing furiously. Although Mercy's face was knit together by fortitude, Alex could tell she was shocked when a gentleman with short, clipped gray hair pulled a machine up to the bed and placed an ultrasound probe on the baby's chest. Alex gave a detailed summary of the baby's history to the cluster of medical providers who took notes on their Bible-thick packets of paper.

"Okay, I think we're good," said one of the fellows, a tall russet-haired guy in cowboy boots and scrubs.

Alex glanced at the baby. His vitals were stable, and oxygen levels were in the low eighties. She peeked at the echo images, pixelated red and blue swirling through the heart, which represented the blood flow direction and confirmed the diagnosis of transposition. The flock of nurses around Mercy had dissipated, and she sat alone, settled into an oversized armchair, quietly observing the attention on her squirming infant.

"He is hungry, I think," she said when Alex knelt beside her.

"Do you need anything?"

"No, thank you, Alex. My aunt will be here soon."

"Okay."

She surprised herself by wrapping Mercy in a fierce hug.

"Call me for anything."

"I will."

Alex left the ICU and, after the double doors thumped closed behind her, she realized that she had no idea where to go or what to do next. A fatigue-infused sadness crept over her. Legitimate despair if she was honest with herself. The adrenaline from the last few days leached out through her feet, leaving her feeling raw and unbelievably tired and devastated about missing Ian. All she wanted right now was to lose herself in his heat. In his lips. In his—

"You just couldn't stay away from me, could you?"

Without checking her momentum, she turned around and launched herself into the arms awaiting her.

FOURTEEN

"My place is only five minutes away," Tim said as they pulled out of the underground parking lot. "You can get some rest, and I'll pick you up after work for dinner."

"Thanks, Tim," she murmured, her forehead melding into the glass of Tim's Honda. The inside of the car felt warm like her own personal greenhouse, and the lure of sleep clouded her vision.

Tim's house was a one-story 1920's style bungalow with a peaked roof and painted gray brick adorned with a purple door. The covered front porch was covered contained a solitary white rocker underneath a powder blue ship-lap ceiling.

When Alex entered the front door, she stood in awe of the living space bathed in natural light from a pair of ceiling-high windows flanking the front door, a light that accentuated the wood grain of the ebony floor. It was so quiet that she heard every creak her footsteps made as she headed toward the guest room. Tim's furnishings were sparse, a solitary leather chair here and a hand-me-down table there. A cardboard village of boxes filled the guest room with a note stuck to one of the boxes.

I wasn't expecting company so soon.
Use my room while you are here.

Alex didn't have the energy to put up a fuss or think of an alternative solution. She dragged her overnight bag into Tim's room, expecting the telltale signs of bachelorhood—socks littering the floor, a pile of unfolded laundry in the corner, rumpled sheets, and the smell of aftershave. Instead, another note stood propped on a bed made to perfection with a navy comforter folded at the end. The room smelled like jasmine and vanilla. She inhaled deeply and unfolded the second note.

Take a bath. Drink some water.
And for heaven's sake eat something.
I'll see you tonight. T

Alex's laughter echoed off the stark white walls. She took her time in the tub, finally ridding herself of the bone-deep cold she'd acquired on the airplane. In her favorite pair of fleece pants and a sweatshirt embroidered with Baylor College of Medicine, she curled up into a ball at the end of the bed, tucking her lower half under the comforter. In the descent into the abyss of sleep, she thought of Ian and wondered just how much longer their lives would accommodate their parallel paths before something had to give.

"I didn't bring anything remotely appropriate for dinner," Alex called to Tim as she rummaged through her sparsely packed weekender bag.

"We're just going around the corner to a Tex-Mex place with a patio."

Tex-Mex on the patio—her favorite. A pang of homesickness hit her. Between riding the waves of her new job and the reemergence into a blossoming romance, she hadn't slowed down long enough to miss her old life, her friends, her home. It all rained down on her at once and the carefully wrapped ball of loneliness she kept tucked away began to unravel.

Alex quickly threw on faded bootcut jeans and a black t-shirt, her lion pendant sparkling happily around her neck. As she was braiding her still wet hair, Tim knocked on the door. She had to blink back a few tears before answering. What in the world was going on with her hormones? Was it simple nostalgia, or did part of her long for a different life? An easier one.

An unbidden reel of images forced their way into her consciousness. She and Tim as partners at work and in life, managing hectic schedules but fitting each other into every second of their downtime. Running or biking on the weekends and stopping at little mom and pop joints on the way home for brunch. Cozy post-call nights in front of a fire watching a movie. No long-distance calls at every hour of the night. No weekend rendezvous that failed to materialize. No separation by space or time zone. Emotional and physical availability. Real life rather than dreams.

She brushed the heel of her hand against her errant tear ducts. She could have had all of that and she had chosen otherwise. She had always been happy with her choice. Ian would always be her choice. But still the gaping void of loneliness prevailed, and once it had opened, it was hard to force it closed again.

"You okay?" Tim bent down his head to study her face.

"Yes. I'm good. Just eye irritation from the plane." Alex blinked fiercely and plastered on a smile that took a little more effort than usual.

"Okay. Good, because I have someone I want you to meet."

Alex strolled next to Tim on a street that rolled gently downhill toward the main thoroughfare of his neighborhood. October evenings in Atlanta in Tim's microvillage of Morningside were exquisite. A light wind ruffled the towering oak trees whose leaves had just started to turn a beautiful reddish-gold.

The smell of freshly baked bread and community hit her nostrils as they rounded a bend. Sets of parents with their ducklings in tow strolled down a street filled with independently owned boutiques and small-scale restaurants. Alex swallowed past a lump in her throat as a pair of middle-aged women in baseball hats zoomed past them on an evening run, their purple shorts rippling as they jogged in sync.

"This is it," announced Tim, pushing open a heavy oak door that emptied them onto a small outdoor patio surrounded by a wrought iron railing with a perfect view of the Atlanta skyline.

A hand shot up in the air, waving frantically at the sight of her and Tim, well, mostly Tim. Tim flashed a smile, and Alex followed him over to the red metal table already decked out with a giant basket of crisp tortilla chips and a bowl of chunky salsa.

Before any introductions were made, the girl catapulted out of her seat and wrapped her arms around Alex's shoulders, pulling her in for an embrace. She was possibly the most petite human Alex had ever seen, short but perfectly proportioned, like a doll Alex could have placed in her pocket. Her head barely made it to Alex's chin, and her hair smelled like a field of ripe strawberries in summer.

"You must be Alex," she said with the hint of a southern belle accent. "Tim's told me so much about you."

"Alex, this is Cara." Tim threw an arm around the girl's narrow shoulders.

"Hi, it's lovely to meet you."

Alex smiled warmly and sat down stiffly on the edge of her chair. *Wow.* Tim hadn't wasted any time. Alex studied her from across the table as Tim plopped down on the seat in between them. She was beautiful with large blue eyes, perfectly done makeup, and long chocolate waves that had just the right amount of natural curl. Her longest layers hung over her shoulder, ending right above her cleavage, which was visible in the off the shoulder cropped peasant blouse she wore with a pair of skinny jeans.

Alex's stomach lurched as the young girl threw back her head in laughter when Tim whispered something in her ear. Physically, she favored Alex so much that she could have been her little sister—a more fun, less exhausted, prettier version of Alex herself.

"What can I get you?" interjected a middle-aged waitress.

She had a red dye job with visible roots and a gap between her front teeth that made a whistling noise when she talked. Right now, she was Alex's most favorite person on the planet.

"Margarita," she replied. Maybe two.

Two hours and one more margarita into the evening, Alex felt as light as a feather and just as silly as the goose it came from.

"And do you remember when Beth when out of town and we filled every inch of her desk with sticky notes written by the night nurses?" Tim wheezed.

Alex tilted her head back in laughter. She and Tim had been cackling like two gossipy old women for the better part of an hour.

"I'm pretty sure one said, 'buy a llama and use its fur to warm the ice in your veins.'"

Beth, their uptight, high maintenance friend from fellowship training who tortured them at every opportunity, had taken a job in Seattle. She and Alex were cut from very different bolts of cloth. Right now, though, Alex missed her blunt, pointed commentary and constant hair tossing.

"I remember finding someone making out with one of the anesthesia residents in the supply room," Alex teased and ignored the eye twitch Cara had developed over her peach-infused cocktail.

"We were not making out," Tim protested. "She was helping me find the tube exchanger."

For some reason, Alex found his statement profoundly funny and felt the room spin as she smashed her face into Tim's bicep to stifle her laughter. Cara openly glared at them across the table, her doe eyelashes framing the distasteful expression in her baby blues. Alex opened her mouth to offer an apology, but instead, a jaw-cracking yawn arose from the depths of her throat.

Covering her hand with her mouth, she quickly mumbled "jet lag" and glanced over where Tim had refocused his attention on Cara. Her face had lit up like a Christmas angel in response to Tim's beacon of a smile.

"I'm going to walk back and get some sleep," Alex announced over the scrape of her metal chair against the concrete.

"I can walk you. You shouldn't go alone," Tim responded.

Cara's face crumpled in disappointment under the calm visage of her perfect foundation.

"Tim," Alex drawled. "I live in a country with wild animals. I think I'll be okay." She observed the palpable aura of chemistry between the two of them. "It's a perfect night. You two have fun."

Before any further protestations could be made, she turned on her heel, grateful for the sensible sneakers she had worn, and escaped through the squeaking gate of the patio and onto a dimly lit street.

As Alex strolled through the night's chill, she took a moment to put her heart under a magnifying glass—like in medical school when they had sliced tiny slivers of heart tissue, plating them on glass slides and scrutinizing their characteristics under a high-powered microscope. What would she discover if she could study her own? Lonely or not, she should be happy for Tim. He was settled in a great career with a new house and a new life and a new...whatever Cara was.

Instead, she had blown into town like a proper *saboteur*—drinking too much, laughing at their inside jokes, and probably dredging up the few insecurities that Cara possessed. She had never wanted Tim the way she wanted Ian, but she did want him. She wanted his sun-like radiance to warm her icy palms and his wit to lift her spirits. She wanted the security of the uncomplicated. It was terribly selfish. She had used Tim for too long as a surrogate for a real relationship with a man.

With Tim, she never gave anything she hadn't wanted to give. She had never been required to change or sacrifice or exist anywhere that was emotionally uncomfortable. Tim loved the small part of herself that she allowed him to see and that was enough for him.

But it wasn't enough for Ian. Ian treaded in the deep waters of her psyche. Ian had incinerated her exterior to reveal the best and worst parts of her. It was painful and wonderful and real. Ian wanted more, even more than she was willing to give sometimes.

As she twisted the knob to enter Tim's house, she felt an overwhelming sense of loneliness but desired nothing more than to be alone. A quiet realm of solitude where she could swim naked in her loneliness and avoid hurting anyone with it.

"Go get checked into your flight. I'll wait right here."

Tim had insisted on parking and waiting in the bustling airport lobby while she received the appropriate clearance to return to Botswana. When she finally made it through the snake's tail of a line at the ticket counter, he was waiting at the entrance to security, hands shoved in his jean's pockets, his tall frame leaning against the glass window of a little shop selling paperbacks and magazines. His face broke into a lopsided grin when he saw Alex, and he crushed her into a hug. He smelled like warm biscuits on the porch.

When she emerged from the cocoon of his embrace, she refocused on the words she needed to say.

"Tim, I'm sorry about last night. I hope Cara—"

"Don't worry about it, Alex. She's fine," he interrupted. "She knows we're old friends."

Alex brightened, and her nose burned with emotion. "I've just missed you."

"I know. Me too," he said solemnly. "But I'll see you again in February for the critical care meeting?"

"For sure. Take care of Mercy for me."

"I will and Alex," he said, kissing her on the top of the head before directing her toward the security line, "try to call once in a while."

Sweat dripped down her back in linear tributaries that joined together to form a pool at the band of Alex's shorts. The dust kicked up by the soles of her sneakers briefly aerosolized before settling onto her lower legs, glomming onto the moisture of unevaporated sweat.

Every year at the tail end of October, as Botswana entered the brink of summer, the glowing halo of the sun threatened to burn up everything in its path. The grass withered into brown clumps, and the animals retreated to the remaining spotty water holes in the Okavango. Alex peeled the hem of the t-shirt, clinging to her abdomen for the hundredth time to allow some air to circulate over her skin.

The pediatric ward census had been low the last few weeks since she returned from Atlanta, giving her time to catch up on reading, and unfortunately, plenty of spare hours to pine after Ian. They tried to talk every night. She would nestle into the pillow mountain at the head of her bed and spent a solid hour unwinding her day for an attentive Ian, who, despite his complete lack of medical knowledge, had excellent conversational skills. As she jogged toward home, Alex replayed last night's witty banter.

"So, what did you do today?"

Music was playing softly in the background, something in French, and Ian dialed down the volume so he could hear her answer.

"I taught the interns how to cardiovert someone, diagnosed a baby with meningitis, and fulfilled my lifelong goal of cutting out the perfect construction paper spider."

Halloween was coming that weekend and, with it, a visit from her best friend. She looked forward to splaying herself open like a book to Rox. Rox who wouldn't judge her for being selfish with Tim. Rox who would understand her loneliness despite her adeptness at being alone. Rox who would help her navigate the uncharted waters of solidifying things with Ian.

"Cardiovert. Sounds sexy," Ian had murmured huskily.

"Oh, it is. So sexy it's shocking." She had snickered into the phone unashamedly.

"Feel free to cardiovert me anytime," he had responded, the wanton heat diffusing through the phone and settling over her, just as it did now during her ridiculous run during the hottest part of the day.

Who had actually cardioverted whom, she wondered? She hadn't realized her heart could mount such a response to another human like she did to Ian.

When she arrived home, drenched in salty seawater sweat, she fired off a quick text to Rox as McCartney frantically drug his tongue over her shins as if they were lollipops.

Can't wait to see you tomorrow

Every year while the children scattered throughout the neighborhoods of Gaborone wearing fairy costumes or decked out as pirates, collecting sweet treats from willing neighbors, the adults who still wanted to be children gathered at Ex-Pats, where they indulged in treats of their own. Usually the liquor-infused kind. Tonight, Alex, in full costume, marched through the throng of glittering tulle and painted faces on her way to the annual Ex-Pats "Drink and be Scary Party."

As she watched the last rays of sun-suffused glow disintegrate and the children become silhouettes on the horizon, she smartly stepped down the street in red vinyl boots, a cape floating on the breeze behind her, toward the raucous music and carousing that awaited right around the corner.

"Hello Jeff," she said warmly, sliding into the only empty barstool.

Jeff had become portlier over the past year but not any more talkative. The top of his bald head, lobster red from the demands of the already large crowd, came level with Alex's face as he bent down to retrieve something from under the bar. A glistening amber bottle appeared in front of her, and she flashed Jeff a grin.

"Thanks."

"Haven't seen you in a while."

His South African accent sounded comforting, like a dish of mac and cheese—heavy on the cheese. She and Rox had frequented Ex-Pats last year, claiming the same barstools every Friday (and sometimes other weeknights) that they weren't working late at PM. Since Rox had moved to London, Ex-Pats didn't hold the same appeal anymore. It honestly made Alex wince. As she glanced around, Alex was flooded with memories of late-night conversations over beers and waxing poetic under a starlit patio after a little too much tequila.

Rox had found her happily ever after, and Alex was genuinely thrilled for her. Still, sometimes Alex longed for the era when they were in the same place in life—two optimistic lady doctors taking on the world without truly knowing what the future held.

Alex tipped up the beer and guzzled it. Beads of sweat were already collecting on her bit of exposed decolletage. She was typically very conservative with her fashion sense, but, somehow, on All Hallow's Eve, dressing out of the ordinary became socially acceptable and no one batted an eye.

The barstool right next to her was abruptly vacated, and Alex quickly claimed the limited commodity by plopping her blue shoulder bag on its smooth wooden circle. She smiled to herself as she tipped her beer to her lips and surveyed the growing crowd, their limbs already seduced by the beats of the African rhythm floating from the makeshift stage outside. This night had Roxanne Clark written all over it.

Glancing at her phone, she noted the time. Rox should be landing any minute and be here within the hour. She released the tension in her shoulders, letting the alcohol induce its muscle relaxant effect, and felt herself swaying to the beat of a heavy-handed guitar player.

Between sips of beer, she checked her phone with the diligence of someone with obsessive-compulsive disorder. When she drained beer number two and still hadn't heard from Rox, a gnawing worry took root in the pit of her stomach. She punched in the digits that she could have dialed in her sleep. No answer. Alex fired a quick text.

Where are you? Everything okay?

Three dots flashed for what seemed like an eternity before a message finally graced her screen.

Hey sweetie, something's come up with Nic and I can't make it but have fun tonight, and I'll call you tomorrow.

At that moment, various emotions washed through Alex in competition for dominance. The chronic loneliness and constant work stress had morphed the glass bottle holding her emotions into a sieve, and she oozed a combination of disappointment, irritation, and downright despair. Alex swiveled around on her stool and met the onslaught of a growing crowd. In a room full of people, she felt entirely alone.

"Turn that up for me, mate," shouted a voice a few stools away from hers.

Jeff obliged with a silent nod and an outstretch of his beefy hand toward the television that hung precariously from one of the rafters. A sports commentator ticked off the most popular headlines from the day, including which American football teams were rising in the division ranks and which college teams had won that day.

"And in the world of soccer, Nicolau Brizido, a solid member of Arsenal FC since his college days, has been purchased by Tottenham Hotspur."

Alex whipped her head toward the glowing pixelated screen to catch a few shots of Nic scoring various goals over the years and running like a gazelle across the soccer pitch. This must be the "something" with Nic that came up.

Slumping in disappointment, Alex threw her bag over one shoulder, adjusted her cape, and had almost made it to the door when a pair of steel cable arms grabbed her from behind.

FIFTEEN

Her first instinct was to run, but like a flightless bird, she was grounded. An arm stretched across her chest, and another encircled her waist, pulling her into the form behind her. Her neurons kept firing out options but at an excruciatingly slow pace. Various words like the action bubbles in a graphic comic appeared and disappeared in her head. Run. Fight. Use your brain that costs more than most people's luxury cars. Her pupils dilated from the stress response as her adrenal glands poured adrenaline into her bloodstream.

"I thought Wonder Woman was supposed to be invincible."

A delectable smell, tiny microns of scent carried on words, reached her nostrils. *Bourbon.*

As the arms relaxed their hold enough for her to wiggle free, Alex spun around and locked the awaiting, hungry lips with her own. For a moment, she forgot that they were in the smack middle of an inquisitive room of people and let her insides turn to warm pulsing liquid desire. She exhaled a light groan as Ian darted his tongue quickly into her mouth. Mounting a massive amount of willpower, she separated from his mouth and noticed the lust-filled hooded eyes boring into her face.

"Every superhero has her kryptonite," she said, "and you're mine."

Alex reconnected for the briefest brush of her lips to his, but it was enough to set her blood on fire. He slid his thumbs down her bare arms until he reached her hands, where he interlocked their fingers. With a devilish look in his eyes, Ian cocked his head toward the back room, and they began to weave and bob through the crowd toward the luxurious silence that awaited. This private alcove at Ex-Pats was used for private parties and high-profile meetings, and now, apparently, secret rendezvous with one's long-distance lover.

This room was thick with memory. It had been where she and Ian had shared a drink after a very riveting dart tournament, a night that had been the catalyst for a chain of events that had changed her life. She headed over to the private bar where reserve bottles of wine and crystal glasses refracted the light from the one overhead sconce.

Turning to see if Ian had followed, she observed him quietly closing the heavy wood-paneled door and attaching the top latch with a definitive clink. She put her hands on her hips and the blue spangled material of her shorts that hugged them.

"What are you doing here?"

"I happened to be in the neighborhood and decided to drop by on my way to Mongolia."

Ian surveyed the door and, satisfied that it would hold up to any intruders, began making his way slowly toward Alex like a predator stalking its prey.

"Botswana is not on the way to Mongolia." She smirked, and his lips twitched in response.

"I know, but it was worth an extra night of traveling to see you."

"So, this is some kind of extravagant, last-minute transcontinental tryst?" she asked.

"Something like that. Is that okay?"

"Absolutely," she breathed.

He placed his palms on either side of her face, and his eyes drunk her in, flitting to each section of her face in consecutive order and finally landing on her lips. There was a question mark in his eyes, and Alex felt the urge to unearth the words he wasn't saying.

"What?" Alex asked quietly.

"Later," he said, dropping his hands and using them to vault himself behind the counter. "What will it be, oh mighty Wonder Woman?"

Alex squinched her eyes shut with a degree of embarrassment. For some reason, it had seemed like a grand idea to dress up as her favorite superhero tonight.

"Surprise me," she said, sliding into one of the chairs lined up at the bar.

"Oh, I plan to," he said, disappearing underneath the bar for a moment before reappearing with a bottle of flaxen-colored liquid that looked like bottled sunshine.

He slid the bottle toward her, and she examined the label. Tequila—a brand called Avión. He began slicing limes, running a knife through their thick rind, and filling the air with the delicate odor of citrus.

"Rox was supposed to be here tonight," Alex admitted, taking the liberty of pulling the cork stopper from the bottleneck and pouring a splash of golden liquid into a pair of crystal cylinders as tall as her index finger.

"I know," Ian said as he pushed a silver tray in her direction, a display of lime wedges circling a mound of coarse salt resembling a tiny ski hill.

"Is that why you're here?"

"No," he admonished, walking around the bar this time to take the stool next to her. "I had my own reason for coming, thank you very much."

She eyed him skeptically and picked up her shot glass. He snaked his fingers around her wrist to stop her, plucking the glass from her grasp with his other hand.

"What?" she said in mock exasperation.

"I'm going to show you the reason."

Ian pulled her wrist up toward his mouth, exposing the tender pale inside, and swept his tongue across its surface. Jets of electricity surged up her back, past the tightly fitting corset she wore, and up into her hairline. Leaving a trail of moisture along the path of her radial artery, he picked up his head, a remarkable flame-worthy glow in his eyes. He took a pinch of coarse sea salt from the little mound on the tray and sprinkled it over her wrist, and then took his time laving his tongue over its inner surface to retrieve the salt.

Alex clenched her thighs together to staunch the heat that arose between them—the heat that was being kindled into an inferno with every sweep of Ian's tongue. With a wicked smirk on his face, he threw back the tequila shot and then stuffed a lime wedge into his mouth. Alex joined him, a trail of burn joining the one already coursing through her middle. The rush of alcohol into her bloodstream combined with a month's worth of longing spiked her heart rate and her boldness.

Licking her lips, she leaned over and removed the lime wedge from Ian's front teeth, a satisfying spurt of sour citrus coating her taste buds. He wasn't smiling as his hands encircled her waist. His tongue darted out onto his lips, and Alex imploded inward.

She desperately wanted to taste the remnants of salt on those lips and feel the drag of his wet heat on every single inch of her body.

He easily lifted her onto the bar and wedged himself between her legs, burying his head between her breasts. She felt his warm breath on her exposed cleavage. Tipping up his chin with her fingertips, she claimed his mouth for her own, hot with desire and traces of salt and tequila wherever she explored with her lips.

As their kiss deepened, she momentarily forgot where she was and began dragging the hem of his t-shirt from his waist to expose the tensile muscles of his lower back. His lips had taken on a new lust-filled fury as he worshipped the space between her jawline and her collarbone. His hands crept up her back and began undoing the laces of her costume corset.

"Wait...Ian," she laughed into his hair.

He slowed down but didn't stop the lips that were now precariously close to her heaving breasts. She tilted her head back in ecstasy. "As awesome as this is," she groaned, "I'm not sure the owner of Ex-Pats would appreciate us using the backroom as a private sex den."

"Trust me," Ian said, peering up at her with hooded eyes. "He doesn't mind."

"Do you know the owner?"

"I am the owner."

Alex's head snapped back into a neutral position, her eyes wide with shock.

"You bought Ex-Pats?"

"I did." He shrugged sheepishly, the tousled ends of his raven hair tickling her skin like fluttering feathers. "I'm sentimental if you haven't noticed."

A part of her heart melted right there, exquisite tenderness pooling right into her chest cavity.

"Does this mean I get free drinks?" she teased.

"Absolutely not," he scoffed, "but you don't need to keep paying with your credit card."

"Oh really. What are you charging me these days?"

Alex's lips widened into a broad smile that stopped mid-stretch when she caught the ravenous look in his eyes as he roved her body. Her body that was form-fitted into an outfit that she would have never worn where people would recognize her. She wrapped her long legs, clad in knee-high red vinyl boots, around his waist and pulled him toward her until the only things that separated her skin from his were two very different types of textiles. She could not be close enough to him. Her skin would not stop begging until every receptor fired with his touch.

In an accelerated flurry of limbs, she yanked his t-shirt over his head while he managed to undo the laces and bracket clasps of an entire corset and fling it to the ground. His chest felt hot and damp from the combination of exertion and the warm night and so perfect against her own. She groaned in anticipation of what came next as he unzipped her boots and disposed of her shiny spandex shorts. His mouth went immediately to her lace underwear, not even bothering to remove them before he put his mouth to work.

"Are you absolutely sure you want to get on an airplane?" Alex sat up in bed purposefully allowing her tousled chocolate waves to cascade down her front and barely cover her breasts.

Ian glanced up from where he was shoving items into a small carry-on, a spark igniting from the fresh kindling of her half-naked body. Ian groaned lightly and zipped his bag closed with a flourish.

"I do a lot of things I don't want to do lately." He made a sound halfway between a laugh and a cough.

"Why so many trips to Mongolia?" she inquired.

"Trying to get some things tied up there with the new mining cooperative before—"

"Before?"

"Before I'm needed in London for a while during the transition."

"So, you decided to take your dad's place when he retires?"

"It's what makes sense. It's the natural path for my life...what I was always meant to do."

He sauntered over to the bed, already fully dressed in dark jeans and a white button-down, every hair in place, having made his transition into the heir to a mining fortune and all the responsibilities that came with it. He tipped up her chin, his eyes already bidding her an unfortunate farewell. Alex knew she wouldn't have another opportunity. She snatched the glittering gold lasso from last night's costume off her bedside table and began winding it around his wrist.

"Wonder Woman has a magic lasso," she explained solemnly. "When it's touching you, you have to tell the truth."

"I thought this might be some new kinky side to you I had no idea existed." He cocked an eyebrow and was unable to hide the intrigue in his eyes.

Alex smiled nervously and flushed a deep hue of pink.

"There's time for that," she admitted, and his pupils dilated at least a few millimeters. "But for now, I have a question for you."

"Okay. Should I be worried?"

"No." Alex shook her head. "Of course not."

"Do your worst." He flashed her a rueful smile.

Alex took a cleansing breath before she catapulted the words into the atmosphere.

"Rox thinks that you are lonely, and you want me to move to London." She bit her lip nervously. "Is that what you want?"

She peered upward into his face trying to invoke an inner calm that she didn't feel. His brow furrowed, their thickness rising together onto the deepening lines of his forehead. He sighed and settled into the spot next to her on the bed, unwinding himself from the coils of her truth talisman.

"It's one thing to know what I want, Alex. It's another thing entirely to ask for it."

Alex wandered through her rented flat for the better part of the day, going from room to room, picking up objects and putting them down with no real purpose. McCartney trailed after her for a while but then grew tired and curled up in a prime spot on the cool kitchen tile to wait out the peak heat of the day. Every few minutes, she checked her phone. She wasn't expecting Ian to call—he was on a plane headed to the bitter cold of the *taiga*. But she had thought that Rox would.

Every time she glanced at a blank screen devoid of missed calls or texts, a pang of distress pierced her. She was in a constant feedback loop of phone checking and a further descent into melancholy. When her wandering finally landed her in the bedroom, she collapsed into the unmade bed, drawing Ian's pillow from last night into an embrace. It smelled like him, a fresh, clean scent with hints of sandalwood. Right now, tucked into the haven of her bed, she felt protected from the change on the horizon that was coming for her like a masked horseman.

Her choices splayed out before her like spindles of a spiderweb, each a precarious journey down the path of her life. It had always been easy to deny herself luxuries and comforts, even the comfort of companionship. She had placed everything on a sacrificial altar to achieve an endpoint—with the endpoint being to finish medical training and choose a career path. Well, here she was. A certified pediatric ICU doctor with an incredible opportunity to make a difference in thousands of children's lives and it wasn't enough.

Admitting that felt like the most asinine disappointment of her entire life. Ian was asking her for something without actually asking. He had said nothing more on the subject. Instead, he had kissed her with a lingering goodbye and wordlessly left her in the doorway, ducking into the black SUV that would whisk him to the airstrip where his private airplane was waiting for him.

Alex had wanted nothing more at that moment than to indulge in insanity and join him. What kind of human was she if part of her wanted to abandon her commitments and jet around the globe with her billionaire boyfriend? A selfish one.

With guilt as a prime motivator, she arrived at the hospital on Monday morning prepared to launch herself into work, devoting every ounce of her intellect and investing every cell of her being into her patients.

"Good morning, everyone. I hope you had a good weekend. What do we have on the ward this morning?"

As they traveled bed to bed, like a slowly moving amoeba with white-coated podocytes, the interns relayed to Alex the admissions from the weekend as well as the kids who remained in the hospital from last week. A four-year-old with dehydration from diarrhea, a two-year-old with pneumonia, a nine-month-old recovering from meningitis, and a ten-year-old boy who had a nasty cut on his leg from a farming accident. The surgeons had explored it last night, and he was febrile this morning but had been appropriately started on antibiotics.

Everything seemed to be working like clockwork. The children were improving. The nurses were charting their progress. By mid-afternoon, Alex was bereft with the absolute lack of activity. She flipped through every chart in turn and paused at each patient to relisten to each set of lungs. She even took down the dressing for the boy with the leg trauma, secretly hoping to see the first signs of infection, a red puffiness of the tissues or a thin green ooze coming from the wound edges. No such luck. The puckered skin between the interrupted vicryl sutures looked pristine.

Lucia sat at a nearby desk, her head bent over a stack of articles Alex had printed for her, highlighting the sentences that appealed to her.

"Do you need anything, Lucia?" Alex asked with rising hope that something would be amiss, and she could redirect her energies.

"No, Dr. Alex," she replied, glancing up briefly.

"Okay, I'll just go grab a drink. Be right back."

Alex headed out into the sunshine-filled afternoon and, after snagging the last two Diet Cokes from the cafe, settled into the sturdiness of the familiar stone bench she used to share with Rox. Nostalgia gripped her, and she reached into the depths of her white coat to retrieve her phone. One missed call. How did she miss that? She pressed the little notification rectangle, and her phone automatically dialed the number.

"Hi there, love," sung a radiant voice that sounded crystal clear despite the thousands of kilometers between them.

"Hi Rox." Alex felt a strange tightening in her throat and clenching of her stomach that had never before occurred when talking with Rox. "How was your weekend?" she asked flatly.

"Oh, you know...insane. Nic got bought by some other team— the something or the something. It was a media frenzy around here. We tried to meet some friends for dinner last night and had to bail out the back of the restaurant afterward into an alleyway."

"Sounds exciting." Her tone bordered on sarcastic. Alex scolded herself. What was wrong with her?

"How was yours, dear?"

"Ian showed up unexpectedly."

"I know. So romantic. Did you guys talk about you know what?"

"We didn't talk that much," Alex admitted. "But I think I managed to confirm some things."

"Like?"

Alex sighed, annoyance suddenly rising like bile into the back of her throat. "Like the fact that he plans to be in London to take over the company...and he wants me there too."

"Oooh, I knew it. I hope you don't mind, but I contacted a gal pal of mine at Great Ormond Street, and she thinks they might be posting an ICU job soon. And she forwarded your CV to the director."

Despite the balmy day, Alex felt a cold creeping toward her fingertips, and it wasn't from the lukewarm silver can she held.

"Why would you do that?" she asked quietly.

"I assume you want to work when you get here."

Alex allowed an awkward silence to settle over the conversation.

"Just because it was easy for you to pick up and leave everything and everyone here in Botswana doesn't mean it's that easy for everyone."

"It wasn't easy for me," Rox said defensively.

"It really does seem that way. While you have been glamming around London, your surgical skills lab has completely fallen apart, not to mention the staff education and the maternal outcomes. It's like the minute you left, you completely forgot about this place."

"I haven't forgotten. I just have different priorities right now. Nic—"

Alex cut her off. "Nic is a grown-up with a hugely successful career surrounded by a crowd of sycophants at every turn. He can share you with the other people in this world that need you."

She could feel Rox's anger rising on the other end of the phone and did nothing to placate it.

"I don't expect someone who has never prioritized relationships to understand what it takes to be a good wife...or a good friend."

"What in the world does that mean?"

"It means, sweetie, that if you can't learn how to put the people you love as a priority, you're going to lose them...and not just Ian this time."

As her words sunk into the depths of Alex's soul, like the Titanic as it plummeted to the bottom of a freezing Atlantic, she heard her name being called through the insulation of hundreds of feet of water.

"You can't keep going rogue for weeks at a time and become so sucked into your job that—"

"Wilde! Wilde! I have a job for you."

Samantha Drake was striding across the short brown stubble of grass, the hem of her canvas white coat flapping in the breeze like a surrendering flag.

"I have to go, Rox," Alex said and clicked disconnect before any more words could be exchanged.

"What's up?" Alex shouted, shielding her eyes from the glare of the mid-afternoon sun. She was grateful to be distracted, if only momentarily, from the unease that had settled into her bone marrow.

"I have a premature baby that needs labs pronto. The nurses

have stuck him a dozen times with no luck."

Great. Something she could do.

Drawing blood was something of a heroine act, especially if scores of people had already failed. As a pediatric ICU doctor, Alex was accustomed to swooping in and saving the day with an expert poke into an artery that was no bigger than a strand of hair.

Alex surveyed the baby, small and premature but not born so early that he couldn't survive. Dark purple islands coalesced along his feet and the crook of his elbows where numerous needles had been plunged into his thin skin. Kate, the fresh-faced flaxen-haired medical student, stood by the crib, butterfly needle connected to a syringe suspended from her hand. She stared at it as if it had appeared there by mistake. Alex took it from her and set it on the mattress.

"Hold his leg just like this," she instructed Kate. "I'll just stick the femoral artery, and we can be done with this."

Sam nodded at Kate, and she wound her long fingers with nails freshly coated in a deep crimson around the baby's ankle.

"All right, little guy. Just one poke and it's over." Alex thrust her butterfly needle into his groin, right through the skin overlying his thumping pulse, and a spurt of bright red blood began filling up the syringe. "How much do you need?" Alex asked.

"Five milliliters...give or take," Sam answered, her usually gravelly voice softened with a touch of awe.

"Done," said Alex perfunctorily and pulled the needle from the skin, careful to apply pressure with a gauze pad to encourage clotting.

In the next instant, several things happened at once. Kate prematurely released her hold on the baby, who decided to make up for his last few moments of immobility by kicking furiously. In her attempt to reestablish her hold on his leg, Kate whacked Alex's forearm, and the sharp blood-stained end of a glinting needle wound up buried two-thirds deep in the meat of Alex's palm.

SIXTEEN

"Ouch," Alex yelped and reacted quickly, yanking the silver offender out of her hand.

"What?" Sam asked as she unfolded her arms, letting them hang loosely at her sides.

Alex put down the needle-syringe combo and ripped off her purple glove. A pinpoint but noticeable puncture wound stared back at her like some grotesque one-eyed monster that was sharing space with the anterior surface of her thenar eminence.

"I got stuck," she sighed, more annoyed than anything and surveyed the room for the nearest sink.

Kate, still engrossed with controlling an infuriated infant, refused to look at her, strands of hair partially covering the flush spreading across her cheeks. She cast a few furtive glances in Alex's direction.

"Go wash that off right now," Sam commanded.

"I will. I will." Alex headed for the nearest sink and soaped up her hands, letting the cool water flood the area.

She was just about to dry off with the nearest towel when Sam appeared with a bottle of betadine, grabbed her hand, stuck it over the sink, and began pouring. An orange-brown river swallowed up the pallor of her hand as Sam held it in an iron-clad grasp.

"Don't you think this is overkill?" Alex wrinkled her nose. She had never liked the smell of betadine.

"It's not. That baby's mom is HIV positive."

Alex's body quieted until she was still enough to appreciate every slow, definitive heartbeat. Every heartbeat ejecting an adequate aliquot of blood out to her tissues that would ensure the highest level of functioning for whatever arduous task awaited her.

Numbers swarmed her cerebral cortex—transmission statistics and viral loads and variables that she couldn't quantitate. Had this mother been receiving antiretroviral therapy while she was pregnant? Sam must have been reading her thoughts.

"We just started her on therapy when she came in for delivery," Sam muttered quietly, "and the baby will need AZT."

They wouldn't know for many weeks whether the baby would seroconvert or not. Alex flipped on the faucet handle and rinsed the betadine from her hand, creating a whirlpool of dilute yellow-brown swirling clockwise around the drain. With uttermost calm, she dried her hands and began walking toward the door.

"Where are you going?" Sam called after her.

"To finish seeing patients and then home," Alex said, not bothering to turn around.

In reality, she had to make one more stop. Her fist hesitated a moment before she rapped on the outside of Dr. K's compressed wood door. She shook her head to overcome her intrinsic shyness. Needing a prescription for antiretroviral prophylaxis was a good reason to interrupt someone's day.

"Come in," boomed the rich mahogany voice.

"Dr. K, I'm sorry to bother you—"

"You are never a bother, Alex," he said, not looking up from the stack of papers on his desk, spectacles perched on the very tip of his nose. "Now, how can I help you today?" His brown eyes, swimming in kindness, surveyed her face as he waited for her to speak.

Alex sat down, the yellow vinyl chair squawking in protest. "I was helping Sam, and I got stuck with a needle. I'm going to need prophylaxis."

"Oh, Alex. I am sorry." His forehead developed an extra furrow before his sparse salt and pepper hairline started.

"It's okay," she answered automatically.

But it wasn't. She had known the risks when she signed up for this job, and no matter what happened, she still wouldn't change her decision to come here. Explaining that to Ian, however, was going to be an entirely different matter.

He pulled a sheet of paper from his drawer and scribbled down some instructions.

"We have a protocol for this," he informed her. "Take this to the hospital pharmacy, and they will get you what you need. Testing will happen today and in six weeks."

"Thanks, Dr. K. I'm sure it will be fine."

"I am sure it will be."

He bent down over his papers, pushing his wire-rimmed glasses up onto the bridge of his nose as Alex noiselessly exited the office.

After the second needle of the day punctured her skin, this time with the express purpose of withdrawing an obnoxious amount of her blood, and Alex had filled a paper bag with medication bottles, she headed home to spend the remainder of her evening curled up with McCartney and some mindless television. She eyed the neat row of chalk-white pills laid out on the counter. Seven pills twice a day for six weeks until her second test came back negative...or didn't.

Alex pushed down the negativity rising like acid in her stomach. Armed with diligence and a giant glass of cranberry juice on ice, she swallowed them one by one, their hard edges softened by the juice's thickness. She had never been able to swallow pills with plain water and, other than occasional binges of ibuprofen for migraine headaches, she never took medicine at all.

Later that night, when she writhed between her sheets, battling a nausea that threatened to catapult her from her bed and into the bathroom, she knew she had done this to herself. What had made her feel like she deserved this? Was it all the horrible medicine she prescribed to children? Medicine that made them sick to their tummies or gave them rashes or made them so exhausted they couldn't leave their beds. Was it because, deep down, she had some masochistic fantasy of understanding exactly what it was like to be a patient so that she could arise to a new level of doctorhood?

Or was it because for a split second, she had imagined what life would be like if she left all this behind? If she moved to London and became the jet-setting, high-profile girlfriend of a billionaire philanthropist. She sat up too quickly and leaned over the bed, heaving the contents of her stomach all over the hardwood floor. The universe was punishing her. She just didn't know for which transgression.

Sometime around two in the morning, Alex awoke, shivering in damp sheets that had absorbed her sweat over the last few hours. Stripping the sheets, she tossed them into a pile and added her clothes before huddling in a lukewarm shower. Exhausted but refreshed, she flung open the window to circulate the bad humors out of her bedroom.

McCartney gave her a thorough sniff and once satisfied, flopped back down on the floor to finish whatever canine dreams he had been having of romping through fields and rolling in disgusting piles of zebra manure. She didn't own a second set of sheets, one of the many tasks that had slipped her mind over the last decade while she was pounding an infinite, never-ending quota of medical facts into her brain.

Instead, she rummaged around in the closet where a flat square of soft pink material beckoned her hand. It was as soft as a foal's muzzle and baby pink like the color of ballet slippers and freshly spun cotton candy. The cashmere cardigan had been a gift from Rox during their first Christmas living abroad, away from their families and comfortable traditions. Even though it was hot as Hades outside, Rox had insisted on gifting her something that would remind them both of being tucked inside with a roaring fire while snow dusted the outside world.

Untying the designer price tag, Alex slipped it on over her pajamas, feeling a quick release of endorphins as her skin responded to the softness. Rox had always known how to shop for herself and Alex. She had chosen clothing items that Alex hadn't even realized she would like until she put them on. Somehow, they were always a perfect fit. Like Ian. Rox had even chosen Ian.

But this bold effort to blaze a path for Alex's future. That was a line crossed. In doing so, Rox was trying to justify her own life choices. Alex had always made her own decisions and the subsequent rewards or consequences were hers to own. However she magically melded the two loves of her life—Ian and medicine—was hers to decide.

Rox didn't call that night or the next or the one following, but Ian did, and Alex reinforced her nerves with steel when she hit answer next to his glossy image on her phone.

"Hello from the coldest most desolate place on the planet," crackled a husky voice through the speaker.

"Where are you?"

"Near Murun. About three hundred miles west of Ulaanbaatar. The reception here sucks."

"What are you doing all the way out there?"

"I don't know if you realize this, but most people frown on developing mining sites near major metropolitan areas."

"Very funny. Good thing I'm wildly attracted to sarcasm."

"I suppose that is a good thing. I mean, why else would you be with me? It's not my devilish good looks or the life-changing sex."

Alex laughed, her first real laughter bubble in days. After the argument with Rox, every second of every day had taken on a shade of gray.

"It's your mind actually. Brainpower turns me on."

"I have a completely new understanding of the phrase screwing someone's brains out now."

"Speaking of which..." Alex bit her lip until she tasted a droplet of blood.

"I miss you," he blurted, and the crackly connection suddenly dissipated into a moment of perfect vocal clarity.

"I miss you too." Alex's voice cracked like an egg over a frying pan.

Sensing that the mood was shifting into deeper emotional waters, Ian began a monologue about the mining site and the progress. He always liked to keep things light over the phone and usually filled their talks with sexual innuendo. *Just say it, Alex.* But forming the words felt like chalk in her throat.

"I'll try to call as much as I can, but there's a lot going on here. Is everything set for Christmas?"

Dr. K. had graciously granted her request for three weeks off to spend Christmas and New Year's with Ian in London. In a fatherly way, he tried to protect her from working too hard and burning herself out.

"I'm all set. I'll be there on the twenty-second."

"Please remember to pack your stamina because I am going to give you the most unforgettable—"

"Ian," she interrupted, and he immediately paused. "It's probably a good thing that we're apart for the next few weeks."

"Why is that?"

"Because I had a little mishap at the hospital."

"What kind of mishap?"

Alex cringed and scrunched her eyes shut.

"The kind where you get stuck with a bloody needle."

He said nothing. No interjection. No questions. Just quiet breathing. She forged ahead.

"I was doing a blood draw on a baby with an HIV positive mom—"

"I don't need to hear anything else."

Alex stopped short, the rest of her well-planned monologue

dying in her throat.

"I shouldn't be surprised at the ways you continue to sabotage your life...but I guess I am."

In times of crisis, Alex reverted to the safe part of her brain that could spout statistics and medical facts.

"The likelihood of transmission is actually very low." Her voice was methodical and quiet, the same voice she used when explaining a diagnosis to a patient's family.

"But it's not zero."

"No. It's not."

She choked on the words, remembering a dream she had last night of being presented with a pill to swallow the size of her fist. She supposed it was the Efavirenz she was taking and its neuropsychiatric side effects.

A din of voices and the revving of an engine erupted in the background.

"Listen, I have to go. The crew is waiting on me."

"Okay. I love you," Alex whispered, but only empty static remained.

During her psychiatry rotation in medical school, Alex learned an extensive amount of what she had then considered useless information on how people deal with unacceptable feelings—psychological strategies, so to speak. In layman's terms, they were referred to as defense mechanisms. As each foot struck the pavement, she ticked them off in her head. Denial. Regression. Projection. Rationalization. Sublimation. Intellectualization. Compartmentalization. The last three were her trusty go-to's.

Sublimation—she glanced down at the swift cadence of her feet, the electric blue running shoes rising and falling methodically, the strain in all four muscles of her quadriceps group as she bent her head into the wind.

Intellectualization—she repeated the practiced sentences she had planned to offer up to Ian about the risk of transmission being less than one percent. *But not zero*, her subconscious nagged. She turned the street corner, and PM popped into view on the horizon.

And then there was compartmentalization—just stuff it somewhere dark and esoteric on the outer rim of her psyche as long as possible.

"How's it going Lucia?" she asked the slim young intern who maintained a vigil to a desk piled high with charts.

"Dr. Alex. I did not recognize you in your...outdoor attire."

Lucia peered over the metal jackets containing a novella of information on each patient—vitals, labs, daily progress notes. Alex reflexively folded her arms across her chest. She rarely showed up to the ward clad in a t-shirt and wispy running shorts, but her internal alarm had resounded while she was running, and she didn't want to ignore it...or maybe she just didn't want to be home alone.

"Do you need any help finishing notes or need me to check on any of the kids for you?"

"No." Lucia chewed her lip thoughtfully.

Alex remained quiet, regarding her face as she struggled with whether to ask for help. It was a common problem among young doctors and a developmental stage that everyone had to endure. Ask for too much and one became known as incompetent and unsure. Ask for too little and one was aggressive and over-confident.

In medicine, Alex had spent entire years acquiring critical thinking skills that had to be applied in a time-sensitive matter. Knowing what to do when the time arose was crucial, but she had also realized that maturity as a physician also meant knowing limitations and when to ask for help. With encouraging eyes, she regarded Lucia as she struggled with that very concept.

"Maybe," Lucia finally blurted, and Alex smiled.

"Tell me the story," Alex urged as they parked themselves in front of the bed space of a young boy with hair trimmed so short that his head was almost bare, wearing a striped tank top and cutoffs.

He was silent, but his face was pinched as if in pain, and his breathing labored with an audible grunt at the end of each exhalation.

"This is a seven-year-old boy who presented with fever, malaise, and cellulitis of the right leg."

Alex nodded encouragement. "Okay, tell me what you've done so far."

Lucia wrinkled her brow in concentration. "I started antibiotics yesterday—clindamycin—but he is not any better, and I am repeating his labs because they all seem very abnormal."

Alex picked up the chart clipped to the end of his bed and began flipping through the sheaf of papers held together by a flimsy paperclip. As she flipped, her eyes absorbed every piece of pertinent data, filling in the gaps to complete the clinical picture. Blood culture was negative, but the platelet count was dangerously low. His sodium was low as well, and his kidney numbers were elevated. It seemed like a cut and dry case of cellulitis that had evolved into sepsis.

Alex tried and failed to ignore the intuition tugging on her like a child on his mom's pant leg.

"When did you say he came in?" Alex asked.

"Yesterday," Lucia answered promptly.

"Well, the antibiotics may not have kicked in yet. Let's give him a dose of vancomycin and ceftriaxone to broaden our coverage."

Alex tiptoed around to the head of the boy's bed, noticing that his eyes had sagged closed while they had been talking. She put the back of her hand to his forehead. The skin was so hot that it scorched her. She grabbed a stethoscope and pressed it to his chest. His heart rate was rapid and frantic as it tried to push oxygen-carrying red blood cells out to starved tissues that were fighting for their existence.

"Can you show me the wound?"

Lucia rotated his left hip so that Alex could get a bird's eye view of his calf, revealing a blistered strip of skin surrounded by an island of red, angry tissue. Alex's phone called out to her from the pocket of her shorts, and she ignored it and snapped on a glove to probe the wound.

The boy's eyes fluttered open as she pressed on his calf, and instead of soft, pliable muscle, her fingers were met with tissue as hard as stone. An area of skin as big as the tip of her pinkie had opened up near the distal part of the calf, an ulceration with a shaggy yellow base. As Alex probed further, her intuition was no longer tugging at her pant leg, it was jumping up and down howling in her face.

"Can you grab me a flashlight?"

Lucia returned with a compact torch that they used when the lights dimmed at night and the nurses needed to tend to one patient without waking the others. In the faint sunlight trickling through a dusty window, they had both missed it on the first pass but the flashlight beam on the boy's skin illuminated it plain as day.

"What is that?" she asked Lucia as she pointed to two evenly spaced puncture wounds on the boy's mid-calf, staring at them like two pinpoint pupils with halos of blistering flesh.

SEVENTEEN

Envenomation. Her phone buzzed like a starving mosquito, and she swatted the screen to silence it. No wonder the antibiotics had done nothing. They might as well have given him saline for all the magic they could work against the bite of a venomous snake. This was not a clinical situation she had anticipated. Sepsis, pneumonia, diarrhea epidemics were in her comfort zone. She had no idea what kind of pit vipers were indigenous to Botswana.

"Lucia, I need you to call the surgeon on call. This wound needs to be debrided."

Alex yanked out her phone. "I'll get busy with Dr. Google."

She noticed multiple texts from Rox and a missed call but swiped them off her home screen. Compartmentalization made easy via technology.

Precisely five minutes later, Alex had scrolled through a surprisingly thorough summary of poisonous snakes found in Botswana thanks to the African Snakebite Institute Website. Various types of cobras, black mamba, something called a boomslang, and the puff adder, the snake responsible for more snakebite-related fatalities than any other. She clicked on the picture of the tan sausage body with black chevron stripes up its scaly back. Local cytotoxicity, which would explain the tissue injury. Low blood pressure from plasma leakage. Coagulopathy. A bite from this snake would explain everything.

Lucia had returned, her mouth set in a grim line. "The surgeon is busy now, but he will come over after his case."

Alex had a sudden thought. "Lucia, can you ask the boy what happened to him?"

Placing gentle hands on the boy's shoulders, she roused him awake, his face contorting with pain as he immediately cried out for his mother.

"I'll grab him some morphine," Alex called, already halfway to the supply cabinet.

She returned with the syringe, holding his writhing arm with one hand while Lucia whispered rapidly in his ear in Setswana. Pushing a small amount of narcotic into his IV, a soothing elixir for the excruciating pain that would only worsen over the next few hours, Alex felt a growing dread take root.

"Open the bag saline and just let it run in," Alex instructed Lucia as she took a seat in the creaky office chair behind the only computer terminal on the ward.

"What did he say happened?" Alex asked as she searched the hospital's electronic formulary for "antivenom."

"He said that he skipped school and was playing in the brush with some friends. He remembers being bitten but did not mention that part to his mother."

Poor little guy. Alex's heart squeezed. He was probably afraid of getting in trouble for missing school, and now what should have been a consequence-free childhood mistake could end his life.

"Why is there no antivenom listed here?" Alex asked, annoyed at the slowly moving green letters inching up the black screen.

"I know it's very expensive, and I don't know if we keep it in the pharmacy or not," admitted Lucia.

Alex knew who would. Her fingers were already dialing. The sound of splattering of water met her ears when he answered the phone, and she could hear children giggling gleefully in the background.

"Dr. K?" she ventured before his rich voice rose above the din of the water.

"Yes, Alex. Sorry, I am watering my gardenias, and the grandchildren decided to run around under the hose."

Alex smiled. She remembered craving any water activity during the long Texas summers growing up.

"Do we keep snake antivenom here at PM?" she blurted, her mind not able to focus on idle chatting at the moment. He hesitated for one second, then two, and Alex realized she was holding her breath.

"Yes, I believe we might," he said smoothly. "Check in the pharmacy refrigerator at the very back."

"Thank you, sir," Alex gushed, then, in her fumbling haste,

accidentally disconnected the call. "I think that's the first time I've hung up first," she mused, giddy as she raced down the back hallway through a maze of covered sidewalks and emerged at the green double doors marked pharmacy in white block letters.

The cramped space was illuminated by a single overhead light that cast dancing shadows over the rows of neatly labeled bins of glass bottles and the pill dispenser station in the corner. A humming noise drew her to the back of the room where a white refrigerator sat, the promise of a life-saving elixir inside. Alex flung open the door, pushing aside various bottles until she found a box at the very back labeled SAIMR polyvalent snake antivenom. *Jackpot.*

As she was ripping open the box to count the vials inside, her phone emitted an obnoxious ring. Roxanne again. Somewhat guiltily, Alex sent her straight to voicemail. There were three vials inside, not a lot, but at least that would be a start. Holding up her coveted prize, she rotated it in the dim incandescence of the refrigerator light. Expiration date 11/2007. She checked each vial in turn. They were all expired.

"Give him another liter of fluid," she called to Lucia while she paced around the ward holding her phone to her ear, a delightful stream of background music that mocked the urgency of her call to the South African Vaccine Producers.

The boy's blood pressure had dropped precipitously in the last hour. The fluid boluses and the morphine were mere bandages for the inevitable. He was dying right in front of them.

"South African Vaccine Producers. How can I help you?" clipped a woman's voice in a thick South African accent.

"Hi, this is Dr. Alex Wilde. I'm a physician at Princess Marina in Gaborone, and we have a really sick kid who I believe was bitten by an adder."

"So, you're calling to obtain antivenom then?"

"Yes, we had some here, but it's expired."

"How many vials do you need?" she asked.

"I don't know," Alex mumbled. "Maybe ten or so?"

"Each vial of antivenom is seventeen hundred Rand. How will you be paying?"

Paying? Alex had not thought this through to conclusion. Of course, they would require payment. Seventeen hundred Rand was about a hundred American dollars...times ten would be around a thousand dollars. *Bloody hell.*

"Credit card," she stammered and then rattled off her credit card information by memory.

"Excellent. We will ship by medical courier and have it to you in about twenty-four hours."

Twenty-four hours? Alex's stomach twisted into another knot.

"This kid will be dead in twenty-four hours."

"Then you are welcome to come pick it up yourself."

Within the hour, Alex had changed into jeans and a t-shirt and was driving into the inky black hole of night headed south toward Johannesburg. She had dropped McCartney off at Mary Lou's, her bristly hexagenerian neighbor from nowhere Kentucky.

"Not this time, boy," she had said, patting McCartney on the head before relinquishing his leash to an impatient Mary Lou.

Much like Alex, McCartney loved road trips, but an eight-hour roundtrip that extended into ten hours because of stopping for McCartney to relieve himself was not something she could afford. Mary Lou, already dressed down to striped cotton pajamas, had coaxed him inside with a piece of leftover bacon.

The memory of the pungent, spicy scent of overcooked bacon made Alex's stomach growl, and she reflexively reached into her cupholder for the frosted can of Diet Coke that awaited her there. She chugged a quarter of it in one fell swoop, wishing that the Coca-Cola company would catch a clue and add just a bit more caffeine punch to their popular concoction.

Smiling, she wiped her mouth with the back of her hand. It had gotten her through worse. Thirteen years of all-nighters—first in college then in medical school, then in critical care training, where staying up all night performing delicate tasks like threading a catheter into unwilling vessels was part of her regular life. She had learned to titrate her caffeine to perfection, enough to promote wakefulness but not enough to cause shaky hands.

As she sped farther away from the city lights, the businesses grew sparse and soon only the twin beams of her headlights lit the path in front of her. Occasionally a grazing animal would startle, and she would catch its sclera, glowing eerily white in the otherwise pitch black. She didn't mind the dark. It reminded her of starlit nights in the heat of the Texas summer, winding through backroads with Natalie using the evaporative power of the wind to cool their sun-soaked skin after a day at the pool.

Natalie had been her best friend growing up, all the way through high school, and then Alex had faded into the abyss of studying to get into med school and then the life-altering decade of medical training. When Alex had seen her at her father's funeral last spring, Natalie had been welcoming and gracious. They had spent a night and two bottles of wine reminiscing about their teenage years and catching each other up to the present.

Alex rolled down the window part way and allowed the wild night air with its exotic scents to stream over her face. Glancing to the left at the empty passenger seat, she thought how Rox would have loved this mad dash to a city four hours away for a pricey dose of antivenom that would be completely worth it when they saved a little life. Had they drifted apart so much in the last few months that they couldn't bridge the monumental gaps between their lives? Alex still felt the sting of their last conversation. Of Rox's abandonment of everything in Botswana for a different life. Of Rox's abandonment of her.

To be fair, Rox had not understood the depth of Alex's distress when she casually canceled her plans to visit. Alex had not revealed how badly she needed a voice of clarity to discern her future and to dissolve her loneliness—a loneliness that not even Ian's love could force out of existence. It was a basic female need to have another female decipher the spiderweb complexity of life and provide a single thread of connection as a stabilizing point to one's pathway.

Alex had come to depend on Rox as that stabilizing point, as the eyes that could see what she could not. As the voice of love and clarity. On a whim, she dialed Rox's number, but it went straight to voicemail. Words tumbled around Alex's brain, but none exited her lips, and she hit end without leaving a message.

Alex pressed the round buzzer outside the plain brick facade for the third time and tugged pointlessly on the handles of the pair of glass doors marking the entrance to South Africa Vaccine Producers. It was nearing midnight, but she had been told that the security guard would let her in to retrieve the precious box labeled with her name at the front desk.

Finally, a stately man in a blue uniform tall enough to adorn the Christmas tree topper wordlessly inserted a metal key into the door and twisted open the lock. Adrenaline shooting into her fingertips,

Alex hastily removed the lid from the nondescript brown box labeled "Alex Wilde" and removed the cold packs to count ten vials of liquid gold in the form of SAIMR polyvalent antivenom.

"Thank you. Thank you so much," she shouted as she hustled past the uniformed gentleman who had not left his post by the front door, receiving nothing more than a slight nod in return.

Once safely back in her truck, she nervously inserted the key in the engine fully expecting something terrible to happen like a dead battery, but it responded with a resolute groan, and she murmured a prayer of thanks. Glancing at her newly acquired passenger in the front seat, she fired a quick text to Lucia.

I got it. On my way.

An astonishing three hours and forty minutes later, a full half an hour ahead of schedule, Alex whisked her clanking package through the peeling gray doors of the pediatric ward and plopped it ceremoniously on the corner desk. The room was eerily quiet except for a few hushed cries here and there from restless babes who weren't used to sleeping apart from their mothers. Lucia, stone-faced and weighed down by the burden of exhaustion, emerged from the supply room and stopped short when she saw Alex. Alex felt her stomach twist, an emotional if not physical case of intestinal volvulus.

"What happened?" Alex's voice, gravelly from dehydration, sounded foreign to her ears.

"The surgeons felt like they should debride the area before infection set in." Lucia paused, casting her eyes to the worn spots on the floor where countless marks from the wheels of stretchers were etched into the linoleum. "He did not survive the operation," she finished.

Alex slumped into the nearest chair, suddenly drained by more than just a harrowing past twelve hours.

"I got here as soon as I could," she whispered, knowing she had foregone eating and drinking so that she wouldn't have to stop for anything but gasoline.

She had driven at breakneck speed that was probably not entirely safe. It was the cold soul-sucking emptiness she always felt when her efforts weren't enough, and tragedy snuffed out a child's light. The cut of death was definitive and cruel and as poisonous as any snakebite. But without the benefit of antivenom.

Alex killed the truck engine in her driveway just as the sun peeked its halo over the horizon. After lingering in the steam of a shower and donning fresh clothes, she trudged the quarter mile down her paved street to where McCartney was probably lolling his tongue at Mary Lou's feet, hoping for a decadent strip of bacon to magically fall into his mouth.

Before she had even rapped on the painted blue door, Mary Lou had opened it just a crack and a frantic wet nose poked through, followed by a russet-colored head. Alex heard a deep-throated laugh of someone who had spent a decade smoking at some point.

"He missed you."

Alex knelt down onto the front porch next to a box of recycling. "I missed you, boy," she said tenderly, his molten brown eyes acting as a salve for her grieving heart.

Mary Lou widened the empty space in the doorframe, allowing the exquisite odor of frying bacon and biscuits to pummel Alex in the face. Mary Lou with her dyed blonde pixie cut and laugh lines etching beauty into her face, her sharp tongue, and her even sharper mind, reminded Alex of her former program director in Philadelphia.

Dr. Gibson had always served as an insightful critic when it came to Alex's life choices. She had devoted a lifetime to her career, forsaking all of life's other offerings like relationships, a path Alex was once forging for herself. Until Ian.

"Come on in." Mary Lou appraised Alex up and down. "You look like you could use a drink."

Alex blinked in surprise. It was only eight in the morning. In the past, when she was this exhausted and grief-stricken, she would make an excuse, preferring her solitude with her hound rather than making idle chit chat. But intrigue, and the fact that she currently had zero alcohol in her own house, led her to follow Mary Lou's flowing tunic into the interior of the living room.

Mary Lou led her to a back patio with cobbled together mismatched furniture consisting of a painted metal table and two wobbly wooden chairs with stretched zebra hides for the seats. Alex brushed a layer of dust off the chair nearest her while McCartney darted off to investigate the scents left behind from the overnight visitors to Mary Lou's yard.

It was a space like Alex had never imagined existed behind the plain crumbling stucco facade. Rows upon rows of rosebushes bright with buds of every color filled the entire backyard. Alex surveyed the delicate heads of pink and white and yellow blooms, their faces seeking out the morning sun. The fragrance was intoxicating. McCartney, nose to the ground, explored the far reaches of a stone wall that extended to the rear of the garden. No wonder he loved it over here.

Mary Lou reappeared carrying a tray piled high with fluffy biscuits supported by a barrier of crisp bacon and plunked it down in the middle of the table. Turning on her heel as if remembering something, she returned, clutching a pair of tall glasses, a small bottle of orange juice, and a ridiculously large bottle of vodka.

"This is my good stuff," she proclaimed, popping the stopper out of the vodka bottle and filling each glass about a third full. "Bought it in St. Petersburg a few years ago."

She poured in the orange juice next, and a mouth-watering citrus odor competed for olfactory dominance. Alex took the glass she offered and sampled it. The liquor's burn was quenched just enough by the juice, but it was still strong.

"Whew," she exhaled, the vapors rising from the back of her throat, and Mary Lou cackled in response, taking a gulp from her own glass.

"No one makes vodka like the Russians," she confirmed and slid into the seat next to Alex.

They sat in complete silence for several minutes, both sifting through their thoughts and eluting the disarray of their souls with alcohol.

"It's magnificent back here," Alex finally said and earned a side glance from Mary Lou, her hoop earrings swaying with the movement.

"I love roses," she said after a beat. "Their beauty is sexy. Irresistible. They draw you in with their vulnerability and then stab you before you can get too close." She emitted a low laugh and removed a slice of bacon from the pile. "Bacon?" she asked, raising her eyebrows.

Alex shook her head. Bacon was one of those foods that invoked a very dichotomous response. Although the smell was appealing, Alex had never understood how people could enjoy a slice of fried up fat so much.

"I never really acquired a taste for it."

Mary Lou tore through half the slice with her teeth. "It's not an acquired taste, honey. People either love it...or they hate it."

Mary Lou swallowed and then added a splash more vodka to her glass. "So, what's twisting up your panties today?"

Alex emitted a soft laugh and took a long drag of her drink. Mary Lou knew what Alex did for a living. and had a solid understanding of her lifestyle from her late-night requests to walk McCartney. But they had never had a real conversation that scratched below the surface.

Alex knew she was a retired social worker from eastern Kentucky who spent six months of the year in Botswana volunteering at the local orphanage. She had never spoken of any family, and the few times Alex had seen the inside of her living room, she had observed only pictures of Mary Lou surrounded by a gaggle of girlfriends in various exotic locations—a dude ranch, a beach dotted with domed huts, a remote mountain trail littered with backpacks.

As the alcohol dissipated into her bloodstream and disassembled her frontal lobe, Alex felt her tongue grow thick with words. Where could she even start? She blew her held breath into her drink, causing ripples to occur on the surface.

"I...I had a bad day at work."

Mary Lou eyed her critically, the amber flecks in her eyes emitting sparks. "Honey," she said, reaching down to pass a writhing McCartney a piece of bacon. "A manicurist has a bad day at work. A florist has a bad day at work."

Here goes nothing, Alex thought wryly, taking an uncharacteristic dive into the dumpster fire of her life that she had been letting build for the past few weeks.

"I lost a patient," she began weakly. "A little boy who we thought had an infection but really was bitten by a venomous snake, and then our hospital had no antivenom." Her words picked up speed, thought after thought, tumbling over itself in a race to cross the finish line of her lips. "And then I charged a thousand dollars-worth of antivenom on my credit card and drove to Johannesburg and back to pick it up...only to find that while I was gone, the little boy died." She inhaled shakily. "Meanwhile, my best friend in the entire world is mad at me for being emotionally unavailable, and my boyfriend is in the far reaches of Mongolia, also pretty mad at me after finding out that I got a needle stick at the hospital and now I have to take six weeks of antiretroviral prophylaxis until my HIV test comes back negative...or doesn't."

Alex furrowed her brows. "And before that, he made not so subtle indications that he wants me to move to London, but I have a commitment here and patients that I'm not ready to leave and I haven't even figured out how to be a girlfriend much less a—"

She paused to catch her breath, the word caught up in the net of her throat and sliding back down before she could say it.

Mary Lou poured vodka into her glass until the remaining orange juice became opaque.

"Like I always say," she said, staring out into the expanse of her garden, "when life gives you lemons, ask for tequila."

EIGHTEEN

"Come on...pick up," Alex muttered, trudging through the early morning mist toward the peaked roof of the hospital up ahead.

"You have reached the voicemail of Dr. Roxanne Clarke. Please leave your name and number and I—"

Alex had listened to that exact message many times over the last few weeks, sometimes leaving a message and sometimes just hanging up. She scrolled through the list and counted. Thirteen calls in total to Rox made every single morning for the last two weeks. Rox had texted a few times with a generic "call you back" or "can't talk now." A far cry from her usual messages filled with witty humor and sisterly advice.

Alex sighed and slipped her phone into her shoulder bag. She and Rox had never gone without talking for this long, and Alex felt like she was starving and couldn't quite be satiated by interaction with any other human.

Even her conversation with Tim the other night hadn't fulfilled her. She had called to check on Mercy and the baby. The surgery had gone well, and he had made it through the post-operative period with flying colors. He remained in the cardiac step-down unit to gain some weight before the team would clear him to fly back to Botswana.

Of course, before she had a chance to tell Tim the tale of her harrowing drive to Johannesburg in the middle of the night, their conversation was interrupted by Cara's insistence that Tim pay attention to whatever binge television show they were watching.

"I'll be right there, babe," he called to the doll-sized beauty, and Alex detected notes of tenderness in his voice. "I have to go, Alex. Can I call you tomorrow?"

"Sure," she said. "Of course."

She had hung up feeling a twinge of jealousy for how close they had become, the ease of their existence, and their uncomplicated normalcy.

Ian usually checked in every few days, which temporarily satisfied the perpetual burn in the back of her throat. The unspoken questions tethered their usual lighthearted banter. Ian hadn't asked again about the unfortunate needle stick, and Alex didn't burden him with the details of her daily gastrointestinal distress from the medication side effects. He also hadn't mentioned anything else about Alex moving to London...or what the future held after taking over for his dad next year. Alex wasn't sure if she was disappointed...or relieved.

She would be seeing him in exactly—she glanced down at the glow of her phone screen—one month from today. Would he ask for what he wanted? Would he expect answers? What answers would she be ready to give? Not all her GI distress could be blamed on medication.

"Dr. Alex, I have a question," called a voice from the covered concrete corridor. Her head whipped around to a panting Lucia, walking with vigor to catch up with her. Alex hadn't realized she had been moving that quickly. "Can you teach me about pediatric sepsis?"

"Of course," she answered smoothly, her face erupting in a smile.

Finally, something she *could* answer.

Sepsis as a final common pathway was the most common cause of death for children under the age of five in Botswana. In her time there, Alex had witnessed a fair share of kids with skin that burned to the touch, inflamed, and writhing with fever, as bacteria coursed through their bloodstream pursued by an army of immune cells intent on destruction.

The fascinating and terrible fact about sepsis was that the damage from the body's immune response was sometimes as life-threatening as the damage from the bacteria itself. It affected every organ system as every single cell in the body struggled to extract precious oxygen molecules from a less than ideal blood supply to continue functioning.

"The key to sepsis is early recognition," Alex said as she stood in the wedge of growing sunlight from the only window in the ward. "There *is* such a thing as the golden hour. Early access to antibiotics and appropriate fluid resuscitation can reverse the effects of bacterial sepsis and lead to survival."

Movement at the group's periphery caught her eye, and a blonde bun atop a pale face took its place among the interns. Alex continued, the words emerging slowly from her lips, one eye trained on the newcomer whose eyes shifted between the floor tiles.

"Sepsis can start as pneumonia, diarrhea, a urinary tract infection, or a primary bloodstream infection. What symptoms indicate that a patient has sepsis?" A hand shot up among the white-coated interns. "Lucia?"

"Fever, high heart rate, low blood pressure."

"Absolutely," Alex replied. "Kate," she said, seeking to make eye contact with Sam's medical student. "Can you tell me what antibiotics you would choose for a child with suspected sepsis?"

Kate shifted uncomfortably for a moment before answering. "Something broad spectrum that would cover a variety of bacteria."

"Okay," Alex responded. "Which ones exactly?"

Alex's phone buzzed dramatically in her pocket before Kate could answer. *Rox.*

"Hey guys, I need to take this. Talk about the pros and cons of various antibiotic choices until I get back."

Hushed murmuring began behind her as Alex hustled toward the metal doors of the ward.

"Rox. How are you?"

"I'm fine." Her voice was flat and even, utterly devoid of its typical sparkle quality.

Alex swallowed and willed herself to press further.

"What's going on?"

"I just called to—"

A sudden tug on Alex's sleeve made the phone tumble to the floor.

"Dr. Wilde, they need you over at bed seven."

Alex nodded furiously and picked up the phone. "Rox, I have to go, but I'll call you tonight."

Rox sighed through her nose in response. "Sure, Alex."

And then the connection was severed.

"What's going on?" asked Alex to a small crowd of interns and crisp nurses forming a halo around one of the cribs.

Shelo, who had been promoted to a bedside nurse position at Alex's urging, was busy spiking a bag of IV normal saline while one of the interns dangled a stethoscope over a squirming infant.

Alex snuck a hand between the crib rails to wrap her fingers around the tiny wrist. Her skin was cool to the touch. Cool with a rapid-fire pulse that barely tapped the pads of Alex's fingers. Alex slid her hand up the baby's arm to find the brachial pulse in the groove between her bicep and her humerus bone. That one was a touch stronger but not much.

Lucia flipped open the chart dangling from the end of the bed. "This is a four-month-old admitted last night for observation for fever, diarrhea, and poor oral intake."

"The first thing," Alex said thoughtfully, "is to decide if this is sepsis and she needs immediate attention. Who thinks this is just diarrhea and a dehydrated baby?"

A few hands in the group shot up.

"Who thinks this could be sepsis?"

Lucia raised her hand, followed by Kate's pale one. Alex gave a wry smile. "I think so too. We have fever, high heart rate, fast breathing, and impaired perfusion."

"How can you tell the perfusion?" The question was lofted into the air by Dev, a tall thin intern with black rectangular glasses perched on the bridge of his nose. He used his index finger to push them up farther. He had always reminded Alex of a young Sydney Poitier.

"It's all in the wrist," she said, winking at him.

When approaching a child, Alex frequently employed a method taught to her by one of her favorite mentors. She lowered herself to eye level and picked up the patient's hand, placing a few fingers along the inside of the wrist. She demonstrated this to Dev and the rest of the group.

"In five seconds, I can evaluate skin temperature, heart rate, and capillary refill to the hand. A baby's lifeforce is her pulse. It gives me an indication of her stroke volume—the blood being pushed out with every beat of her tiny heart. Is it a normal happy tapping thrum, or does it feel thready...or barely there at all?"

Four pairs of brown eyes were transfixed on her as she waxed poetic about the radial pulse.

"Kate and Lucia," she directed, "you have one hour to improve this baby's condition before she likely deteriorates. Shelo already has a head start."

Shelo split her red lips into a smile as she filled a syringe with a clear solution and began pushing it into the baby's vein through her IV catheter.

As Alex reviewed the remainder of the patients with the other two interns, she frequently ping-ponged back over to the baby to check on her progress. Fluid to fill up the proverbial tank. Early antibiotics. Reassess for organ perfusion. Add adrenaline to improve the cardiac output. Repeat.

On her third visit over to the crib where Kate, Lucia, and Shelo huddled over the baby, Alex noticed that the baby's heart rate was coming down nicely, and she had produced a generously wet diaper.

When the kidneys were happy, Alex was happy. She placed two fingers on her wrist and two on her upper arm, noticing a significant improvement in the quality of each pulse—like two tiny drums in a crescendo that preceded the finale of her survival.

"Excellent job, ladies. Early recognition and early reversal of organ dysfunction led to a good outcome. I'm really proud of you."

A small smile crept to the corners of Lucia's mouth, and Kate whooshed out a sigh of relief.

"Since things are under control, I'm heading to the airport to pick up someone."

Tomorrow was Thanksgiving, and Alex had sent her mom an early Christmas present in the form of a roundtrip ticket to Botswana. She had even convinced Janie Wilde's boss to give her the next two weeks off to enjoy a rare glimpse into a beautiful country and Alex's life.

"Isn't tomorrow some American holiday where you eat a ton of food and watch sports on television?" Lucia asked.

Alex chuckled softly. "Something like that."

As she strode toward the door, beckoned by the promise of freedom and a four-day holiday, Alex detected the shuffle of footsteps behind her.

"Dr. Wilde?" mewed a soprano voice.

Alex turned. "You can call me Alex, Kate."

"Okay...sorry," she stammered. "Dr. Drake always wants to be called Dr. Drake."

"Well, I'm not Dr. Drake." *Thank goodness.*

Kate stared at her suede flats, a rosy blush climbing into her cheeks. "I just...I wanted to say that I'm sorry...for the needle stick."

Alex felt an unexpected surge of empathy and tenderness for the young, still naive medical student. "It was an accident, Kate. Just bad luck."

She nodded her blonde head, blinking furiously. "I think you are a great doctor. I hope I can be half as good as you are someday."

"It takes time, but everyone comes into their own. You just have to want it bad enough."

Kate nodded again, letting the advice sink in below skin level.

"Do you want to come over for Thanksgiving tomorrow? My mom is flying in, and she's a great cook."

Her blonde head snapped up. "That would be great. Could I invite Dr. Drake too? I don't think she has any plans."

Alex inhaled sharply before southern hospitality got the best of her. "Sure," she answered slowly, drawing out the word into multiple syllables.

Alex made a mental note to ensure that she was at least half a bottle of wine in before Sam arrived tomorrow.

"I can't believe I'm here!" gushed Janie as she and Alex sat on matching stools surrounded by a mound of potato peelings.

"I can't believe you packed sweet potatoes in your luggage," Alex snickered, staring at the freshly peeled mound of cubed orange tubers piled up on her kitchen island.

"It's not Thanksgiving without sweet potato casserole," chided Janie, scooping up the pile and dumping it into the only steel pot that Alex owned. She twisted the knob on the gas range, and blue flames leaped out from the burner.

Alex must have let out an audible sigh because Janie twisted her head of ginger hair and squinted her eyes into slits. "What's Ian doing for Thanksgiving?"

Alex played with the pile of reddish-brown peels, bulldozing them into a neat pile with her fingers and raking them into the trash.

"He won't back in London until tomorrow, so probably enjoying a meal of Thanksgiving mutton and fermented mare's milk."

"Where in the world is he these days?" Janie asked, drying her hands on a dishtowel.

"Mongolia."

"He's been there quite a bit this year," Janie observed.

Alex felt the furrow on her brow deepen. "He has. More than he's ever been anywhere else, I think."

Previously, Ian had bounced around the globe between the

Devall Foundation's various charities in sub-Saharan Africa and the office in London. But during the last six months, he had canceled all his appearances at social events and charitable functions. Alex only knew this because she had snuck a peek over his shoulder and caught an email from him to Lydia. She had no idea what was so different about this particular mining site, and her curiosity was piqued.

Alex caught Janie observing her curiously as she picked up a knife to begin peeling and slicing apples. She wanted to say more. She wanted to tell her mom about her suspicion that, when Ian takes over for his dad, he will want her to move to London. She wanted to delve into her conflicting life paths and how she was struggling to reconcile them. She wanted to tell her about her rift with Rox and the needle stick and the fruitless trip to Johannesburg for the anti-venom, but she had always protected her mom from the woes of her life.

The grief heaped on Alex's head was mostly self-inflicted, and she had always preferred to travel this road solo, letting her mom emit a sunshine that she did not overshadow.

"So, what's new in Cole's Church?" Alex asked, fishing a second knife out of the drawer and relaxed as her mom rattled off the latest juicy gossip that involved someone's cow and another person's unfortunate incident with its left hoof.

Alex wandered over to peer out the yellow floral curtains of her front window and took another sip of her wine, an indulgent sharp chill filling her oropharynx with an anxiety-reducing delight.

"Anybody here yet?" Janie called from the kitchen, her voice mixing with the comforting sounds of pots being stirred and the opening of the oven door to reveal the lovely scent of apple pie bubbling in a homemade crust.

McCartney emitted a short staccato bark just as Alex caught sight of Mary Lou striding up the pebbled drive, a bottle in one hand and a dish in the other. She had just enough kyphosis to make her appear stooped in her men's denim shirt and cargo shorts that showed a little too much pasty white leg patterned with varicose veins. Mary Lou had told her once that the best part of getting older was not giving a rat's ass about what anyone else thought. Alex hoped she acquired even a pinch of that type of boldness as she aged.

"Mary Lou," Alex called over her shoulder.

Holding back McCartney by the nylon collar with one hand, she popped open the door latch with the other. Janie was already on hand to collect the items from Mary Lou's precarious grasp.

"I'm Janie Wilde, Alex's mom. Please make yourself at home Mary Lou," Janie chimed as she whisked off to the kitchen to recheck the marshmallows crisping over the top of the mashed sweet potatoes.

"I will do just that," Mary Lou crowed, and Alex caught her eyeing the chilled glass of Chenin blanc Alex had abandoned on the coffee table.

"I'll pour you a drink," Alex said, grinning and scurried into the kitchen while McCartney gave Mary Lou a thorough sniffing.

"Open the bottle I brought," Mary Lou called in a gravelly voice. "It's to die for."

Alex wrestled the cork out of the bottle and poured a hefty amount into two stemless glasses. "Mom?" she asked, proffering the neck of the crystal-clear bottle toward Janie, who was heaping melted butter on a pan of rolls.

"Just a little for me," she said, and Alex poured a splash of the ballet pink liquid into a third glass.

Alex had rarely seen Janie sip anything that wasn't sweet tea with lemon. She flipped over the bottle to read the label. "This is from Delaire Graff."

"From the who, sweetie?" asked Janie.

"Only a high-end luxury wine estate in South Africa," appraised Alex as she handed a glass to Mary Lou.

"Cheers." Mary Lou clinked her crystal rim to Alex's, a sly smile playing at her lips and a wink to go with it.

The rose-colored liquid danced across Alex's palate as an entire love story took place in her mouth. It now topped her favorite French Sancerre as the best wine she had ever tasted. Alex swirled the pink liquid around her glass, admiring its transparency.

"I'm pretty sure I could fill up a bathtub with this and drink my way to the bottom."

A laugh resembling more of a cackle escaped Mary Lou's throat. "I'm pretty sure I did that once."

Alex's eyebrows jumped to the top of her hairline, not quite sure whether to believe her or not. Before she could respond, a knock burst through the quiet followed by McCartney's incessant barking.

Alex opened the door to find a neatly dressed Kate, wearing a midi-length suede skirt and silk white top.

"I wasn't sure what to bring," Kate said as she balanced a cardboard box between outstretched palms.

"Anything is fine. Come in and meet everyone," Alex said, peering around her silhouette to look for Sam. "Is Sam...uh...Dr. Drake coming?"

Kate shook her head, the waves in her shoulder-length hair flipping to and fro. "No, she said she had things to do at the hospital."

Alex felt an instant wave of relief, immediately followed by regret and a curious sadness for the brash redhead who might be a worse workaholic than Alex herself. "Well, maybe we can wrap up a plate and drop it off for her."

The words sounded hollow to Alex's ears, but she did have reasonable goodwill toward Sam, especially after she had helped with Mercy's baby.

Introductions were made, and the foursome settled into conversation and heaping plates of southern delicacies like sweet potatoes topped with melted gooey marshmallows, green beans straight from Janie's vegetable garden, and tender bits of turkey breast smothered with an amber gravy. As dinner progressed and the wine continued to flow long after that first bottle of rosé had been emptied, the clink of forks was replaced by raucous laughter and disinhibited wit, led mainly by Mary Lou.

Alex held a green bean aloft. "Mom, how did you not get arrested in customs for bringing fresh produce from a foreign country?"

Janie shrugged and said, "I told them I had nothing to declare except that it was my first time out of the United States and I was excited to be here. I guess they thought I looked innocent."

Mary Lou slapped the table, the rouge of her nose and cheeks deepening with each subsequent glass of wine. "That reminds me of the time I tried to smuggle bourbon into Myanmar. I had them convinced that this is what mouthwash looks like in Kentucky."

The entire table roared with laughter, and Alex felt the dizzying heights of an early buzz from the alcohol and the human connection and camaraderie she had desperately missed for the better part of a year.

"Ms. Wilde, this food is incredible. How did you make these rolls so fluffy?" asked Kate, tearing a hunk from the golden-brown top.

"It's all in the wrist," replied Janie evenly, startling when Alex and Kate erupted in an unexpected fit of laughter.

NINETEEN

"Hey you," murmured a throaty voice through the receiver of Alex's phone.

She had fallen asleep on top of her iPhone, knowing Ian would call the minute he landed in London. She hadn't wanted to miss it. Luckily, answering her phone when she was dead asleep had become an occupational requirement.

"Hi," she yawned, still sluggish from the calorie-packed dinner and copious glasses of wine she had consumed earlier today. "Are you back in London?" Alex asked, sitting up in bed and rubbing the matting from her lashes.

"I am. Just got off the plane and waiting for my driver to finish with the luggage."

"You're spoiled," Alex teased.

"Hey now. I've been slogging through ice and snow for weeks. I deserve it."

"Mmm," Alex murmured. "I'm sure that someone has already handed you a newspaper and a glass of bourbon."

"As a matter of fact...no. The bourbon is waiting for me in the car."

She could hear his smile over the phone and gravitated to the lightheartedness of this conversation compared to their recent ones. "Everything sounds perfect."

"The only thing missing is you."

Alex sucked in a breath, holding her words and her exhale long enough that the moment passed. A sound squeaked from her throat but was drowned out by Ian's next words.

"So, how was Thanksgiving?"

"We had a feast courtesy of my mom."

"How is dear Janie?" Ian asked.

He and Alex's mom had bonded over their mutual over-protectiveness when Alex had been injured on a humanitarian mission to Haiti last year.

"She's good. Exactly the same," Alex said as she heard a deep voice in the background.

"Mr. Devall, we're ready for you."

"Tell her I said hello."

His voice drifted off, and Alex suddenly couldn't bear the thought of losing this shred of flimsy cellular connection she had to Ian. Her heart rate spiked, and her mouth dried into a prune.

"Ian...I just...I can't...I am so..." she floundered.

"I know," he replied smoothly. "I love you too."

"Where is this place again?" Janie asked, shielding her eyes against the noonday sun.

"We should be there any minute. Let me know if you see a sign."

Alex downshifted the truck and crept along the dusty highway sweeping her head from side to side in search of the entrance to the game reserve. A splintered wooden sign caught her eye, and she deftly steered the groaning V-8 engine onto a driveway thick with mustard-colored sediment amidst a jagged overlay of rocks.

After enduring several bumpy miles inland and muttering a few choice swear words, Alex maneuvered the truck into a parking lot surrounded on three sides by squat one-story buildings, one of which extended outward with a canopy roof overlying a cluster of picnic tables. An animated yellow lab mix hustled over to the truck and began sniffing the exiting occupants. Alex bent down and offered him a quick scratch. Meanwhile, Janie strolled over to what appeared to be a ramshackle office building with an open window and peered inside.

"Hello?" she called into a room, empty of occupants except for a pudgy orange tabby that hissed from its lazy perch on the windowsill.

"What a grump," Janie remarked as the cat shot through the air past her face and scuttled off behind building number three.

As Alex was pulling her phone out to message the guide that they had arrived, a billow of dust appeared in the distance, thrust up behind the oversized wheels of a golf cart barreling toward them. It skidded to a stop near a maintenance shed, and a gangly youth in his twenties hopped out, followed by a second dog. This one was a small brown terrier that yapped a quick greeting to the strangers and then promptly leaped from the vehicle to pursue the stick-straight tail of the orange tabby. Alex and Janie exchanged a smile. Being surrounded by animal antics made them feel right at home.

Alex had grown up surrounded by a rag-tag assortment of rescue animals that she or Janie had discovered while exploring the woods near their home or had been casually deposited at their doorstep. Alex had dreamed of becoming a veterinarian as she grew up playing animal hospital with the various pets she and Janie had nursed back to health. She supposed she had become a vet of sorts—a vet to little human animals that couldn't speak or advocate for themselves.

A smile stretched across her face as she recounted the animals from her childhood—Henry, the crow with the broken wing that she had kept in a shoebox; a despondent coyote pup; an array of stray dogs and abandoned cats; and one Christmas even a baby deer who had lost his mother to a hunter. A singular experience had catalyzed the course of her life from vet school to med school. Not a pleasant one and not something worth dredging to the surface on such a lovely afternoon. Some memories needed to stay buried.

"Dumela!" called a deep-throated voice as the guide loped toward them with legs quite possibly as long as a baby giraffe's.

Alex shielded her eyes against the noonday sun to catch a better glimpse of the silhouetted man in a khaki uniform smattered with mud and a pearlescent smile that exuded joy.

"We're here for the safari on horseback," she said hesitantly and received a vigorous nod in response.

"My name is Mel. I am the guide. Go ahead and hop into the car."

Alex would hardly call the four wheels held together by a steel frame and two vinyl bench seats a car, but it was probably safe for off-highway use. She motioned to her mom to join her, and minutes later, they clung to the steel bars for support while their heads knocked together like a pair of watermelons.

He skidded to a halt in front of a wood plank stable, its doors thrown open to allow a breeze to circulate through the stalls. A rectangular paddock with a central pile of golden hay edged out from behind the stable where a few sinewy horses were pulling up the sparse green blades protruding from cracked earth.

"The horses are already saddled and waiting in the barn," Mel shouted, peering over his shoulder to assess his passengers, possibly to ensure they were both intact after the drive through a wicked piece of terrain.

"Great. We're really excited to be here. It's my mom's first time in Botswana."

"Hopefully, it's not her first time on a horse," Mel laughed, his pecan-colored skin parting to reveal a smile that belonged in a toothpaste commercial.

"Hardly," Alex replied.

Alex had forgotten how spectacular it felt to be on the back of a horse with a thousand pounds of power and speed between her legs, rocking to the gentle sway of her mount's hindquarters as he picked his way across the savanna. She had chosen the taller, more formidable horse—a bay that was probably just over sixteen hands with lively chestnuts for eyes and a dark forelock that swept sideways in the wind. Janie rode just ahead of her on a dappled gray mare holding both reins in one hand like she had for years as a child and then teenager, growing up on a working cattle ranch in south Texas.

Alex's grandparents had both died before she could remember her visits to the ranch where her grandfather was foreman, but she had a framed photo of her first time on a horse as a six-month-old baby sandwiched between a horse's prominent withers and her mom's midsection.

They had never been able to afford a horse of their own, but, as a teenager, Alex had begun working in a barn in exchange for lessons. Soon, she become well known for her natural horsemanship and was often asked to exercise the horses that belonged to others in their small community. Even without formal lessons, she felt more comfortable on the back of a horse than walking on her own two feet.

She clicked her tongue a few times and pressed her calves into her horse's sides to urge him into a trot. "Having fun, Mom?" she asked when they had caught up to Janie.

"You bet, sweetie," her mom answered, a gust of unexpected wind sending her ginger bob ruffling over her face.

They walked in silence for a while with only the sounds of hoofbeats as an accompaniment to the stillness of the day, baking in the sun while skirting the horizon for a sign of wildlife. Mel followed along but was allowing them a wide berth, close enough to keep them on course but far enough away to provide privacy.

As they emerged over a ridge, a rippling water pool came into view, the dirty gray water churning with the velocity of hoofs and lapping tongues. She glanced at her mom and tilted her head toward the menagerie of animals jostling for a spot at the only source of drinking water for miles. Because they were on horseback, their scent would be masked by the overpowering musk of horse. Alex held her breath as they crept close enough to smell the pungent odor of animal perspiration and aerosolized earth.

A herd of elephants thrust their trunks into the pool, splashing the bent heads of the zebra next to them. A small herd of springbok skittered around the opposite side of the water, taking tiny sips as they roved their eyes about for predators. A pair of kudu with twisting horns and delicate stripes pranced to the water's edge, causing a flock of sandgrouse to scatter. Unperturbed, the horses bent their head to the ground, whuffing about in search of a grassy snack.

"I want to talk to you about something," Janie said, staring straight ahead at the National Geographic episode brought to life in front of them.

Alex, who had pulled out her phone and was busily snapping photos, stilled and felt an ice ball start to form in the pit of her stomach. The last time Janie had said that phrase, it was followed up by the news that her estranged father had died. As a physician, the worse possible scenarios flitted through Alex's brain in quick succession—cancer, maybe breast cancer, or worse, metastasized breast cancer. She forced an exhale.

"Sure." She snuck a quick glance at Janie, who began to move her lips before any words exited them.

"About getting married."

In a moment of both extreme relief and utter astonishment, Alex felt the ball of ice extend to the fingertips loosely holding the leather reins and was surprised when actual snowflakes failed to exit their tips.

"Ooookay."

She drew the word out interminably and wondered why Janie, who had never pried into any aspect of Alex's dating life, wanted to talk about the one thing she was keeping closest to her heart right now. So close in fact that it coexisted with every heartbeat of every second of every day since Ian had alluded to the idea when they were driving back from holiday in Mozambique.

"Peter," Janie began, and Alex's eyes crossed with confusion and then revelation, "has asked me to marry him."

Alex exhaled a breath a cloud of sublimated ice. "That's great, Mom...really."

Alex had not spent very much time with Peter and exchanged even fewer words. He was naturally introverted, similar to herself, with a quiet steadfastness that had stabilized Janie's life once Alex had left Texas for training in Philadelphia.

"I wasn't sure I wanted to share my life with anyone after what happened with your dad."

Alex nodded in empathy. Living in a house with an abusive drunk lunatic had almost claimed both their lives.

"But Peter is different. Kind. Easygoing."

"Do you love him?" Alex asked, trying to get a glimpse of her mom's face.

Janie turned in her saddle, her cheeks rosy from the wind and sun, and a girlish grin lighting up her face with bright youth.

"I do."

Her eyes shone and Alex felt a pang of foreign jealousy. How uncomplicated it all seemed. The natural next step after falling in love with someone. It could never be that easy for her and Ian, could it?

Over the next few weeks, time sped up as Alex transitioned between work at the hospital and spending evenings with her mom cooking dinner or watching movies on her laptop. She had even taken her to Ex-Pats one night, casually avoiding the backroom that she and Ian had turned into their private sex den a few months before. Her mom became animated after one glass of wine and received more than a few admiring glances from Jeff the bartender.

Now as Alex entered the airport, she couldn't ignore the despair gnawing at her insides.

"It feels like you just got here," Alex said, throwing her arms around Janie's petite shoulders.

When she released her embrace, Janie's eyes swam with unshed tears.

"I wish I could stay longer," she sniffed, brushing the back of one hand against her pale lashes.

"I'll see you again in February, Mom. Only two months." Alex flashed two fingers at Janie's drawn face.

"That's right. You're coming to Texas for that big medical meeting."

Alex pulled Janie's roller bag up to the counter and handed it to the attendant. "I'm mostly coming for a wedding." She grinned, catching the small but detectable smile flashing across her mother's porcelain face.

After escorting her mom through security, Alex hugged her tightly and waved. The image of her petite frame and oversized shoulder bag disappearing into the airport melee was still forefront in her mind as she wound through congested streets toward the hospital. The secure comfort of her mom's presence had exposed more than a few cracks in her seemingly well-adjusted façade. Surface cracks that threatened to expose the crater underneath. Cracks that needed a fresh coat of plaster in the form of a hospital full of sick kids.

Even at the peak of her exhaustion during her first year of fellowship, Alex had never dreaded coming to work. She had a little ritual. In the steps between her apartment and the sliding glass doors of the looming children's hospital, her dread transitioned to excitement—three hundred and forty-three steps where fear and exhaustion crumbled away beneath her sneakers and was replaced by a healthy anticipation of the challenges that the day promised.

Once she stepped into the ICU, a frenzy began in her neurons as she put together each patient like the pieces of a scattered puzzle. She went head-to-head with perilous pathology and beat it back while maintaining grace and composure. Badassery took dedication.

The rubber of Alex's running shoes struck PM's linoleum and her nose inhaled the scent of cleaning solution and healing wounds. She was home. At least for the time being. Her white coat swished against the ivory bed railings as she squeezed between two cribs. A curious toddler stared at her with wide almond-colored eyes as she placed her hand on his distended abdomen.

"How are you feeling, buddy?" she asked softly as her fingertips explored the contours of his distended liver.

His eyebrows furrowed, but he remained quiet as she tried to mask her physical exam as an attempted tickle. The child squirmed and emitted a squawk as her hand pressed deeper into the cavity.

"I think he needs an abdominal ultrasound."

Alex whirled around to assess the face that belonged to the

familiar voice. Mercy stood a few feet away, face alight with a joyful smile. Alex doused her hands in hand sanitizer before grasping both of her outstretched ones, pulling her into a brief but warm embrace.

Opening her stance, Mercy revealed the covered baby carrier at her feet, using her hand to draw back the thin curtain of ikat material. Alex knelt to the floor to drink in the sight of the sleeping baby. He was perfectly angelic with cheeks that had rounded out over the last few months and absolutely no remnants of his ordeal except for the linear scar like a permanent zipper running down the middle of his chest.

"He's perfect," Alex murmured as she felt her index finger stray to stroke the back of his tiny hand.

"Thanks to you."

Alex glanced up to catch the trembling of Mercy's lower lip and an unshed tear accenting her usual steady demeanor. Alex brushed her palms over her powder blue scrub pants and rose to her feet.

"Hardly just me."

Mercy responded with a tight nod, and Alex caught a glimpse of the mountain of stress her friend must have shouldered living with relatives in a foreign country away from husband while her newborn son underwent open-heart surgery. A barely perceptible cry found its way to their ears, like the first early morning roar of a lion cub, and Mercy averted her eyes to the handle of the carrier.

"I better go," she said. "When he wants to eat, he does not take no for an answer."

Alex followed her to her small green sedan, flinging open the creaking door to help facilitate the infant's transition into his car seat.

"Thank you, Alex," Mercy said as she sunk into the driver's seat.

"Anytime. I'm also a very qualified babysitter if you ever need one."

They exchanged a smile, and Mercy reached in her purse to fish around for something, extracting an ivory envelope with "Dr. Wilde" visible in delicate cursive on the back.

"An invitation to the christening next weekend," Mercy said, answering the unspoken question in Alex's eyes.

When the dust had settled from the rubber tire's trauma to the shale parking lot, Alex removed the blue cardstock from the interior of the envelope. Her eyes scanned the page until they became glued to the name scrolled in large font about halfway down.

Thabo Alexander Moloi.

TWENTY

"I can't believe I'm missing your birthday...again," Ian lamented.

Alex glanced down at Ian's frozen still on her phone as she listened to his forlorn yet somehow incredibly sexy voice on speakerphone. She finished putting in the diamond earrings he had given her last Christmas.

"You'll just have to make it up to me when I see you next week," she replied with a hint of coy.

"Any plans to douse yourself in champagne with a random guy?"

"Tim was not some random guy," she complained as she adjusted her navy shift dress and slid on her nude heels, the same outfit she had worn to her graduation from fellowship.

It hung awkwardly on her now. Her subtle curves had hollowed out over the past few weeks with constant nausea from her daily regimen of antiretrovirals.

In a strange way, she was grateful for the experience—the unexpected walk in the shoes of her patients. On the other hand, she would not be sad when it was over. Right at this moment, a vial of her blood was sitting in the PM lab ready to answer the sentinel question that would propel her future in one direction...or another.

"I'm not going to let it happen a third time. Next year is going to be completely different," Ian promised.

Alex wondered just how different. She had not let herself ponder a future with Ian until she had her test results. The entire situation, although stressful, had given her a much-needed reprieve from the mental circus of contemplating their future. Could two lives align like stars in a celestial event where she could be with the man she loved and continue the work that she loved?

"I have to go. I'm going to be late for the christening."

Her finger dangled over the end button but would not submit to the willpower to push it.

"Not yet," Ian blurted. "Just let me hear you breathe...then say my name again."

"Ian?"

"One more time."

"Ian."

"Alex."

Alex felt her chest fill with expectant breath that floated out of her suddenly buzzing lips.

"Ian."

A molten warmth grew in her abdomen until it spilled over into her pelvis between her thighs, weakening the tautness of her calves until she was tempted to kick off her heels. The hand that rested on the navy linen of her sheath dress inched precariously close to the dormant volcano between her legs.

"Alex."

She clapped her hand over her mouth to stop herself from groaning and clenched her thighs together. Still, a small noise escaped from the back of her throat.

"I'll see you soon," Ian said in a husky voice, and then he was gone, and all that remained was empty static and torrential desire that would remain unrequited. At least for now.

The christening was a beautiful affair in a small white stone church just north of the town center. Alex sat at the back in the sweltering heat, thankful that she had foregone pantyhose for bare calves. No one seemed to notice, especially not the ladies marching in, sliding into cushioned rows next to their friends waving fans constructed from spare paper.

A part of Alex had always been deeply spiritual, and she was comfortable here surrounded by stained glass and an oversized painted cross hanging from the pinnacle of the pulpit. She found herself caught up in the timbre of rich voices singing in Setswana, the melodies creating a sea of grace and tranquility that reverberated off the sanctuary walls.

In this place where hope abounded and grace permeated every heart, no one was more exemplary of this than the minuscule gentleman with the horizontal scar snoozing in his mother's arms despite the noise and heat.

After the service, Alex noticed that Mercy was engulfed by a crowd of family and well-wishers. She offered her a wave and edged to the periphery of the crowd, where she escaped out of the front doors held ajar with a stack of hymnals.

"Alex! Dr. Alex," echoed the deep baritone of Dr. K, and she paused on the church steps.

She turned around to spy him hurrying toward her.

"I need to give you this," he said without fanfare, his obsidian eyes trained on her face as she plucked the white letter-sized envelope out his hand.

"What is it, Dr. K?" she asked, although she already knew the answer.

"Your lab results," he replied evenly.

"Oh, thanks."

She mechanically opened her shoulder bag and stuffed the envelope inside like it was a grenade capable of exploding at any moment.

"I'm sure everything will be fine, but Alex—" He placed a fatherly hand on her shoulder. "If you need anything, you know where to find me."

She met his gaze but quelled the upsurge of emotions so that her eyes were calm...steady.

"Thanks, Dr. K."

As Alex drove into the late afternoon sun, she glanced periodically at the potential fuselage poking out of her powder blue shoulder bag. She circled Tlokweng circle three times before jerking the wheel toward the exit, accelerating like a wayward electron on a parabolic path that would lead her to Ex-Pats.

Settling into the seats that she and Rox used to share sent a wave of nostalgia crashing over her. Longing gripped her. They hadn't spoken in over a month. A few texts here and there were hardly surrogates for conversation or apologies.

Alex plopped her shoulder bag with its obtrusive occupant down on Rox's seat and defiantly kicked her heels onto the floor with a clatter. She couldn't help but remember thrusting off these very same heels the night she had grieved to Rox after thinking she ruined her chances to win the Devall Foundation grant. Rox had chastised her into empowerment. *Shoes on...game on.* The words still tumbled around her brain when she needed a boost. There was no one better at inspiration than Rox.

Jeff extended a beefy arm in her direction, wiping down a long segment of wooden bar with deliberate strokes. "What can I get for you, love? It's on the house."

He smiled knowingly, and Alex assumed he had found out that Ian had purchased his work establishment, which also meant he knew about her and Ian. Her cheeks pinked in embarrassment for the several trysts they had shared in the backroom.

"Just white wine tonight," she said, flicking her eyes downward.

Moments later, with a glass of perfectly chilled Chenin blanc in her hand, Alex stared at the white envelope propped against a pile of round coasters and, for the hundredth time, wished Rox was here. Her index finger had poised over her phone several times, but each time she hesitated. Alex studied the picture of Rox she had snapped at her wedding last June. Rox had been a vision—elegance itself in an ivory and blush gown as she floated toward her groom like the dawn meets the day.

She stuffed her phone back into her leather bag. The last thing she wanted was to burden Rox with her drama, at least not until they had repaired their friendship and bearing each other's burdens once again became an expectation.

Alex emptied the glass of wine, the sharp edges of her grief only slightly dulled as it entered her bloodstream. She motioned to Jeff, and he began making his way toward her, slinging his bar towel over his shoulder with a smile. A movement caught her eye, and a formidable shape exchanged itself for her shoulder bag on the seat next to her. Her annoyance spiked, and she swiveled around, abruptly banging her knees on the undersurface of the bar in the process.

"That seat is...taken," she finished slowly, processing the muscular form of one very tall and very agitated redhead.

Samantha Drake shifted her eyes around the perimeter of the bar. "Since I don't see your fancy boyfriend, I'll assume you were saving it for me."

Alex shrugged and rolled her eyes, rotating to face forward where Jeff stood, ready to provide her with a much-needed second drink. Sam's eyes flitted to the paper envelope stamped with the Princess Marina logo.

"Are you going to open that or just let it taunt you to death?"

Alex ground her molars together. "I haven't decided."

Before she could react, Sam snatched the envelope from the bar with a freckled hand and pulled out the single sheet of paper inside.

"Hey!" Alex sputtered, unsure of what to do next.

She wasn't quick enough to reclaim the contents, but before she could decide her next course of action, Sam's eyes had finished scanning the page.

"It's negative."

"Really?"

Alex grabbed for the paper to see for herself and fixated on the dot matrix printout: HIV-1,2 antibody.....NEG. A ball of stress like tightly wound twine began to unravel in her chest.

"Did you come tonight to be here when I found out my test results?" Alex asked, suspicious of Sam's actual intentions.

Sam shrugged and ran a long-fingered hand through her fiery red pixie cut. "I had to make sure I didn't totally screw your life up."

"Wow—thanks," Alex responded, shocked at the admission of almost-caring from Sam.

"Another round of the same?" interjected Jeff, swiping Alex's empty glass and replacing it with a fresh one.

"Actually, Jeff," she said, smiling as newfound wings emerged from her heart. "I'll have a champagne." Alex glanced at Sam, who had splayed her arms out onto the bar as she scrolled through a list of emails on her phone. "Make that two."

Happy Birthday to me.

Alex circled the pediatric ward like a mother hen, offering words of encouragement and guidance as the interns scribbled furiously in charts and reviewed lab results, trying to piece each patient together into a sensical diagnosis with an expected course and treatment plan. She stopped to examine a young girl with braided pigtails, running her hands over the raised red papules covering her mid-abdomen. Encircling the girl's neck between her palms, she felt the various sized lumps creating a mountain range of lymph nodes extending from the back of her neck to her trachea.

"This one just came in this morning, Dr. Alex."

Without removing her scrutinizing eye from the young girl who languished in the bed, skin moist from fever, Alex snuck her stethoscope onto the girl's chest and heard her heart pounding a frantic rhythm. It was regular but entirely too fast.

"Diagnosis?" she asked into the space between her and Lucia.

"I was thinking group A strep infection."

"I agree," said Alex, nodding. She ran her fingertips over the stippled rash again. "This rash looks like scarlet fever."

Strep infections could be mild or exceedingly dangerous if the bacteria entered the bloodstream before antibiotics could control their multiplication. It could also lead to a condition known as toxic shock, where the body exploded with inflammation in response to provocation by certain types of bacteria known as superbugs. Alex grabbed her chart from its spot hanging on the bed railing and flipped through her scant paperwork inside.

"What's been ordered so far?" she asked.

"We ordered penicillin."

"High dose?"

"Yes." Lucia's lips worked themselves into a smile.

"And what about for her dehydration and lower blood pressure?"

"A fluid bolus. The nurses are retrieving the saline from the supply room."

Glancing at her watch, Alex noticed the time. If she wanted to make her flight to London, she would need to leave in about five minutes. She looked at the girl again, wrapping her fingers around her limp wrist, palpating the desperate pulse underneath a pale swatch of skin. A large stone turned over in her stomach as she contemplated her options.

Shelo appeared with a bag of saline, expertly stringing it up onto the slim hook tacked into the wall plaster and used her thumb to open the roller so that the crystalline drops turned into a steady rivulet of fluid.

"We can handle this, Dr. Alex," Shelo announced over her shoulder, her signature red lips pressed together in concentration.

"We know exactly what to do. You have taught us well," confirmed Lucia. Alex stepped back from the bedside, glancing from one bright-eyed, passionate woman to the other.

"I guess you do," she said with a smile, her chest bursting with pride.

Alex slipped her cab driver an extra bill as she skirted around to the trunk to retrieve her single suitcase.

"Merry Christmas," she called buoyantly through the open

window, and he responded with a stern nod of his bald, sweaty head.

As she strode over to the check-in counter, she had an overwhelming moment of triumph that she had had the foresight to drop McCartney off at Mary Lou's before she left for work this morning.

After gifting him with an early Christmas present of a brand new stuffed squeaky toy, he had made off like a bandit, intent on destroying the reviled creature before Alex had even left for the hospital.

Mary Lou's living room was in a state of disarray. Half-wrapped packages littered her floor, and short sticky strips of packing tape were stuck in neat rows on the edges of her end table. A small artificial tree decorated one corner, wrapped in a colorful strand of lights and turquoise tinsel.

A wistful nostalgia gripped Alex's insides as she was flooded with memories of cozy Christmases shared with her mom in the small white house on the perimeter of Cole's Church. Without any extended family, the holidays had always been a quiet affair but full of love, nonetheless. She wondered if Mary Lou had any plans this year.

Alex spread open the mouth of the brown paper grocery bag and began removing the items she had toted down the street—a tin containing an assortment of cookies she had baked herself and a long box wrapped in red paper depicting a montage of cartoon reindeer skating across a frozen pond.

"Thanks for offering to take care of McCartney for the next few weeks, Mary Lou," Alex said. "I really appreciate it."

Mary Lou picked up the cookie tin and shook it, and then examined the long box. "Can I open it?"

Alex nodded even as Mary Lou was ripping off the paper to reveal a crystal bottle with an iconic horse and jockey decorating the top.

"A bottle of Blanton's. I knew you had good taste."

Alex smiled as Mary Lou fingered the facets in the bottle and flipped it over to read the label.

"Well, Ian does," Alex replied. Ian had a certain predilection for bourbon, so she had known exactly who to ask when shopping for Mary Lou.

"I expect you'll make good use of your time in London with...what's his name...Ian."

She drug out the "I," her east Kentucky accent adding a few extra syllables to his name.

Alex blushed as she imagined precisely what they planned on doing every single night they were forced indoors by the unforgiving London frost.

"I hope you packed something to keep you warm," she continued. "Not that you're going to need it." She closed her right eye in a knowing wink.

The pink in Alex's cheeks deepened to a solid fuchsia as Mary Lou began rummaging around the packages in her living room.

"Ah...found it." She extracted a flat package wrapped in pink tissue and a single flat red cord of ribbon. "It's nothing fancy," she interjected as Alex removed the tissue paper and gasped.

It was a beautiful handmade scarf using Botswana's national colors of royal blue and black and white. She held it to her face, the luxurious feel of the material caressing her cheek.

"I had some extra Alpaca yarn lying around," Mary Lou said nonchalantly, but Alex couldn't help but notice a smile tempting the corners of her lip-lined mouth.

"Thank you, Mary Lou. It's beautiful," she said, wrapping the material around her neck.

"It'll keep you warm if your boyfriend isn't up to snuff," she cackled in her throaty ex-smoker voice.

Now, at the airport, Alex fingered the edge of the fringed scarf as she stepped up to the luggage drop-off, heaving her overstuffed bag onto the scale.

"Looks like you made it under the weight limit," remarked the more than middle-aged man standing ramrod straight behind the counter.

"Excellent," Alex muttered, wringing her hands from the finger strain induced by carting the bag through the airport.

Normally, she wasn't a heavy packer, but she needed layers and a heavy coat to survive the weather in London, plus she had stuffed in her Christmas gifts as well, hoping they would survive the trip on the airplane without being crushed.

Ian, as always, was impossible to buy for. For Christmas last year, Alex had bought him cufflinks shaped like the Millennium Falcon, mostly to remind him of his brother Ryan, who loved Star Wars as a kid. Ian had watched it with him all summer after he had become ill with heart failure. The last complete summer of his short life.

The hectic blur of starting her job and dealing with work drama, Mercy's baby, and her mishap with a needlestick hadn't afforded her a ton of shopping opportunities. Luckily, she had happened onto something sentimental while she was in a village last month taking blood samples. Ian's gift was situated in the bottom of her shoulder bag, surrounded by scratch paper, a tube of lip balm, and a paperback she had been meaning to peruse.

"Oh." The agent with ramrod posture cleared his throat and peered at Alex over rectangular-shaped lenses. "Your flight is quite delayed."

No! Every cell in her body protested. She had chosen this late afternoon flight so that Ian could fetch her from the airport, and they would have an entire day together before they were due at his father's house for the holiday festivities.

"How delayed?" she said evenly, trying to contain her disdain for all things associated with the airline industry at the moment.

"It looks like—" He scrolled through a few screens with a repetitive strike of the down arrow. "A few hours at most."

After receiving his tight-lipped smile, Alex stalked toward security with the knowledge that if her flight left at all that day, it would be a Christmas miracle.

Exactly six hours and thirty-nine minutes later, Alex accepted her personal Christmas miracle in the form of an airborne plane among the stars, the faint lights of Gaborone fading in the distance as the wing dipped toward the city as they turned north toward Europe.

She settled into her seat, huddled into her scarf and a navy pullover sweatshirt, her ears filled with the orchestral Christmas music that was like comfort food for the auditory center of her brain.

And then she let the rest of her mind fill up with questions for Ian. It was time to lay all the cards on the table. She just hoped that when that happened, they both had a winning hand.

TWENTY-ONE

A black sedan flashed its lights twice, and Alex reflexively raised her palm. Despite the cramping in her lower back muscles and the bitter cold seeping through her jacket, Alex's insides fluttered nervously when she realized it was headed toward her spot on the pavement. A gentleman in all black, a woolen cap pulled low over his forehead and scarf waving in the breeze, leaped out of the driver's side and threw open the rear door of the car.

"Dr. Wilde?" he asked in the most soothing of British accents.

She nodded, her face split into a grin as he collected her suitcase and gestured for her to enter the vehicle. With the blood pounding in her ears, she slid onto the leather seat, depositing her shoulder bag onto the floor and surveying the interior—which was empty. Disappointment as potent as any drug flooded her veins. Black cap man poked his head into the rear door.

"Mr. Devall sends his regrets that he could not collect you himself."

Alex willed her eyes to meet those of the driver. "Why didn't he?" she asked, so quietly that she was surprised that he heard her over the rumble of engines and squawking horns.

"I suppose because he had to socialize at the soirée."

"What soirée?"

"The holiday party Mr. George Devall throws every year. If we leave now, we'll make it just in time."

He closed the door with a *thunk*. Alex settled in, her forehead pressed against the frosted glass of the window as they sped through a snowcapped downtown London, leaving it behind for the rustic elegance of the Devall property in Waltham Abbey.

When Alex was ushered into the familiar foyer, the scene that met her eyes was unlike anything she had ever witnessed. The entire house had been transformed into a winter dreamscape complete with iridescent snowflakes of various sizes hanging from the exposed rafters. A giant pine tree draped in warm white lights and swathed in powder blue ribbon took center stage amidst a throbbing crowd of guests dressed in holiday finery plucking delicacies and champagne flutes from the silver trays. A stirring melody from the corner took wing, and Alex recognized the first bars of "Joy to the World" played by a string quintet in tuxedos.

Underneath a layer of grime and exhaustion, she felt like the passengers on the Titanic who enjoyed the orchestra right up until their ship sank into the depths of the Atlantic. She spied Ian as he sipped a glass of bourbon by the fireplace in a deep blue velvet dinner jacket and light blue shirt that matched the ribbon on the tree, his hair glossy and tamed for the evening. He was the picture of someone about to slip into the shoes of a business mogul. He threw his head back in laughter and set down his glass, the flames in the stone fireplace roaring behind him. A slim arm reached out to steady herself on his jacketed forearm, the porcelain arm of an exotic beauty sharing in the moment's hilarity.

I don't belong here. The words flashed through her stream of consciousness, and she observed the scene from the shadows of the foyer. A perfect little snow globe universe with Ian drinking and laughing accessorized by a woman that added to the night's glamour. The only thing missing was the powdery fake flakes.

When Ian caught her in his peripheral vision, she watched him excuse himself politely from his companions and start making his way toward her, deftly dodging the animated partygoers and scurrying waitstaff. Alex didn't miss the slim hand that squeezed his bicep as he exited the group.

"You made it," he murmured, palming both sides of her face with hands that had been warmed by fire and liquor. She closed her eyes and let his warmth permeate the frost that had collected on her face. Equally warm lips brushed her own in a kiss that did nothing but kindle desire in the reservoir of her pelvis. She momentarily forgot they were standing in a room full of people exploding with holiday cheer.

"I did," she whispered, her eyes fluttering open.

Ian's eyes were scanning the room, his hands leaving her face to gesture to a couple in the corner who was trying to get his attention.

"Sorry about all this," he said, one hand reaching up to tuck a strand of hair behind her ear. "My dad throws this holiday party every year and—"

"It's beautiful," she interrupted. "I just didn't expect it."

Alex swallowed her disappointment at the fading vision of spending the evening cozied next to Ian with a crackling fire and a hot chocolate. An intimate moment that would have allowed her to broach the subject of their future.

"Do you want to get changed?" He leaned down, his lips barely brushing her earlobe. "No one will miss me," he whispered huskily.

Alex peered over his shoulder at the expectant faces taking consecutive turns to glance in their direction. "No," she replied firmly. "I can manage. I won't be long," she added when a shadow of disappointment disrupted his countenance.

"Follow me, miss," commanded a voice from a woman that Alex remembered as George Devall's house manager. Her hair, perfectly coiffed, sat atop her head in a faded bun, her neck adorned with pearls over a silk navy blue suit. "Your bags have already been taken upstairs," she added when Alex frantically scanned the entryway.

Ian blew her a kiss as Anne led her up a welcoming wooden staircase that spiraled upward to the second floor. Even in sneakers, her feet made little sound on the perfectly polished walnut. As she neared the top, she stole a glance back at the party scene below. Ian had returned to his former spot next to the fireplace along with the dark-haired beauty who shamelessly handed him his unfinished glass of bourbon but not before she had helped herself to a sip.

"Right this way," Anne said in a clipped tone. Alex tore her eyes from the scene below to meander down a never-ending hallway of plush rugs and ornate works of art, finally ending up in front of a walnut door and a brass knob with a notable patina .

Alex entered the spacious room, and like a specter, Anne faded into nonexistence with only a faint click of the door signifying her exit. The guest room was elegantly furnished with a large four-poster bed along one wall, crisp white sheets already turned down, and navy pillows arranged three rows deep along the head. The vaulted ceiling seemed to continue forever and boasted a transparent circle at the very top, a small but effective skylight that allowed a few moonbeams to reach the floorboards.

An ornate dresser filled the wall opposite the bed, and Alex noticed that her suitcase and shoulder bag were there next to it on a small bench. As she unzipped her suitcase to begin unpacking, she noticed that framed photographs filled the dresser top—Ian with his arm slung around Nic who was wearing a soccer jersey; Ian in graduation attire posing stiffly with his father; Ian in a tuxedo holding Clementine, his Jack Russell terrier; and then one that brought a prick of tears to her eyes. A glossy photo of her and Ian from New Year's Eve last year, fireworks erupting behind them on a London rooftop. She kept the same one on her own dresser.

Curiosity struck her, and she gently pulled open one of the dresser drawers to peer at the contents. It was chock full of folded men's undershirts and boxer briefs. This had to be Ian's room.

A secret thrill coursed through her, and she removed one of the shirts and held it to her face, drinking in the scent. She squinted into the dim lamplight at her reflection in the vintage full-length mirror next to the dresser. If she was honest, it left quite a bit to be desired. Especially if she was competing with the vixen from downstairs.

Sighing, Alex began extracting the contents of her suitcase one by one. She hadn't expected a lavish party, but with Ian, she never knew what to expect and was learning to pack accordingly. Emerging with two dresses, she stood in front of the mirror examining their merits.

One was a simple black wool sheath dress with a pretty V neckline. The other, a complete impulse purchase with Rox during a post-holiday sale two years ago, was a strapless red number in thick silk with a sweetheart neckline and fitted silhouette that ended just above the knee. Remembering the slim porcelain hand running amok over Ian's arm, she tossed the black one back over the open suitcase. Definitely the red.

Less than an hour later, Alex carefully made her way back down the stairs, this time in proper holiday attire, her gold strappy heels clicking with every downward step, hair swept off her face in a top knot to display the sparkling studs in her earlobes and her delicate décolletage.

The inkling of a migraine pulsed behind her right eye, and she attempted to stave it off as she entered Ian's line of sight. Her lips flirted with a smile when his jaw dropped several inches. He met her at the foot of the stairs, hand meeting hers in midair and brushing her knuckles with his lips before giving them a tiny nip with his teeth.

"You look—" Ian appraised her, a ravenous look overtaking his features.

"Did you run out of adjectives?" Alex asked, offering him a flirtatious wink.

"Unbelievably sexy? Visionary? Ravishing? Goddess-like?"

"Any of those will do." Her face blossomed into a smile that held all the promised joy of the night ahead.

"I want to introduce you to a few people," he said, steering her through the crowd.

Before they made it terribly far, a hand clamped onto Alex's shoulder, a hand belonging to a beaming Rachel, Ian's director of children's programs at the foundation. She and Alex had struck up an easy friendship during their trek into the Kalahari last year.

"Alex," she squeaked and flung her bare arms around Alex's waist.

"It's great to see you again, Rachel," Alex said, pulling back so she could get a better glimpse of her friend dressed head to toe in an emerald jumpsuit with dangling emerald earrings to match.

"How have you been?" Rachel bubbled. "You look amazing in that dress."

Alex caught the infectiousness of her exuberance and smiled. "I've been great. You look beautiful. Is Rahul here with you?"

After a devastating breakup with his fiancée last year, Rahul had found his true love in Rachel, his work partner with the sunny disposition. Rachel scanned the crowd and pointed at Alex.

"He's over there getting me a cocktail." She blew him a kiss, and he waved shyly in return.

Alex noticed the sparkle thrust into her line of vision, a sparkle emanating from the vintage square cut diamond ring on Rachel's hand.

"We're engaged, by the way," Rachel laughed, noticing the look of surprise cross Alex's face.

"Congratulations," Alex stammered as Rachel cut her eyes to Ian, who loomed over them.

"Thanks." Her face glowed as she talked. "We're thinking next Christmas. I've always wanted a December wedding."

Ian's hands tightened on Alex's bare shoulders. "Sorry, I have to cut the girl talk short, as scintillating as it is," joked Ian, earning an eye-roll from Rachel. "But I have to steal Alex."

Rachel surprised her by enveloping her in another hug.

"Don't be a stranger," she said and then bounced off through the crowd toward Rahul, who was holding her drink aloft like a trophy.

Ian steered Alex toward a handsome couple sipping champagne, their arms wrapped around one another.

"Alex, this is Colin, a partner in the legal division, and his wife, Jessica."

The introductions abounded as Ian swept her through the room, and she did little but nod and smile. Meanwhile, the noise escalated her headache to the point of brutality. Even moving her mouth caused her pain. Her stomach roiled at the thought of food, and she refused each tray the waitstaff thrust in her direction. She desperately needed a Diet Coke and a handful of ibuprofen. As she traipsed behind Ian, she kept glancing toward an opening that might be the kitchen.

Alex was just about to excuse herself when a shapely silhouette in a silver dress, barely held up by a pair of spaghetti straps, appeared in front of them. In strappy silver sandals, she was a head taller than Alex but with delicate bone structure and almond-shaped eyes that popped with a smear of silver eyeshadow. Her glossy black hair was parted down the middle and cut in an angular bob that accentuated her cheekbones. In horror, Alex watched as she boldly planted a kiss on Ian's cheek, precariously close to his mouth.

"I can't believe you've been keeping her to yourself all evening," she exclaimed in a proper English accent as her eyes riveted to Alex. "She's absolutely stunning."

Alex recoiled slightly when the silver vixen leaned down to place soft shimmery lips on both of Alex's cheeks. Ian put his drink to his lips, wholly unruffled by the interaction.

"Alex, this is Soo-Yun. She's working in Mongolia with us."

"Nice to meet you," Alex said evenly, not bothering to extend a hand since she could still feel residual lip gloss on both cheeks.

Soo-Yun clapped her hands on both Alex's shoulders, peering intently into her face. "Ian has not been able to shut up about how wonderful you are." Then, she added, "Remember Ian, when we were in that little bar outside Murun, and you ordered a round of shots and that guy—"

The silver beauty's exotic face contorted in laughter, and much to Alex's surprise, Ian joined in, practically doubled over in mirth. In one smooth motion, Soo-Yun snagged a pair of champagne flutes from a nearby server. She proffered one in Alex's direction.

"Champagne, love?"

Alex shook her head, her mouth paper dry and the pounding in her head accentuated with every word coming out of those luscious lips.

"Ian?"

Alex watched the scene unfold slowly as he plucked the crystal flute dancing with golden bubbles out of her hand.

"Cheers, then," she said, clinking her glass with Ian's.

The clink sent a hot poker of pain through Alex's right eye, like her frontal lobe had been skewered. Extracting her hand from the crook of Ian's elbow, she began edging away toward the nearest doorway.

Ian planted a smooth kiss on her face, missing her lips entirely. His breath smelled heavily of bourbon, and his eyes appeared glazed over as he asked, "Everything okay?"

"I just need to take a few ibuprofen. Be right back."

Alex forced a smile and felt his concerned gaze burning into her back as she fell into line behind one of the white-clad servers hoisting an empty tray above the stylish heads and retreated to the kitchen.

"Can I help you miss?" inquired a well-groomed gentleman in a white jacket with gold buttons and white gloves, no less.

Alex skidded to a halt, not realizing the speed she had picked up between the main room and the kitchen entrance. "I need a glass of water or a Diet Coke if you have it." She might empty all the cash in her purse for the ice-cold burn of diet soda coating the back of her throat.

He nodded curtly. "I'll see what I can do, miss."

While she waited, she surveyed the kitchen that stretched from one end of the house until it transitioned into a formal dining room on the other end. It was the most updated room she had seen in the house with sleek modern, high-efficiency appliances, a chef's range with all eight burners lit with undulating blue flames, and a central island covered with half-empty bottles of various libations.

The countertops were also modern, a black quartz that contrasted nicely with the white cabinetry and the light gray uniformly square stones that comprised the floor. She briefly wondered if Mr. Devall also liked to cook. Ian seemed to enjoy it the few times they had been in the kitchen together. He had completely ruined cheese omelets for her for life. She would never be able to find another so rich and mouth-watering.

"Do you prefer still or sparkling?"

Alex looked up from her admiration of the floor tiles to find a silver tray perfectly balanced with an array of beverages, including a single silver can with notable red lettering.

"Still is fine," she said, reaching out to collect the glass bottle of water and the coveted soda can. "Thank you."

She smiled so broadly that the gentleman averted his eyes, a blush forming on the bald spot on his crown.

After washing down a handful of painkillers with the so-bad-it's-good Diet Coke, Alex exhaled in relief. No matter what happened, in exactly one hour, the little orange tablets would tame the inflammation around her neurons and take the edge off her pain. As for the rest of her headache, she would let Ian take care of that. She blushed in her giddiness, imagining the hours after all the guests had departed and she could finally be alone with Ian...and his talents.

"What are they putting in a can of soda these days?"

Embarrassed, Alex sought the face for the soft, musical voice that had just spoken. "I had a headache," she began sheepishly, "but I'm feeling better now."

The man put out a smooth brown hand, a hand that matched the color of eyes situated under heavy lids and bushy white brows.

"Tony Chen."

"Alex Wilde," she replied. "Do you work for the Devall company?"

"I do. I have been Mr. Devall's top engineer for many years."

"That's incredible. What are you working on lately?"

"I'm in charge of the Mongolia project."

"Oh, so you work with Ian?"

"Ian?" His brows furrowed, forming a single fuzzy line. "He helped us set up the cooperative, but he hasn't been involved much lately." Tony accepted a bottle of beer from a passing tray. "He'll come around again when we are done with the actual construction."

Ice flooded Alex's venous system, and it took all her willpower to maintain a minimum level of composure. "Oh, then you work with Soo-Yun?"

"Who?"

"Never mind." Alex waved her hand, fluttering it between them like a drunk butterfly. "It was lovely to meet you, Tony."

Leaving her beverages on the nearest counter, she pivoted on her heels and headed back into the fray of the party.

When she finally located Ian, he was standing near the Christmas tree surrounded by a gaggle of partygoers emitting chuckles and gasps as he regaled them with some involved story. And he wasn't alone. Soo-Yun, in all her exotic glory, stood within breathing distance, her head thrown back in laughter, her arm thrown across Ian's back. If a sparkling diamond suddenly evolved into a person, it would look exactly like her.

Alex's respiratory rate accelerated as she threaded through any empty space she saw in an attempt to edge closer to the stairs. Closer to a refuge where she could process her exploding thoughts. Twenty more steps. Then ten. She dared a glance over her shoulder. She wasn't sure if Ian had seen her weaving among the guests. Her heel bobbled right as she reached for the banister, and she almost lost her balance.

"Alex."

The faint trace of her name floated through the din as she struggled to slide her foot back into her shoe. *Oh, screw it.* She kicked off both gold sandals into a shadowy corner next to the stairwell and headed up the grand staircase.

By the time she entered Ian's room and closed the door behind her, her chest heaved with breathlessness from the metabolic demand of emotional overload. She took a moment to condense the random words sprouting in her head into one word—betrayal.

If Ian hadn't spent most of last year in Mongolia working for his dad, then what exactly had he been doing? Maybe Ian had never changed. Maybe this is who he was—who he had always been—and she was a complete idiot.

TWENTY-TWO

The bedroom door creaked open, and Alex didn't bother turning around. In the mirror next to the ornate dresser, she could see Ian edging toward her, a pair of discarded heels in one hand, a bottle of champagne in the other.

"I thought I would bring the party to you," he said, smirking as he held the champagne aloft, the mist still swirling up from where the cork had popped.

Alex whirled around, searching his face, half expecting him to realize the reason she had fled the festivities. There was nothing. No hint of remorse at being caught. Nothing except for a piercing blue gaze that danced with amusement and burned with the blatant disinhibited desire offered by too many alcoholic beverages.

"How's your headache?" he asked, brows furrowed in concern.

"No better, no worse."

Alex instinctively pushed her thumb into the supraorbital notch of her right eye. Ian sidled over to her, extending the champagne.

"Want me to make it better?"

He reached behind her and set the champagne bottle on the dresser, leaning over so that he grazed her jawline as he spoke. Despite her anguish, her knees wilted in response, and she placed her palms on the dresser's rounded edge for balance. She steeled her mouth when his lips found hers, willing herself into a statue of unresponsiveness. For the briefest of seconds, she opened a slit between her lips, and Ian playfully darted his tongue inside.

"Ian..."

"Mm-hmm," he murmured as he moved his ministrations to the tender groove along her trachea. She positioned her palms flat against his muscular pectorals and created some distance between them.

"Ian," she repeated sharply. "What have you been doing in Mongolia?"

His head snapped up, and he absorbed the acerbic look on Alex's face. "Because you haven't been working for your dad."

He narrowed his eyes, a smirk elevating one side of his luscious mouth. Alex's anger flared. She had expected remorse not arrogance. She let loose her next several sentences like flaming arrows toward Ian's expensive button-down.

"I met the guy in charge of the Mongolia project, and he says you haven't been involved in a while. And I have no idea how Soo-Yun fits into the picture because he didn't seem to know her at all." She crossed her arms to shield herself from the ricochet of her emotional overload. "But apparently you do, since she has spent the entire night groping you."

Ian's mouth quirked at the mention of Soo-Yun, not arousing the least bit of humor from Alex.

"You think this entire time—" He paused to place his lips close enough to hers that she could smell the spice of bourbon on his breath. "While you've been saving the world, driving to another country for snake potion, getting stuck with dirty needles, and making last-minute trips across the ocean with a woman and her baby, I've been goofing off in central Asia with a Korean architect?"

Architect? Ian reached behind her, pressing his body close to hers until she felt the swell in his pants against her lower abdomen. He took a long swig of champagne straight from the bottle.

"Maybe." She unfolded her arms, but she held them flaccid against her sides.

"I haven't."

"Then what—"

"Shhh."

He ran his fingertips over her trembling lower lip.

"No...more...talking."

Ian took a lengthy swig from the champagne bottle and put his lips to hers. She tried to resist, but his momentum forced them open, and a liquid bubbled into her mouth, her tongue floating in a delightful effervescence.

For one blissful moment, Alex forgot the swell of anger and hurt in her chest as it ebbed, along with the throbbing in her temples. She swallowed the champagne, but the taste lingered as Ian explored her mouth, sending all manner of sensations sizzling into her lady region.

Despite the lack of resolution, she wasn't entirely disappointed with the evolution of this conversation.

Ian hiked up her leg around his waist, which elevated the hem of her dress to an indecent height, exposing the thin silk of her panties. His finger taunted the elastic edge, not quite slipping underneath, and began to outline her contours slowly, lazily. Her pulse thrummed in her core, and she bit her bottom lip to keep from groaning. And then, ever so delicately, Ian slipped two fingers inside the top of her panties and massaged the tender growing swell between her thighs. At this moment, all she wanted was him to want her the way she wanted him.

As she felt the brush of his fingers into her welcoming center, the spasm that came with it carried all the fear and yearning of the last few months, shifting her emotional tide into wanton lust. Alex ran her palms over the tensile strength of his thorax and hooked her fingers into the spaces between his opalescent buttons, yanking until buttons struck the back of the door.

Ian growled as he shrugged the shirt onto the floor and then stepped back from Alex to pull off his white t-shirt. Her eyes drank in the sight of his etched mid-section, and she reached backward and unzipped her dress. She stepped out of the crimson silk, folds of material settling onto the floor like petals of a rose and launched herself into his arms.

Fervent kisses landed like a shower of tropical rain, hot and wet, all over her face and neck. Then he kissed her deeply—so deeply that her head spun, and she startled when her back suddenly met with something soft and pliable.

Ian expertly removed the remaining shreds of her undergarments as she settled luxuriously into the mattress. When he laid his body over hers, she interlocked her fingers with his, closed her eyes, and opened her quivering thighs, arching her back to the feel of his taut skin over sinewy muscles.

No words. No noise. Just skin.

The music had quieted, and the final voices had faded from downstairs when Ian cracked the door to the hallway. Alex burrowed further into the layers of cotton sheets topped with a thick duvet, the ache in her head finally extinguished by Ian's skillful ministrations. He had pulled on a pair of flannel pants in addition to a t-shirt for his foray into the house.

"I'll be right back," he whispered, leaving Alex to burn with afterglow and unanswered questions.

Several long minutes later, Ian returned with a slim laptop case and a plate piled with party food. Alex had barely eaten since she left Botswana and her stomach growled in anticipation. She sat up in bed, pulling on Ian's discarded white t-shirt.

Greedily accepting the plate from Ian, she balanced it on her lap while inspecting its contents. An assortment of rolls, cheese, olives, and a giant slice of chocolate cake. She picked up the fork nestled in the middle of the plate and thrust the tines into the center of the cake. A dark chocolate crumb made perfectly moist by the inclusion of a middle layer of chocolate mousse. Her eyes closed in gratitude.

"Don't think that this makes up for anything," she said, inserting her fork into the cake slice.

"I thought that's what the sex was for."

Ian smirked and plopped down next to her.

"I'll talk...you eat," he commanded, and she eagerly complied.

He cracked open the lid of his laptop and began dragging his forefinger over the mousepad.

"I *have* been in Mongolia this whole time," he began, the backlight of the screen reflecting off his retinas, "but I wasn't working on the mining co-op. I was working on this."

He spun the screen toward Alex, and she began to analyze the details of a partially constructed building that rose at least five stories in height. The structure was covered in a neat brick and lined with windows that ran uniformly parallel on each floor with a large set of double doors marking the front entrance.

"It looks like—" she paused, and her breath caught, "a hospital."

"It is."

He clicked to the next picture, a close-up of the lettering on the outside—the Benjamin Ryan Devall Hospital for Children. Alex stared at the screen as Ian clicked through a slideshow of photographs of the building's progress.

"When I was traveling through Mongolia last year, I realized that, outside of Ulaanbaatar, there weren't really any options for sick kids, so I used some foundation funds to purchase the land, and we started construction last summer. It's opening in the spring."

Alex continued to stare, open-mouthed, as he continued.

"Soo-Yun is a friend from college and a world-famous architect. She's been helping with the details of the construction."

"She probably wants to help you with more than that," Alex muttered, giving Ian a sideways glance.

"I'm pretty sure she's taken."

"Is her boyfriend aware of that?" The words felt like acid on Alex's tongue.

"No." A mischievous grin erupted on Ian's face. "But I'm pretty sure her girlfriend is."

Alex's ears did a double take. "Oh."

"Brigitte is a designer. She's been with us too...working on the interior."

"Wow. I just assumed...I guess I am a raving lunatic," Alex admitted, licking a thick dollop of frosting from her fork.

"No more than usual, baby," Ian said, plucking the fork out of her grasp and using it to shove a heap of cake into his mouth.

Christmas dawned, and the entire front lawn appeared crisply white, enveloped in the saint-like beauty of freshly fallen snow. Alex sat in the window seat of the library snuggled into a wool blanket, amazed that any remnant from last evening's soirée had vanished. Only the stately tree remained, the scent of pine traipsing through her olfactory nerves.

Ian had gone out to shovel snow from the circular drive so the catering van could make it into the driveway. Alex had watched him expertly flinging piles of snow into formidable mounds while she perused a novel that she had randomly picked from the shelf. *Outlander* by Diana Gabaldon. Scottish history, time travel, a medical heroine, a dashing Scottish Lord—what more could a girl want in a vacation book?

When Ian stomped in, discarding his outer layers as he strode over to the window, she grinned at the flush in his cheeks. The blue in his eyes seemed brighter today for some reason.

"I didn't know billionaires shoveled their own driveways," she teased.

"Only on Christmas."

He smirked and leaned down to kiss her, his frigid lips lingering on her warmth. They heard the crunch of tires on snow-covered gravel as a black van labeled with "Catering by Cathy" in block letters skidded to a stop in the driveway.

"Just in time." Ian pressed his lips to the corner of her mouth, the light coating of stubble on his jaw shockingly abrasive on the peachy softness of her cheek. "Hungry?" he asked, his eyes alight with wicked intent.

"Famished," she breathed, but she didn't necessarily mean for food.

She hoped that last night had been the mere appetizer to the next several weeks of being intertwined in all of Ian's extraordinary appendages.

The Christmas brunch that spread over the entire extent of the sixteen-person dining room table could have fed Santa and all his elves. Platters of baked goods including croissants and mini-muffins, danishes with puffed edges bordering a central dollop of cream, and piles of fruit cascaded from a three-tiered silver tray. Crystal bowls of various condiments like jam and whipped butter accessorized the larger platters of eggs and sausages.

George Devall was already there, dressed in a navy sweater and matching slacks, the collar of an ivory shirt visible around his neck. A friendly crinkle developed around his eyes when he saw Alex.

"Allow me, my dear," he said and pulled out a dining chair with an elegant formality.

Alex hesitated before sitting, recalling his gracious manners the last time—in fact, the only time—she had visited his homestead. She had come in search of Ian. Instead, she had discovered he had left the United Kingdom for Mongolia. Mr. Devall had given her a letter he found wedged in the glove compartment of Ian's car, a letter that had given her hope that she and Ian would find a way back to each other. In his subtle way, George Devall had nudged them together. She loved him for what a wonderful father he had been for Ian.

"Thank you for having me. Everything is so beautiful."

"Just like you, my dear," he said, winking conspiratorially as Alex sat delicately onto the ivory cushion.

"She's way too young for you," Ian said as he took the seat next to Alex and began helping himself to a pile of eggs.

"Then too bad I'm not younger." Mr. Devall strode gracefully around to the other side of the table, picking a seat across from Ian.

Alex viewed the plate in front of her that Ian had heaped with winter berries, a pile of eggs, and a croissant stuffed with cream. She ate silently, reveling in the quick, easy banter between father and son.

They were obviously close. For over a decade, it had been just the two of them.

It made Alex miss her mother, and she scribed a mental note to call her as soon as it was morning in Texas. Mr. Devall cleared his throat, and Alex glanced up to see that he was watching her while taking a sip of his coffee.

"Ian has shown you his personal project in Mongolia?"

Alex nodded, a beaming smile spreading across her features. "He did. The hospital is phenomenal."

"When did you say it would be operational, Ian?"

Ian lounged casually in his chair, sipping his own coffee.

"Probably spring. March, I think."

His eyes glowed with excitement as he shared the latest construction progress with his dad.

"We will have to have some sort of dedication, I think," responded Mr. Devall, rubbing his hand over the fine carpet of white facial hair covering his jawline.

Ian stole a glance at Alex, who was busy tearing her croissant into bite-sized pieces.

"Interested in making a trip to Mongolia in March?" asked Ian, his eyebrows waggling with excitement.

"Wild horses couldn't keep me away."

She smiled and then shook her head in disbelief, a prick of unexpected tears suddenly invading her visual field. She reached across the table to squeeze Ian's unoccupied hand. It might have taken almost two decades, but Ian had dealt with the death of his younger brother by taking sublimation to a whole new level.

This was the true heart of the man she loved beyond reason. Underneath the arrogance, sex appeal, and charm, he truly desired to make a difference in this world. She had once shamed him, accusing him of being someone with massive resources who refused to see what was good in the world. What was worth fighting for. How things had changed since that night at Ex-Pats.

Ian grinned, free and boyish, his cheeks still rouged from the bitter cold outside, and squeezed her hand between long slim fingers.

"I was hoping you could help me get things started once the hospital opens," Ian said.

Alex cocked her head quizzically. "How so?" She had just assumed that, with his resources, he had a team of experts at his beck and call.

"Doing what you do best," he cooed and offered his best smile. "Taking on a hopeless cause and turning it into something spectacular."

Ian's dad snorted into his breakfast and cast one gentle eye in his offspring's direction. "If your recent success is reflective of your abilities, my dear, this hospital is sure to succeed," offered Mr. Devall, his face partially hidden by a cloth table napkin.

Alex still could barely conceptualize the prospect of a freestanding children's hospital soaring above the plains, kissing the azure sky outside of Ulaanbaatar. Alex had been to Mongolia once as a pediatric resident. She had worked as part of a surgical team performing open-heart operations on children to fix congenital defects.

The country was beautiful, vast and wild, and unlike anything she had ever seen before. Other than a few central urban collections, Ulaanbaatar being the biggest, it was open country, home to the world's last true nomadic civilization. The impact of a children's hospital that could revolutionize healthcare for kids living in remote areas would be profound.

Still, she had made a commitment to PM, to the staff and the kids. A commitment not easily broken. An unease settled over her that she tried to disguise behind a heartfelt smile launched in Mr. Devall's direction.

"Everything is beautiful here, mom. You would love it."

Alex smiled into the phone as she pressed her forehead to the chilly glass of Ian's bedroom window. A thick crust of snow lay on the sidewalk below, and she watched families huddled together as they braved the descending twilight to schlep over to the lighted homes of loved ones for Christmas.

Shortly after brunch, she and Ian had loaded her luggage into a black SUV for the trip back into London. She had no idea how they were spending the remainder of her vacation. Although she was bereft to say goodbye to Ian's father, the privacy offered by Ian's London flat beckoned. George Devall had placed his hands on her shoulders, planting a kiss atop the crown of her head as they departed, a gesture that twisted through her with both discomfort and comfort. She supposed she had never learned to accept acts of kindness from father figures.

"I know I would," Janie answered. "It's so warm here I watered all the flowers in shorts."

In their inconsequential town of Cole's Church, Texas, Christmas weather could be anything from snow to downright balmy.

"What do you and Peter have planned?" Alex asked, huddling further into her pink cardigan.

"Not too much. I baked a pie, and we're going over to his sister's later."

Janie sounded thoughtful. Alex knew the holidays evoked a nostalgic sadness in them both.

Christmas had always been their favorite holiday, a day of catching up while the kitchen was filled with the delectable smell of sugar cookies and the delicate evergreen of the tree decorated with homemade ornaments courtesy of juvenile Alex.

Medicine had claimed Alex's holidays for the past decade, and Ian had claimed this one.

"I'm sorry I'm not there, Mom, but I promise you next Christmas for sure."

"I'm holding you to that. Maybe you can throw in Ian too."

Speaking of Ian. A warmth descended on her in the solid form of Ian's front pressing against her back, his hands settling on her hips, warm breath with a notable spice riding on the air molecules of her next inhale.

"Merry Christmas, Janie," he called into the phone.

"Merry Christmas, Ian."

Janie's voice expanded with excitement at the sounds of Ian's low timbre, and Alex rolled her eyes.

"Sorry for dominating Alex's holiday this year, but we'll see you at the wedding."

Alex side-eyed him in surprise. "I didn't even invite you yet."

"I invited myself." He shrugged and then cocked his head toward the phone. "Bye, Janie. See you soon."

"Bye, Ian. Bye, honey."

"Bye Mo—"

Before she could finish, Ian had plucked the phone out of her hand and tossed it onto the bed behind them.

"Hey, what's the rush?" Alex playfully punched him in the bicep. Ian tilted his head toward the door.

"Follow me, and I'll show you...and bring my Christmas present that you've been lugging around."

"How did you— never mind," Alex grumbled but snatched her shoulder bag from the floor and followed Ian into the hallway and up the spiral staircase leading to the roof.

A blast of frigid air penetrated her sweater, and she cursed herself for not having her coat nearby. The roof patio where they had celebrated New Year's Eve last year had been transformed into a cozy outdoor wonderland with a roaring fire pit made from a large block of rectangular white stone with glass sides that enclosed a ripple of blue flames. The outdoor furniture had been piled high with woolen blankets, and a bucket of champagne on ice rested on a table between two cushioned chairs.

"Did you do all of this?" Alex asked incredulously.

"Maybe. Here," he said, picking up one of the plaid throws and tossing it around her shoulders. "I know you're cold, but the view is—"

"Completely worth it," Alex finished, drinking in the sight of upper-crust London decked out in holiday garland and twinkling lights as far as she could see.

In the corner of her eye, she could see Ian reaching into his coat pocket for something, and she momentarily stood in shocked silence. But when his hand emerged, it merely held a small rectangle of cardstock.

"Merry Christmas, Alex."

She accepted it between her frozen fingers, staring down at the postcard depicting a white sandy beach and turquoise water, two happy-looking stick figures sketched on the sandy shore.

"Is that supposed to be us?" Alex chuckled.

"This looks exactly like you," said Ian in a serious tone, pointing to the stick figure sporting pigtails and a bikini.

Alex burst out with a stream of giggling, and Ian's solemn face transitioned into a smile.

"I promised you a trip for New Year's, and that's exactly what this is."

When Alex stared at him open-mouthed, he continued. "We have a place in Virgin Gorda, in the British Virgin Islands. I thought you might enjoy spending some time lounging on a beach without a care in the world."

Alex reveled in disbelief. That's exactly what she needed. That and a daily private audience with Ian.

"You are too much. This is too much...but I can't wait."

His face glowed with elation, and Alex knew she had rarely witnessed anything more heart-wrenching.

"Here."

She thrust her hand into her shoulder bag until her fingers met with the smooth wrapping paper of Ian's gift. "I never know what to buy you," she said shyly as she handed him the box wrapped in red paper bearing a white ribbon.

Ian's fingers tore through the paper and flipped open the box, all the while a smile playing on his lips. When he removed the hand-carved elephants, a male and a female, their trunks intertwined, his fingers lingered over their imperfections, and he breathed a sigh as if resolving something that had been weighing heavily on him.

"I got it in a village outside Gaborone," Alex explained.

"I love it," Ian said and leaned over to kiss her.

Before their lips met, Alex froze when a notable high-pitched ping met her ears, her eyes immediately riveting to the statue.

"Oh no," she moaned.

A hind leg had broken off the bull elephant and landed on the ground. Alex bent down to retrieve it.

"That's exactly why I put it in my carry-on." She frowned as she examined the damage.

Ian took the statue with its missing appendage and placed it gently on a side table.

"Don't worry about it. There's only one thing I wanted for Christmas this year anyway."

"What's that?" Alex asked, flicking up her gaze to find him staring intently at her, the flames from the fire pit dancing in his irises. And suddenly, she knew exactly what he was about to say before his lips formed the words.

"I want you to marry me, Alex."

TWENTY-THREE

A thousand thoughts flitted through her brain like a flock of winter geese, but instead of being able to discern them, all Alex heard was the chaos of one thousand pairs of flapping wings.

"Ian—" she breathed.

She felt herself hyperventilating, consumed by the fog of alkalosis as she exhaled the majority of her body's carbon dioxide. And then, like an idiot, she started spewing questions in the most random of orders.

"What about my job in Botswana? I assume I would have to quit and then where would I work? Would I work at all? If I don't work, then what was it all for...all the training and sleep deprivation and sacrifice?"

Ian began running one hand through the errant tufts of his glossy black hair.

"You could work if you want," he offered.

"And if we live here, how often would I see my mom? Between work and you and traveling. And what if everyone thinks I'm a huge poser? The humanitarian doctor who marries her rich boyfriend and lives happily ever after."

"I think that's the point."

Alex regarded his face—one brow furrow away from crestfallen as he simultaneously tried to reign in whatever emotions surged under the surface. Her heart hurt with the kind of pain people felt when their coronaries spasmed and restricted the blood flow to struggling cardiac muscle.

"I'm not saying no."

"I know."

"I'm just saying maybe not right now. I need some time to process everything. So much has changed in my life."

"I know. Take all the time you need."

Although his voice was strained, he placed a gentle kiss on her forehead then reached for the bottle of bourbon. Everyone had a way to self-medicate. If bourbon was Ian's, then tonight champagne could be hers.

Alex awoke groggy and naked. One glass of champagne had quickly become another...and another...until the night devolved into her and Ian seeking solace in the one sure thing that superseded all others— the power of physical chemistry. They had poured their unspoken words and torrential emotions into the singular purpose of achieving mutual bliss.

Alex tried to untwist the lower half of her body from the sheets, thrashing like a bug caught in a web, until she wriggled free and realized that Ian was not there.

"Ian?"

Her eyes scanned the room in search of her jeans and cardigan before she remembered that they were exactly where she had left them the night before—on the roof. With the sheet as a makeshift gown, she hobbled over to Ian's carved mahogany dresser and extracted a t-shirt and a pair of plaid boxers.

She had just pulled the soft navy material over her head when Ian appeared in the doorway, already showered and dressed in jeans and a casual black button-down. She stared at the spot on his throat right above his sternum, such a sensitive part of the body where the trachea entered the thorax before branching out into each bronchus, and she suddenly had the urge to press her lips there and revive the exquisite sensations of the night before.

"For once, you're the early bird." Alex pressed her entire front against his chest, letting her arms curl naturally around his middle and her cheek dive into the softness of his shirt.

"It's not that early," he teased, cradling her head against his chest, "but you looked so peaceful in your drunken, over-sexed stupor that I didn't dare wake you."

"I wasn't the only drunk one," Alex grumbled.

She tried to push away from him, but he only hugged her tighter, her efforts flimsy against the steel cables of his arms.

"You get really vocal when you're drunk, by the way."

Her cheeks flamed as she recalled bits and pieces of last night. It involved more than a few *Ian's* and *yes's* and *don't stop's.*

"If only it was that easy for you to say yes to everything like you say yes to—" Ian mused.

"Okay, okay!" she squealed.

This time Alex succeeded in pulling out of Ian's embrace as she chastised him with a glare and a gentle slap on his pectorals. He was chuckling, a smirk decorating his features, but his eyes failed to flash with amusement. Instead, they were flat, like a still pool, and almost solemn. Alex inhaled sharply through her nose, still smelling the vapors of Ian's bourbon, and placed her palms on his biceps.

"Are you okay? I mean after—"

"You mean after I asked a girl a really important question and I'm still waiting on the answer?"

"Yes." Alex averted her eyes and chewed on her bottom lip.

A finger tipped up her chin as Ian bent his head to meet her gaze.

"Hey," he said softly. "I told you to take all the time you need, and I meant it."

He brushed his lips against hers, but it was rushed and mechanical and not near enough to undo the gripping anguish that wounded her delicate cardiac silhouette.

"I need to tell you something. Soo-Yun called this morning."

Alex vaguely remembered the phone ringing as the first light of dawn appeared through Ian's bedroom window.

"There's a problem at the build site, and I need to go take care of it."

"You're going to Mongolia?"

"Just long enough to get this issue taken care of. A day...two at most."

Alex blinked furiously to ward off the sting of emerging tears.

"Is this because of last night...because I—"

"No," he said firmly, sandwiching her face between warm palms.

His eyes scanned her face. Eyes that had always been able to breach the imagined or the actual distance between them.

"I'll be back for New Year's Eve and then I'll whisk you away on my fancy plane where the only thing you need to worry about is what drink to order next."

His smile was short-lived but genuine.

"What should I do while you're gone?" Alex asked, clasping her hands together behind his back. A simple gesture but a way to ensure that she kept him close while she could.

"Whatever you want—devour the library, run a thousand miles, organize my DVDs."

Alex rolled her eyes in faux exasperation.

"And here's a thought," he said, pulling her tighter into a full-frontal embrace, "go make up with Roxanne."

Less than an hour later, a pitch-black SUV pulled up on the narrow lane in front of Ian's three-story flat. As Ian gracefully toted his compact luggage to the door, checking his carry-on a second time for his passport and wallet, a rising panic swept through Alex's nervous system carried from neuron to neuron on a wave of despair. He turned the knob, heaving the door into a mini-snow bank, and handed his bags to the driver waiting to retrieve them.

"I'll be just a minute, Mark."

The man nodded and turned on his heel to deposit the bags in the car.

By the time Ian rotated halfway to face Alex, she had already launched herself into his arms, sending greedy hands upward around the back of his neck. She pulled back an inch and appreciated the snowflakes on his exhale before allowing her emotions and her lips to run wild over the contours of his mouth. He groaned and deepened their kiss with the ferocity that she desired and truly needed at that moment.

A kiss that would imprint Ian on her soul. A kiss that could sustain her while he was gone. She wasn't ready to let him go. She would *never* be ready to let him go. And right then, she had her answer.

Alex stared out the window long after the car had disappeared from her view. She continued to trace patterns on the moist glass and reimagine the parting with Ian. She had poured her heart into that kiss. When she replayed the events in her mind, he had paused to catch his breath from lip ravaging, and she had bravely blurted out the word burning a pathway through her brain.

"Yes."

Ian stilled, and Alex's pupils grew to the size of grapes as she fully absorbed the shock on his face.

"Yes, what?" he asked slowly, enunciating every syllable so that no mistakes could be made.

"Yes," she repeated, her eyes shining as his face transformed into its own sun.

But it hadn't happened that way. Ian had paused to catch his breath, and the word had remained in her mind, lit up like a flashing marquee. Instead of speaking, she leaned in to kiss him again, to use the soft but effective power of lip seduction to make him feel her love. He moaned softly and cupped her face, winding his fingers into her still damp hair hanging in loose waves. There was a desperate intensity to their kissing that was new. It both thrilled and terrified her.

Alex wished she was not so cerebral. She wished that she was just a woman kissing a man—a man whom she loved more than oxygen. But she wasn't just a woman. She was also a physician, and others would bear the consequences of her decisions.

When Ian finally pulled away, his cufflink had gotten caught in her loose waves. They had shared a giggle as he unwound the wet tendrils. She caught the sparkling detail in her peripheral vision and pulled his wrist to eye level.

"You're wearing the cufflinks I got you."

"I always wear them when I travel," he responded resolutely.

He stepped out into the snow, pausing in the doorway to meet her lips once more in a tender but not satisfying enough kiss that would have to sustain her for the next several days.

His lips brushed the folds of her ear with a feather touch as he whispered, "See you soon, baby."

Alex's breath created an expanding patch of fog on the window that looked out from the quaint library onto the street level. Amidst her restlessness, the usual medicinal quality of solace had become simply annoying. Her thoughts hammered in her ears as she tried to dissect her head from her heart, knowing full well that separating the two was impossible.

She loved Ian beyond reason but saying yes to marriage meant saying no to everything else in her life. It meant saying no to her commitment in Botswana. It meant saying no to ever living near her mom. It meant saying no to decades of training, preparing, becoming.

Alex feared all the unknown variables a life with Ian entailed. If she left Botswana, the work she had done over the past two years would unravel—which is exactly what had happened with the obstetrics program now that Rox was no longer there.

How could she be asked to make a decision fraught with so many consequences? Only one person in the entire world would be able to lead her through the entanglements of her thoughts and shine the light of clarity on her path.

Alex picked up her phone and tapped the picture of the blonde-haired diva in her wedding gown before she could change her mind. It had been over six weeks since they had talked, and their last conversation had erupted into surges of grief and betrayal from both sides. Alex held her breath and wrapped an arm around her middle as her abdominal muscles clenched.

"Hello?"

"It's me, Rox."

"Sorry, I can barely hear you."

Alex detected a rising din in the background of children laughing at a rich voice swelling with intonation as it told a story. It sounded like Nic.

"Where are you?" Alex asked.

"Nic's parents' house with about fourteen of his cousins and their children."

"That explains the noise."

"I'll be back in a minute," she heard Rox shout to someone, and then a door closed, blocking out the cloud of noise. "Much better."

"Rox...I...about what I said, I didn't really mean it."

"I know, love."

Alex plunged ahead, knowing that she wouldn't have Rox's attention for much longer.

"I feel like we've drifted apart, and I don't want that, and I need help with figuring things out with Ian and our future...and you are the only person in the universe who could understand."

Rox said nothing for a moment. Alex could imagine the lip pursing and nail drumming that was happening on the other end of the phone.

"What I can tell you is this. I'm happy with my life and my choices. What I had to sacrifice doesn't compare in the least to what I gained. Change isn't always what you expect it to be. It hurts less and more than you think it will...but somehow, it's all worth it. There is nothing selfish or cowardly about putting love first, and the rest of the world understands that. But in a relationship, there is no room for regret, and resentment is like poison. It's up to you to find a way to reconcile the rest of your life when you love someone and agree to become a partner."

"What if I'm not ready to become someone's partner?"

"None of us ever are. We just decide to be...because the alternative is not an option."

Alex heard a staccato knock through the phone and Rox's muffled, "Be right there."

"I have to go, Alex. Dinner and all."

"Thanks for the advice, Rox. Maybe we could get together when you get back. I'm staying at Ian's right now." She paused and then added, "I miss you."

"Sure, Alex. I'll let you know." Roxanne sighed heavily. "I've missed you too."

Running was always a good idea. Alex kept repeating this to herself as she slogged through the leftover Christmas powder that was devolving into slush. Wetness had seeped through her Brooks into her socks, and she tried to ignore the tingling chill in her feet as she rounded the outskirts of Hyde Park. She had left a trail of footprints from Ian's front door down to Knightsbridge and had wound through a promenade lined with bare trees, ending up on the far side of the park near the Princess Diana Memorial Playground. She stopped briefly to watch a mom corral two children who had been running a perimeter around an oversized pirate ship before collapsing in a snowbank, a crystal cloud of aerosolized snow appearing in the air around them.

What would it be like to live here? To work, to raise children, to intertwine her life with the man she loved? Would her life resemble a dream realized, or would it always be missing something? Would she go to bed at night longing to hear the muffled whines of children tossing in their metal hospital cribs or the squeak of Lesede's leather shoes on the linoleum floor?

Sure, she could travel to Botswana or any other location for her global health career, but how effective could two or three visits a year be for the advancement of pediatric medicine?

More than anything, Alex had grown to love her job there. Pleasure was watching the interns grow in knowledge and expertise. Pride was working alongside them to provide mechanical ventilation to their very first patient and succeeding. Adventure and hope waited around every corner, even when she tried for a miracle and failed.

The little boy she was watching lost his woolen knit cap in the snow, revealing an unruly shock of dark hair, and his laughter reverberated through the frozen mist. Alex wondered what Ian had been like as a boy. Carefree and curious? Naughty but kind-hearted?

Ian was so much more than the man she had met almost two years ago in an expatriate bar in Botswana. Back then, she had only seen his outer surface. Attractive but arrogant. Charming but flippant.

But now...she knew every inch of his superior skin with exquisite detail. She knew that kissing the tender spot just beneath his ear aroused him the most. He liked chocolate chips in his pancakes but didn't like them in cookies. He avoided texting in lieu of talking on the phone if he could, and the sight or scent of a hospital still made his heart race with anxiety.

Despite being a light sleeper, he wasn't an early riser. Bourbon was his preferred drink, but he secretly loved rosé wine and baths—usually together. He tried to hide a superb work ethic behind a robust social calendar, but Alex had phoned him many times in the middle of the night while he was awake into the wee hours of the morning bonding with his laptop.

His greatest fear was abandonment, which wasn't surprising considering that his mother had walked out on him. He had religiously avoided female attachment since that day. Until Alex. He had held onto her with a force that defied logic and reason, even when she had not held onto him.

But what she loved the most—Ian had the heart of a dreamer.

The little boy caught her staring and waved jubilantly in her direction with a tiny hand engulfed in a blue mitten. She waved tentatively back, a slow smile unfurling over her frozen face.

Alex had let Ian go once, and she wasn't about to make the same mistake again. She wasn't the same woman she was a year ago. And at that moment, she answered a question that had been plaguing her since realizing she was in love with Ian. Who would she become as the wife of a billionaire-philanthropist, a reformed playboy with a tender soul, a spectacular lover, and friend?

The answer was: exactly who she was supposed to be. A woman who knew how to love and be loved. A woman who wasn't afraid to accept the blessing of the unexpected. A woman who believed that any dream she could imagine could become a reality.

When she picked up her speed and left the park in the distance, she ran with a specific destination in mind. *Home.*

TWENTY-FOUR

"We're leaving first thing in the morning, so I'll be back in plenty of time to kiss you at midnight."

For once, their conversation was devoid of the background noise of grinding tires and shrill beeping. Noises that she had assumed were related to the mining site but now knew were, in fact, coming from the construction site for the children's hospital.

"I'm counting on it," Alex said, a spectacular giddiness rising into her throat. "Where are you right now?"

She heard him groan.

"In the North. In a literal epicenter of frozen tundra."

Alex closed the door to Ian's refrigerator, cracking open the plastic cap on the water bottle she had retrieved.

"What are you doing all the way up there?" she called to her phone on the kitchen island surrounded by her haphazard attempt at a sandwich.

"Nobody is up here at the mining site right now except for our Mongolian team so Tony and I are checking things out before we leave."

"Tony Chen?"

"Yeah, how do you know Tony?"

"I met him at the party," Alex trailed off as she gave Ian a moment to fit together the pieces of last week's party debacle.

"Aah. Right before you stormed off to my bedroom all hot and bothered."

"How was I supposed to know you were secretly building a state-of-the-art children's hospital instead of working for your dad's company?" she retorted.

"You weren't until I was ready to surprise you," he muttered.

"Consider me surprised." *Beyond surprised.*

"This will probably be my last trip for a while. The hospital is almost finished, and Soo-Yun's girlfriend is taking care of the inside details."

Alex's heart floated into her throat at the thought of spending the remainder of her vacation draped over Ian with nothing but the sound of ocean waves for conversation. He cleared his throat like he wanted to say something else, and then silence ensued.

"I hope you like it," he murmured.

"I already love it."

"And I love you. Alex—" He paused as if whatever was circling his consciousness couldn't quite find a place to land.

"I love you too, Ian," Alex interrupted.

And the question she knew he couldn't yet ask remained: but do you love me enough? *Yes*, she thought. *Yes, I do.*

Alex spent the twenty-four hours before Ian's arrival scurrying around his flat in a deluge of nervous energy and purpose. Every counter was sparkling. Every book in place. She had even dusted the piano keys. Although the house was empty of all other beings, Alex still felt it necessary to tiptoe down the spiral stairs to the basement where Ian had an industrial-level wine cellar plus his secret stash of aged-to-perfection bourbon.

A blush bloomed in her cheeks and in her lady parts when she edged around the dimly lit backroom to dig through the crates stuffed with wood shavings for the exact bottle she wanted. Her eyes flicked to the shadowy wall at the very rear of the room where a memory lay etched in the woodgrain—a memory and her handprints. If walls could talk, they would describe Ian's eyes as they raked over her barely-there black lingerie. They would whisper the spectacular noises of their New Year's Eve tryst from last year, now absorbed into the aged wood.

Dusting off her prize from the bottom of the box, Alex held it up to the light to admire the chestnut hue and the golden flecks as the light struck the amber liquid inside. Ian drank bourbon in times of celebration and in moments of devastation. Tonight, would belong in the former category. On a whim, she snagged a bottle of champagne as she passed the massive wine wall and headed upstairs with both bottles tucked safely under her arm.

The celestial spirits had fallen into line with Alex's plans because the night was perfect. Cloudless and windless, the sky had erupted into a spectrum of stars, creating a rare but stellar view from Ian's rooftop. It was a beautiful night for fireworks of all kinds.

The air was crisp with anticipation, as was Alex's fluttering stomach. For the third time, she rearranged the snacks and beverages displayed across the stone tabletop. Settling into one of the patio chairs with a glass of Sancerre to calm her nerves, she giggled to herself as she imagined Ian's trajectory through the house until finally finding her waiting for him on the roof.

On the first floor, she had strung up a happy birthday sign with an arrow pointing up to the second floor, where Ian would find a birthday card leaning against the bottle of bourbon. She had left an empty glass and a note instructing him to pour a drink and keep going.

On the sideboard next to the rooftop stairs, Alex had decorated a small round birthday cake with fireworks in strips of multi-colored buttercream framing a single word. *YES.* She had drawn an arrow on a sheet of paper pointing toward the stairs to the roof, where she would be waiting.

Alex grinned uncontrollably as she imagined the look of shock that would dominate his features when he saw the cake. He would race to the rooftop to seal their future with a searing kiss.

Over the last few days, she had examined every life permutation, and the only one that wasn't an option was a path that took her farther from Ian. She had no idea what their future held or how she would reconcile loving this man and succeeding in her career, but one thought burned brighter than any other—she and Ian would do it together.

Despite the frigid temperatures, Alex glowed with an internal warmth as she downed the remaining golden drops in her wine glass and then glanced at the luminous numerals on her phone. It was nearing ten o'clock, and Ian had not even texted that they had landed. Alex frowned, her mood transiently doused by Ian's tardiness. Surely if the flight had been delayed, he would have called. She rose to warm her hands, passing them back and forth above the blue flames of the fire pit, rapt anticipation in her spine as she balanced on one of life's many precipices. Everything was about to change.

The door to the roof creaked open, and Alex paused as a thrill flooded into her toes. Her hands, now toasty warm from the flames, smoothed the front of her wool coat, and she tucked a stray hair behind one ear as she prepared to be captured into the whirlwind embrace of a pair of weary but electric arms.

But when she turned to greet Ian, her smile faltered as Roxanne's face set behind a mask of holiday make-up appeared from the dark stairwell. Recovering quickly, she strode over to her friend, the heels of her leather boots sounding eerily hollow against the patio flooring.

"Hi Rox," she said, smiling and leaning in to place her arms around Rox's bare shoulders.

Holiday glamour was Rox's specialty, and, tonight, she didn't disappoint. She was wearing a strapless pink bustier top and black cigarette pants with matching pink satin heels. Her sleek blonde bob had grown out over the last few months and now brushed her shoulders. She tilted her head and a pair of drop diamond earrings sparkled even in the dim patio light.

"It's so good to see you." She inhaled a whiff of Rox's floral perfume as she tucked her chin over Rox's bare shoulder. "I didn't even know you were coming by," Alex added, pulling back from her friend with a furtive expression.

"I didn't either," Rox admitted then cast her eyes to the horizon where a few premature fireworks had erupted into the skyline.

"I can't believe you remembered," Alex murmured.

When Alex had left Botswana, she and Rox had promised that they would spend New Year's Eve together no matter what. A pact to ensure that the bond of their friendship stayed alive—no matter what else had changed in their lives.

"Every year, Alex," Rox said and pulled her into another solid hug.

That was when Alex noticed the fresh tears springing from her eyes and the slump of her usual perky shoulders.

"What is it?" Alex asked, alarmed. "Are you okay? Is it Nic?"

"Let's go downstairs." Rox's voice shook, and an alarm resounded through Alex's consciousness.

As Alex followed Rox to the main floor, cold dread seeped first through her feet, then up and up until it gripped her around the waist. Nic was waiting for them in the kitchen, frantically scrolling through his phone, his typical cheer completely absent, having been replaced by quiet melancholy. He glanced up when they entered the room and wrapped his long arms around them simultaneously like a pair of dolls.

Alex could smell the grief. It was palpable, like a shroud thrown over them. Her pulse slowed so dramatically that she thought it might stop, and the even voice that came from her lips sounded foreign.

"What happened?"

Nic cleared his throat, his thyroid cartilage bobbing up and down erratically like the words were stuck there, strangling him.

"I got a call from Ian's dad. He was notified that there was some kind of premature blast at the mining site in Mongolia. A faulty fuse of some kind that made the explosion happen a day earlier than planned."

"Was anyone injured?" Alex's blood rushed through her head.

"George sent a crew to examine the wreckage, and they found someone named Tony Chen. He was too far gone by the time they got to him."

Alex's brain skipped backward to Ian's smooth voice on the phone this morning: *Tony and I are checking things out before we leave.*

"Ian was with him."

A silent wail grew inside her chest until it blocked out every other sensory input. She couldn't see or hear or feel the floor beneath her feet.

"I know," said Nic. "They haven't found him."

"So, he could be...he could still be..." Alex gulped.

"Yes, absolutely," Rox said, tears freely running down her perfectly rouged cheeks. "And we should hope for the best."

The trio huddled in Ian's living room, Nic and Rox under a blanket on the couch and Alex tucked into the leather club chair, knees pressed into her chin and eyes glued to the flatscreen television hung on one wall. BBC News was providing exclusive coverage of the mining accident and the unknown whereabouts of Britain's most beloved reformed playboy.

Every so often, a glossy photograph of Ian would flash onto the screen, his face always captured in a smirk as if he was sharing a private joke with the camera. A woman's smooth undulating voice erupted from the television speakers amid the background of an aerial view of a pile of rock surrounded by all-terrain vehicles, their blue lights flashing in the mist.

"Tragedy struck in northern Mongolia yesterday when a premature blast occurred at a mining site belonging to the Devall

Corporation and claimed the life of engineer Anthony Chen. Fortunately, no other workers were injured. However, well-known businessman and chair of the Devall Foundation, Ian Devall, has yet to be found."

Although Alex remained perfectly still on the outside, her mind hummed with hive-like activity. Was it even possible that Ian was alive? Had he been far enough away from the blast that he was injured but survived? Could he have been found and taken to a local hospital where he was unconscious and unable to communicate?

A list of potential injuries scrolled through her brain like a ticker-tape—long bone fractures, head injury, pneumothorax, crush injuries, splenic laceration. All of which were potentially survivable if proper medical care could be delivered. Timeliness was everything in trauma.

Alex stared at the layer of snow covering the Mongolian steppe. Hypothermia was devastating to someone with traumatic injuries. It induced shock, acting as an anticoagulant so that patients continued to bleed from the inside out.

Misplaced images of medical school flashed into view. During her trauma rotation, she worked at the county hospital, a place her friends had referred to as the "world's receptacle for all human suffering." It was where she had learned how to shove a chest tube into the victims of gunshot wounds and place splints on complex fractures. It was where she pushed an innumerable number of stretchers down poorly lit hallways to the CT scanner and sat with the on-call radiologist who pointed out the white blotches of intracranial hemorrhage caused by the blunt force trauma of a car accident.

The shrill ring of Nic's phone interrupted the silence, and Alex's intestines clenched reflexively. Nic put it to his ear before it could ring again as Rox dug her manicured nails into his other forearm.

"Hello?"

Alex strained to hear the voice on the other end of the phone, her knuckles turning white while she gripped the blanket.

"Okay. I'll let her know." *Click.*

Alex stared at Nic, steeling herself for whatever might exit his mouth.

"That was George. He's in the air on his way to the site."

He looked over at Alex, his green eyes solemn and tender.

"He said to tell you that a team is combing the area. If Ian is alive somewhere, they'll find him."

He set his jaw in determination, the same face Alex had seen him use while losing a football match. She wished finding Ian only took sheer force of will. They had enough in this room to find him a million times over.

"What about calling all the local hospitals? He might have been taken to Ulaanbaatar," Alex proposed.

She knew that UB had the only trauma hospital in the entire country. Seemingly relieved to have a new focus, Rox leaped to her feet and snatched her phone from her purse.

"Come on." She motioned to Alex. "Let's go upstairs. I can help you make a list. We'll call every single hospital in the entire country if we have to."

They sprawled out on Ian's oversized bed with a map of Mongolia pulled up on Alex's laptop screen with every single hospital annotated by a green hatch mark. Rox furiously scribbled in a notebook procured from Alex's shoulder bag while Alex clicked on each green mark in turn to find the contact information. After a full half an hour of clicking, they had compiled a list of thirteen hospitals within a geographic radius of two hundred miles, including all the hospitals in UB, that might have admitted an unidentified John Doe with multisystem trauma.

Alex had scrutinized the website of the nonprofit she had worked with in UB a few years ago on a congenital heart surgery mission. They had an excellent section for commonly used phrases in Mongolian that unfortunately did not include how to say, "Did you happen to admit a patient from a mining accident?"

Rox held out her phone. "Do you want to start calling or should I?"

Alex hesitated and then accepted the phone. "I'll do it," she stammered. "Thank you, Rox. I'm so grateful that I don't have to go through this alone."

Tears filled Alex's eyes for the first time that evening, and she choked down a sob. Across the menagerie of scattered papers and electronic devices, Rox pulled her into a hug.

"You're never alone, sweetie, and I'm so sorry—"

Her voice cracked like an icy river that had just seen the first glimpse of spring. "I'm so sorry," she said again, pulling back to wipe the streak of mascara running down one cheek, "that I ever made you feel like you were."

Alex nodded and used her palm to wipe her tears. "I'm sorry too. Sorry for everything," she sniffled. "You are my elephant."

"I'm your what?" A hint of amusement curled Rox's lips.

"Elephant," Alex repeated. "Female elephants...they bond for life."

A wave of emotion washed over Rox's elegant face, and her lips trembled as she nodded then cracked a sideways smile.

"Only your brain would feel the need to add a bit of animal trivia to the moment. Now start hitting some digits."

Rox squeezed her hand tightly as Alex shakily entered the country code for Mongolia.

An hour later, they had dialed twelve hospitals with one to go. Alex had saved the best for last, the largest hospital in UB, and the most likely place a smaller hospital would send a trauma patient that needed higher-level care.

"Hello...I need to speak with the nurse manager."

"I can help you," said a smooth voice in perfect English.

Alex's heart soared, and she struggled to speak slowly.

"I am looking for a man who was brought in with injuries from an accident. He has dark hair and blue eyes, and a tattoo on his forearm," she added quickly.

"Let me check with the registrar."

Alex held her breath, her eyes flicking to Rox, who held one hand over her mouth to stifle her emotions. After what seemed like a short eternity, the phone connection clicked, and the woman was back.

"We have a man meeting that description. Are you family?"

Alex had no breath for words, and she struggled to croak out a response. "Yes...I'm his...wife."

Rox cocked one shapely brow.

"Hold, please."

Rox erupted in questions, and Alex waved a hand to shush her while she pressed the phone receiver into her ear cartilage. One breath...two breaths...three...and then a man's gravelly voice came through the speaker.

"Hello?"

"Ian?" Alex shouted through tears, and Rox nearly fell off the bed as she scrambled to her knees.

"No, this is David...David O'Malley. Who is this?"

Alex's heart plummeted into the depths of an endless, dark void.

"I was looking for someone. My...husband," Alex said slowly. "When they put me through to you, I thought you might be him. He was injured in a mining accident yesterday and—" She paused, unsure why she was babbling to a perfect stranger.

"Oh, I heard about that. I'm terribly sorry, love. What a tragedy."

Alex swallowed and found that she had no more words. No more oxygen molecules to devote to the metabolic demand of emotion. No more anything. She pressed end while he was still in mid-sentence.

TWENTY-FIVE

One week passed. Then two. Then three, with each day only a slightly different version of the one before. Ian's dad called every morning with an update on how many square miles the search team had covered and how many hospitals he had personally visited to look for Ian and leave contact information in case he showed up there.

After three weeks, the search team called it quits since it was unlikely that anyone could survive alone in the tundra with injuries and zero supplies. Gradually the rubble was being cleared from the blast site, but it would be months before all of it would be removed to reveal whatever horrors it encased. Alex refused to believe that Ian was buried under a mountain of jagged rock. It wasn't likely anyway. Even Tony hadn't been anywhere near the actual explosion but had been struck in the head with a high-velocity projectile.

Alex moved through her days methodically: answer phone, return emails, put food into mouth and chew, perform basic hygiene, and repeat. Dr. K had called and offered her as much time off as she needed, and Tim had called a few times, but she hadn't had the energy to call him back. She had returned his worried text messages to ensure him that she was okay. But she was far from okay.

When Janie had called in a terrible fit of sobs, Alex had spent an hour reassuring her with false hope so that she didn't worry herself into an emergency room visit. And every night, she and Rox stayed up well past midnight dialing various hospitals. Sometimes a repeat of the original thirteen and sometimes venturing outside the geographic zone around the mining site. Only when her eyes closed of their own accord, forcing her brain to disconnect from the outside world, did she sleep.

Morning time was sacred. The first thirty seconds of every day when particles of sunlight shone through Ian's bedroom window and she believed that all of this was a bad dream. She expected to roll over to find Ian snoring lightly beside her, his lips full, his face in its most peaceful state.

This morning, Rox's indelicate sleep talking had woken her, and Alex slipped out of bed, silently making her way downstairs to start the fancy Italian coffee machine that sat on the corner of the kitchen counter. Espresso had become their drug as she, Rox, and Nic had hunkered down in Ian's flat to await any tidbit of news. Alex had packed her things three different times, intending to be on the next flight from London to Ulaanbaatar, but Rox had talked her out of it. If a swarm of ex-military hires couldn't find Ian, what hope did she have?

When she made it downstairs, Nic was already up, dressed in a tracksuit and speaking in low tones over the phone as he nursed a mug of steaming coffee. Alex mechanically opened the refrigerator and removed a carton of eggs and began cracking them into a bowl.

"That was George," Nic offered when he hung up the phone.

"What did he say?" Alex continued breaking eggs, watching the shells split apart and the golden drops collect in a puddle at the bottom of the bowl.

"He's back in London."

Alex nodded and blinked rapidly to quell the tears. If Ian's dad was back in London, then it meant he had given up searching and he believed Ian was gone.

Alex furrowed her brow. "I want to go see him."

She began whisking the eggs, pouring her emotion into a silver tool that swirled through the viscous sun.

"We can take you today," announced Rox, who was simultaneously yawning and twisting her hair up into a wayward topknot.

She floated down the stairs in matching pink silk pajamas, looking more like a page from the Victoria's Secret catalog than the sleep-deprived best friend of a girl who had just lost the love of her life.

Alex nodded graciously and dumped the eggs into a warm pan where, after a faint sizzle, the edges immediately began to set.

"Did the search and rescue team find anything at all?" Alex asked, gripping the porcelain teacup in her palms to extract warmth from the searing caramel-colored liquid within.

George Devall put his cup to his lips and sipped loudly. He looked tired with a haggard countenance that couldn't quite be covered up by a white shock of well-groomed hair and a neatly trimmed beard. The lines around his brown eyes had deepened into well-defined grooves, and his hands trembled ever so slightly as he lowered the teacup to its matching saucer. Winston and Clementine, a pair of usually lively Jack Russell Terriers, rested at their master's feet, their brown and white heads flush with the hardwood floor as if they too were weighed down by the atmosphere of grief.

"I am afraid not," he answered.

"There has to be another option. Something we haven't thought of."

"We searched the area ten times over. The hospitals. Every ger within a hundred miles."

"It doesn't make sense. He wasn't even supposed to be there. Why would he have been near the blast?"

"I haven't a clue, but that seems to be the only explanation."

The only explanation for why they couldn't find him. Because he was still there...buried under a pile of rubble.

"I won't give up. I can't. Not until we know for sure."

"Neither will I," he said and reached for his drink, not the tea he had been sipping but the glass of bourbon next to it. "We'll keep searching for as long as it takes."

George Devall's eyes stared into a time and place that Alex couldn't see. She took that as her cue to leave, joining Nic and Rox, who loitered in the foyer. The ride back to London was solemn, as if the purposeful energy of the last few weeks had been spent, leaving only heavy grief in its place.

Alex immediately retreated to the shower when they arrived at Ian's brownstone, relishing in the scalding temperature that was endearingly painful. Somehow the somatic pain soothed her because it manifested how she felt on the inside.

When she trudged down to the kitchen in her black sweatpants and damp hair, Rox and Nic had ordered pizza and were busily opening the box lids and sliding slices onto dinner plates. Nic opened the bottle of bourbon—Ian's special bourbon that Alex had left on the kitchen counter. For the past three weeks it had held up the edge of an unopened birthday card. The smell of the amber liquid wafted through the air as the particles aerosolized when they splashed against the bottom of a glass. Nic held his drink aloft.

"To Ian," he choked, and Rox slid a protective arm around his waist. "Gone but never forgotten."

He swallowed the entire glass in one gulp, the strap muscles of his neck bulging with tension.

Ian's voice came unbidden into Alex's head, a memory stirred by the scent of bourbon and longing. *I may be leaving, but I'm not going anywhere.* He had uttered those words to her on a dusty Gaborone airstrip when their story was just beginning. He wasn't gone. He couldn't be. He still felt too real. She could still smell his scent on the t-shirts in his top drawer. Her skin still tingled where he had last touched her. The taste of bourbon and promises still lingered on her lips.

Her doctor brain accepted reality. Based on the circumstances, survival was unlikely. Her heart, however, continued to press forward in beautiful hope...for a miracle. She suddenly felt desperate to give Ian a placeholder in their reality. A substance to his absence. She poured a half glass of bourbon and tried to stare through it at her friends on the other side.

"Did you guys know that once Ian served me bourbon in a Star Wars glass?"

Rox quirked her face as if Alex had lost her mind.

Maybe she had.

"And also in a red plastic cup." She smiled at the memory. "I accused him of having bourbon stashed all over the planet."

Nic filled his glass almost to the brim as a slow smile spread into his chiseled cheekbones.

"We were on a trek through the Andes one summer when Ian was in grad school. We were young and stupid and didn't bring near enough water." Nic handed his glass to Rox, whose glossy lips took it with ginger acceptance. "We spent the last day surviving off the bottle of bourbon Ian *happened* to find in the bottom of his backpack." Nic shook his head and chuckled.

"Why bourbon?" Rox mused, a smile twisting up the corner of her mouth.

"The sex appeal," both Alex and Nic said at the exact same moment and then erupted in a fit of laughter.

"Our entire lives, women just fell over themselves trying to be near him," said Nic. "Except for you, Alex. I remember the first night he met you. I met up with him at the bar later, and he was...different. A spark was in his eyes. And for once, he completely ignored every female within striking distance."

"He didn't even know me then," Alex retorted, her throat burning with the continued onslaught of bourbon.

"Oh yes, he did."

Alex glanced up, a complete wave of shock settling over her features. "What?"

"Ian always did his research. He knew exactly who you were, where you were from, and what you did at PM."

"He never told me. I acted like an idiot when we met."

"I think he used the phrase 'awkward in the sexiest way possible.'"

Laughter tried to escape around the lump forming in the back of Alex's throat. Rox tittered between sips of bourbon.

"He had Alex all kinds of twisted up...in the worst and best way," Rox said.

"He wanted you from the first moment he laid eyes on you and he never stopped. He needed someone like you in his life," Nic added.

"He still does," Alex whispered.

The words left her lips unintentionally, but it made them no less true. Rox peered at her with concern as an awkward silence ensued. As much as Alex loved Rox and Nic, they would never understand the abyss of pain that waited for her when she believed without a doubt that Ian was gone and never coming back. Even a crack in her fortitude would rip open a gaping wound that would never heal. It would be the death of her, and this time, she didn't know if she could rise from these ashes.

Alex tucked a strand of hair behind one ear before she bent down to insert the slim glinting end of a needle into the crook of a little boy's elbow. A torrent of burgundy blood flowed into the corresponding syringe, and Alex exhaled with satisfaction as the boy squirmed, causing her to tighten her grip on his arm.

"All done," she said, extracting the needle when she had enough.

She deposited the syringe in the cooler next to her and then grabbed a Snoopy bandage from the box next to it.

"You did an amazing job!" she exclaimed, winning a small smile as she applied the dressing. "I'll see you next time."

He was the very last patient of the day in their mobile clinic in a remote village two hours south of Gaborone. Shelo, now a full-fledged nurse at PM, had already packed up most of the supplies into the truck. Alex had spent more days than not making regular visits to the outlying villages to deliver medications, draw blood samples, or perform testing for people who rarely made it more than five miles from their homeland. The hospital had been too confining. She preferred the fresh air, the new scenery, and the freedom of being on the road. She wanted to practice medicine where she felt most at home—in a field of grass.

Spending time in the villages reminded Alex of being a child in Texas. When she was growing up, she loved roaming the fields so much, her mom was convinced that one morning she would wake up completely transformed into a horse. By that time, she had been pretending she was a horse for the better part of third grade, galloping during recess, eating only oatmeal and salad, raising her head to sniff the wind while she practiced being in the correct lead around a corner. Janie's friend from church had discovered her obsession with all things equine when she found Alex doodling wild ponies all over her sermon notes one Sunday.

Terry had let her hang out at the barn, providing a few basic horsemanship lessons in exchange for small chores. Alex groomed the five horses she kept for showing, washed an endless pile of saddle pads, and swept the sawdust from the barn's interior. The chores had never felt like work because Alex loved everything about the barn—the sound of a hoof pawing at the hay strewn over her stall, the sweet musk of horse, the thin layer of dirt that coated everything, including every inch of her by the time she left after school every day. Terry recognized that Alex was a natural, with hands that were easy on the reins and a horse's tender mouth, a steady seat, and a quiet confidence that horses responded to. After a few years, Alex became adept at riding all the horses at the barn, but George was her favorite.

He was the biggest horse in the barn—a seventeen-hand chestnut Thoroughbred that had failed to make it at the racetrack and had been turned into a classy jumper. Classy but near retirement, which meant he only wanted to perform when he felt like it. But on the days when the sun shone brightly and a crispness entered the air,

Alex would take him out on a loose rein and let him fly.

"Dr. Alex?"

Alex realized Shelo was peering down at her curiously as she was arranging ice packs over the blood samples.

"I'm so sorry, Shelo. What did you ask me?"

"Are we finished for the day?"

"Yes, I think so."

Shelo parted her lips, painted berry red today with matching fingernails, her brown eyes shifting to a patch of grass next to Alex.

"I am very sorry about your—" she paused, her brows knit together to summon a vocabulary word, "loss."

Alex nodded without speaking, accustomed to the apologies, condolences, and hushed whispers she had endured since arriving back in Botswana two weeks ago. Ian had been missing for five weeks but she still believed he could be alive somewhere. The empty landmass in northern Mongolia was vast and filled with nomadic clusters of people hunkered down for the winter with their sheep.

George Devall messaged her every day with the progress of the new team he had hired to search for Ian. They hadn't found him...but neither had the crew at the blast site.

"Thanks. We're still hoping he's out there."

And there it was. The same expression. This time on a different face with high cheekbones and long doe lashes, surprise mixed with concern topped with an overwhelming dollop of pity. Dr. K had looked at her similarly, his eyes bulging over the top of his spectacles when he had cornered her outside the small hospital cafe. He had handed her a foam cup, modestly warm from its contents of red bush tea and asked, "Can we sit for a moment?"

Alex had been in a hurry to return to the pediatric ward to check on a patient with pneumonia, but she had acquiesced and sat on the nearest bench. He had sipped his tea noisily before speaking, taking time for his train of thoughts to come to a stop at the station.

"We have not had a chance to talk since—"

"Since I got back from London?" Alex finished.

"How are you, Alex?"

Her well-rehearsed speech began as easily as hitting play on a song.

"I'm fine. So far so good, I guess. We're still searching the area. There's a lot of land, and it's really cold, so the progress is slow, but we're hoping for a good outcome."

For once, Dr. K had not been able to concoct a reply. He simply stared at her while he sipped his tea with the same expression that Shelo now bore. Like she had completely lost her mind.

By the time Alex finished unloading the blood samples at PM and checked on a few patients, the sun was setting behind a halo of pink clouds. She made it to Mary Lou's in record time to pick up McCartney, who scrambled out of the gap between the front door and Mary Lou's silhouette.

"Come on, boy," she called as she wrenched open the passenger side door.

George phoned her every night with an update, and she didn't want to miss his call.

"You got a bee in your bonnet?" called Mary Lou in her gravelly voice.

"No. Maybe. I have some things to do at home," Alex answered.

"I made a pot of potato soup if you want some."

Alex couldn't remember the last time she had been hungry.

"No, thank you. I'm okay."

"You're gettin' awfully thin," Mary Lou said.

Alex shrugged and shut the door behind a wriggling McCartney.

"It's hard...losing someone."

Alex whirled on her, a vortex of anger surging from her middle and right out of her mouth.

"I haven't lost anyone. Why does everyone just assume that Ian is gone? We have a plan. We have hope. I'm not giving up on him."

Alex balled up her fists at her sides and cast her eyes upward where the sky had just begun to turn dark. When she looked back at Mary Lou, she was shocked by the hardness in her gaze, the immobile stare devoid of sympathy that she usually received.

"Well, he's not here, is he? Which means that wherever he is, he's gone. You deal with it your way...but don't lose yourself in the process."

She turned around and strode into her house, her flowery kimono flapping behind her.

"Damn it," Alex swore when she looked down at her phone and noted two missed calls from George. She quickly pressed redial but was sent straight to his voicemail.

As McCartney whined and paced the hardwood floors of her bedroom, Alex traded the phone for a red marker and began shading the inside of a circle drawn southwest of the mining site, which was the most recent location of the search and rescue team.

Dime-sized red circles dotted a map of Mongolia hung on Alex's wall like an eruption of measles. The diameter extended far beyond the epicenter of the blast at this point. George had told her that the team was combing the countryside from ger to ger with an interpreter and Ian's photograph, hoping to glean any information. Someone like Ian would be sure to stand out, even if he was injured and even if he couldn't communicate.

Alex clung to this last shred of hope that was like a spider's silk thread, a mere wisp yet formidable. She couldn't let it go. Lately, it seemed she and George were the only ones holding on this tightly. She rushed home every day to hear any bit of news, and he never disappointed. His smooth voice filled the phone receiver with legitimate hope in the form of information.

McCartney curled up in the corner, aggressively licking his front paw, and when Alex stooped down to examine it further, he emitted a sudden yelp.

"Hey boy, what's going on?"

She turned his paw over to reveal the stub end of a rosebush thorn protruding from the soft pad of his foot.

"Wait here," she commanded, but as she edged into the bathroom, McCartney followed, limping and whining with every step. Alex rifled through the drawer until she found her best pair of tweezers. In one swift motion, she pinned McCartney's russet paw between her knees and plucked the thorn out in its entirety.

McCartney's yelp filled the small space, resounding off the bare walls before he turned to apply his own salve to the paw in the form of his tongue. Alex smiled. It reminded her of the time she had removed an acacia thorn from Ian's hand during a trip to the Kalahari. It had been the first time they had truly been alone in the tender early stages of getting to know one another. There were a lot of firsts that night.

Alex could still describe every detail of their first kiss. It was wild and magical and terrifying and perfect. Something that perfect couldn't disappear from the world like it never existed.

Tugging open the vanity door, she began fishing around in a plastic box for a tube of antibiotic ointment. Instead, her hand closed on a cylindrical object wrapped in plastic, and she pulled it out. She frowned as she stared at the woman's hygiene product and began flipping a mental calendar in reverse. She had always been irregular, blaming a stressful career or overdoing it on the running, but this time it had been a while. At least before Thanksgiving.

Her veins turned to ice, and her fingers shook as she began to scroll through her phone.

"Hello?"

"Sam, I need your help."

TWENTY-SIX

Alex's knees shook as she huddled under a thin sheet, naked from the waist down while she waited for Sam to finish up a C-section in the operating room. The room was dark and windowless, the only light coming from a hurricane lantern perched atop a stack of medical journals.

No one used this space anymore. It had become a landing place for mismatched furniture and donated supplies, like the Room of Requirement in Harry Potter. A pile of suction canisters filled up the corner, and one entire wall was lined with boxes brimming with chest tube kits and various types of suture material. Dusty medical textbooks covering every topic from tropical diseases to pediatric dermatology were stuffed into a set of bookshelves.

The couch on which Alex reclined had been shoved into a shadowy corner. Sam had taken the liberty of covering it with a set of fresh sheets before barking Alex a few instructions: "Strip from the waist down and wait here until I come back with the ultrasound machine." The transition from doctor to patient, from in to out of control, from the clarity of decision to something that resembled Schrodinger's cat, had frayed Alex's nerves into an unrecognizable mess.

A lifetime of emotions had coursed through her on the drive to the hospital—disbelief, fear, and finally, a spark of excitement. An excitement that felt out of place yet completely normal. Her life had been devoid of anything so perfectly miraculous that she couldn't help but wonder every time she felt the slightest twinge in her abdomen. Could it be possible? Would she lose Ian only to gain a baby? His baby. Their baby.

Sitting there in the dark, she let her imagination run wild and picture herself with a dark-haired blue-eyed baby perched on her lap, fisting her hair and giggling at a stuffed monkey. A little piece of Ian that she would always have, no matter what happened.

Sam banged through the door. "Sorry, that took so long. My grandmother sews faster than that med student."

"You have someone new?"

"Yeah, Kate left at the end of December, and they sent me some total jerkwad know-it-all from Boston."

She rolled her eyes and made a lousy attempt at a Boston accent, and Alex released a faint smile. Sam shed her white coat, tossing it on the back of the couch, and plugged in the ultrasound machine, green lettering immediately flashing across the screen. She still wore her surgical cap, a few spiky pieces of ginger hair peeking out of the back.

"May I?" she asked, her tone professional and emotionless, as she pointed to the square of unoccupied couch next to Alex.

"Sure." Alex scooted over to give her room.

Sam pulled the sheet down to Alex's lower pelvis and palpated gently before squirting a thin film of gel below her belly button. Alex remarked at the extreme cleanliness of her hands, her neat cuticles and finely trimmed nails rounded to perfection without a speck of dirt or grime in sight. Surgeons always had the most perfect hands.

"So—" Sam drawled.

Alex braced herself for whatever extract Sam's sharp tongue was about to fling her way.

"The billionaire boyfriend knocks you up and then goes and gets himself killed. What a douche."

The barbed comment unexpectedly struck a chord of humor with Alex, and a tiny snort escaped her nose. Sam's mouth quirked as she placed the probe low in Alex's pelvis, dragging it side to side then up and down. Alex scrutinized the grainy screen, trying to discern a lifeform from the shades of gray that evolved with every swipe of Sam's hand. Sam hit a button to emit a Doppler signal, a maneuver that would detect the presence of the tiniest of hearts no bigger than her fingertip. Alex held her breath until she heard a faint *whoosh-whoosh*. As her heart rate spiked, so did the frequency of the noise, and she realized that she was hearing her own heart pushing blood into her arteries.

Sam scanned a few minutes more before she stuffed the probe back into its holder. "You're not pregnant."

Alex nodded, feeling immensely idiotic for even considering the possibility.

"You're probably just irregular from all the stress," Sam clipped.

Alex nodded again, shutting her eyes to stave off the hot tears desperately clamoring for a way out of her lids. How ridiculous to mourn something that you never had. To cry over a baby that never was and never would be.

Tears streamed silently over her cheeks, carrying the anguish of the last few weeks. The tumultuous roller coaster that had become her life's trajectory. And then arms circled her in the world's most awkward...and most appreciated hug.

"I'm here in the lobby. Come on down, and we can walk over together."

Alex finished putting in her diamond earrings and smoothed her hand down the front of her navy sheath dress. Her complexion left something to be desired. It was pale and haunted. Her cheekbones had become a touch more prominent, and the dark circles under her eyes a shade more purple over the last few weeks.

"Okay. Be there in a minute."

She pressed end on the call, Tim's elated face disappearing from view. It would be good to see him. More than good.

When she descended the stairs to the Four Seasons hotel in Austin, Texas, and let him engulf her in an embrace, it was a balm to her soul that she desperately needed. Like the sun had suddenly emerged over the horizon and chased away the night. He pushed away, holding her at an arm's distance, and scrutinized her appearance.

"You look like hell. How've you been?" he finished tenderly.

She shrugged and glanced over his shoulder at the mounted longhorns adorning the wall above the hotel bar.

"Worse than the time I had multisystem trauma in Haiti during an earthquake?"

She smiled the briefest smile at her half-hearted attempt at a joke. Tim's eyes said it all as they filled with a concern that made her grief deepen. He tried to hide it behind his usual wit.

"I have just what you need," he said, wrapping long arms around her shoulders, "an afternoon filled with research talks on the lung microbiome and genetic heterogeneity in sepsis."

Alex gave a light snort. "Sounds perfect."

She and Tim settled into the back of the largest room at the Austin Convention Center in fold-out burnt orange chairs. Alex sighed and began jotting notes to herself on the Society of Critical Care Medicine-issued notepad she had received in her welcome packet. Focusing her willpower into her ballpoint pen, she scribed interesting points made by each speaker. Distracting her grief away via work-related activities had always been her fallback. It had always worked. Until now.

Every few minutes, a wave of grief would surge and then ebb, like a midnight ocean right before a storm. Since the accident, she felt like an intangible spicket was twisting on inside her, emptying the tank of her emotions. A drop here. A gush there. Until she barely felt anything at all. A voice droned behind the podium, and another set of digital slides with a blue background flashed on the screen.

"Recently, there have been several discoveries in inflammatory biomarkers that predict mortality from acute respiratory distress syndrome."

As her lids began to droop, Alex shifted again in her seat and stretched out her legs that had been tucked under her chair. Tim's long lower extremities filled the entirety of the space between their chairs and the row in front of them. Her shins fit perfectly underneath his calves and served as her only source of warmth in the otherwise frigid conference room. Her eyes flicked to the clock, then back to her scrawled notes, then to her phone, then over to Tim, whose soft brown eyes deviated in her direction. She made a subtle movement with her head toward the exit, not expecting him to see it, but he did.

At the sound of polite applause signaling the start of the next talk, Tim rose to his feet with a feigned look of importance and began striding toward freedom written in bright red neon. Alex scrambled to follow, dropping her notebook once and her shoulder bag twice before weaving through the disgruntled row of physicians in their business casual attire.

When the afternoon Texas sun struck her face, and the door closed with a resounding bang behind her, the emptiness waned the tiniest bit. Tim stood on a street corner a few feet away, his gangly arm held aloft while a yellow cab zipped up to the empty curb in front of him. As Alex approached, he swung open the door.

"Where to, Dr. Wilde?"

Alex slipped into the car, pressing the back of her head against the bench seat and inhaling the scent of tacos and hospitality that was her home state.

"Anywhere I can sit outside and drown myself in a margarita and eat my body weight in guacamole."

"You heard her," Tim said to the driver. "Do your worst."

The driver smiled and pulled into a steady stream of feeder road traffic.

The day was uncharacteristically warm for a Texas winter. The best and the worst thing about Texas weather: its propensity to do exactly what it wanted when it wanted. The driver had dropped them at a shabby pink building in downtown Austin that didn't look like much from the front, but when the hostess led them to an outdoor patio, Alex thrilled at the site of an empty table painted bright turquoise partly shaded by an oak tree with cafe lights strung above it. Alex picked the chair nestled in a bright spot of afternoon sun and kicked off her heels before collapsing into its metal frame.

Moments later, a fresh basket of tortilla chips ringed with three types of salsa in red melamine bowls and a margarita the size only found in the Lone Star state stared at her from the center of the table. The first sip was the perfect blend of chill and tang and salt with a background hint of tequila. She existed in a moment of perfect silence and let the tequila drown out almost two months' worth of sorrow. The only feelings she had left were painful ones. She would rather not feel anything at all, if only for one night.

Tim twisted the cap off a second beer. "I'm really sorry..."

"Not tonight," Alex interrupted.

"You don't want to talk about it? Because if you do, that's okay." His molten brown eyes searched hers fervently.

"I don't," she replied evenly. "Maybe someday but not tonight."

He nodded and shifted his gaze to the label of his beer.

"Tell me something about life in Atlanta. Anything. Everything."

A wan smile crossed her lips right before the next swig of her drink burned the roof of her mouth with the potency of tequila.

"I got a dog," Tim said sheepishly.

"Really?" Alex narrowed her gaze. Tim had never struck her as the pet-loving type. "What kind?"

"A rescue. A Great Dane, actually. She looks like a small cow."

Alex suppressed a giggle.

"It was Cara's idea. She thought it would be nice for me to have something to come home to every night."

Alex maintained a straight face even though her eyes threatened to roll upward. After meeting Cara during her brief trip to Atlanta with Mercy, Alex was sure that the "something" Cara wanted Tim to come home to was *her*.

She settled deeper into her seat and listened to Tim babble about the adventures of puppy ownership and then the challenges at work in the pediatric ICU and balancing all of that with a social life. Taking a mental foray into Tim's life proved to be a much-needed distraction from her own, and she barely noticed when the waiter slid a second margarita in front of her.

"I was working on Christmas Eve, and I ran home to check on her. That dog was laid out on the couch, up to her neck in a box of leftover pizza." He laughed deeply and took a swig of his beer. "She doesn't like Cara. Every time we try to sit down, she squeezes right between us. And forget about Cara sleeping next to me."

Alex raised her eyebrows. She hadn't realized that Tim and Cara had become that serious.

"She's just jealous and wants you all to herself." Alex winked at his face, whose features had blurred over the last hour. "Who wouldn't?" she added, and Tim cocked a brow.

The words had barely left her lips before Alex chastised herself for such a careless comment. Tequila had always loosened her inhibitions, but this was uncharted territory. She had never let Tim believe they were anything more than great friends, even when he had kissed her last year. She had told him that it would always be Ian. But now, a voice from the dark corners of her mind whispered, Ian was gone.

Her straw slurped the last traces of margarita from the bottom of her glass as night descended on them. Alex rose, grabbing her shoes from under her chair but not bothering to put them on her feet. She motioned for Tim to follow.

"Let's get out of here."

As they strolled arm in arm through downtown Austin, the city was just coming to life as young professionals poured out of their office buildings and apartments to join the Friday fray. Alex's head snuggled next to Tim's muscular arm for support. She was in a dangerous place. A place where consequences did not exist. Where the only thing that mattered was soothing the massive ache inside. And right now, Tim was her opioid. He was warm and real—actual skin she could touch, arms that could embrace her, and a voice that lived outside her own head.

His mouth was moving, and she laughed even though she couldn't discern his words. When they walked past an open doorway that led to a dark, cavernous interior, a few music notes filtered to their spot on the sidewalk.

"Let's go in here."

Alex grabbed Tim's hand and led him into the dimly light bar where a band was assembling on an elevated platform before a gathering crowd. Pushing through the throng, she headed toward an empty leather couch, where they collapsed as the first chords of an acoustic guitar vibrated through the air.

The band was good, technically talented with a strong lead singer who fulfilled the look and sound of Americana singer-songwriter. Alex settled into the leather cushions with a beer and lost herself in the lyrics.

"Let me kiss you one more time before I have to forget you," crooned the singer on stage.

She could feel Tim's eyes on her. She closed her lids and swayed to the rocking beat. Or maybe the room was swaying and she wasn't moving at all. When she felt a hand on her bare knee, she didn't think twice about taking the warm, strong fingers and interlacing them with her own. She needed this. To feel close to another human. Just for a little while.

An arm descended on her shoulders, and she didn't pull away. Instead, she nestled in closer. She had never realized how clean Tim smelled, like fresh laundry left out in the sunshine. Her head lolled onto his chest, and she could hear the rapid thumping of his heart through his button-down.

Something propelled her forward—a desire to lose herself in any pleasurable sensation that could make her momentarily forget her tragic life. She picked up her head, and his lips were right there, beckoning her. Enough tequila made everything seem like a good idea. Her top lip brushed his bottom one as her pulse thrummed along with the beat of the music.

"Alex," Tim whispered, the movement causing his bottom lip to drift across hers.

She tried to snake her arms around his neck, but he caught them and returned them to his chest.

"Alex," he repeated more firmly.

She halted and blinked without speaking.

"There was a time when I would have given anything...*anything*...to have a go with you like this." He flitted his eyes to the floor nervously, and his chest heaved a sigh. "But I'm with Cara. I really like her, and I think we might actually have something. A future."

The cold sting of reality smacked her in the face, and she struggled to unwind herself from Tim.

"Alex, what are you doing?"

"I don't know. I'm...I'm so sorry, Tim."

Picking up her heels, she began striding for the door before the fountain of tears came.

"Alex, where are you going? Alex!"

When her bare feet hit the pavement, she ran before Tim could follow.

The bar was nice, upscale, and unknown to the general public. Alex had accidentally stumbled upon it while searching for a pharmacy to buy a bottle of ibuprofen. Who knew there were actual bars named "The Pharmacy"?

Sad eyes and a twenty-dollar tip to the host landed her an ideal spot on the end of a sleek granite bar where a large Diet Coke and four teeny orange tablets waited for her command to solve her oncoming migraine. She swallowed each one consecutively, a trail of bitterness extending into her esophagus. What was wrong with her?

Alex had once told Ian that she was a terrible person. Maybe it was true. She sipped her soda, truly appalled at what she had done to Tim. She had been desperate to feel something—anything—besides pain and grief but not at Tim's expense.

The bar had begun to fill with a few patrons seeking an after-dinner cocktail: women in designer mini-dresses and stilettos and men in dinner jackets and concert t-shirts or button-downs. The tantalizing notes of contemporary jazz floated through the melee. This was urban chic at its finest. Her eyes swept the room and landed on a strikingly familiar profile. She did a double take. Maybe the tequila was affecting her vision. No such luck.

Logan Paine, dressed in a navy sports coat and jeans, tipped back a martini glass at a corner table. A shock of chestnut hair flopped over on his forehead as he met her stare. Remembrance flared as a vision of him slicing oranges behind a bar in Tanzania. She had been trying to find Ian after an argument, and Logan had served her a drink while she lamented over the tragic events surrounding an attempted elephant heist.

Despite his most charming efforts in Tanzania, Alex had left Logan staring after her as she scooted off to find Ian. There was no way he would remember her.

Yet now, she observed him across the crowded room rising from his seat and making a beeline toward her spot at the bar. She averted her eyes to the floating cubes of ice in her glass of diet soda. As he slid into the seat next to her, she could smell his cologne, a woodsy scent like freshly chopped cedar.

"How about a drink, Dr. Wilde?" He emphasized the word doctor.

"I have one," Alex retorted, putting the glass rim to her lips.

"I can see that, but I bet you could use a different kind."

He motioned to the bartender, who scurried over with a flourish and plopped two Shiners down on square white napkins.

"Anything else for you, Mr. Paine?"

Logan glanced at Alex, who shook her head decisively. She watched him grasp the neck of the beer bottle and take a long draw, his neck cartilage bobbing up and down as he drank. When he was finished, he swiveled in her direction, his honey-brown eyes seeking an audience with her own.

"I heard about what happened, and, for what it's worth, I'm really sorry."

Alex turned her focus to the Shiner label and blinked against dry eyes.

"Ian never liked you," she muttered.

"Hmm. Probably because I'm better looking," Logan quipped, receiving a well-deserved snort from Alex.

A movement caught her eye, and Logan slid a hand across the bar to stroke the back of her knuckles with a gentle thumb. A completely unbidden shiver trickled down her back at the intimacy of his gesture.

"I know we don't know one another very well but—" He bit his lower lip before continuing. "You are way too beautiful to stay sad."

His words rang with sincerity, and a depth of empathy filled his eyes. "You want to...go somewhere?"

Alex looked away, but she didn't move her hand from under the soft stroking of his thumb. Something was definitely wrong with her. She had descended into madness if she was making moves on Tim and even considering spending an evening with the egocentric CEO of a travel company. She couldn't believe he had even recognized her from their brief meeting in Tanzania last summer.

"I'll go somewhere with you," Alex said evenly. All emotion drained from her face as she turned to face his gentle expression. "When hell freezes over."

His face changed from soft to lit up with amusement, and a low laugh escaped the back of his throat.

"Come on. It won't be what you expect. I promise."

She eyed him warily but slipped her hand into the one he offered and allowed herself to be led out of the pharmacy.

"I wasn't entirely prepared to go on a nature hike," Alex grumbled.

Several streets and one unmarked path later, Logan hiked ahead of her up a natural limestone staircase. The scrubby vegetation scraped against her shins as they ascended above the city, where she could appreciate the moonlight reflecting off the Colorado River.

"It's not too much farther," Logan called. "My offer to carry you still stands."

"No thanks," Alex muttered as she stumbled over a large rock.

When they emerged into a clearing, Alex could barely make out a few scattered stone picnic tables and grassy clumps. As she explored farther, following Logan to the very edge of the mini mountain they had just climbed, the view became spectacular. The orange glow of the Capitol framed by the downtown skyline on one side and the Colorado River, winding lazily through the western part of the city on the other. And above them hung more stars than she could count.

Logan turned his face toward the sky. "When I was a kid, we'd go out to my grandparent's ranch. My sister and I would climb up on the roof and just lay there under the stars. So many stars that we couldn't even count them."

Alex nodded, remembering her own childhood and her fascination with the Texas sky.

"I used to think nobody outside of Texas could see so many stars in the night sky," Logan said.

"They can't." Alex smiled, venturing nearer to the cliff's edge and taking in the exquisite panorama. In a moment, she added, "For some reason, everything seems better in Texas. The sky. The land. The—"

"Queso," Logan finished, and they both shared a laugh.

He bent down to pick something off the ground, a shape that he turned over in his hand a few times before he handed it to Alex.

"Why are you giving me a rock?"

He shrugged and began searching the ground for another one. When he found the right candidate, he lobbed it into a dramatic arc through the air before it plunged into the water, creating a cascade of ripples.

"It's just something I used to do as a kid when I needed to work things out in my head."

Alex furrowed her brows. "Throwing rocks into the water helped you achieve mental clarity?"

"Something like that." He gave her a sideways glance before tossing another one into the river. "Let's see what you got."

The smooth stone was just the right density as she weighed it in her hand. Motor memory kicked in as she extended her elbow behind her and thrust her arm forward, releasing the stone at the perfect moment so that it sailed through the air before parting the water in the middle of the river. Logan let out a low whistle.

"Didn't see that coming."

Alex bent down and picked up another one, pitching it through the air as soon as she was upright and then another and another until her chest heaved from the effort.

"See, I told you? Feel any better?"

Alex giggled hysterically. "Not really, but it's nice to know I haven't lost my throwing arm."

As she hurled the final rock over her head, her momentum carried her forward until one foot slipped on a segment of loose pebbles, and she landed in a heap right on the edge of the cliff face. Logan held out a hand, trying to stifle a chuckle, and she grabbed it.

"Thanks."

"That's what friends are for," he said, pulling her upright.

"Are we friends?"

She noticed he hadn't let go of her hand and was gently tugging her into his body.

"If you want to be."

"I don't," she whispered, right before crushing her lips to his.

It only took him a second to overcome his surprise, and he responded with a frenzy of lip ravaging. She opened her mouth wide, and he didn't hesitate to thrust his tongue inside. One taste of heat and lust. One taste to satisfy the grief monster. She had to be closer to him. The cricket song thumped in her ears, and the stars spun as she wound her arms around his neck.

"What do you want, Alex?" he asked when their lips separated for breath.

Ian. What I want is Ian. She froze into a statue, and then for the second time in one night, she started to run with no idea where she was headed.

It had started to drizzle, changing the crisp evening into a muted blur of people jostling for a position beneath the building overhangs under a halo of streetlamps. Alex didn't mind the rain. It dripped down her hair and face, carrying with it the depravity of the night and her shamefulness. For a girl who had gone her entire life with only a handful of dates, it seemed that every man within ten feet of her became sucked into her gravity. When it rained, it poured. And the only thing she felt was wet.

As she passed a halogen sign atop a glass-enclosed shop, she paused, staring at her sopping reflection. The dramatic script of the sign beckoned to her with its bright colors. If the grief monster wanted pleasure, she was going to give him pain. She pushed open the door and went inside.

TWENTY-SEVEN

Warm hands caressed her own and pulled them to even warmer lips. Her eyes fluttered open. Sunshine streamed through her hotel window, framing a face with unruly raven hair and flame blue eyes.

"Ian?"

"I've been gone for barely two months, and you're a mess." He smirked at her and bit her fingers playfully.

"How did you get here?" she asked, confused and groggy. It was impossible to make her mouth move fast enough to expel her words.

He held up one of her fingers and sucked on its tip. "Making out with Tim...again." Alex cringed inwardly. "And then spending the night with Logan Paine."

He stared at her through narrowed lids, but there was no anger in his expression. Only amusement.

"Wait, I didn't—" Alex fumbled with her words.

"Shhh. It doesn't matter. Now kiss me."

He leaned over, and she met his lips—soft luxurious lips that she would never stop kissing.

A brusque knock resounded through her head, a relentless pounding straight through her temples. She struggled to open her eyelids that were heavy with eye makeup and grime and leftover rain. She was alone. The room cast in gloom from the early morning fog. The space on the bed next to her empty.

The knock sounded again, matching the internal pounding in her head from last night's debauchery. She peered at the lily-white inside of her left forearm, where a fresh bandage lay plastered over how she had ended her night.

Smelling of tequila and shame and streaming with a fresh coat of raindrops, Alex had pushed open the door to Screamin' Demons and was met with the sound of incessant buzzing, like a hive of bees busy at work. The man at the front with a steel bar piercing through one eyebrow and ink sleeves for arms gestured toward an empty green vinyl chair in a mirrored corner.

"What will it be, love?" he said in a coarse British accent.

She hesitated for a moment and bit her lip in consternation. What was the rate of hepatitis B transmission again? He smirked and held up a notebook containing samples of his work.

"Butterfly or let me guess—Chinese characters on your lower back?"

She pushed away the heavy three-ring binder. "Can you write in Cyrillic?"

In the early morning light, Alex ripped the bandage off her arm to reveal the ink permanently etched under her first layer of skin. Small but noticeable. The letters contrasted nicely with her skin. *Ian*—written in neat Cyrillic block characters.

Pulling a sweatshirt over her head, she reluctantly schlepped to the door and opened it. Tim stood there, a bright expression on his face, proffering a steaming cup of chai tea and a brown paper bag. A smear of chocolate rested on his lower lip.

"I brought you chocolate croissants," he said, waving the bag in front of her face.

"It looks like you helped yourself to one."

Alex's lips stretched open into a smile as Tim wiped his lips on the back of his hand.

"Can I come in?"

Alex groaned but stepped aside so he could enter the room. He thrust the bag into her chest as he passed her and immediately flopped down on the bed. Her stomach grumbled, and she opened the bag to inhale the buttery contents.

"Go ahead. Eat your shame," Tim said as he reclined on a pile of pillows. Alex sighed heavily and shut the bag.

"Tim, I'm so sorry. I—"

"Listen," he interrupted, "it's not your fault that I'm completely irresistible."

Alex smiled and blinked away a few tears, but not fast enough for Tim to miss.

"Come here." He motioned for her to settle in next to him on the bed.

She sat down, keeping a decent amount of distance between them, but he pulled her into his side anyway. She rested her head on his chest, out of melancholy rather than lust. *Sans* alcohol, everything seemed like a bad idea.

"I love you," he whispered, putting his chin on top of her tangled hair.

She sucked in a breath, intending to speak, but Tim got there first.

"Don't...say anything."

"I didn't—"

"I don't even want to know what you were going to say." He hugged her tighter so that she was unable to lift her head and see his face. "I love you enough to be exactly what you need right now."

"What do I need right now?" Alex didn't know the answer to her own question.

"A friend."

Alex took the S curve just a little too quickly in her rental car, and the rear tires fishtailed on the gravel shoulder. On all sides, she was surrounded by grassy fields dotted with cedar trees and frolicking cows. Above her, the blue sky hovered like an aquamarine jewel, crystal clear and cloudless.

"Something is wrong with me," she shouted above the twangy country song on the radio.

"There's nothing wrong with you, love, except that you never learned how to grieve properly, but who has?" Rox's melodic voice emanated from the speaker on her mobile phone. "You're human and humans need other humans," she added.

"I don't," she muttered, half hoping that Rox didn't hear her.

"Yes, you do. Where are you now?"

"Somewhere between Austin and Cole's Church."

"What time is the wedding?"

"Not until four, so I have plenty of—"

Rox's picture disappeared from the face of her phone, as did all her phone bars when she rounded the next bend and slowed at a stop sign.

"Time," she finished, saying the words to the empty air.

"Searching for signal" flashed across the top of her phone. It was good to be home.

The church was decorated with delicate sprays of baby's breath and yellow roses from the local florist shop affixed to the corners of the pews with large white bows made from tulle. A lavender ribbon was wrapped around the stems, the loose ends fluttering with the breeze blowing through the open doorway. Peter stood calm and stately in the front of the church near the altar, his bald head glinting with the sun that filtered through the stained-glass windows. He was dressed in a pair of dark jeans and cowboy boots, the ensemble escalated a notch by the navy dress jacket and crisply ironed shirt he sported. A smattering of friends had gathered for the occasion. Alex spied a few ladies from church as well as Natalie's mom who blew her a kiss from the end of the fourth pew.

Natalie was supposed to be here, but she had an issue arise with the sale of a Dallas estate and had to cancel. It was just as well. Alex didn't really feel like seeing anyone, even her best girlfriend from high school. She tugged on the lace sleeve of her lavender dress. It didn't entirely extend beyond her elbow, not even close to covering up the artful ink that now decorated her forearm.

Ian. His name looked beautiful in Cyrillic, and, although it had been a rash decision borne of a night of tequila and regret, she loved seeing the reminder etched permanently underneath her skin. Her phone vibrated inside her clutch, and she fished it out.

You should have never kissed me.

Her pupils dilated as she stared at the text from Logan. She had been drunk and vulnerable and so humanly needy that it disgusted her. No one could ever replace Ian. Before she had the chance to drop the phone back into her purse, it vibrated again.

It's all I can think about.

Her mind absorbed the words, and the memory of soft lips and a rim of coppery stubble under a skyful of Texas stars paralyzed her.

"Alex?"

She whipped around. "Yes, I'm here. What do you need?"

Her mom looked stunning with her ginger hair pulled off her face, wearing a floral day dress with tiny navy flowers that complemented Peter's coat.

"I'm ready," she stated firmly, looping an arm through the space between Alex's elbow and her thorax.

To the tune of Canon in D emanating from a crackly speaker in the back of the church, Alex walked down the aisle next to her mother and deposited her in Peter's presence. Amid hushed murmuring, most likely regarding her most recent life's tragedy—that or the fresh tattoo displayed on her arm—Alex slid into the first burgundy pew. Her mom smiled, utterly enraptured by Peter's kind face and oblivious to her surroundings, including the even droning of Pastor Brian.

"And these three remain: faith, hope, and love. And the Lord's people said—"

"Amen," Alex mumbled along with the rest of the guests.

"Bow your heads with me in a prayer."

Alex closed her eyes, but all she could see was a reality that would never be. What would it have been like to marry Ian? To say yes to a future beyond her wildest dreams. To have their children. To grow old and more in love. The steel blade of grief pierced right through her heart. She didn't know how much more she could bleed.

Alex ran her fork through the white cake with the pastel buttercream flowers for the hundredth time without taking a bite. Dumping her uneaten confection in the nearest trashcan, she hurried into motion, eager for any task that could distract her from the weighty burden of her grief. She began to refill glasses and deliver cake slices to the small crowd gathered around Janie and Peter. But interacting with the townspeople had its consequences.

In Cole's Church, nothing happened without everyone spreading the latest gossip and then talking about it in public in hushed whispers. The congratulatory gestures soon descended into "did you hear about" as soon as her back was turned.

"Are you sure you're okay, sweetie?" Janie's voice trilled over the rumble of the diesel engine of Peter's truck.

"I'll be fine, Mom."

Alex had agreed to dog-sit Hank and Delilah, her mom's two enormous Labrador retrievers, while she and Peter spent their wedding night at the famed Inn on the River.

"I'll see you tomorrow."

She leaned in the window to give her mom a quick hug and waved enthusiastically, a smile plastered over her face as they disappeared into the distance. *I'll be fine, Mom.* How many other times had she uttered those words over the last three decades? Her first day of school, when she left for college, after leaving Texas for Philadelphia, as she boarded the plane for her first international medical trip, when JR died, and at least a hundred times over since Ian. This time though, her words were hollow, merely a reflex to deflect worry.

That evening Alex mechanically went through the motions of pouring dog food into enamel bowls, refilling water bowls whose contents would be eagerly sloshed onto the linoleum and watering the few indoor plants her mom kept throughout the simple kitchen. For February, the night was unusually warm, and she left the backdoor open to experience the inklings of an early spring.

Janie was impeccable about her housecleaning. Everything was spotless and organized and Alex had nothing else to do but converse with her thoughts. The house of her childhood: of umpteen birthday parties, late nights crouched over her homework at the kitchen table, even later nights with the rotary phone pressed to her ear to drink in every word Natalie had to say, Saturday mornings leaving a note stuck to the fridge when she left for the barn, Sunday mornings frantically shoving a piece of buttered toast in her mouth before church.

The house was infused with memories that no longer soothed her nor grounded her. She had lost that girl. The girl who gripped ambition. The girl who chose forward momentum over dwelling in tragedy. The girl with a neatly charted course for her life.

Before Alex knew where she was headed, she found herself in her mom's truck, windows down, passing through the minuscule downtown of Cole's Church. It was empty, completely lifeless, apart from a few secretive teenagers gathered under the porte-cochere of a hamburger joint. She remembered those nights.

At the stoplight, she turned west, bumping over a set of railroad tracks before winding down a serpentine lane that led to the middle of nowhere. When her tires crunched down the familiar shell driveway between two densely populated fields of cornstalk stubble, her headlights swung around a bend, bringing the entire scene into view.

The white A-frame church starkly contrasted with the inky black night. She killed the engine to welcome the stillness apart from a few musical crickets. Stepping gingerly onto the bridge, she sat down on the edge overlooking a stagnant creek that reflected a half-full moon on its surface.

A year ago, she had sat here with Ian after her accident in Haiti. A year ago, she had been asked a fundamental human question. *What do you need, Alex?* At the time, she had said freedom. Freedom to choose her path. To be the only one that bore the consequences of her decisions. It had been a cop-out. The response of someone who lived her life in sight of the herd but not actually within the herd.

In all her self-sacrificing glory, she had learned to drift in and out of relationships so that no one actually needed her, and she hadn't needed anyone else. This was what Rox had been referring to during the one and only epic fight of their friendship. Emotional investment had never been easy for her, not like her work ethic or her passion for serving others or her fortitude. Even Rox, who she loved like a sister, had no idea where she had come from or what she had endured.

Once, while running a marathon, a stark epiphany had hit her when she crossed the finish line. While weaving between scores of other runners during the race, she would pace with the same people for miles and even hold short conversations between bursts of breath. But then she would surge ahead or fall behind and fade into the milieu. In life, as in running a race, no matter who she ran with along the way, she would start and finish alone.

She had never needed anyone. Not really. She had never allowed herself to be that vulnerable. Until now.

What do you need, Alex?

I need you, Ian. And you're gone.

She sent a piercing wail into the night, screaming into an empty void and emptying the contents of her heart into a place where they would be absorbed into memory and nothing more.

TWENTY-EIGHT

The stages of grief included the following: denial, anger, bargaining, depression, and finally, acceptance. Every morning Alex woke up to a world that didn't have Ian. She ran with McCartney, showered, and pulled on her scrubs for work. She bought a tea and didn't drink it while going over the overnight admissions with the interns. She floated through her day aimless but purposeful. Existing. Functional. But nothing more. And every night Alex pushed her face into her pillow, praying that if she said his name in her head enough times, her dreams would give her a reprieve from reality.

"Can we get your help with something, Dr. Alex?"

Alex glanced up from the desk where she was jotting a few notes to herself.

"Of course."

She regarded Lucia's expectant face. Lately, she felt like everyone treated her like a bomb that might explode at a moment's notice. Her chair grated against the floor when she pushed back from the metal desk. Trailing behind Lucia, they exited the pediatric ward into the overcast afternoon, passing through a labyrinth of outdoor corridors until they reached the surgical area. When she entered the double doors peeling with pea-green paint, the smell of singed flesh and the sound of whimpering overpowered her.

A cluster of white coats had taken up vigil at the bedside of a young toddler who looked no older than two. His eyes were wide with fear as he observed the ring of strangers staring down at him. When Alex edged closer, she could see the charred flesh covering the better part of his right hand and wrist.

"What happened?"

She directed the question to no one in particular. Several faces regarded her without speaking. Squatting down next to the stretcher, she initiated a game of peekaboo in the spirit of distraction.

"Well?" she barked toward the tallest man who peered down at her through square frames. He looked familiar, and then she remembered he had dated Rox off and on during her pre-Nic obsession.

Dr. Mosweu cleared his throat. "A burn injury."

"I can see that," Alex said in a clipped tone. "How?"

"He reached into an outdoor cooking fire," offered Lucia and Alex shot her a grateful look.

Speaking to surgeons sometimes was more painful than poking her own eye.

"What do you need from me?" Alex asked but already knew the answer.

"Our anesthesiologist is not here today, and we need to sedate the child to debride the wound properly."

"Okay. I'm happy to do it."

Turning on her heel, Alex motioned for Lucia to follow. "Always get a good history before you provide procedural sedation," Alex instructed Lucia. "It may be the only way to anticipate problems and prevent them."

The child's mom was sitting in the corner of the waiting room huddled in a vividly colored sarong that stood out among the white-washed walls and pale-yellow floor. Alex and Lucia sat down as the other two points of a triangle, and Lucia began rattling back and forth in Setswana.

"Make sure you ask about allergies, anesthesia history, last time he ate or drank anything," Alex chimed in.

Lucia just nodded, never removing her eyes from the tearful young woman across from her.

Alex was accustomed to dealing with all brands of parents—hysterical, stoic, or just plain angry—and this woman's reaction seemed out of proportion to the situation. She covered her face with her hands and turned away from them. Alex frowned and tugged on the fabric of Lucia's blouse.

"Tell her it's going to be okay. He will be fine. We'll make sure of it."

"It's not the procedure she is worried about. She recently lost her husband, and this is very stressful for her."

Alex's insides heaved with empathy, and she tried to quell the raw feeling creeping up the back of her throat. A tear escaped her lid, and she dashed it away with the back of her hand before reaching over and taking the woman's hands in her own. They were rough and slender, the hands of someone who worked hard for a living and now had to provide for an entire family. Her blue eyes sought an audience with a pair of brown ones that were the color of freshly tilled earth.

"I lost someone too," Alex whispered.

A language barrier failed to matter. They squeezed one another's hands in understanding, speaking the language of grief instead.

Alex depressed the syringe plunger just a touch more, and the child's breathing transitioned from rapid to slow and regular.

"Hold the oxygen bag over his face just like this."

She positioned Lucia's hands on the facemask so that it made an appropriately tight seal with the tiny nasal bridge and chin. While the surgeons busied themselves with prepping and draping the child's right hand, Alex flicked her eyes back and forth to the small rectangular box keeping pace with the heart rate and oxygen saturation. Every time the *beep beep* would increase its cadence, she infused a bit more medication into the child's bloodstream to dull his response to the stimulation and pain of wound debridement.

With the ketamine coursing through his system, he slept, peaceful and pain-free, and would awake to a freshly bandaged hand that was ready to heal. If only all pain were that easily managed. If only Alex could wake up one morning without the sharp raw edge of grief gnawing at her insides. If only her heart were ready to heal.

"Thanks again, Mary Lou." Alex reached down to scratch the russet-colored head deliberating over the myriad of smells he detected on her scrub pants.

Mary Lou tossed an arm in the air, bracelets jangling down her bare arm. "We've reached an understanding. He doesn't dig up my roses, and he gets all the bacon that he wants."

At the word bacon, McCartney lifted his head and emitted a short whine.

"Speaking of bacon," she said, appraising Alex up and down, "you look like you could use a piece or two."

Alex forced a laugh. "I don't eat bacon, remember?"

"Or much of anything," Mary Lou said sharply.

Alex shrugged and avoided Mary Lou's stern gaze. "It's a basic female right to eat an entire chocolate cake or nothing at all when you're sad."

"How's that goin' by the way?"

Alex's bottom lip trembled ever so slightly. "Ian...is gone."

"But you're not," Mary Lou emphasized.

"I feel like part of me is."

Mary Lou motioned for her to take a seat on the green brocade couch.

"You'll never be the same, that's for sure, but you're still you. Just a little worse for the wear. Loved or not loved. In love or out. You are a woman on a journey, and it's just starting. You're not lost just because you can't see what's ahead of you." Mary Lou paused to scratch the large head nuzzling into her thigh. "Don't let the good stuff pass you by because you're too busy looking behind you to look ahead."

"Is that what you did?"

Mary Lou pursed her lips, the lines around them coalescing into a singular crack at the corner of her mouth. She settled into the sofa next to Alex.

"I lost my sister and my husband in the same day. He and I hadn't been married that long...only two weeks when he went to pick her up from school that day. She lived with us during the week since my parents lived up the mountain, almost an hour's drive from town. It was usually me that picked her up but that day I was sick with a stomach bug." Her eyes grew distant and watery as she spoke.

"What happened?"

"Accident at the railroad crossing. Mechanical failure they called it. The train flew by, and the arms didn't come down."

Alex fixated her gaze on the photograph of the two young women in button-downs and skirts, arm-in-arm next to a broad-shouldered man in a work shirt.

"So, you devoted your life to helping people? Traveling the world and volunteering?"

"Not until later. I eventually got married again. No children or anything. And then when my second husband passed from cancer, I took off into the sunset and never looked back."

She cackled and picked up a photograph of herself astride an elephant somewhere in southeast Asia. "Life never stops, Alex, so you just have to keep on living it."

When Alex arrived home with McCartney, she noticed a strange car in her driveway, a rental from the look of the plates and the cherry red paint coated with a thick layer of travel dust. A not so strange silhouette was taking up the space on her front porch, reclining on an overturned roller bag, the back of her blonde head resting on the door handle.

"Rox?" Alex called and took off in an awkward jog, trying to avoid tripping on McCartney's long limbs.

Rox gracefully popped upright and caught Alex in her arms as she entered the yard.

"What are you doing here?"

"My feminine instinct and our last phone conversation convinced me that you need me, so here I am. Plus, I am your elephant or whatever it is you said I was," she chided, but Alex could hear the notes of tenderness in her voice.

"You *are* my elephant," Alex replied, grasping her in a fierce hug.

"I hope by that you mean I'm intuitive, dominant, and loyal...because I draw the line at wrinkles and a large behind."

Once inside the house, the pair flopped down on Alex's couch, flanking McCartney, who took up the majority of the middle.

"How are you doing, love?"

"I've been better. Not sure I've been worse." Alex wrinkled her forehead.

"There is absolutely nothing wrong with you, by the way," Rox added, referencing their most recent conversation during Alex's drive from Austin to her hometown.

"I'll let you be the judge of that." Alex cringed, and Rox shot her a pointed look.

"Why? What happened?"

"In a nutshell, tequila overdose that transformed me into a raving lunatic."

"Elaborate, please."

"Well—" Alex picked at a thread on the couch where the stitching was unraveling. "First, I threw myself at Tim, who has a serious girlfriend by the way, and then I ran out on him and ducked into what I thought was a pharmacy but ended up being a fancy bar, where I happened to run into Logan."

"Logan Paine?"

"Yes."

Rox cocked an eyebrow. "And then?"

"We talked. We drank. We bonded over our obsession with all things Texas. And then we...kissed."

Rox exhaled, a look of empathy filling her hazel eyes. "How was it?"

"Short," Alex said flatly.

"It apparently left an impression."

"So much of an impression that I ran out into the rain for the second time in one night and—" Alex pushed up the sleeve of her hospital fleece jacket.

Rox grabbed her arm, jerking it upward so she could assess the three letters on Alex's forearm. "I'm assuming this says—"

"Ian," Alex said defensively.

Rox released Alex's forearm and settled back into the couch. "No one would fault you if you wanted to have a bit of fun, Alex. It's—dare I say it—considered healthy."

"I don't need grief sex."

"Maybe you do."

"I'll probably never even see him again, and I could never feel...that way...about anyone other than Ian." She refrained from using the word love.

"But you will see Tim again. Do you have feelings for him?"

Alex paused before answering. It felt so good to get this off her chest to her best friend.

"I love him. I always have...but not the way I love Ian. Tim is comfortable and safe and—"

Too good for me.

"Sometimes comfortable and safe is a good thing," Rox offered gently.

Alex exhaled heavily.

"Ian ruined me. What we have...had—" She paused to swallow. "It consumed me...and now I'm just a pile of ashes waiting to see where the wind blows me next."

As if illustrating her point, Alex jumped up and hurried into the kitchen.

"Do you want something to drink?" she called over her shoulder. "I have white wine. Maybe some red somewhere."

"Just a bottle of water."

The way she said it made Alex pause. When she lifted her head, she spied Rox's sly grin from the doorway of the kitchen.

"You're pregnant," she breathed, a surge of happiness amidst the sliver of an ache in her chest.

"It's early. No one knows yet. Only Nic."

"I'm so happy for you."

"Me too." Rox glanced down at her lower abdomen.

"When are you due?" Alex asked, thrusting a bottle of water into Rox's hand.

"Early September. Plenty of time for you to plan my baby shower."

Alex smiled, the ache deepening a little, and was relieved when her phone's rattling sliced through the air. She grabbed it off the coffee table and flipped it over. It was Ian's dad. She flashed the screen to Rox then swiped to answer.

"Hello? Mr. Devall?"

"Hello, Alexandra."

A silence ensued, and for a split second, Alex thought he might be calling to share a miracle. That Ian had been found somewhere.

"I hope I'm not interrupting your work. I had a bit of business to discuss with you."

Oh. "Of course not, sir. I'm actually at home now."

"Excellent. I'll get right to it. Next weekend is our annual charity event at the Uhuru Elephant Preserve in Tanzania. I believe you and Ian traveled there last summer."

"We did."

It seemed like a lifetime ago. When their relationship still felt fragile. When she had finally revealed her past. When they had bonded over the fate of a baby she-elephant.

"Would you be willing to attend the gala and represent the Devall Foundation?"

Alex hesitated. "Are you sure I'm the best choice?"

"You are the perfect choice," he said assuredly.

"Okay. I can be there."

"Excellent. That brings me to my next request." He paused, and Alex wondered what he could possibly be ready to ask her. "The hospital, Ian's hospital in Mongolia. The dedication is in two weeks. If it is amenable to you, I will charter a plane to take you from Arusha to London, where you will meet up with us and travel to Ulaanbaatar."

Alex's mind was inundated with roadblocks, the most formidable being the time she would be away from Botswana and from work. But she had promised Ian and it was not a promise that she was willing to break. She hoped that Dr. K would understand.

"I would be honored," she said, choking back the emotion rising in her voice.

"Excellent. I will see that you receive the details via email."

"Mr. Devall?" Alex blurted before he could hang up the call.

"Yes, Alexandra."

"Is it hopeless? Is Ian really gone?"

Alex could see Rox watching her from the sofa, a pained expression crossing her face. She didn't want to ask the question, but she needed to hear the words from someone else's mouth. Words that would become a stepping-stone to her new reality—a life without Ian.

He cleared his throat, and then he cleared it again. This poor man who had lost not one but two sons in his lifetime. It was more pain than any human should have to bear.

"Hope lives in the hearts of those who choose it, but yes, I believe that he is. I will see you soon, Alexandra."

His voice had cracked with those last few words before he abruptly ended the call.

Alex took a breath and laid the phone on the table under the scrutinizing gaze of her best friend. It wasn't anything she didn't already know, but it put a lead weight in her chest anyway.

"What did Mr. Devall want?" asked Rox cautiously.

"He needs me to go to Tanzania to represent the foundation at an event and then he wants me to fly from there to London and accompany him to Mongolia for the hospital dedication."

Rox nodded enthusiastically. "Good. This will be really good for you, Alex."

Alex suddenly had a wild idea. "Hey Rox, how long can you stay?"

Never comfortable with asking for things, she hoped that Rox would reach the conclusion she needed.

"As long as you need me to."

"Then I guess *we're* going to Tanzania."

"This place hasn't changed a bit," Rox exclaimed, rotating her head one hundred and eighty degrees to take in the view from the PM courtyard.

"Some things have," Alex muttered, spying the tail of Sam's white coat flapping in the wind, the layers of her red hair grown out over the last few months so that it looked even messier.

"From your tone, I take it that's Samantha Drake."

Alex wrestled with what to say. On the one hand, Sam had been completely antagonizing and insanely difficult to befriend, but on the other, she had been there when Alex needed someone. She hadn't even bothered to tell Rox about the needlestick or the pregnancy that wasn't, and she didn't see the point now.

"She's actually not that bad...just complicated."

Rox began waving her down, and although Sam tried to pretend like she didn't see them, she eventually gave up and stopped in her tracks. Rox was an unstoppable force.

"What are you doing?" Alex inquired.

"While you do your morning errands, Sam and I are going to have a little chat."

Before Alex could protest, Rox was striding across the courtyard to an unsuspecting Sam. Alex felt bad for her. Almost.

Ducking her head into the pediatric ward, Alex took a quick inventory of occupied beds—eight out of twelve contained children hooked up to various IV solutions and oxygen tanks. Her ears detected a very familiar beeping and her stomach leaped into her throat when she saw the child in the corner, breathing tube in place and connected to their only mechanical ventilator. Racing to the bedside, she took stock of every minute detail: correct size breathing tube, correct ventilator settings, equal rise and fall of the chest wall. Everything looked—

"Dr. Alex?" A smooth voice interrupted her thoughts. "How does it look?"

"Perfect," she answered, a slow, genuine smile, filling out her features. "When did this patient come in?"

"Last night," Lucia answered.

"You could have called me. Who did all this?"

"We did," added Shelo, her lips painted fuchsia pink today.

"You have taught us well, Dr. Alex," said Lucia, taking a moment to place her hand on Alex's shoulder.

Alex was still reeling from the sight of the intubated child when she knocked on Dr. K's door.

"Come in," he called. His face, which had been pinched while he concentrated on the computer screen in front of him, considerably brightened when he saw Alex.

"Dr. Alex, what can I do for you?"

Alex picked on her fingernails as she sat in the worn leather chair across from Dr. K's desk. "I need to take some time off, and I know it's asking a lot since I just got back from Texas, and I wouldn't even be asking if it wasn't something for the Devall Foundation—"

Dr. K held up his hand to silence her, and the torrent of words immediately halted. "From what I hear, the pediatric department is doing quite well."

Alex smiled, the scene from this morning filling her with pride.

"Take all the time you need."

"Okay."

Her voice was barely a whisper as she registered his words—words that had been spoken to her before.

TWENTY-NINE

"We're almost there," Alex called to Rox, not bothering to hide the hilarity in her tone at the sight of her friend holding on for dear life in the rear of a bouncing jeep.

"I just hope I still have all of my teeth," she heard Rox mutter as she turned back around to spy the massive tent-like structure on the horizon.

The sun had beat down on their heads for the better part of two hours during the trip from the airport. The air was still and the sky cloudless, and the rushing wind from the jeep's velocity had been welcome. March in Tanzania was the transition between summer and fall when the days were sunny but bearable, flanked by nights that were cool while pleasant.

Josef was waiting for them when they stepped out of the jeep, their clothes and luggage covered in a thick layer of road dust.

"Very nice to see you again, Alexandra."

"You as well, Josef."

They exchanged a smile full of nostalgia, and without another word, Josef swooped in to retrieve their luggage from the rear of the jeep.

"Why did he call you Alexandra?" Rox whispered in her ear.

"It's a long story," she said, a twinge of remembrance hitting her as she recalled how Ian had introduced her to Josef last August.

"Come on. I want to show you something."

Alex led Rox to the covered patio overlooking the elephant herd and scooted a small sofa as close to the edge of the grass as she could for the absolute best view. Rox's mouth opened in a surprised "o" as she flopped down on the couch, no doubt exhausted from the combination of travel as well as growing a tiny human. Alex had told her about the proximity to the elephants at Uhuru, but it was another thing entirely to experience it.

Not more than fifty yards away, a tight herd of four females grazed on the delicate shoots of grass and the piles of hay that had been placed purposefully close to the building. Their trunks twisted playfully as they alternated between eating and gesturing toward one another.

"Don't you wonder what they are gabbing about?" asked Rox, mesmerized by the view.

"Watering hole with the cutest guys?" offered Alex in an attempt at humor.

"Or best mud for fine lines?"

"Maybe how grateful they are just to be together." Alex swallowed hard and stared out at the herd, a singular tear trickling down her face.

"You know someone once told me," Rox continued, "that female elephants bond for life."

She began humming the theme song to Golden Girls, and Alex leaned over to put her head on Rox's shoulder. For the first time in a long while, she felt at home.

"Do you recognize your little one?"

A low, pleasantly gritty voice with a hint of Texas twang drew her attention from the elephant herd to the man standing behind her. His hair was perfectly styled, the coppery strands catching the sun as he stepped in front of their picturesque view. His facial hair was trimmed to a subtle stubble, and the white linen shirt he wore clung to his chest with a light sheen of sweat. Alex's palms turned clammy. As always, Rox was her saving grace.

"I'm Roxanne," she said, jumping to her feet with a surprising amount of energy. "You must be Logan."

"Nice to meet you." Logan thrust out his hand and eyed Alex, who had stayed seated, over Rox's shoulder. "Alex," he said in a raspy voice.

Alex stood, wiping her hands on the back of her jean shorts. Why did she feel so unsettled and nervous? It wasn't like she had done anything wrong. Just out of character, interjected her subconscious. She cocked her head in consideration of his original question.

"I don't actually," she admitted after scanning the group of females once more.

How would he know which one was Ujasiri? The baby elephant that she and Ian had saved. The elephant he had named for her. She would have grown tremendously in the last seven months.

Logan smirked in understanding and pivoted toward the field, extending his arm out and squinting as he pointed toward the smallest female, who was trotting circles around the matriarch.

"There she is. A real lady that one. Just like her mama."

Alex blushed at the reference and the compliment. Feeling every bit of heat in her cheeks, she looked away from Logan toward the beautiful heart-wrenching sight of the she-elephant frolicking in the afternoon sun, spirited and free.

"How can you tell?"

"I've been keeping up with her the last few months."

Alex stared at him with incredulity. Why would he do that?

"Plus, I had the guys paint her feet pink so I could tell her apart from the others." He chuckled at his ingenuity, and sure enough, she could just barely see the splashes of bright pink across Siri's front toes.

"Oh, that was...clever," Alex murmured.

He turned toward her, a faint smile on his lips, his golden eyes brimming with much more to say, but he hesitated, instead, running his tongue over his bottom lip.

Alex felt a hand encase her elbow.

"It was nice to meet you, Logan," Rox said. "But Alex and I need to get ready for tonight."

Alex let herself be maneuvered out of the patio. Rox picked up speed once they reached the grass courtyard that led to their room.

"Did you know he was going to be here?"

Alex shook her head. "No, but I guess I'm not surprised."

"He's...different than what you described."

"Different how?" Alex asked, a little too sharply.

"Hotter," Rox said, and Alex could tell she was mentally appraising Logan's features.

"I wish he wasn't," Alex muttered.

"What was that?"

"Nothing."

After a shower and a much-needed nap for Rox, both ladies admired themselves in the bathroom mirror. Night had brought cooler temperatures, and they had chosen their attire accordingly. Rox looked stunning in a pink silk top and white linen pants, a heavy gold chain looped around her neck. With Rox's encouragement,

Alex had splurged on something new—a white eyelet dress that ended mid-thigh and hugged her curves, with long sleeves that provided her with some warmth.

"It's been way too long," Rox teased. "I forgot how hot you are."

She poked Alex in the ribs, receiving a well-deserved eye-roll in response.

Alex finished fastening the diamond studs from Ian in her ears.

"Well, you're not getting lucky. No matter how many compliments you give me." Alex flashed a small smile as Rox snorted.

"Maybe not me, but somebody else perhaps?" Rox let the question dangle in the air, and Alex attempted to ignore it without biting, which only made Rox up her game. "You deserve some fun. No strings. No judgment. Just think of it as free therapy."

Alex shook her head, pulling a few strands out of her bun to frame her face, and grabbed Rox's hand.

"Nothing is ever free. Let's go."

An outdoor tent had been erected on the front lawn, complete with bistro lights crisscrossing the ceiling and a temporary faux hardwood floor. Most of the guests were clustered around the food tables, which boasted steaming piles of local dishes like fish in curry, rice cooked with coconut milk, and skewers of goat meat roasted over a hot outdoor fire. The melodies of hushed conversations mixed with a background of live acoustic guitar from a gentleman who sat strumming in one corner.

Alex hadn't realized this was such a big event. The American ambassador to Tanzania was there along with one of the secretaries of the World Health Organization. Josef, dressed in a gray suit with no tie, held a drink in his hand, the lights glinting off his perfect white teeth as he shared a laugh. It was nice to see the caretaker so carefree for once. Alex spied Imani behind the bar giving instructions to two young gentlemen who were pouring drinks and serving them not quite fast enough for her liking. She stood with her arms crossed, her face flawlessly beautiful, albeit scowling.

"Can I get you ladies a drink?"

They turned around in unison, Alex's eyes darting over the appealing physical stature of Logan in a honey-colored linen suit that brought out the gold flecks in his eyes.

"Water, please. My throat feels like the Sahara," Rox blurted and dramatically grabbed Logan's forearm.

"Alex?"

Why did her name have to sound so sweet coming from those lips, like honey dripping straight from a beehive?

"Water for me too," Alex replied, and she detected a flare of disappointment in his eyes.

"Coming right up," he said and disappeared into the crowd.

She could practically hear Rox humming with excitement.

"He's got it bad for you, Alex. All you need to do is flip the switch."

"What switch?" Alex hissed, but the tapping of a wireless microphone drowned out her voice.

"Good evening, friends." Josef's velvety voice resounded off the canvas ceiling of the tent. "Welcome to Uhuru Elephant Preserve. Please enjoy the food, the music, the company, and remember to drink responsibly and donate irresponsibly."

A chuckle rippled through the crowd at Josef's dry humor.

"Tonight, we thank our friends and partners, including the Devall Foundation and DreamBig Travel, for their generous support." Josef raised his glass toward Alex and then toward Logan as the lights dimmed throughout the tent. "Have a wonderful evening."

As the guests erupted into applause, the beats of a love song by a new artist from the UK named Ed Sheeran, filled the background and several couples gravitated toward the dance floor.

"You're a lifesaver," Rox said as two bottles of water were extended in their direction. She snatched up both, earning a scowl from Alex.

"Since I failed on your drink—" Logan narrowed his eyes at a nonchalant Rox. "Can I offer you a dance?"

Rox was already moving away from them, shimmying from side to side to a rhythm that existed only in her own head.

"Sure," Alex said.

There was no harm in a single dance. Before she realized what was happening, a warm hand closed over her fingers, leading her gently to the dancefloor. With one dramatic tug, Logan pulled her into his arms, one hand positioned solidly on her mid-back as the beats of the music intensified into their crescendo. She felt as stiff as a store mannequin while Logan swayed next to her, beckoning her body to respond to his signals. He was taller than she was but not by much. His lips reached the level of her nasal bridge so that with his every exhale, she could smell the delicious mint on his breath.

Why was being human so fraught with consequences? Why did humanity feel like such a weakness at this moment? The weakness of need, of another human's touch, of the warmth of someone's skin against her own.

Alex glanced reflexively at her left arm where Ian's name resided, but it was covered up by the sleeve of her dress. In mid-whirl, she dropped her arms to her side, rooted to a spot on the dance floor as the last notes of the song faded. Logan looked at her quizzically, his arms extending toward her.

"I have to go."

Without a destination in mind, Alex began striding toward the nearest black hole in the white canvas tent. As she passed a table adorned with a silver bucket, sweating from being packed with ice, she closed her hand around a slim green bottleneck and pulled out an entire bottle of champagne to accompany her.

Every star in the southern hemisphere lit her path to the barn-style building at the property's edge. She twisted the handle and pushed her full weight against the door. When it gave way, she fell into the blackness headfirst and landed with a thud on her knees.

"Fabulous," she muttered, rising to her feet and feeling the blood trickling from her kneecap. Groping her way along the wall, her fingers closed over a plastic panel, and she flipped the switch. A dim amber overhead bulb provided a small circle of light, enough for her to edge her way to the hallway of oversized horse stalls. She found a five-gallon bucket and flipped it over.

Alex began twisting, first the wire, then the cork, until a satisfying pop echoed through the empty building. Plopping down on the overturned bucket, she put the bottle to her lips and guzzled until she had to come up for breath. A twinge of pain coursed through her leg, and she pulled up the hem of her dress to inspect the damage.

"Damn."

The skin over her left knee was macerated and blood-stained. One more scar to add to her collection. The sound of footsteps caught her attention, and she stopped mid-swig of her overly expensive champagne. Her heart rate spiked for a moment as a surge of adrenaline mixed with alcohol coursed through her veins. Logan's perfect hair peeked around the corner, and Alex relaxed as the fear was diluted out by something else.

"I'm sorry. I just...I was worried."

His voice sang with sincerity, and Alex relinquished whatever hold she had on her inhibitions. She waggled the bottle in his direction.

"It's fine."

He slid over and accepted the offering, putting the rim to his lips and drinking.

"I thought you only liked the hard stuff."

Alex jerked her head upward and smirked.

"I do," she said, a slow whimsy spreading over her face. "Except for champagne. I could literally drown myself in it."

Alex retrieved the bottle from Logan and took a satisfying gulp, her mouth filling with stars. Her head had begun to spin, and laughter bubbled out of her throat as she stood up to hand to bottle back to Logan. Once upright, a fresh stream of blood ran down her shin, and Logan stared at her in alarm.

"What the hell, Alex?" He set the bottle down into the dirt and knelt at her feet.

"It's fine. Just a little scrape," she admonished.

"It looks pretty bad."

"Well, I'm the only doctor here, and I say it's fine."

He reached into his pocket and pulled out a blue handkerchief. Tipping the champagne bottle, he wet the handkerchief and then used it to clean the blood streaks coating her shin. His touch was gentle and deliberate, and Alex had to stabilize herself on the metal bars of the stall.

"Too much champagne?"

Logan glanced up, his eyes like two suns beaming heat into her.

Alex's mouth felt paper dry.

"I only drink champagne on two occasions." She closed her eyes and leaned her head back onto the bars. "When I'm in love...and when I'm not."

"Is that an original?"

He continued to rub the damp material closer to the macerated skin.

Alex sucked in a breath.

"No," she grunted, and suddenly Logan was no longer at her feet but millimeters from her face. She could smell the champagne on his breath. Champagne mixed with desire.

"Coco Chanel," she breathed without opening her eyes.

His lips brushed hers gently, asking permission before continuing. Alex froze, letting the warm fullness of his mouth cover hers completely. She relinquished the hold on her own lips, allowing them to part just slightly. His chest pressed against her and his hands explored up her body to rest on her back. Alex opened her mouth wider, and he used the opportunity to deepen their kiss. He tasted exquisite, like starlight and hope. She focused only on the sensation of his mouth on hers, pushing everything else to the corner of her mind.

Alex felt her bottom lip swell as Logan ravaged it and then began moving down her neck. His fingers found the zipper to her dress, and he tugged it down, exposing her back to heated palms. What was it about another human's skin that felt so incredible? Alex didn't want to think. Every time any thought erupted in her brain, she shoved it aside into the pile. She shrugged her arms out of the loose sleeves of her dress, letting the top fall around her waist, and wrapped her arms around Logan's neck.

"You are...so damn beautiful," he rasped into her ear, and Alex's lids fluttered open when his lips met her collarbone.

Even through the darkness in the corridor, Alex could see the bright white of her skin and the ink she bore on her interior forearm.

"Logan—" At the sound of her strangled tone, he halted his assault on her lower neck. "I can't."

She used his surprise to push her arms back into the sleeves of her dress. He stepped back from her, creating a small column of space, then leaned in to help her zip the back of her dress. His demeanor exuded resignation, and she expected anything other than what she saw in his eyes—kindness, compassion, humanity.

"So, it'll always be only Ian?"

Alex felt like the tattoo on her arm had burned its way through another layer of tissue. She let her veil fall in a moment of unadulterated truth.

"I don't know, but for now, he's all that I see. It's not fair for me to use you as a...distraction," she finished slowly.

"I don't mind being used."

He flashed her a wry grin, and she tried to look down, but his fingers held her chin steady. He leaned in closer and pressed his lips to hers again. She didn't have the emotional bandwidth to stop him. And then it was over and too short to satisfy her longing to be touched, held, wanted, ravaged.

Stop signs adorned with flashing red lights amid a perimeter of orange cones erupted over the landscape of her mind. Her breathing hitched, and the skin around his right eye twitched right before she let him claim her mouth one more time in a kiss that didn't stop the world but did spark some hope that maybe one day—one day far in the future—she could feel again how she felt with Ian. But right now, she had been in love. Consumed by a bright flame until there was nothing left except to begin again. To become again.

As Alex lingered in the enveloping night, she had no answers. No clarity. The farther she walked the blacker the world became until she couldn't see her own path. And she wondered, once someone had experienced an epic love, how could she be content with anything else?

THIRTY

The smell of George Devall's bourbon permeated her olfactory system, and she inhaled deeply to pull every micron of scent from the air. The screech of wheels unfolding underneath the plane catapulted her out of the haven of her memories and her spine straightened as she checked her seatbelt one more time to make sure that it was snug.

"My apologies, Roxanne," said George as he nimbly stood from his seat when its actual occupant arrived in the aisle. "I'll see you on the ground." He and his half-empty bourbon glass made their way carefully back to his seat in the rear of the plane.

Rox flashed him a grateful smile and flopped into the now empty chair. Her face, though beautiful, had maintained a green sheen since they had departed from Arusha.

"Whoever came up with the term morning sickness is an idiot," she said, taking a magazine and wafting it in front of her face.

"I don't think your baby knows when exactly morning is," Alex said, her thoughts drifting to the insanity of the last twenty-four hours.

After leaving Logan in the barn, she had finished her champagne in a patch of grass under the stars. Then, like closing the cover on a book that had been indulgent but purposeful, she strode back into the party, careful to avoid Logan's eyes piercing her from the other side of the tent. For the first time, she couldn't see what was ahead, but she was going to walk toward it anyway...with her best friend beside her.

"Come on," she hissed, tugging Rox away from a cluster of brilliant skirts near the bar.

"Where are we going?" Rox asked, snatching up her water glass. "Anywhere else."

After the promise of an excellent tip, one of the preserve's workmen agreed to drive the pair back to Arusha, where a jet waited patiently on the tarmac to whisk them to London.

In London, they transferred planes, and Rox glanced wistfully toward the city containing her husband only once before following Alex up the rollaway stairs. As the plane slipped into the night, Alex sat perfectly still, marinating in her thoughts while she watched Rox sleep fitfully. She had felt every kiss from the night before a thousand times over until the sensory memory began to fade, and she didn't try to revive it.

"Can I get you anything?" she asked Rox.

Rox fished around in her purse to extract an overly large pair of sunglasses which she perched expertly on her face and leaned her head back into the white leather cushion.

"A warm bath in a beautiful hotel room."

Alex smiled to herself as the ground loomed closer, and she steeled herself for the impact. She loved traveling, especially taking off in a plane on the way to a big adventure, but even more than that, she loved the landing. Feeling the formidable ground underneath her after being weightless in the sky.

The harried group of travelers deplaned one by one, and Alex was last to leave. She tucked her scarf tighter into her wool coat. The frigid air that met her face contrasted with the slice of warmth from the overhead sun in the land of the eternal blue sky.

"Welcome to Ulaanbaatar," called a rich voice holding open the door to a black sedan.

"Thank you," Alex said, sliding in next to Rox. "It's good to be back."

Alex's eyes were drawn to the familiarity of the terrain as the car sped from the airport along a two-lane ribbon of highway toward their hotel. Through her window, she viewed the cluster of high-rise buildings juxtaposed with snow-capped mountains jutting out of the landscape in the distance.

Almost five years had passed since her last trip here. New buildings had sprouted from empty grass-filled lots, and billboards advertising a new bank or a modern shop had multiplied along the narrow highway. Some things had changed—the natural progression of an economy that was doing well in the years after Russian occupation—and, thankfully, some things had not.

The car whizzed past a plain red brick building, completely nondescript from the outside, that housed a hospital in its depths. A hospital she had gotten to know quite well during her time here after her second year of pediatrics residency. The cardiothoracic surgeon at her training institution had been impressed with her dedication, work ethic, and commitment to global health. She had invited Alex to accompany her and a small team of specialized nurses to UB for two marathon weeks of performing as many corrective heart surgeries as they could. Families had come from all reaches of the country, primarily nomadic families who traveled partly by foot, horse, and car to reach the hospital and the source of a new beginning for their children.

The beautiful part of congenital heart surgery was the happy ending. Something that started out utterly broken could be fixed by expert hands and nearly microscopic stitches. Not all kids born with heart disease could be repaired, but for those with holes where they didn't belong or residual connections that should have dissipated, heart surgery was a life-changing miracle.

Alex had never worked harder or longer into a night that extended into the next day, but the richness of the experience thrilled her in a way nothing else had. Caring for this unique population of warrior kids with zipper scars on their chests was life-altering. Once Alex had removed their breathing tubes and supplied them with pain medication, the parents had swooped in, intimately involved in the care and recovery of their children. The moms would bring in large jars of mutton that looked like chunky gray gelatin and scoop spoonfuls into little birdlike mouths.

And afterward, their lives were changed forever—a death sentence changed into a life that beckoned. They would grow up, get married, have their own animals and children. An endless realm of possibilities awaited.

The car slowed to a stop in the circle drive of a five-story building on the west side of town. Located on the very fringe of UB, the only thing between the Hotel Genghis Khan and the mountains was an endless stretch of space. Alex flipped through the red folder Lydia had handed her this morning, finding an annotated schedule inside.

They had dinner and a private performance by the Mongolia National Orchestra this evening and then would be leaving early in the morning to drive out to the hospital for the dedication. Every minute of their stay was carefully scheduled and color-coded for the proper attire.

What a life Ian must have lived as chairman of the foundation. Every second accounted for except for his escapes to Botswana for their transcontinental trysts. Rox's eyelids were descending over her corneas as they entered the suite they would be sharing. It wasn't long before they both passed out on the twin beds for a much-needed battery recharge.

When Alex awoke, the large red ball of sun had almost been reappropriated by the moon. She had slept deeply and dreamlessly until startled awake by the sound of a hairdryer.

"What time is it?" she asked Rox, who was wrapped in a white cotton towel, fluffing her nearly dry cornsilk hair that hung to her shoulders.

"Almost time to meet downstairs for dinner."

Alex, coated in a layer of gritty exhaustion, felt as if her limbs were made of lead.

"Okay," she sighed, wishing that she could fall back into an easy coma and maybe dream of Ian.

"I'll do your hair, love," Rox said sweetly.

Alex put effort into her next smile, intensely grateful for the presence of her best friend.

The night was memorable. After an elegantly prepared dinner served in the hotel ballroom, they headed over to the concert hall. Alex had been quiet and reserved most of the evening, fielding questions from Rachel and Rahul and catching Lydia glance at her once or twice. Rox had commanded the evening, and by the time the lights were dimming for the music to begin, everyone was chuckling or outright guffawing at her most recent escapades.

"And this one time—" Rox clutched her stomach to hold in a laugh. "Nic signed an autograph outside our house, and the man handed him a cat in return—hissing and snarling—the poor thing didn't know what to do."

"What did you do with her?" Rachel asked, her face gleeful and buoyant.

"I was thinking about giving her to you," Rox said pointedly, and the entire group burst into laughter that quickly faded as the lights dimmed and the curtain rose.

The orchestra members were dressed in traditional costumes of thick, buttery yellow robes lined with black felt with a matching hat. They sat perfectly erect, waiting on the conductor to wave his baton. When it finally swished through the air, the hall was inundated with the structured, complex sound of the *morin khuur*—the traditional instrument of Mongolia—otherwise known as the horsehead fiddle.

Alex was mesmerized by the flying fingers and winged bows fluttering over the strings made of horsehair. The rhythm and cadence alternated between a fast canter and an extended trot to a freeform gallop across a grass-filled valley.

A man emerged from somewhere among the buzzing orchestra in a *deel* of red silk brocade and stepped to center stage. The instruments waned into background noise as the throat singer emitted vibratory pitches that waxed and waned like the song of a million grasshoppers under the moon. Alex could feel the music in her chest, in every heartbeat and every thrum of her pulse. Once, she had heard a Mongolian legend that herders used the music of the horsehead fiddle to calm their animals after a stressful experience. Tonight, she nestled into her seat and closed her eyes, letting the symphony of wild horses and freedom work their healing magic.

"Do you have everything?" called Rox from the hallway. Alex tucked the last of her clothing into her small roller bag and made one more sweep of the bathroom before answering.

"Yes, I think so."

George Devall and his entourage, including her, were scheduled to spend the morning at the dedication and then be whisked back to the airport where they would head back to London. George had curtailed their trip, citing a need to be present at a board meeting the following Monday, but Alex knew being here was simply too painful for him...for a variety of reasons.

In the car, while speeding west of the city, Alex had ample time to contemplate her nerves. She began shuffling through her notes, trying to keep her clammy palms from smearing the fresh ink. As they traveled farther outside the city, solitary patches of stubborn ice were separated by a few diligent grasses, poking their way through the hard ground in an attempt to herald spring. Alex was so focused on the changing landscape and the mountains in the distance that she failed to realize the hospital had come into view until Rox squeezed her knee. It was the largest structure for miles and situated on a perfect plot of land that was far enough outside the city to be accessible to the nomadic families and close enough to maintain a robust supply chain.

Alex mentally praised Ian's foresight. At least five stories high, the outside was made from locally sourced blue-grey brick. It was structured but whimsical with rows of oversized windows that peered into the interior and multicolored block letters across the top that read "The Benjamin Ryan Devall Hospital for Children." Soo-Yun had outdone herself.

When their black sedan pulled to a stop in the parking lot, Alex hustled out after Rox, the prairie wind whistling through their legs. Although her wool coat was long, she wished that pants had been allowed. Lydia had specifically written "wear a dress and heels" in bold red letters on her itinerary.

"If you will follow me, please," chirped the Scottish brogue of their red-haired matriarch.

Alex fell into the middle of their group, huddling close to Rox for extra warmth and tucking in the scarf Mary Lou had made her for Christmas.

They entered the exterior glass doors, brand new and spotless, and joined an already growing crowd in the hospital lobby. Alex looked up. From the lobby, she could see every single floor and the exposed staircase that connected them. A collection of plastic orange chairs had been arranged in rows in a sphere of sunlight created by an overhead skylight. Carved wooden statues of sheep and horses and camels that were nearly life-size stood guard over the corridor to the lower-level clinics and emergency department.

"It's meant to represent all things essential to Mongolian culture," a voice said near Alex's ear, a French accent she didn't recognize but reminded her of expensive perfume and violets.

She turned to find a petite woman bundled into a fur-lined coat, her pixie-like face framed by shoulder-length waves with just the right amount of bounce. "The sun, the sky, and the horse," she said, pointing toward the skylight and then the statue of a foal frolicking next to his mother.

"You must be Brigitte," Alex said, casting her eyes over the tiny woman's shoulder to Soo-Yun, her elegant frame easy to pick out in the crowd.

"How ever did you guess?" Brigitte laughed girlishly just as Soo-Yun stepped over to join them. "And this is my beautiful other half, Soo-Yun."

"We've met," interjected Soo-Yun, and she leaned down to kiss Alex on both cheeks. "What do you think, Alex?" she asked.

Alex struggled to choose a singular word to describe seeing Ian's dream as a brick-and-mortar reality. It was perfect. Hauntingly perfect. Every brick an honor to two men that would never see it.

An authoritative-appearing Mongolian gentleman began tapping the microphone, and she saw Rox's hand beckoning for her to join her in the front row.

"It was so nice to see both of you. Excuse me," she said, pushing past them and the thinning crowd to slide into the seat next to Rox.

"Thank you all for joining us here today on this unprecedented occasion."

The voices of the two men, one in Mongolian and the other interpreting in English, rang through the sun-drenched lobby. There was an introduction by the Mongolian Minister of Health and then the newly appointed director of the hospital, a smooth-faced Mongolian woman who had been in pediatric leadership for decades. George Devall gave a short speech about the foundation's inception, its progress, and goals. And then it was Alex's turn.

She felt every inch of cement flooring underneath her nude heels as she stepped to the podium. When she surveyed the crowd, everything around her disappeared. All she could see was Ian's face. She glanced up once at the patch of blue sky on the ceiling. It had all started with eyes as blue as flame. As limitless as the sky.

"When I met Ian," she began, "I thought we couldn't be more different. I had spent my life doing humanitarian work, and he was more of a disenchanted prince." A few uncertain chuckles emerged from the audience, and Alex smiled before continuing.

"He told me once that people rarely made the kind of difference that really mattered. But once he began to believe in himself, Ian proved himself wrong. Once he discovered what was worth fighting for, he made differences that mattered. With this new hospital, his vision and dedication will help thousands of Mongolian children receive proper medical care for generations. Ian changed many lives, including mine."

Alex surveyed the seated guests and skipped over those closest to Ian, especially George, whose eyes watered with the glint of early tears.

"Thank you for your hospitality and congratulations on a lifelong partnership with the Devall Foundation."

The audience erupted in brief but hearty applause, and Alex felt an additional weight slide off her shoulders when she stepped away from the stage.

THIRTY-ONE

Alex sipped her refreshment, some type of freshly squeezed juice that was both tart and refreshing at the same time. Rox stood next to her in sentry position, ready to field off any unwanted questions as she was approached by dozens of people wanting to offer their congratulations and their condolences.

After shaking what seemed like a million hands and offering the few phrases she knew in Mongolian, a voice in her native tongue, with a Texas accent no less, rose above the din to greet her.

"It's good to see you, dear. I can't believe all the good things you are doing."

Rox stepped aside to allow a familiar face into Alex's circle. Miranda Stone. It had been ages. She was one of the lead cardiologists on the mission to Mongolia several years ago and had encouraged Alex to pursue her passion for global health.

"Miranda...Dr. Stone...what are you doing here?" Alex said as she extended her arms in a brief embrace.

"I moved here a few years ago," spouted Miranda proudly, cocking her head to the side in a full smile. The lines around her eyes had deepened in the last few years but only made her more beautiful.

"What?" Alex gasped. "Wow, what have you been doing?"

"This and that," she tossed her head, the blonde shag cut streaked with a minute amount of gray fluttering about the delicate bone structure of her face. "Volunteering in the orphanages, working in a few clinics, helping out the surgical teams that come through," she listed as she eyed Alex with warmth. "I bought a house in town not too far from here, and I met Ian once a few months ago. He was lovely, just lovely, and he offered me a position here, so I start next week as Medical Director of Inpatient Services. I'll be doing direct patient care too, on the ward and in the emergency department."

She prattled on, her mouth barely keeping pace with her thoughts, and Alex smiled, remembering how she conversed at the speed of light, especially when she was excited.

"Wow, that's incredible. I don't think Ian was even aware we were colleagues."

"I filled him in on most of our misadventures."

She winked, and Alex smiled sheepishly, remembering their time in UB, including a trek on a very inappropriate camel.

"This place is really lucky to have you," Alex said wistfully, staring up at clean, white-washed walls and the freshly painted doors.

"You know, if you are interested, I sure could use someone with your skill set to run this place."

Every single neuron in Alex's brain suddenly felt alive. Could she? Even for a few months? The challenge thrilled her and the chance to see Ian's dream transform into a reality was irresistible.

"Wow, I—"

She glanced up at Rox who was trying to keep an impassive face, but Alex could see the encouragement bubbling underneath. It was impractical, not to mention irresponsible, but she couldn't help but think that this was exactly what Mary Lou had been trying to tell her. Time had brought her the clarity to light the path in front of her.

Just as she had been drawn to Ian like a moth to the flame, completely unsuspecting of her fate, she found herself nodding her head in agreement and couldn't believe the next words that came out of her mouth.

"Yes. I would love to."

When the entourage arrived at the UB private airport, Alex sat in the back of the running car with Rox.

"Okay, so what about my stuff? My house? McCartney?"

"I'll get in touch with Mary Lou as soon as we land and sort it out. It will all be waiting for you when you get back to Botswana. And I'm sure she won't mind taking care of McCartney for a few extra weeks. How long do you think you'll stay?" Rox asked quietly.

"I don't know." Alex bit her lower lip between her teeth. "I need to feel out things with Dr. K and PM, but I was hoping for a month or so."

"I think that sounds like a perfect amount of time. Enough time for you to get things started here and enough time to—"

She didn't finish her sentence out loud, but Alex knew what she was thinking. Enough time to say goodbye.

"Dr. K will understand," Rox finished, and Alex nodded her head, suddenly awash with emotion after the events of the day.

"I love you, Rox."

"And I love you. Elephant sisters forever."

Alex let a fresh round of tears fall as she scooted out of the car after Rox. She waved at the rest of the faces of the shocked group as they boarded the aircraft without her. When she looked back over her shoulder before climbing into Miranda's red Hyundai, Lydia glared at her sharply from the oval window. This had obviously not been part of the itinerary.

.

"Thank you for letting me stay with you," Alex murmured as Miranda led her into the simple brick house on the outskirts of UB. "This is probably not what you expected today."

"I had it all planned out. I was hoping I would see you and you would agree to stay and that I would be making you tea at this very moment." She reached over to fill a kettle with water and then plunked it onto the gas stove.

By the time Alex had returned from depositing her small suitcase in Miranda's guestroom, a steaming cup of fragrant liquid awaited her. She touched the rim gratefully to her lips but didn't drink. Miranda sat at a simple wooden table, thumbing through a medical journal and sipping her tea out of a mug that read, "Awesome is as awesome does."

"You hate tea. I forgot," she said, not looking up.

Wow, she had not lost her degree of perception.

"Diet Coke, right? I'll pick up some for you next time I go to the store."

Alex smiled gratefully. Memory still intact as well. "That would be great," she said.

"It's going to be a full day at the hospital tomorrow. The clinics aren't open yet, but the emergency department is. You better wear your running shoes."

Alex looked down at her feet. Thankfully her running shoes were one thing that she always packed. She rarely went anywhere without them.

"I might need to pick up a few things."

"Of course, dear," Miranda answered, running freshly manicured nails through her short hair. "It's still going to be cold here for the rest of the month. There are places up north that are still knee-deep in snow."

"Can you take me somewhere to shop?"

"More than somewhere," she replied. "I'll take you to see my friend at the Gobi."

A short time later, Alex stood half-naked in a curtained dressing room in Miranda's preferred department store, which was no less than seven stories tall, each floor connected by a rapidly moving escalator. Every floor was thematically planned, from the gift shop with everything from goatskin flasks and watercolor art, to the next floor, which contained Maytag washers and dryers. The women's department was on the third floor, and Alex remained stationary while Miranda scavenged the racks for appropriate attire for the next few weeks.

I don't even have enough underwear, Alex thought, and right then, a package of women's cotton briefs came sailing through the curtain. Alex picked them up and scrutinized the packaging.

"Oh, Miranda, I'm probably more of a small than a large."

She heard a telltale snicker. "Maybe back home, sweetie, but not here."

"That makes sense," she replied wryly, thinking of the plethora of petite frames among the Mongolian women she knew.

By the time they left the shop, Alex had amassed the necessities in addition to a few cashmere sweaters, t-shirts, and pairs of jeans. She eyed a pair of sheep's wool-lined boots near the checkout and, on a whim, tossed them onto the counter. Maybe she would have time to explore a little while she was here.

"The key here is layers," Miranda said, sidling up to her at the cashier's counter. Before Alex could answer, she launched into an entirely separate monologue. "Are you hungry? I'm starving. What sounds good? Oooh, I know an Indian place? Do you like Indian food?"

Alex smiled and handed her credit card over to the cashier as her stomach grumbled her answer. "Doesn't everyone?"

An authentic Indian restaurant in UB—who knew? Alex had expected something like the ones she had frequented in Philadelphia with rows of shining trays in a buffet-style service and clusters of tables on colorful carpets. The interior of this restaurant, however, resembled someone's private dining room with intimate tables separated by kantha quilts in vibrant colors. Miranda waved a gregarious hello to a couple behind the bar, who greeted her with nods and waves.

"The owners," she whispered to Alex.

They hadn't been at the table more than five minutes when dish after dish of savory samples appeared in front of them. A rich chicken tikka and a hearty dal not to mention a huge basket of freshly baked naan. Alex broke off a piece and dipped it into a fragrant red sauce.

"If I lived here, I would gain ten pounds." She closed her eyes, luxuriating over the bread chunks with just the right amount of liquid heat from the sauce.

Miranda laughed. "I limit myself to once a week, but," she said with a shrug, "it all comes out in the wash. You look like a few extra pounds wouldn't hurt."

Alex glanced down at her food, and an uncomfortable silence descended. She knew Miranda was treading carefully.

Alex exhaled heavily. "These last few months have been—"

"Total shit."

"Yeah, something like that."

Alex smiled despite the somber turn of the conversation. The waiter plunked two beers in front of them, and Miranda raised hers in a toast.

"Here's to good vibes and better days ahead."

"Cheers." Alex clinked her beer bottle to Miranda's and took a long swig.

She was not lost...and she was starting to see what was ahead of her.

On Monday morning, Alex pulled on the only pair of scrubs she had packed and topped them with a sweatshirt and then her wool coat over the entire outfit.

"Do you have an extra stethoscope?" she called to Miranda, who was busy frying eggs in the kitchen.

"I do, sweetpea. It's hanging by the door."

Alex stuffed the stethoscope, a water bottle, and her phone into her blue shoulder bag, catching her finger on something sharp wedged in the bottom of the bag.

"Ouch," she yelped.

Paper cuts were the worst. She pulled out the offender. The postcard Ian had given her for Christmas. The trip to Virgin Gorda that had never materialized. She chuckled silently at the stick figures he had hand-drawn on the front, especially the one of herself in a bikini with pigtails. Maybe she would go one day.

Miranda drove them to the hospital just as the sun was rising behind them. Alex felt the typical emotional trajectory of anxiety followed by excitement when about to embark on a new medical adventure. Medicine required her to be rested physically, present emotionally, and replenished spiritually. At least she had two of the three going for her this time.

"What should I expect to see?" she asked Miranda as they pulled into the parking lot.

"No telling," she answered. "The typical pediatric crap: respiratory infections, GI bugs, rashes, but some of the kids might be pretty sick. I had a kid the other week who came in after being kicked in the abdomen by a horse."

"Geez," Alex said. "Do we have the right equipment to handle kids with critical illness?"

"I guess we'll find out," she sang as the double glass doors closed behind them.

Alex couldn't believe the scene in front of her. Nurses in various colored scrubs bustled about carrying crates of equipment and supplies. An entire section of the lobby had been converted into a distribution area with a team assigned to allocate pharmaceuticals.

"What should we do?" Alex asked Miranda.

"Come on. I imagine they need help in the emergency department."

The emergency department had been created as an offshoot of the lobby as a place to triage and provide initial therapies to kids who needed admission to the hospital or who could be sent home with antibiotics and guidance. Alex and Miranda joined the fray and set to work checking patient monitors and pulse oximeters, organizing essential emergency medications, and vascular access supplies. Soon, the only thing left to do was wait on their first patient. They sat on the paper-clad exam tables, swinging their legs as they chatted.

"So why did you decide to move to Mongolia?" Alex asked

Miranda as they split a sandwich and a Diet Coke for lunch.

"I needed something different. Somewhere I could make a difference away from the tedious crap in academic medicine."

Alex nodded in understanding. "I know exactly what you mean."

"Doctors," a commanding voice called from the doorway, "we have a patient."

Alex and Miranda scooted off the exam table in unison, chunking the rest of their lunch in the nearest trashcan. In her mind, Alex wondered what it could be—severe sepsis or trauma or respiratory failure. She and Miranda entered the exam room together and smiled when they saw the chubby face of a toddler waddling around and exploring the corners of the room.

"What seems to be the problem?" Alex gestured toward the child, and the mother erupted in a stream of Mongolian.

"What did she say?" Alex looked expectantly at Miranda.

"Constipation."

They worked seamlessly side by side throughout the afternoon seeing everything from feeding difficulties in a newborn baby to a child with a chronic cough. Most children were sent home with their parents, but a few earned an overnight stay for IV fluids or the initiation of antibiotics. The day passed quickly, and darkness had settled over them before Alex realized it. She had stepped out to the lobby to admire the emerging stars through the skylight when one of the nurses called her by name.

"One more patient, Dr. Alex."

Yawning, she stumbled back into the ED and entered the room of a young girl with flowing black hair, probably not quite school-age and cheeks that were rosy from windburn and sun. Her mother stood protectively over her, holding her by both shoulders. Alex knelt to begin her exam. She offered her stethoscope and allowed the girl to run it through her hand before Alex placed it on her chest.

"What seems to be the...problem?"

She choked out the last word, her eyes widening in shock. Reaching out a tentative finger, she traced the glinting metal button on the girl's heavy felt shirt—a button in the shape of the Millennium Falcon.

"Where did you get this?" Alex asked, pointing to the button.

The startled mother stared at her quizzically, pulling her daughter into her side.

"Miranda," Alex yelped, and Miranda appeared within moments, her hands still wet from the washbasin outside.

As she flicked them dry, a few droplets landed on Alex's face.

"Can you ask her where they got this?" Her voice was strangled with emotion. She gestured to the silver button fashioned from Ian's cufflink.

Noting the woman's reticence, Miranda bowed her head and started with a greeting and then explained Alex's interest in the button. The young mother was more than happy to oblige and launched into a story that involved many syllables and even more hand gestures.

Alex almost tapped her foot with impatience as she reined in the thrill of hope blossoming in her chest. They had probably found it close to the mining site. Ian might have dropped it there before—

"She said her husband found it when he went after some goats that wandered off, on the ground up near Lake Khövsgöl."

What? From what Alex knew of Mongolian geography, Lake Khövsgöl, the blue pearl, was in northernmost Mongolia. Nowhere near the mining site. The woman continued to talk, and Miranda interpreted as quickly as she could. Alex kept hearing one word over and over that sounded familiar. Tsaatan. Tsaatan.

"Wait—what is Tsaatan?"

Miranda furrowed her brows, trying to piece together Alex's interest in a coat button. "The reindeer people."

On the way home, Alex fingered the cufflink, turning it over in her palm to examine the details. The little girl had been reluctant to part with her shiny trinket, so Alex had traded her Miranda's stethoscope and a chocolate bar she had found in the depths of her bag. She would not let herself hope that this meant Ian was alive. It most likely meant that someone had found him but not until after his injuries and the harsh climate had claimed his life. The cufflinks might have been taken as a souvenir.

"What did the woman say again?" Alex turned to Miranda, eager to dissect the details of the story once again. Miranda nodded and pressed on the accelerator.

"They were staying north of Murun right after the first of the year when a wolf spooked their herd of goats and scattered them toward the lake."

"Lake Khövsgöl?" Alex asked, and Miranda nodded.

"Her husband went after them on horseback and was gone for the entire day. He returned with the entire herd thanks to the help of a couple of the Tsaatan."

Miranda glanced in her direction as she turned into her driveway and cut the engine. "They tend to winter in the northern tip of Mongolia, right near the Russian border in a remote valley with no roads, no communication, no connection to the outside world whatsoever."

"And he found the cufflink?"

"Yes. He bent down to pick up his horse's reins and there it was."

Alex sighed and let her thoughts percolate from her frontal lobe into the rest of her body. She closed her hand around the silver talisman.

"What are you going to do?" Miranda peered at her with questioning eyes.

"I need to make a phone call."

George Devall picked up on the third ring. It was 3 a.m. in London. Alex felt incredibly rude rousing him, but this wasn't something that could wait.

"Hello?"

"Mr. Devall, it's me, Alex."

"Alexandra, I wasn't expecting a call from you. Is everything all right?" His voice was mildly garbled from being woken from mid-REM sleep.

"It is. I need to ask you something. When you sent the team to search for Ian, how much ground did they cover? Would there have been any areas that were left out?"

George Devall sighed into the phone. "Alexandra," he started, his voice pained, "as you can imagine, I have unlimited resources. Over the last few months, my team searched everywhere."

"What do you mean by everywhere?"

"Every square kilometer of the entire country."

"So, you're saying there's no possible way that Ian is still out there. That the team might have missed something. That there's no hope at all."

She imagined the pinched look on his face and the sadness filling his deep-set brown eyes.

"We can always believe that Ian is out there, and hope that someday he will come back to us...in one way or another."

Alex's grip tightened on her phone.
"Hope is not a plan."

THIRTY-TWO

Alex paced the floorboards of Miranda's cottage home, alternating between scribbling notes on notebook paper, studying the map of Mongolia displayed on her laptop screen, and dialing every single local travel company. Miranda had brewed a pot of coffee that filled the house with a delectable scent. Alex had even choked down half a cup in the spirit of needing all her neurons firing tonight.

"Thank you," she gushed for the hundredth time that night and pressed end on her phone that depicted a rapidly declining battery.

"What did they say?" Miranda asked and settled into her gray suede couch next to her curled-up Dachshund.

"They don't know exactly where the Tsaatan are this time of year. Most people aren't idiotic enough to wade through a forest of tundra to find them. She said it would be best to wait a month or so, and they would make it down to the lake and set up their tourist booths."

"And I take it that's about a month too long?" Miranda stared at her pointedly.

"Absolutely," Alex said, taking another sip of coffee and grimacing.

"It's not that bad," Miranda chided. "You just have to get used to it."

"I've tried. I feel like I'm drinking hot garbage."

Miranda shrugged and laughed, sipping her beverage from a coffee mug that read, "Being a doctor is my superpower."

"So, what's the plan?"

Alex glanced down at the notes she had scrawled. "If you can drive me to Murun, the adventure travel company will pick me up in a van and drive me to the edge of the taiga forest. From there, the lady suggested I find someone willing to lend me a horse that I can take into Tsaatan country."

"You need a guide."

"I know."

"And an interpreter."

"I know." Alex slumped her shoulders. "I know this sounds crazy, but I have to do this." She began stuffing her notebook and pen back into her bag. "Do you know where I could hire a guide and an interpreter?"

Miranda stared at the ceiling for a moment before answering as if weighing a few options. "I know a guy who has taken some tourists up there before, usually in the summer, but I could see if he would be willing to go. He's a little...unconventional."

"Great. That's perfect. I don't care if he turns into a winged monster at night. What about an interpreter?"

"Well, you're looking at the obvious choice."

"Miranda, I would never ask you to go with me. This is...I mean...I'm insane."

"You're bat shit, sweetie pie, but I'm still going with you."

The lines around her eyes coalesced into a perfect crow's foot as they giggled hysterically.

Alex spent the several-hour drive to Murun mentally running through the short list of supplies they had stuffed in the trunk of Miranda's car. She had never been camping, much less on a survivalist suicide mission. She was thankful to the loquacious bloggers who had described in exquisite detail their trips into the frozen forest or *taiga* as the locals called it.

Miranda had picked up a few reams of goat jerky and a jar of peanut butter which would serve as their sustenance for the few days on horseback. Luckily, the thick crust of snow on the ground would provide them with an ample water supply in case they ran short. That only left the potential for hypothermia, frostbite, a random wolf attack or possibly falling off the side of a cliff. The travel company had promised to provide her with a satellite phone that could be used in an emergency. Or if they found Ian.

On the way out of UB, they had pulled into a two-story building enclosed by a partial sun-dried brick wall. A man a full head shorter than Alex, who was thick around the middle with bleary eyes from either sleeplessness or conjunctivitis, fell into the open passenger door and promptly tilted his head back and began snoring. Alex could smell the fumes from his breath wafting through the car, and she cracked her window to diffuse them.

"Is he drunk?" Alex whispered to Miranda above the car's engine and the man's rhoncorous snores.

She wrinkled her nose. "Batu's not much to look at, but he's kind, and he knows the taiga like the back of his hand. He was Tsaatan once upon a time."

"How do you know him?"

Miranda pursed her lips and refocused her eyes on the road. "Sometimes, I have a bad day at work, and I require some...therapy."

Alex thought about her own therapeutic experiences at Ex-Pats with Roxanne.

"He's a bartender?"

"More or less," Miranda winked enigmatically.

Two doctors and an alcoholic bartender set off into the wilderness to find a missing billionaire philanthropist. It sounded like the beginning of a very interesting novel.

"Tell me about the Tsaatan," she prompted Miranda, her voice still competing with Batu's snores.

"I've only heard stories, but they are an ancient culture. Nomadic and completely devoted to raising and caring for the reindeer. They even let them inside their teepees or gers at night when it's cold."

"They raise them like livestock?" asked Alex.

"More like...family. They use them for milk and cheese and transportation."

Alex nodded, remembering the few photographs she had seen online of beautiful children astride reindeer with fuzzy tipped antlers.

"And they prefer to live apart from technology?"

"Not really," Miranda answered. "From what I've heard, they are just as likely to have an iPhone as the rest of the world."

"And how do they feel about outsiders?"

"Mongolian culture is based on hospitality. I can't imagine they would be any different."

But would they rescue an injured man and keep him alive for months? It seemed very unlikely.

The sun reached its apex, and Batu continued to sleep, his head lolling back and forth with the bumps and potholes in the road. Alex's nerves were taut to the breaking point. Either this was going to be the biggest adventure of her life or the most memorable failure.

"How much farther?" she asked.

"We're making good time," answered Miranda, who assessed the gauge on her speedometer where the needle was flirting with the red zone. "We'll be there in less than two hours."

Two hours to Murun, where they would trade the beat-up Hyundai for a van that would deposit them at the edge of the taiga. And then how to barter for horses? She would cross that bridge when she came to it.

They arrived in Murun at sunset and pulled into the parking lot of the Arata Travel Company. A man with a hat pulled low over his brow and dressed in layers of heavy clothing smoked a cigarette, the bright embers of its tip glowing in the dusk. He stood next to a muddy brown omnibus with snow chains wrapped around the tires.

Batu stirred, finally opening his lids and grumbling in Mongolian as he stepped out of the car into the night's descending chill. The two men exchanged greetings, and then he returned and motioned Miranda to roll down the window. He gestured to the van and then asked her something in Mongolian. They volleyed words that Alex couldn't understand for a few minutes before Miranda nodded and rolled up the window.

"What did he say?" Alex asked hurriedly.

"It's too late to leave for the taiga tonight. We need light to see where we are going. There are no roads, only mountain paths, and we don't want to end up at the bottom of a ravine."

Alex groaned inwardly but couldn't see the point in arguing.

"What time can he pick us up in the morning?"

"I told Batu we need to leave early. If we leave by four, we should make it there between nine and ten."

It sounded like a lifetime away, but Alex nodded. "Where do we sleep tonight?"

Miranda motioned to the small office building connected to the parking lot. "Tem said we can spread out on the floor of their office if we don't mind a draft and a bathroom with no shower."

"I've had worse." Alex smirked and exchanged a knowing look with Miranda.

As she fell prostrate into her sleeping bag, Alex welcomed the exhaustion weighing down on her like a ton of bricks. Tem hadn't been exaggerating about the draft. She had worn her clothes to bed, plus her coat and shoes, and still didn't feel warm. She couldn't imagine what the next few nights would bring as they traipsed through one of the coldest regions of the world on horseback. The flooring pressed into her back, and she shifted position for the hundredth time, absorbing the stillness of the night. No matter the conditions, she was grateful for something solid on which to rest her horizontal frame.

Miranda snored lightly in the sleeping bag next to her, but the third sleeping bag was empty. She had hoped Batu would be resting so that he would be sober and ready to go before dawn. But the last time she had seen him, he was sitting outside with Tem sharing a bottle of vodka and swapping stories.

A restless sleep claimed Alex's consciousness as she drifted just below the surface waters of sleep, prepared to emerge at any moment. She awoke before her phone alarm chimed and, after a quick trip to the bathroom for some last-minute hygiene, began to pack up her supplies.

As promised, Tem was waiting next to the open door of the van with a lit cigarette, blowing doughnuts of smoke into the chill. He stubbed it out under his foot and gestured to the inside of the van. Alex slid into a worn vinyl seat, ripped in various places and patched up with duct tape. She noted the absence of seatbelts.

Tem climbed in and gunned the engine, but instead of putting the van in gear, he sat back and opened a newspaper as warmth crept into cabin. *Where was Batu?* Alex looked sharply at Miranda, who shrugged and peered harder into the darkness of the office building window. A wrestling contest between respectful manners and anxiety-driven rudeness ensued between Alex's id and superego. The id was winning by a nose. She leaned her head back and tried to summon a river of calm through her internal frenzy and waited.

Almost half an hour later, Batu emerged, not from the office door, but schlepped around the corner, head bent into the wind, his overcoat flapping open. Alex flared with irritation as he wrenched open the passenger door and the rancid smell of unwashed human and last night's alcohol binge struck her in the face. So that's where he was all night. The crunch of tires on the morning snow as they peeled right off the edge of the parking lot onto an unmarked path toward the mountains was only a slight consolation to Alex's disgruntlement.

For hours they skidded and swerved to a destination unknown. The topography changed considerably as they rose in altitude. The trees became denser, and the snow became thicker, covering everything with a thick white frosting that reminded Alex of the birthday cakes her mom made when she was a kid.

She had no idea what was ahead, but she knew she was on the right path—her path. And she wasn't alone on the journey. She reached over and squeezed Miranda's hand. Miranda with her finely boned features and short layered hair, her thin frame, and rapid, pressured speech. Her joyous eyes and graciousness. Her spiritedness and loyalty.

When they had worked together in Mongolia several years before, Miranda had adopted her as more than a mentee. She had treated her like a daughter and a sister and a friend all wrapped up into one. After they settled the post-operative patients for the evening, she and Miranda would share leftover wrapped sandwiches and socialize. Miranda would talk animatedly about her career and her life and would listen attentively to Alex. At the time, Alex had little to share compared to Miranda who had already been all over the world—Thailand and Kenya and Peru—as she worked with local physicians to improve access to cardiac surgery for kids.

Alex had observed how the rest of the team treated Miranda with reverence and friendship. She had admired this brand of kinship and longed for it in her own life. And she had found it with Tim and Beth, then Roxanne, Mercy, and Mary Lou, even Sam. *And Ian.* With Ian she had experienced a vulnerable intimacy, a friendship, and a love like she had never known.

Alex was thrown forward off her bench seat when the van skidded to a stop. *Rrrrr.* The tires spun without creating forward momentum, and large globs of mud spattered the windshield. Tem jumped out and flung open the sliding door to the back of the van. He gestured and said something terse in Mongolian to Miranda. She jumped out, slinging on her backpack.

"We're walking from here, sweetpea."

For some reason being out on the terrain, stumbling along behind the others with her backpack felt infinitely better than being inside the van. Every inhale was the purest air she had ever breathed, and she imagined that the freshly fallen snow had never seen footprints before hers. They walked single file through a scattered clump of trees, and over the next rise, Batu began waving and shouting. Alex broke into a jog, her heart rate picking up speed along with her steps, and when she reached the crest, Lake Khövsgöl came into view.

Alex saw a wisp of smoke drifting upward from a large, felt-lined ger that was surrounded by a cluster of smaller gers. Alex had never been inside one, but the thick felt panels comprising the outer walls made them look incredibly cozy. She knew that a one room ger usually housed an entire family and was filled with colorful wall hangings that paid homage to their ancestry. A few of the men milled outdoors tending the animals and glanced up as their motley group approached. Tem and Batu broke off and approached a man holding the lead rope to a rangy-looking pony.

Alex watched nervously while the men bantered back and forth. How hard would it be to convince these guys to loan her a few horses? They would need at least four. One for each rider and one to carry supplies.

"What are they saying?" Alex nudged Miranda.

"I don't know." She shook her head as she tried to refocus on the words. "The dialect isn't familiar to me."

Alex wandered into the small village, and a little boy popped his head out of one of the smaller gers. He was dressed in a traditional blue deel, his hair cut short under a fitted hat. He flashed her a smile, and Alex gave him a wave. One of the smaller ponies stood next to his ger, rooting his nose through the snow to get at a few stubborn grasses that sprouted underneath. The boy grasped a handful of mane and swung a leg over the pony in the same motion, heading off in a stalwart trot.

Horses were a way of life here and considered sacred in Mongolian culture. Everyone learned to ride before they could walk properly. This was as close as Alex had ever been to one, and she critically observed its characteristics. The Mongol horses were small but well-built, bred for their resilience. Their fortitude.

"Alex," Miranda called, and she tore herself away from the grazing ponies to hustle back to her friend's side. "We're good to go."

A slight man with graying temples held the lead ropes to four saddled horses, and Alex felt the tension build inside her. This was it. It was actually happening.

Tem accepted the lead ropes, and Alex reflexively began evaluating the options to choose her mount. Two of the horses were chestnut brown with a thick layer of winter hair and long shaggy manes. The third was a dappled grey, a rarity among Mongolian horses and stockier than the other two with excellent hindquarters.

And the fourth was deeply ebony, jet black all over with a mane rippling over his neck that had never been trimmed. Alex peered into his eyes when Tem led him past her. He tossed his head wildly, fire inside the depths of his black eyes. But there was also purpose, intelligence, and fearlessness.

Reaching out a hand, Alex brushed her fingers along his velvety soft muzzle. In response, he skittered his lips over her hand, searching for a treat. She grabbed his bridle and softly blew a fog of breath over his nostrils, and he answered with a warm gush of air onto her cheek.

"I'll take this one," she said, and Batu chuckled, pointing at her and then at the horse. Alex looked to Miranda for interpretation.

"That's a stallion. A man's horse, not a lady's. He's a wild one."

"Then he's perfect for me," Alex replied quickly, patting his neck.

She took the reins from Tem and tossed them over the black beauty's neck. Batu shrugged and accepted the reins of the grey, and with surprising agility, mounted up. Tem and Miranda loaded the supplies on one of the bays, and then Tem handed her the reins to both horses. He began speaking in a low voice, and Miranda nodded, accepting whatever he was saying. Alex looked on inquisitively. Tem held up three fingers, and Miranda glanced at Alex.

"What does that mean?"

"We have the horses for three days," she explained "Tem will meet us here to pick us up."

Three days. That wasn't near long enough, but it was the best she had.

Tem looked right at Alex and then jerked a thumb at the black horse tossing his head at the end of the leather reins.

"I hope you are a good rider," Miranda interpreted.

Alex smiled and swung herself into the saddle, settling there and shushing her mount.

"I *am* from Texas."

THIRTY-THREE

Alex nudged her horse along, encouraging a brisk trot to catch up with Batu, who was several lengths ahead of her. The going was slow, not far from treacherous, and the experienced ponies picked their way through snowbanks, fallen tree limbs, and rocky outcroppings as they continued to gain elevation. They took turns holding the lead rope of the pack pony that carried their supplies including a set of saddlebags for food and water and the rolled-up felt they would use as a makeshift tent.

Several hours into their journey, Alex could no longer feel her feet. She dropped her stirrups so that she could scrunch up her toes inside her boots without her horse thinking she wanted more speed. He certainly was responsive to her every movement. Every time she shifted in the saddle, she felt his back muscles tense and his haunches bunch underneath her, ready to explode with power at the slightest encouragement. If Ian were somehow transformed into a horse, it would be the one between her legs.

When she caught up with Batu, she noticed that his chin was tucked into his chest, stuffed into his coat like a turtle, and his eyes were closed. Was he sleeping? She bristled with annoyance again. They might not have been able to get a better guide at such short notice, but they couldn't have done much worse.

"Excuse me, Batu?" she said warily. "Should we stop and let the horses get a drink somewhere?"

He merely grunted in response. Miranda rode several paces behind her. She tried to pantomime river by undulating her hand to and fro, finally earning a hard stare from Batu. And then the forest rang with laughter, and he wheeled his horse to the right and motioned his hand for Alex and Miranda to follow.

A few more miles dodging and weaving between coniferous trees brought them to a river covered with a thin sheet of ice that moved languidly, pushed along by the undercurrent. Mongolia was right on the verge of transitioning into spring, and soon this narrow strip of ice would receive a gush of melting snow from the mountainside and turn into a torrent.

Alex slipped off black beauty, her boots crunching in the frozen earth when she hit the ground. "Come on," she encouraged, the horse balking before allowing himself to be led to the water's edge. Alex found a sturdy branch on the ground and began breaking up ice chunks to expose the freshwater underneath. She dropped to her knees and removed her gloves to scoop a mouthful of the river water. It was so cold that it crystallized her veins, and she treated herself to another mouthful.

Her doctor brain shook its finger at her. It was never a smart idea to drink river water because of the parasite burden. She had acquired *Giardia* more times than she could count from her travels over the years, and it wasn't pleasant. The water here, though, was different, pure and untainted. Quivering black lips joined her at the water's edge as her black mount snorted into the swirling river and then imbibed a few sips before tossing his head.

Batu had stopped upstream with his back to her, and she noticed a stream of liquid arcing out from his midsection and carving a pattern into the snow. Miranda arrived next to her, puffing out a freshly exhaled breath as she dismounted.

"Is he always this...charming?" Alex wrinkled her nose and jerked her head toward Batu, who had leaned down next to the water's edge to fill a leather carafe.

"Absolutely. You should see him when Arsenal is playing Tottenham Hotspur," Miranda replied. "He was passed out for three days afterward and had to cancel my appointment."

"Appointment?" Alex looked at her sharply.

"He's a dentist by training. Did a killer job on my root canal."

Alex's eyes bugged out of her head. "I thought you said he was a bartender."

"He's a dentist who owns a bar in town."

"Is that how you met?"

"Yes."

Miranda flushed pink when she mentioned the bar, and Alex wanted to press further but decided against it.

"So, he's an Arsenal fan," Alex said, squinting at the sun

beginning to settle on the horizon.

Once Batu found out that Alex not only knew but was good friends with Nicolau Brizido, the most famous Arsenal footballer in history, she gained a tremendous amount of status in his eyes. While they set up their camp for the night, he badgered her with questions via Miranda, his face taking on an animated appearance that made him seem years younger. He was reasonably handsome once he wasn't drunk or hungover. His face, broad with prominent cheekbones, sported a light sprinkling of dark facial hair with eyes that were chestnut in color and contained equal parts amusement and toughness.

Alex observed Miranda trying to hide a grin while he talked. There was definitely something cooking there, and it wasn't just an excellent root canal and an after-dinner cocktail.

Alex untacked the horses while Miranda and Batu struggled to erect the circumference of the ger that all three of them would share. She hobbled the horses' front legs together with nylon binding so that they could graze but not stray too far during the night. They were deep into the taiga. The winter home of the Tsaatan couldn't be far away, and tomorrow they would find it.

As she stared at the flames of their small fire later that night and watched the yellow, orange, and red dancers sway to a melody she couldn't hear, she let herself be hopeful for the first time since finding the cufflink. It was a hopefulness, though, mixed with a hefty dose of reality. She knew that it was much more likely that she would find out what happened to Ian rather than find Ian himself. But hope was like a pearl—the more she abraded its surface, the larger it grew.

Alex huddled into her sleeping bag after a dinner of goat jerky and a bag of peanut M&M's she had stashed in her backpack that she split three ways. Miranda slept peacefully beside her, a wool hat pulled down low over her eyes for added relaxation. Batu, on the other hand, sat cross-legged on the floor at the doorway to the ger. His broad back faced her, and she could hear the slosh of liquid as he took gulp after gulp of what was most likely not water.

A wolf released a mournful howl into the night, followed by a series of yelps and guttural growls. The horses whinnied nervously, and she could hear them pawing at the frozen ground. Batu peeled open the hanging doorway of the ger and introduced a wedge of moonlight into the interior. His face stayed impassive, but he brought two fingers to his lips to procure silence, rotating to make sure Alex saw the gesture.

At first, she thought she imagined the delicate sound of snow crunching under something light-footed, but then she heard a whine and then another that coalesced into a symphony of growls. A painful yelp resounded through the clearing as a hoof met with the soft underbelly of a wolf. She could hear the horses snorting and stamping as they whinnied loudly amidst the onslaught of the wolves. Throwing back her sleeping bag, she crawled to the doorway and the formidable body blocking it. She tried to open the flap, desperate to do something to protect the horses from the predators outside.

Batu shook his head and motioned for her to get back. Even though he was right, she stared at him hard and pointed toward the tragedy unfolding right outside their tent. Expressionless, he lifted a flask to his lips and jerked his thumb backward. Alex seethed and wrung her hands but retreated into the far corner of their dwelling. She covered her head with her blanket as she heard an animal's last groan and a sickening thud as it was brought to the ground.

At the first sign of impending dawn, Alex threw back the flap to the tent to check on the horses, first discovering the bloodstained ground where one of their horses had been killed by wolves and then the streaky ribbons of maroon that disappeared into the forest where they had drug the carcass. She woke Miranda to reveal the events of the night before and, with their jaws set in determination, they backtracked toward the river to find the rest of the horses.

"I must have been in a coma last night," Miranda said, puffing a breath out as they climbed over a dead tree blocking their path.

"Have you seen Batu this morning?" Alex asked.

"No, I don't even remember him leaving."

"Figures," Alex grumbled, thinking of the amount of alcohol he must have consumed while having a front-row seat to equine murder. "I just hope he didn't get so drunk that he fell in the river and drowned."

Miranda stifled a laugh and then straightened up her face when she caught Alex's glare.

"We have to find the Tsaatan today. Tomorrow is going to be cutting it too close, and then Tem is picking us up, and this is over." Alex's voice sounded shrill to her ears.

"Don't worry," Miranda said softly. "I trust Batu. He knows exactly what he's doing. Let's turn around and try the other direction."

They searched for the better part of an hour with not so much as a footprint to follow and then headed back to camp to try the other side of the forest. Alex could no longer tell when her feet struck the ground, and black disappointment covered her like a shroud.

When they entered the small clearing, Alex startled at the sight of the ger that had been disassembled and neatly rolled up and Batu stamping his boots over the embers of a dying fire. The remaining three horses had been tacked up, including Alex's black one, who pawed the ground as the women approached. Batu spat into the snow and threw a leg over one of the bays.

Alex eagerly mounted her precious black and extended a hand to Miranda so she could join her.

With three horses left, they would have to ride double so that the other bay could carry the ger and saddlebags.

"*Yaavtsgaaya*," instructed Batu and trotted off into the forest.

"I assume that means 'let's go'," Alex whispered to Miranda.

"More like...get your ass in gear."

Alex urged her mount forward through thick snowbanks and over fallen limbs, and every time he thought about slowing, she brushed her heels against his furry sides. Batu had taken up his typical riding stance of head lolling side to side and eyes closed. Periodically, he would pull the leather-bound flask out of his boot and take a hooch.

Alex felt pressured, like a huntress closing in on her prey, and her anxiety was seeping into her mount. He startled and tossed his head at every shadow and had tried to unseat her and Miranda more than once. She had refused to let the group pause for lunch, and now, in addition to being cold and bone-tired, they were also hungry.

Alex looked up at the sun directly over them, praying for it to infuse some of its warmth into her skin. The forest was thick, but it didn't entirely block out the blue sky, offering them some frame of reference for their direction.

Speaking of direction. Maybe the ketones building up in her system were playing tricks with her mind, but she could have sworn they had passed that rock already. She narrowed her eyes. They had absolutely passed that rock over an hour ago because she had thought to herself how artsy of God to make a rock shaped like a giant jalapeño pepper.

"Hey," she called into the space ahead of her. "Hey," she repeated, digging her heels into her horse's sides so that he sped forward. "Batu," she said when his face came into view. "Are we going in circles?"

One eye popped open and observed Alex with its marble-sized pupil surrounded by a conjunctiva bursting with red. He grunted in response.

"Because I know that I've seen that rock before."

Batu grumbled a string of Mongolian and gestured toward Miranda.

"He says that we are following the spirits of his ancestors that still roam these woods. That we must submit to the guidance of the heavens if our journey is to be successful."

"Maybe that was true in the year 1287, but in 2011 we have something called a GPS," Alex said coldly and then dismounted so quickly that Miranda almost toppled off. She dropped her reins and slid her hand over the leather of the black's bridle.

"I am counting on you," she said, boring her eyes into Batu's, eyes that pleaded with him to understand her level of desperation. "I lost someone that I have to find."

Alex saw Miranda's sympathetic gaze out of the corner of her eye. Batu continued to stare at her, and she wasn't certain, but she thought she detected a realm of empathy in his eyes.

"Please," she implored, allowing his horse to nuzzle her ear.

With a definitive grunt, he spurred his horse forward, and Alex watched him form an exaggerated arc in the snow dust. He dropped his reins and held his hands out to his sides, circling not one but three times before he dismounted swiftly and bent his ear to the ground. He called to Miranda, and Alex peered at her expectantly.

"He says we will stop here for the night."

Alex nearly boiled over with rage. They had not covered enough ground today, and only half a day remained before they would have to turn back—and that's if they rode the entire night to meet their three-day deadline.

"I don't want to stop here," she shouted at the top of her lungs. "I want to keep going."

She had half a mind to head off on her own, frozen forest or not, and take her chances with hypothermia and predatory wolves. Batu barked at her in Mongolian.

"You will stay," interpreted Miranda, "and help me call on the White Heaven through fire."

"Do what?" Alex responded, throwing her hands up.

Miranda shrugged and dropped her gaze.

"Did I mention Batu is a dentist by day, bartender by night, and a weekend shaman?"

What the hell am I doing? Alex grunted as she and Miranda hoisted a thick tree limb onto a rapidly expanding pyramid of logs, under the direction of Batu, who was seated on an overturned saddle gesturing with his hands.

"What now?" Alex asked Miranda.

"He wants it bigger."

"What man doesn't?" Alex muttered, earning choking laughter from Miranda. She stomped back into the thick of the forest and seriously considered offering a certain hand gesture as her reply but didn't.

She and Miranda had spent the better part of an hour compiling small twigs and brush and then stacking tree limbs upright to erect a legitimate bonfire. By the time it was completed to Batu's liking, Alex was freezing and had long ago lost sensation in her toes and fingers. The frigid phantasm had kept spreading until her teeth chattered and her abdominals were sore from violently contracting.

Batu had finally made himself useful and tied up the horses so that they didn't bolt at the first sign of fire. Horses hated fire. They either became paralyzed with fear or fled on winged hooves and wouldn't stop until they exhausted themselves. Alex shuddered at a long-ago memory of hooves pounding against wood and neighs turning to screams.

A bottle was suddenly thrust into her line of sight, a clear liquid sloshing up and down like ocean waves. Batu extended a shaky hand toward her, proffering the bottle. She accepted it into a gloved hand and sniffed the contents. *Whew!* The vapors almost bowled her over.

"What's in here?" she mused aloud.

"Probably *arkhi*. Also known as milk vodka," Miranda answered. "Batu keeps his own still for his many experimental varieties."

Batu gestured to her, encouraging her to take a sip. Alex held the cold rim to her lips and tried not to inhale too deeply.

"Please tell me I'm not going to go blind from this." She took a swig of pure liquid fire and coughed as it sizzled down her esophagus.

Batu laughed aloud, a hearty sound that rocked the nearest tree limbs, and despite the raw feeling in the back of her throat, Alex laughed too. She took another small sip for good measure before handing the bottle back to Batu and received a nod of approval. He tipped the bottle up, guzzling the contents before plunking it into a little nest of snow and then disappearing into the ger.

Night had crept up on them like a specter. The orange hues of the evening sky had already transitioned to shades of purple. She and Miranda sat huddled with a sleeping bag thrown over their shoulders and wrapped around their fronts to evade the chill. The cold had penetrated so deep into her body that her heart itself felt made of ice—an ice heart pumping glacier temperature blood to frozen tissues.

"What's the warmest place you've ever been?" asked Miranda, trying to distract her from the cold.

Alex filed through her memories—the Kalahari, that beach in Mozambique, the sweaty Texas summer nights with no air conditioner. And then she saw images of Ian pulling her hand to his chest on a balcony in Paris, the two of them tangled in sundrenched sheets in her tiny apartment in Philadelphia and ripping clothes from one another in a hayloft in Tanzania. Despite the cold, her cheeks filled with a warm flush, and her lips curled upward.

"He was that good, huh?" Miranda ribbed her with an elbow.

"He was...epic."

Alex pulled the bottle of vodka from the snow and choked down another gulp, and then handed it to Miranda. Tinkling laughter bubbled up as Miranda raised the bottle to her own lips.

"Aah, Batu makes good stuff," she said, wincing a little.

Alex gave her a sidelong glance. "Is he good at anything else?"

The alcohol was starting to sublimate the ice in her veins. Her tongue already felt thick, and her hands didn't feel quite as cold as they should. Miranda nursed the bottle and stared off into the trees, where there was nothing to see except for the ensuing darkness.

"Mm-hmm. Quite good actually."

"Well, I hope so because so far, he's a really crappy guide."

Their laughter launched into the night, so abrupt and high pitched that it scared one of the horses and his hind legs skittered through the snow. Hugging one another for warmth, they continued laughing, tittering into the inky black of their sleeping bag cave until Batu emerged from the ger.

"What the—?" The laughter died in Alex's throat.

Batu had donned a black mask that completely covered his face with a curtain of black beads in strands that glinted in the starlight. A festive arrangement of eagle feathers poked out of the top of his head in various vectors. As he crept past them, Alex noticed that he carried a drum in one hand and a small mallet in the other. Where had he packed all of that? She twisted around to look at Miranda, who motioned her to be silent with two fingers. With one swipe of his arm, the entire bonfire burst into flames.

"Holy sh—"

"Shhh!" Miranda hissed into her ear.

The beat of a drum resounded through the clearing. *Boom. Boom.* Batu revolved around the fire, worshipping the flames as he kept perfect time on his drum. He threw his head back, a guttural noise escaping his throat, and the cadence quickened. His words peaked and dipped, up and down, like mountains and valleys were being spewed from his lips. All the while, his drum accompanied him. He beckoned the flames. He protested to the sky. It was ethereal.

Alex followed his movements, finding herself seduced by the drum and heady with the spirits—both the ones in the bottle and the ones around them. She suddenly found herself throwing off the sleeping bag and wrenching out of Miranda's grasp to approach the fire. She knelt at its base, the wet ground seeping through the knees of her pants and focused on the flames. The heat scorched her face as the cold clawed at her back.

What would she see if she stared into the flames? She didn't realize the drumming had paused until she felt a hand under her elbow, jerking her to a stand.

THIRTY-FOUR

Her eyes wouldn't open, and the ground beneath her oscillated like she was at sea. Her cheek was entrenched in a divot in the ground, completely flush with the dirt. Reaching out to the warm body next to her, she found Miranda's back through the sleeping bag. What had happened last night? She struggled to remember, like inserting a key into an old crusty lock. It required quite a bit of jiggling before it popped free.

Alex had been staring into the fire when Batu had pulled her upward by her arm. He held out both hands in front of him as if asking for charity. He thrust them under her nose, and she began backing away.

"Ask him to explain, Miranda."

He and Miranda exchanged a few phrases while Alex put a little more distance between her and Batu. Miranda handed him the vodka bottle, which he inserted into the beaded curtain to take a lengthy sip.

"He needs you to offer your turmoil to the spirits. Do you have anything of Ian's?"

Alex sighed, reaching into the zippered pocket of her down parka and removing the silver cufflink. Before she could change her mind, she plopped it into Batu's outstretched hands. He rolled it between his palms, chanting something under his breath. Her heart wailed as he tossed it right into the fire.

"And now something of yours," Miranda added.

"Of mine?" Alex squeaked. "I don't have anything with me," her voice trailed off, "except for this."

She reached down past her layers of clothing to finger the lion pendant around her neck. *Something to remember where it all started.* That's what Ian's note had read when she pulled the glittering lion pendant out of the robin's egg blue box. She could still remember how her chest had vibrated with the lion's roar during their first kiss in the Kalahari. The spark that had lit her on fire. It had started with lions, and now it looked like it might end with them too.

Unclasping the necklace, she dangled it above Batu's palms, admiring how the gold caught the firelight. He accepted it into his palms, rubbing it between them and chanting melodically before also tossing it into the fire. He thrust his arms upward, fanning the smoke with his hands, and resumed his orbit around the fire. Miranda brought Alex the almost empty vodka bottle.

"Here."

"Thanks," she replied. "What happens now?"

"Batu will send up the smoke of your sacrifice as an appeal to the spirits to help us find Ian."

"What should we do?"

"Finish the vodka."

Alex peeled one eyelid open with her thumb and forefinger. Finishing the vodka had turned out to be a bad idea, but it had dulled the pain and kept her oblivious to the cold for most of the night. They had all three sat around the fire until it turned to ash, with Batu miraculously producing an additional bottle of spirits when the first one came up empty.

Alex sat up and pulled a few twigs from her hair. What had she been thinking? She crawled over to the flap of the ger and opened it. The day was cloudy but already infused with sunlight. She cursed under her breath. Most of the morning had passed while she was comatose from vodka that bordered on being considered poisonous.

Leaping from the tent, she scurried past the horses, who eyed her curiously, and headed toward the river. With every footfall, a deeper level of annoyance struck her tendons. Instead of spending every second searching for a sign of the Tsaatan, Alex had allowed them to stop for a Shaman ceremony that she was pretty sure Batu used as an excuse to get rip-roaring drunk and pass out.

She would never again see the cufflink or her necklace...or Ian. A wave of despair washed through her, but her eyes, gritty from smoke and dehydration, failed to generate a single tear. Or maybe she had reached the point where she didn't have any tears left.

Finding a bare spot on the ground, she degloved and knelt to dip some of the ice-cold water from the stream. She splashed it on her face, the shock of the cold reviving her frazzled neurons from last night's shenanigans. She stared at her reflection in the small rippling pool framed by chunks of ice. It stared back at her impassively. *I'm not lost. I just can't see what's ahead of me.*

The back of her neck prickled with anticipation. Someone was looking at her from across the river. As she slowly picked up her head, she met the eyes of the woman staring at her, her head cocked to one side, her hand patting the white furry neck of her mount—a white reindeer.

The woman had a moon-shaped face, her cheeks beet red from exposure to the elements, her body covered by a purple satin deel and a magenta scarf thrown over one shoulder. She nodded a greeting to Alex, and when Alex waved slowly, her lips parted in a tremendous smile. The reindeer had fur as white as the winter's snow and a pair of antlers so extreme that they almost touched the woman's face. He regarded her calmly as if she were no more than an extension of the ground like a rock or a tree stump. Alex scrambled to her feet.

"Are you Tsaatan?"

The woman gestured toward the reindeer, and Alex stifled a laugh. Of course, she was.

"We've been looking for you. Stay right there!" She flapped her hands, pointing toward the woman's spot on the other side of the river. "I'll be back."

Alex tore through the dense thicket of forest to reach the clearing where Miranda and Batu were most likely still sleeping. Miranda was up, crouched over the ashes from last night's ceremonial bonfire, digging through them with a stick.

"Miranda—" Alex was breathless. She gulped oxygen like it was disappearing and bent over until her hands rested on her knees. "Follow me."

Miranda, her face awash with concern, jumped to her feet and grabbed Alex's outstretched hand.

"Where are we going?" she yelped as they trotted over the terrain. Alex carelessly pulled her forward.

"The river. I found a woman," Alex huffed, "with a reindeer."

As if on cue, the woman held up one hand to the newcomer, and Miranda skidded to a stop.

"*Sain baina uu.*" Miranda waved and walked the rest of the way to the river's edge.

The woman smiled and began speaking rapidly.

"What is she saying?" Alex asked.

"I don't know. I'm terrible at the northern dialects and the Tsaatan speak Dukha."

Like a gift from heaven, Batu came lumbering out of the forest then, still staggering from the effects of the libations the night before. He scrubbed a hand over his face, rubbing some soot onto his cheeks in the process. He stopped short when he saw the reindeer, his face transforming with awe and reverence. He called to the woman, and they conversed back and forth for a few minutes with Alex and Miranda watching them like a tennis match. Batu pointed at Alex and then said something to Miranda in Mongolian.

"This woman will take us to her village, and we can ask her family if they know anything of Ian."

This was the first strong lead since they had left UB. They had found the Tsaatan. Although it wasn't the same as finding Ian, it was something. The tiniest pearl of hope.

"This is amazing. Tell her yes and thank you. Wait—" Alex paused. "Why do you look so defeated?"

Batu began gesturing and pointing downriver, and Miranda held up her hands to slow down the pace of his speech.

"We can't get across the river. It's not frozen solid anymore. The horses would fall right through the ice."

"What about farther down?"

Miranda shook her head. "There's nowhere to cross for hundreds of kilometers. It's what makes this area so remote until summertime when they can swim across or the dead of winter when it's frozen solid."

Alex began nodding her head, an idea of pure insanity taking shape. A mantra beat its way into her head like last night's drum. *Live wildly. Love recklessly.*

"I'll be right back. Don't let her leave," she instructed her companions.

When Alex returned, she was toting her backpack containing a water bottle, a useless iPhone, and a satellite phone she hoped would come in handy.

"Alex, what do you think you're doing?" Miranda asked pointedly as Alex took her backpack and tossed it to the opposite riverbank.

It landed with a thud.

"I've come too far," she grunted, bending down to tuck her pants into her boots, "to turn back now."

"That's incredibly romantic of you, but this is not Last of the freaking Mohicans," Miranda objected.

Miranda's voice became shrill as she continued to protest. Batu merely raised his eyebrows as Alex trotted upriver a few paces to find a stretch of virginal ice without any cracks. She flopped onto her stomach near the bank and slid the front half of her body onto the ice.

"That's not going to hold your weight, Alex," Miranda shouted.

"I guess we'll find out," she muttered, not necessarily loud enough for anyone to hear.

Head then chest. She crept forward. *Knees.* And then ever so slowly, her entire body was suspended on a thin sheet of ice. She moved at a snail's pace, digging in with her fingertips and pushing with her toes in the most excruciating plank she had ever done, gaining an inch here and a half an inch there.

Alex was thankful that she couldn't see Miranda's horrified face behind her. Halfway there, she heard the first whine of protest from the ice. Everything faded around her, and she centered her strength, her sheer force of will, and every ounce of fortitude she possessed, to deliver precise instruction to her muscles. Contract. Relax. Move forward one more inch.

Alex focused her gaze on the ice below her eyes rather than the bank ahead of her, and she didn't dare look behind her. She was within an arm's length of the bank when a groan tore through the ice, and the lower half of her body plunged into the water. It was so unbearably cold that she gasped and could not command her chest to relax enough to exhale. It immediately soaked through her clothes and weighed her down. Her arms burned with the exertion of keeping her upright, and somewhere outside the frenetic atmosphere of her brain, she could hear Miranda and Batu shouting.

When Alex was a child, she had survived a flood. As a teenager, she had escaped a fire, and now she had become a woman. A woman who had lived and loved and lost. She had known real love and real tragedy, and, through it all, she continued to rise. She wouldn't stop now on account of some godforsaken ice. She exhaled forcefully and scissor-kicked her legs to propel herself upward.

Flinging her arms in front of her, she began grappling for anything within arms' reach until her fingers closed around a magenta scarf. With surprising strength, the Tsaatan woman yanked on the other end of the scarf until Alex felt the ground, formidable and solid beneath her face. She dropped her forehead to the dirt and kissed it.

Behind her, Miranda and Batu were making noises worthy of waking the dead. Alex scrambled to her feet on unsteady legs that still had not gained full circulation.

"Are you okay?" shrieked Miranda.

Alex shot her a thumbs-up then cupped her hands around her mouth. "Head back with the horses, and I'll call you from the sat phone when," she paused, deciding whether to correct herself, "I find Ian."

Alex's hands tightened around the woman's thick midsection and balanced precariously behind the saddle of her snow-white reindeer as he dutifully carried his passengers over the tundra. With a single lead rope attached to a woven halter, the woman was able to guide the reindeer through the terrain, adding an occasional bump with her heels when he became distracted and slowed his pace. The country had opened with hospitality as they left the forest behind for a dipping valley covered in pristine frost.

Despite her legs quaking from being soaked to the bone, the ride was exhilarating, and she was almost sorry when they arrived at a cluster of five makeshift teepee-like structures. She slid off the reindeer after the woman, who only glanced back once to make sure Alex was following.

When she disappeared into one of the tents, Alex was unsure whether to follow until she popped her head out and motioned for Alex to enter. The inside was surprisingly warm from a fire burning inside a clay stove in the middle of the floor. Colorful tapestries and furs lined the walls. A slender man with short-cropped black hair, long sideburns, and a thin mustache picked up a ladle and stirred whatever bubbled on top of the stove. It smelled delicious, and Alex's stomach rumbled.

The woman tugged on the man's turquoise shirtsleeve, and he regarded Alex with wide eyes full of curiosity and kindness. She gestured to Alex and then launched into an involved monologue, explaining—Alex assumed—the reason an American was elbows deep in the wintry taiga right now. He seemed confused and began shaking his head. Alex's spirits plummeted.

She began frantically tucking her hair behind her ear, her brain still fuzzy from the insanity of the last twenty-four hours. With how little water she'd drunk today, she was probably bordering on kidney injury, which was ironic since she had almost drowned earlier. Reaching in her backpack, her hand searched for the cylinder of her water bottle but instead closed over the cool rectangle of her phone. *Jackpot.*

Alex pulled it out, praying there was enough battery left, and, with frozen fingers, pressed the on button. It took ages for the bitten apple to disappear, but once it did, she flashed her phone up to the couple, her home screen displaying Ian, in all his pixelated glory. It was a photo she had snapped of him at Christmas last year when his hair was mussed from the wind and his cheeks held a light blush from the cold. His full lips were parted enough to show his straight teeth. And his eyes, as blue as a Mongolian sky, were filled with mirth and mischief.

Slim brown fingers wrapped around the phone and tugged it out of Alex's grasp. The man's eyes squinted at the photo, and then he peered at the woman who threw up her hands in response. Alex smiled and shifted her eyes away. They were obviously married. When she looked back, the man was digging into the pocket of his pants. His face broke into a toothy smile when he found what he was looking for and thrust it toward Alex. A tiny silver replica of the Millennium Falcon.

Frantically, she nodded her head and pointed at the cufflink and then at Ian's picture. He tried to deposit the bit of silver in her hand, but she gave him a resolute no and pointed at Ian, begging him with her eyes to understand. He rubbed the black stubble on his chin and glanced at his wife. She launched into a passionate speech using the heel of her hand to point northward and then finished with her hands on her hips. The man grunted and then headed out of the tent.

Alex waited, venturing as close to the fire as she dared, her knees still quaking from her damp clothing while the woman observed her calmly. She couldn't imagine what she looked like with her face streaked with dirt, wearing wet clothing, and smelling like yesterday's garbage. The woman regarded her with solemn eyes, and Alex had to stop herself from hugging her and thanking her for saving her life. She doubted the woman's hospitality extended to physical affection with a bedraggled urchin of a human. Instead, Alex wrapped her arms around herself while she quietly prayed for warmth. While her eyes were closed, she felt the fluttering of cool silk across her face and opened them to find the woman wrapping her magenta scarf around her shoulders.

A cold gust struck her as the flap of the canvas tent was flung open to reveal the slender husband holding the lead rope of a saddled reindeer with tawny fur and mile-high antlers. He extended the rope in Alex's direction. She took it willingly and put a gentle hand on the soft muzzle craning through the doorway. The man grew excited as he gestured northward and pointed to Alex and then the reindeer. Alex bit her lip and shook her head. She had no idea what he was trying to tell her.

"He wants you to take the reindeer to the frozen valley," a sunshine voice outside the tent said. Alex stepped out into the sunlight.

The voice belonged to a young girl mounted on the back of the snow-white reindeer with smooth skin over prominent cheekbones and eyes alive with youth.

"You speak English?"

The girl nodded.

"I attended school for two years in Ulaanbaatar before coming back here to be with my family." Her eyes roamed over her parents and then to the reindeer dotting the landscape. "I'll take you where you need to go."

The frozen valley was a four-hour ride due north through mostly flat, open terrain where the depth of the snow increased the farther they traveled. It was a remote, poorly accessible region of the taiga where a cluster of Tsaatan families gathered to manage the winter together until spring when they packed up their belongings, including an entire herd of reindeer, and traveled south to Lake Khövsgöl to take advantage of tourist season.

Alex gripped her calves around her reindeer, clutching the single rope in her left hand and holding onto the saddle with her right. The first hour had been unsteady as she had experimented with different positions in the saddle that would promote rather than inhibit the forward momentum of the reindeer. It wasn't like riding a horse at all. Horses had broad backs and hefty hindquarters that absorbed some of the kinetic energy of travel. This was entirely different. She could feel every footfall, every exaggerated movement. The more

HK JACOBS

she tried to move with the reindeer, the more unbalanced she became.

Tuvshinbayar rode ahead of her, graceful and still, like she was merely an extension of her reindeer. In dark jeans, rubber boots, and a parka, she looked like any regular schoolgirl. Her ebony hair whipped behind her, partially blocking her face as she turned around and flashed a smile at Alex. She emitted a clucking noise, and Alex's reindeer transitioned into a slow trot as he obeyed the command to catch up with his comrade.

"This is harder than it looks."

Alex exhaled forcefully as her behind struck the saddle when the tawny reindeer downshifted to a stop.

"It helps to start early in life." Tuvshin smiled broadly. "But it's not too late for you."

"I considered myself a decent horse person until today. Any advice?"

Alex gripped with her calves as the reindeer lurched forward once again.

"Pretend you are the reindeer," she said simply and urged snow white into a faster walk. "Just over this hill is a long stretch of flat land, and then we're almost there. The valley is right below us."

The knots in Alex's stomach tightened. She was on the precipice of the conclusion to this insane and wonderful journey, and the only thing to do now was hold on tight. She and the reindeer skittered down the hill as a pair into a panorama of mountains, regal and snow-capped, and a wisp of smoke coming from the valley that nestled up against them. Alex rocked back and forth as they sped into a precarious trot and then into a full run. The wind whipped against her face, and she bent down to clutch the neck of her reindeer, pushing her legs behind her so that they moved seamlessly with his. For a moment, she completely forgot she was human.

When she was growing up and learning to ride, her instructor had emphasized control and precision—always being a step ahead with the proper command to signal the horse of his next move. She was diligently aware, quiet with her hands and never moved if she didn't have to. A natural, Terry had said. But when she could escape the indoor ring for the countryside, she and her chestnut horse grew wings and became something else entirely. Girl and horse. One body. One spirit.

Alex felt the downshift in the reindeer's gait as Tuvshin slowed to a walk at the first sign of the village. She felt the curious stares from the children lying on the ground using their reindeer pals as pillows and from the women crouched down squeezing milk from swollen udders. She offered a tentative wave and received a few upright palms in return.

Tuvshin dismounted and left her reindeer to mill about the others. She peered into an open teepee to find a grandmotherly woman with white hair pulled tightly under a silk kerchief, stirring a giant vat of thick bubbling cream. Tuvshin offered her a greeting and accepted the ladle from her and began stirring in slow, purposeful arcs.

"This is Emee. She is everyone's grandmother."

Emee held a pair of withered hands out to Alex, accepting her grimy ones in return. After a heartfelt squeeze, she tottered out of the tent, a limp on one side and notable kyphosis from years of bending over.

"Follow her," Tuvshin instructed.

Emee led Alex to the very back of the compound, past the lazing reindeer and napping children, to the very last structure with a doorway flap that was pulled closed and tied with a nylon string. The only evidence that someone might be inside was a pair of boots sitting outside the doorway and a puff of black smoke rising from the center. Emee gestured to Alex, repeating something in Dukha over and over.

Alex felt every heartbeat pounding in her chest. She was terrified of what she might find inside the tent but more terrified of not knowing.

With a shaky hand, she reached out and tugged the string holding the flap in place. She stepped into the small enclosure, eyes adjusting to the dimness.

"Ian?"

THIRTY-FIVE

Alex adjusted the lace sleeve of her dress, smoothing it over the tattoo on her left forearm. Although her mom hadn't said anything, Alex knew Janie's silence didn't equate with approval. She took a long, scrutinizing look at herself in the mirror and tucked a wayward strand of hair behind her ear.

Ears. They were missing something. She dug her hand into her blue shoulder bag and extracted the diamond studs. She was just inserting the first one when the creak of a floorboard startled her, and she almost dropped it into the crack at her feet. Rox approached her cautiously, her gait less precise now that she had a small bump showing in the base of her belly. She wound an arm around Alex's waist.

"It's almost time."

"I know," Alex replied.

"Are you ready?"

"No," Alex admitted guiltily in a moment of unabashed honesty.

"Take all the time you need, love."

Rox winked and removed her arm from around Alex's waist to adjust her garment, a deep blue dress of pure silk that looked incredible with her figure. Baby bump and all.

"I have something for you," Alex said and thrust her hand back into her shoulder bag, extracting a light blue box tied with a silk white ribbon.

Rox snatched it greedily and pulled off the bow. Her eyes filled with delight as she discovered the treasure inside—a delicate gold chain on which hung an elephant charm.

"I bought myself one too," Alex admitted sheepishly.

Rox pulled her into a hug, and this time, in the highest heels Alex had ever worn, heels of a deep blue satin to match her eyes, her chin fit nicely on Rox's shoulder instead of on her swollen breasts.

"Elephant sisters for life?" she asked Rox.

"And maybe longer." Rox pulled away frantically, looking around for tissues as her eyes began to fill with tears. "I can't ruin my makeup," she yelped. "I need something. Quick!"

For the third time in five minutes, Alex rummaged around in her bag, this time pulling out a magenta scarf. A scarf that had borne streaks of dirt, sweat, and possibly a blood spot or two.

"Here," she said, handing Rox the scarf. "A few more tears on this thing won't matter."

A hateful gust of wind whipped through her still damp clothing straight into her bone marrow. Alex removed the magenta scarf from around her neck and scrubbed her face with it. It came away stained with dirt. She balled it up in one hand before reaching out her other hand to pull the string that would open the doorway to the tent.

"Ian?" she whispered as she stepped into the enclosure.

A figure stirred, a supine figure on a bed made from logs and covered with a mound of blankets. The mound shifted, and Alex rushed to the side of the bed and knelt to the ground. A face emerged from the rumpled quilts, a mass of raven-colored hair framing a face with more prominent cheekbones than she remembered covered by a light carpet of facial hair. An ugly jagged scar traversed his forehead in its final stages of healing.

"Ian?" she breathed, but his eyes didn't open.

His lips parted, and he emitted a small moan and then a garbled sentence.

"What?" she asked, tilting her head closer to his lips.

"I said—" He spoke clearly now, his eyelids popping open to reveal the sky-blue hue inside. "Did you have enough time to think about your answer?"

What? And then she dropped her head on his chest and smothered her hysterical laughter. Laughter that shortly devolved into a stream of shameless tears pouring down her face.

"I did," she said through muffled sobs.

"And?"

She picked up her head and regarded the face she thought she would never see again apart from her dreams.

"Yes," she croaked, smiling through a tsunami of tears.

"Say it one more time." His cracked lips spread into a smile, and he closed his eyes.

"Yes. Forever, yes."

Alex watched Rox dab her eyes with the magenta scarf, a gift from Tuvshin's family once they had made it back to their village to await transportation to Ulaanbaatar. One call on her satellite phone straight to George Devall's secretary in London had earned them door-to-door helicopter service from the taiga to a hospital helipad.

The helicopter landing in the middle of northern Mongolia, its rotary blades whipping the grass and scattering snow like tufts of cotton, had made quite a scene. The kids had absolutely loved it. The reindeer, not so much.

Settled into his hospital room, under the careful watch of the most militaristic nurse Alex had ever known, Ian received the proper imaging studies and was committed to bedrest until deemed otherwise. Plenty of time for Alex to hear his entire saga.

Ian had been at the mining site when the explosion happened. He remembered hearing a giant boom and then the earth shifting with a seismic wave under his feet, a momentum that catapulted him to the bottom of a nearby ravine. He didn't remember anything else for weeks. Not being rescued by the Tsaatan or transported to the frozen valley. His first memory after the accident was waking up to an oversized tongue licking the wound on his head. A tongue belonging to a reindeer.

With both of his legs broken, he spent the next few weeks in excruciating pain. He still couldn't bear weight when Alex found him after almost three months in the taiga. Without the ability to walk or ride a reindeer and no cell service or outside contact, Ian knew he was stuck there until the spring when the Tsaatan would slowly make their way back down to Lake Khövsgöl.

"Fracture non-union," Alex informed him, holding the X-rays of his tibia up to the fluorescent light on the ceiling. "You really need more calcium in your diet," she teased, and he rolled his eyes from his upright position in the bed.

"Do reindeers count as dairy? I've had enough reindeer milk, reindeer cheese, and reindeer yogurt to last me a lifetime."

Alex walked over and gently sat on the edge of his bed. "As soon as your dad gets here, we can fly you back to London. You're going to need surgery and probably a plate and some screws."

"Great," he muttered. He adjusted his position, his face becoming ashen with the effort.

"Are you still in a lot of pain?" Alex asked.

Ian reached up and palmed her cheek, the flames dancing in his bright blue eyes.

"Not anymore."

On their final evening in Mongolia, Alex feigned taking Ian for a stroll around the hospital in a wheelchair and instead pushed him out to the curb.

"So where are you taking me? I hope there's food...and bourbon," he grumbled.

"I can't promise either one, but there's something I want to show you."

When Miranda pulled up in her cherry red Hyundai, Alex deposited Ian in the front seat with Batu's help.

"Ian, this is my friend Miranda and her...uh...my...friend Batu."

Batu clapped Ian on the shoulder as he slid into the backseat. Alex squeezed in beside him, and he waggled his brows as he slipped a flask out of his overcoat. She wrinkled up her nose when he offered it to her.

"Not tonight." Alex grinned, using one hand to push the leather flask back toward Batu. He shrugged and instead extended the flask toward Ian, who snatched it up and put it to his lips.

Alex smacked him lightly on the shoulder. "You're admitted to the hospital. You can't drink!"

"I not only can—" He took a swig and coughed as the fumes hit the back of his throat. "I will," he croaked, and the entire car burst into laughter.

Miranda drove them out of town, and as the sky transitioned to a deep violaceous hue, the hospital came into view over the ridge. Ian, who had been joking with Batu in broken Mongolian, suddenly became quiet as they pulled into the parking lot. From the brightly lit windows, they could see nurses scurrying back and forth, a few transporting patients on stretchers. He cleared his throat, and Alex leaned up to wrap her arms around his neck and place her lips close to his ear.

"Look at you...making a difference after all."

He chuckled softly, and she moved her lips to kiss the tears on his cheek.

"*Tulgatsgaaya,*" barked Batu, holding his liquor source aloft. He took a swig and passed it to Ian.

"Cheers," Ian replied, taking his own sip, "and thank you."

"This thing smells awful," Rox complained, tossing the magenta scarf back into Alex's bag.

"I imagine it does," Alex murmured. "Sorry, it's all I had."

"Well, since it's your wedding day, I'll let it slide."

The rich timbre of a pair of cellos coming from a speaker wafted through the open window.

"Time for me to make my entrance," said Rox, tossing her hair back and nearly tripping over the makeshift cosmetic counter they had constructed from an overturned church pew. "This baby really has me off balance." She turned and winked at Alex. "See you at the altar."

Rox opened the door of the white A-frame church with a squeak, allowing the sun to penetrate through the dust motes and create a path on the floorboards that led right to Alex's feet.

The Devall Company plane had come to fetch them in UB, and Alex had bid a sorrowful goodbye to Miranda and Batu and the Tsaatan friends that she might possibly never see again. Ian had an emotional reunion with his father, and by the time they landed in London, George Devall had hugged Alex at least thirty times.

Ian underwent surgery the next day at King Edward VII's hospital and spent another week recovering before they begrudgingly discharged him to Alex's care. He had become increasingly popular with the nursing staff, who fell in love with his quick wit and irresistible charm.

After a quick call to Dr. K, Alex arranged for a sabbatical of sorts so that she could personally oversee Ian's recovery. Despite his privileged upbringing, Ian had an excellent work ethic for anything he was passionate about, including walking. With a bit of encouragement from Alex, he had only been home a week before he could stagger from the couch to the kitchen of his London flat. He had been immersed in the aqua therapy pool at the gym one day in late April when a decisive look crossed his features.

"What are you doing next weekend?" he asked Alex, who was sitting on the side of the pool thumbing through the third book in the *Twilight* series.

"I don't have plans," she replied, ruffling his damp hair.

"You do now," he said, eyes burning bright with fervor. "We're getting married."

An entire entourage had flown to Texas. Alex and Ian, along with George Devall, Rox, and Nic, were picked up at the airport by a joyfully tearful Janie and a quietly emotional Peter. Janie and Rox had insisted that they dump the men at home and whisked Alex to the closest bridal shop to search for a dress.

The only shop within twenty miles of her town happened to be owned by Natalie's mom, who had the best sense of style in the entire county. It was small and dainty and only slightly bigger than Ian's closet, but every corner was filled with nuptial treasures. Dresses in every shade of white and ivory and the sparkling accessories to match. While Alex and Rox flipped through the racks, Eloise, in a floral blouse and pencil skirt, a measuring tape around her neck like a scarf, floated through the shop, gathering various options for Alex to try.

"Indoors or outdoors, dear?" she called from the back storeroom.

Alex furrowed her brow and said, "outdoors," just as Rox said, "indoors."

"I thought you always wanted to get married in your church," Rox said.

"I did, but then I had an even better idea."

Alex took one more look at herself in the mirror they had borrowed from her mom's house. The Chantilly lace of her dress was the perfect shade of suffused white, and the silhouette fit her frame nicely with a high neckline that covered up her entire front while plunging in the back until it ended in a flourish near her feet with a short train. She could barely see the blue satin heels peeking from underneath. They had been a gift from Rox.

When the melody changed tempo, she put one heeled foot in front of her and headed toward the doorway. Today she could see her path clearly, her path to the rest of her life with whatever joy and sorrow it would bring.

Alex stepped into the sunlight, immediately swallowed up by the fragrance and melody of spring. Even through the music, she could hear birds chirping. The field to her left was overgrown and unkempt but boasted the height of wildflower season, dense with blue and fiery red blooms. Lady Bird Johnson had once said, "Where wildflowers bloom, so does hope." What did anyone really have in the end anyway? Love and hope...and family. She looked out over the rippling creek and the wooden bridge that held just about everyone she loved most in the world. *Her herd.*

All eyes were trained on her, but she only had eyes for the man in the linen ivory suit, his raven hair ruffling in the slight breeze. Even from her vantage point from across the bridge, she could see his eyes—as blue and limitless as the sky above them. A perfect Texas spring day. A perfect day for a wedding.

His broad smile coaxed her forward, and she took a precarious step onto the first wooden plank of the bridge. Nothing short of a miracle propelled her forward without toppling over. She quickened her steps until one heel became wedged in a knothole, leaving her glued to the bridge about five feet short of her goal.

At the sound of light snickering, she shrugged and sheepishly stepped out of both shoes, leaving them in the middle of the bridge, much to Rox's horror. The wood felt warm and deliciously firm against the soles of her feet, and she skipped forward to take Ian's free hand while his other balanced gingerly on a cane.

"It's a true blessing when man and woman come together to join in marriage," drawled Pastor Brian. The rest of his words faded into the background as Ian pulled her close.

"You are the most beautiful creature I've ever seen," he whispered.

Alex sighed and squeezed his hand even tighter. Despite hating being the center of attention, she didn't mind it when Ian shared her spotlight. With him there, she felt undeniably calm, wrapped in more layers of love than anyone could ever want. She peeked at her mom. A neat stream of tears marched down her face as she clutched Peter's bent forearm. Rox unabashedly sobbed into a designer handkerchief while Nic patted the growing swell in her lower abdomen. And George Devall, who towered over the crowd, beamed his sunshine smile down at them all.

An exchange of vows, an exchange of rings, and now all that remained was to seal the deal.

"You may kiss your new bride, Mr. Devall."

In a flourish, Ian dropped the cane to his feet and palmed Alex's cheeks which glowed with a rush of warmth. Unable to wait, she met his lips halfway, the feel of his mouth sending a ripple of desire right into her bare toes. Good kissing made everything else disappear. And this wasn't just good. It was life-altering, world stopping, rather die-than-be-without-it, *epic* kissing. She encouraged him to part his lips just a little so that it bordered on inappropriate, and he groaned softly. He pulled back and met her forehead with his own.

"What am I going to do with you?" he teased.

"Love me," she said and averted her gaze to the bridge. "And try not to die anymore."

"I won't if you won't."

They shared a chuckle before he tipped her chin up to kiss her again, softly but purposefully, and she felt the heat under the taut skin of his lips. Since his rescue from the taiga and the long recovery from complex orthopedic surgery, they had not been able to consummate their reunion. Alex had thought she might incinerate from desire.

To her astonishment, Ian bent down and scooped her up to his chest and, amid a cacophony of cheers and whoops behind them, began to carry her toward the car.

"Ian! You shouldn't be doing heavy lifting."

He rolled his eyes. "You're not heavy."

"You're terrible."

"But you love me anyway."

"I do."

She leaned down to give him another lingering kiss.

"Almost there."

He took one more step and deposited her at the car, a rental to get to the airport and the awaiting private plane that would whisk them to a month of paradise at Ian's place in Virgin Gorda. Ian palmed her the keys.

"Driving is another matter."

"I got this," Alex replied and slid into the driver's seat of the sleek black BMW.

As the car crept along the shale until it ended at the start of the paved two-lane road, Ian's hand trailed down the bodice of her dress, his fingers caressing the bare skin of her back.

"It will only take us an hour to get to the airport," she chided.

"Maybe," he said, his voice low and husky, "I can't wait that long."

His gaze lingered on her exposed back and then up to her face, where she could see the flames building behind his irises.

"Isn't there somewhere we can go?"

His smirk released a torrent of butterflies from her middle.

"I know a place," she said softly and pulled out onto the country road.

His eyes sparked with excitement.

"You're becoming a wild woman," he murmured as he leaned his head into the seatback, leaving a hand between her thighs.

The wind blew through his open window scattering the pieces of his hair into a tousled mess. She laughed and guided the car past a field of swaying bluebonnets. She wasn't becoming one. She had always been a wild one.

EPILOGUE

"I hope you know that I'm never moving from right here," Alex groaned.

She lay reclined in a chaise with the sun permeating her skin with the most luxurious warmth. From Ian's cottage overlooking an inlet beach, the only thing they could see for miles was turquoise water and white sugary sand. Her black bikini was almost dry from their latest foray into the water, but her hair remained damp and stiff from the salt left behind in the evaporative process.

Ian playfully nipped her on the prominence of her pelvic bone. "Let's go in town and grab some lunch."

Alex groaned again and scrunched her eyes shut. Her entire body felt heavy and sedate. It had been a phenomenal two weeks in Virgin Gorda. They had barely left the villa. Her cheeks filled with heat, remembering the intensity of their wedded bliss.

"What are you thinking about?" Ian teased, and Alex realized there was a slight arch to her lower back.

Embarrassed, she sat up quickly, a tingling rush coursing up her spine, and pushed her sunglasses to the top of her head. Ian, still recovering from the fractures he sustained in Mongolia, used his chaise to push himself upright. He extended a hand in her direction.

"I know a great little ceviche place."

Alex shoved her arms into her white linen shirt and took his outstretched hand. He hauled her to her feet, her other hand connecting with his shirtless chest. The simple act of reconnecting with his skin had her head buzzing and her heart pounding. She tipped her face upward to the sun and the ocean's sky, her lips hungrily encasing Ian's lower lip. When his lips parted, she thoroughly explored his mouth and the taste of salt and ravenous desire. Her stomach rumbled, and he ended their lip lock too prematurely for her liking.

"I knew you were hungry," he said.

"Hungry for you," she replied, biting her lower lip in a blatant attempt to entice his interest.

He brought her hand to his lips and kissed her knuckles before tugging her behind him.

"Come on. We can't survive on saltwater and sex." He turned back to give her a delightful smirk. "As much as I would like to try."

"You're not the only one," Alex grumbled but smiled and let herself be led out to the yellow Jeep waiting in front of the house.

Alex tilted her head back and let the wind whip through her beachy waves and the thin linen of her shirt, fluttering around her torso like a pair of wings. They drove parallel to the beach, past a stretch of land richly verdant from the recent rains and unoccupied except for a few feral goats. Only a few miles into their journey, Ian whipped the Jeep onto a sandy lane that deposited them into a surprisingly full parking lot. The ramshackle building was painted bright turquoise and had a thatched roof that looked like it wouldn't survive the next strong gust of wind that blew through.

"It's still here," Ian said, gesturing to the screened-in shack. "I haven't been here in years."

"When was the last time?" Alex asked, floating a hand over to stroke Ian's forearm.

"Five years ago or so. My dad took me sailing, and we ate here just about every day. Well, I ate, and he delivered not so subtle hints about how I needed to get my life in order."

Alex smirked. "It seems like you did."

"I did."

A faraway look entered his eyes, the same one he always got when he envisioned the past, but Alex had a feeling that this time, he was thinking about the future. *Their future.*

"Any idea what you want to order?" Ian asked her.

They had chosen to sit outside on a covered patio at a remote table apart from the rest of the crowd where Alex could sit in a little patch of sun.

"Everything," she mused, flipping through the multi-page plastic menu.

Ian suddenly thrust his hand up in the air in greeting and used the table to push himself to a stand. Alex looked behind her to see an amicable man, deeply tanned with a short peppery buzz cut, motioning for Ian to join him at the bar.

"Friend of yours?" Alex asked, smiling.

"Yeah. Eddie, my dive instructor. I can't believe he remembers me. Good guy. He moved here from London about thirty years ago and never left." He leaned over and kissed the top of Alex's head. "Mind if I go say hi?"

"Of course not but bring me something with an umbrella when you come back."

"Your wish is my—"

Alex interrupted him by pulling him into a kiss. "And don't forget it," she whispered as he lingered on her lips before shuffling over to the bar.

Despite his energy, he still bore a significant limp in his left leg. Alex furrowed her brow. They would need to get him back into physical therapy when they got home.

Home. That was a construct she hadn't dared let herself imagine. Without a doubt, home was with Ian, wherever that was going to be. London. Botswana. Mongolia. Since the wedding, they hadn't discussed anything beyond their next meal, but soon, they would be faced with the logistics of their life. His job in London. Her job in Botswana. And their mutual commitment to the hospital in Mongolia that Ian had built, and Alex had promised she would support. No matter what, she belonged with the beautiful man bathed in sunlight with his head tilted back as he laughed freely. They would figure it out...together.

Her eyes drifted to his tall silhouette leaning over the surface of the bar as he listened to his dive buddy talk animatedly. He was thinner than he used to be but still had delicious muscle definition in his lower back. Lean muscles that became evident when the wind blew and his linen shirt flapped sideways. He looked completely edible in threadbare khaki shorts that hung low on his hips and a few days' worth of stubble decorating his jawline.

Since being here, his skin had bronzed in the sun, overcoming the pallor and dark shadows under his eyes. He looked vibrant and not at all like someone who had been stranded in northern Mongolia for three months with multiple fractures. Two identical maroon lines extended from his knees down to his ankles on both legs—the only indication that anything had happened to him at all.

When Ian returned, he placed a tall glass of flamingo pink liquid in front of her, complete with a cherry floating on the top that had been skewered by a nifty paper umbrella. Alex took a tentative sip through a straw as Ian slid into the seat next to her. The sweet nectar enveloped her palate right as the vapors struck her in the nose.

"Whew," she said, wiping her lips with the back of her hand, "what is in this?"

Ian eyed his own glass of pink and swirled it a few times. "Some kind of rum punch. A special blend of Eddie's, I think."

"If I drink all of this, I'm either going to be curled up under the table or dancing on top of it," Alex joked.

Ian raised his eyebrows and put his drink to his lips. She plucked the cherry from the toothpick umbrella and popped it into her mouth. She mashed the sweet fruit between her teeth to release the juices and then began absentmindedly flipping the stem around with her tongue. She could feel Ian's eyes on her.

"Can you—?" he asked.

Alex furrowed her brow in concentration, using her oral muscles to manipulate the cherry stem into a solid knot. Ian had no clue that she and her high school friends, Justin and Natalie, had once spent an entire summer competing over who could find the cherry in their soda and then tie the fastest knot. It was hardly fair, but she was enjoying Ian's wide eyes and the way his tongue darted out onto his lower lip. With a flourish of her fingers, she plucked the knotted stem from her teeth and laid it next to her glass, smiling smugly.

"That was insanely hot."

"Too bad we didn't stay at the beach house." Alex let her eyes rove over Ian.

"We can be back there in exactly two minutes, and I can have your clothes off in one."

He held up his index finger and then tapped her on the nose. Her stomach flipped deliciously, a sensation that she was becoming very accustomed to. Maybe even addicted to.

"Just let me—" started Alex and was interrupted by a gravelly voice belonging to Eddie.

"Pardon me everyone. No need to panic, but does there happen to be a doctor here today?"

Alex hesitated for a few seconds, willing someone else to push back their dining chair. *Damn.* She flicked her eyes up at Ian, who casually sipped his drink while he raised an arm into the air.

"Right here, Eddie," he called, pointing a finger at Alex.

As Eddie weaved through the seated guests, Alex stood up, tugging her denim shorts farther down her tanned thighs.

"I'm Eddie," he said, thrusting out a hand covered in flat brown sunspots.

"Alex." Alex shook his hand and gave him a wide smile.

"Follow me, Doc," he said, pivoting on his heel and motioning for Alex to accompany him.

"I'll save your seat, cherry pie," Ian whispered as she bent down for a swift kiss.

Alex trailed behind Eddie down a set of wooden stairs leading to the beachfront where blue and white striped chaise lounges sat in a neat row. One of the chairs was occupied by a woman in the recumbent position, hands folded neatly over her abdomen, a large white umbrella shading her face from the glaring sun.

"One of our regulars, a snowbird from up north somewhere that owns a house not too far from here," Eddie explained. "She nearly passed out walking up the stairs to the restaurant, and our hostess made her lie down."

"What's her name?" Alex asked as they approached the still form.

"Margaret...Margaret Levine."

The voice, crisp and prim, echoed from inside the cocoon of the umbrella, and Eddie nodded in recognition.

"I've brought you a doctor, Margie," announced Eddie. "Now be a dear and tell her what's going on with you."

"There is absolutely nothing 'going on with me' Edward," she replied in a clipped tone. "The sun was much too hot for my walk this morning, and I became a bit dizzy."

Alex edged around the umbrella to get a better view of her patient. She was dressed in white linen pants and a long-sleeved black blouse. A set of pearls adorned her neck, and a wisp of dark bangs fluttered beneath a black silk scarf tied over her hair. She looked to be in her late fifties, elegant and refined, with perfectly polished red fingernails and skin as creamy as alabaster despite living in a beach community. Alex knelt at the edge of the chaise, her bare knees sinking into the sugary sand.

"Hello, Ms. Levine. My name is Dr. Wilde, but you can call me Alex."

Margaret remained in her reclined position, the majority of her face covered by a pair of Chanel sunglasses.

"You, my dear, look nothing like a doctor."

Alex gritted her teeth but smiled. "I'm sure I don't, but I am a doctor. An ICU doctor. Can you tell me what happened?"

"I already told you."

Her thin lips tightened into a singular red line, deepening the grooves around her mouth. Alex ignored the woman's tartness and transitioned into ultra-professional mode.

"Have you felt dizzy before?"

"Of course, who hasn't?" she snapped

"Did you have chest pain?"

"No."

"Shortness of breath?"

"No."

"Nausea?"

"Only since this conversation started."

This was going nowhere.

"Can I take your hand?"

"If you must."

The woman thrust her hand toward Alex, an enameled bracelet bearing a gold "H" spinning on her bony wrist. Alex enveloped the hand into her own, cool despite the warm day. She slid her fingers under the bracelet and detected a thrumming pulse that was regular but not quite strong enough for her liking.

"Have you had enough to drink today?" Alex asked softly.

"Hardly," the woman answered, a small smirk forming at the corners of her mouth.

"Can we get you something?" Alex asked, casting a questioning look at Eddie.

"I'll take a whisky sour made with Macallan's, Edward," the woman said primly, pulling her hand from Alex's grasp.

Alex sighed and narrowed her eyes, noting the woman's expensive taste in whiskey.

"You need some water first," Alex chided, and Eddie chuckled in the background.

"I will have water," she proclaimed, smoothly removing her sunglasses and turning her head toward Alex. "It will be frozen and surrounded by whiskey."

She had a piercing gaze and ice blue eyes, eyes that looked startlingly familiar. Alex was mesmerized by her face that, although aged, was finely boned and beautifully symmetric. A movement near the stairs caught her eye, and she spied Ian, linen shirt flapping in the breeze, showcasing his chiseled middle.

"Need anything?"

Alex stood up and cupped her hands around her mouth. "Can you bring some water?"

The elegant woman grunted in protest. He nodded and, less than a minute later, carefully limped down the stairs with two bottles of water.

"Thanks," Alex breathed, brushing the hair out of her face before accepting both plastic bottles over the still form of the woman, her hands clenching her sunglasses.

"You're really getting better at stairs."

"It helps living with a doctor." He smiled brilliantly and ruffled her hair.

"Here you go," Alex said to Margaret, offering her one of the water bottles.

What little color that existed in her complexion drained as she stared at Ian, her pupils dilating until only a rim of blue existed in her eyes.

"Ms. Levine, this is my—"

"Hello Ian," she interrupted, and Ian looked down, fully taking in her features, his face turning to utter stone.

"Hello, Mom."

Mom?

COMING SPRING 2022

After overcoming tragedy, Alex and Ian enter their first year of marriage, deeply in love and ready for life's next adventure. But nothing could have prepared them for the challenges that will threaten to expose every weakness in themselves...and their newly forged relationship. The highly anticipated conclusion to the Alex Wilde Series coming in Spring 2022.

Also by HK Jacobs:

Wilde Type (Book 1 of the Alex Wilde Series)
Becoming Wilde (Book 2 of the Alex Wilde Series)

Connect with us on social media!

www.hkjacobs.com
Instagram: @hkjacobsauthor
Facebook: Author HK Jacobs
Twitter: @hk_jacobs
Pinterest: Author HK Jacobs
Goodreads: HK Jacobs

ABOUT THE AUTHOR

HK Jacobs is native to a small town in Texas that gave her both roots and wings. She holds a Doctor of Medicine from Baylor College of Medicine and a Master of Public Health from the University of Texas. She is a board certified pediatric critical care physician whose passion is traveling the globe caring for seriously ill children in low-middle income countries. She currently resides in Texas, where she continues to balance the many roles in her life—mother, physician, humanitarian, dreamer, and author.

Made in the USA
Columbia, SC
24 September 2021

46101991R00200